Vi Agra Falls

VI AGRA FALLS

A Bed-and-Breakfast Mystery

Mary Daheim

WILLIAM MORROW
An Imprint of HarperCollins*Publishers*

HarperCollins books may be purchased for educational, business, or sales promotional use. For information please write: Special Markets Department, HarperCollins Publishers, 10 East 53rd Street, New York, NY 10022.

FIRST EDITION

Designed by Rosa Chae

Library of Congress Cataloging-in-Publication Data

Daheim, Mary.
  Vi Agra Falls : a bed and breakfast mystery / Mary Daheim.—1st ed.
    p. cm.
  ISBN 978-0-06-135154-9
   1. Flynn, Judith McMonigle (Fictitious character)—Fiction. 2. Bed and breakfast accommodations—Fiction. 3. Northwest. Pacific—Fiction. I. Title. II. Title: Vi Agra Falls.

PS3554.A264V53 2008
813'.54—dc22   2008008634

08 09 10 11 12 OV/RRD 10 9 8 7 6 5 4 3 2 1

To Bud and Betty,
who have won the Best In-Laws in the World Award
for the forty-second year in a row.
How did I get so lucky?

Vi Agra Falls

1

Judith McMonigle Flynn stood on the front porch of Hillside Manor, took a deep breath of fresh summer air, and gazed around the cozy cul-de-sac on the south slope of Heraldsgate Hill. It was a perfect June morning with pink and white dogwood trees in full bloom, maple trees swaying in the soft wind, and rosebushes bursting with new buds.

"Nice," she said out loud. Not too warm, she thought, and so peaceful. The only sound was the chirping of baby birds in a nest that Mama and Papa Robin had built in the branches of a cotoneaster bush by the east side of the house. All the weekend B&B guests had left by eleven o'clock on this last Monday of the month.

Judith was about to go back inside when she heard a rumbling noise. A plane overhead? A helicopter? A herd of stampeding buffalo? The sound grew closer. She leaned on the porch railing and saw a huge truck pulling into the cul-de-sac. It stopped in front of the second house from the corner. Judith went down the front steps to see the big black and red letters on the truck's side: GROOVING MOVING, INC.

"What's going on?" a voice nearby called out.

Judith turned to see Arlene Rankers coming out of her house

on the other side of the laurel hedge. "I don't know," Judith replied. "Are Rudi and his girlfriend moving out?"

Arlene's pretty face puckered into a scowl. "If they are, I should've known about it. Cathy keeps her ear to the ground when it comes to the real estate business. Surely my own daughter would've told me."

Judith gestured at the two burly young men who had gotten out of the truck. "They're going to Rudi's rental. I think their lease is up about this time of year."

"That's right." Arlene started across the pavement that curved in front of the Rankerses' house and the B&B. "Let's find out."

Judith hesitated. She was as curious as Arlene, but lacked her neighbor's brashness in posing awkward questions. Then again, there were times when Judith didn't want to know the truth. The moving van's arrival was one of them.

"Arlene!" called a voice from farther down the cul-de-sac. "Wait!"

Rochelle Porter, who lived on the other side of the Rankers, hurried to the middle of the street where Arlene stood with her head cocked to one side like a curious bird. "What is it, Rochelle?" she asked.

Rochelle motioned for Judith to join them. "Last night I couldn't sleep," Rochelle said, lowering her voice. "Gabe got a crazy notion that he wanted some real soul food. He made chitlins with vinegar and some kind of hot sauce that practically set my mouth on fire. For a black man who was raised right here in this city and hasn't been farther south than Disneyland, I don't know why that fool husband of mine comes up with these peculiar cravings." She shook her head. "I was up half the night with heartburn. About three in the morning I saw lights over in Rudi Wittener's house and a big U-Haul. Rudi's girlfriend, Taryn, came outside, and the movers started hauling furniture from the house to the truck." Rochelle gazed at the newly arrived moving van. "Look, they're unloading the truck. Somebody else must be moving in."

Arlene stamped her foot. "I'm going to strangle Cathy! She should have told me! I'm never the last to know!"

Judith suppressed a smile. Arlene was right: she was indeed the font of all knowledge, rumor, and gossip on Heraldsgate Hill. Long ago, Judith had dubbed her neighbor's store of information as Arlene's Broadcasting System, or more briefly, ABS.

"Maybe," Judith said soothingly, "Cathy doesn't know. It's odd to move out in the middle of the night. Why would they do that?"

Arlene glared at Judith. "*You* wonder? Not as much as I do! And," she added, marching off toward the van, "I intend to find out!"

Rochelle laughed and shook her head. "Arlene's got more nerve than a peanut merchant. I admire her gumption."

Judith nodded. "Me, too. She's a terrific neighbor."

Both women stopped talking as they watched Arlene's animated conversation with the brawny movers.

"Bus?" Arlene shouted. "What bus? The nearest stop is a block and a half over on Heraldsgate Avenue."

One of the men threw his hands in the air; the other stomped off toward the ramp that had been propped up behind the van.

"Oh, for heaven's sake!" Arlene exclaimed. "If you people can't speak English, at least show me your work order! My husband's the block watch chairman around here. *We have to know.*"

With a heavy sigh and sagging of broad shoulders, the mover who'd remained by the curb came around to the driver's side of the van and opened the door. He returned with a clipboard and shoved it at Arlene.

"'Buss'?" Arlene snapped, looking up from what Judith

presumed was the work order. "You don't spell 'bus' with two esses."

The man tapped his finger several times on the sheet of paper.

"Oh," Arlene said, more quietly. "That's the person's name. Carry on. Or lift on. Or . . . whatever you people do." She headed back to Judith and Rochelle.

"Someone named Billy Buss is moving in," Arlene announced. "He's from Oklahoma. There was a handwritten note attached to the work order. I think I got the gist of it. It indicated that Mr. Buss was anxious to be in the house by today, which, I suppose is why Rudi and Tara had to move on such short notice. I hope they got a break on their rent. I was never fond of them, but fair is fair, after all. This Buss person sounds very demanding. I hope he's not a musician."

"Amen," Rochelle said with fervor. "Rudi and his violin just about drove Gabe and me crazy as a pair of three-legged chickens."

Judith agreed wholeheartedly. "His outdoor practice sessions, especially when he did them in the nude during the hot weather, upset all of us, including my B&B guests."

Arlene shot Judith a dark glance. "And that wasn't the worst of it," she said pointedly.

"It wasn't," Judith responded with a grimace. "I'm still trying to forget about that whole wretched episode."

Rochelle's smile was ironic. "You and your dead bodies. If it wasn't so terrible, it'd be funny."

Judith frowned at Rochelle. "You wouldn't say that if you had to contend with the state B&B association. They almost took away my innkeeper's license after the murder involving Rudi Wittener and his hangers-on."

Rochelle's expression grew somber as she put a hand on Judith's arm. "I know. I'm sorry. It's just that you . . . well, you have sort of a . . . *habit* of getting involved in those things."

"Some habit," Judith murmured. "I hope I've gotten over it by now. I'm not as young as I used to be."

Rochelle looked rueful. "Who is?"

"Mary Alice O'Flaherty," Arlene said. "You may not know her, Rochelle, but she goes to our church. She was forty-eight for the past seven years, and now she's forty-two. Amazing."

Judith and Rochelle both managed to keep straight faces. They were used to Arlene's occasional off-the-wall remarks.

"Lordy, Lordy," Rochelle said. "That *is* amazing."

"Mary Alice doesn't look her age," Judith noted, which was true. Mary Alice looked more like seventy-two than forty-two.

The three women paused to watch the movers carry a red brocade Victorian loveseat into the rental house.

"Gaudy," Rochelle commented. "That thing looks like it belongs in a whorehouse."

Arlene's blue eyes widened. "You don't think . . . ?"

Rochelle burst out laughing. "No, of course not. This is Heraldsgate Hill. With our skyrocketing real estate prices, not even first-class hookers could afford to move in."

But Judith was suddenly struck by an equally unsettling thought that wasn't exactly unconnected to excesses of the flesh. "Excuse me," she said. "I have to see how Phyliss is getting along." Smiling weakly, she headed back to Hillside Manor just as her cleaning woman appeared on the front porch, shaking out a dust mop.

"Heathen goings-on," Phyliss said, her thin lips pursed in disapproval. "Look at what's coming out of that moving van now. A bar!"

Judith turned to see the men rolling a sleek portable cherrywood bar down the ramp. "That's what it looks like," she agreed bleakly.

Phyliss leaned her scrawny frame on the dust mop. "Does this mean the naked fiddler's been hauled off by Beelzebub?"

"I'm not sure what it means," Judith said glumly. She gazed out into the cul-de-sac as Arlene and Rochelle walked off to their respective houses. "What's taking Joe so long at the hardware store? All he had to do was buy some lightbulbs."

Going back inside the house, Phyliss shrugged. "You know men—they go hog-wild when they see all those fancy tools and tin buckets and nuts and bolts."

"True," Judith said vaguely. She wandered into the kitchen, trying to concentrate on the tasks she performed in the course of her typical innkeeper's day. For the second time that morning, Judith checked the computer at the far end of the counter to see if there were any new reservation messages. Three requests had come in during the past three hours, two for late July, one for early August. The B&B was perking along nicely during the peak travel season, but she still felt uneasy. While she was responding to the latest inquiries, Joe breezed in through the back door, loaded down with brown Full House Hardware bags and carrying a sink plunger.

"What," Judith asked, "is all that? And don't we already have six sink plungers?"

Joe set the paper bags on the kitchen table and twirled the sink plunger like a baton. "None of them are like this baby," he declared. "It's what they call 'modular modern.' See how the handle curves? And look at the difference in suction." He shoved the plunger into the sink and gave it a couple of pushes.

Nothing happened.

"And?" Judith said, her dark eyes wide with feigned interest.

"Well . . . " Joe paused and then shrugged. "Of course it's not going into action. The sink's not plugged. Just wait until it is."

"If our summer excitement is based on unclogging a drain," Judith said, getting up from the chair by the computer, "I'd prefer something a little more dramatic."

Joe pulled the plunger out of the sink. "You're bored?"

"No," Judith replied. "Of course not. I'm just . . . wondering about something."

Joe's green eyes regarded Judith with curiosity. "Such as?"

"Did you see that moving van in the cul-de-sac?"

"I did. Is that for Mrs. Swanson?" Joe replied, referring to the elderly Japanese-born widow who lived on the corner.

Judith shook her head. "No. She's not moving in with her daughter until around Labor Day. Rudi and Taryn moved out last night," she went on, and recounted what Rochelle Porter had seen.

"Odd," Joe remarked. "Then what's that van doing over there . . . ?" He grimaced. "Do you know who's moving in?"

"Somebody named Buss from Oklahoma," Judith said. "Arlene saw the work order."

"Ah." Joe looked relieved.

Judith smiled. "Yes, I know what you're thinking. The thought occurred to me, too. I assume you haven't heard anything from Florida lately?"

"Not since Christmas," Joe said, removing some hinges from one of the hardware store bags. "You saw the card, too."

"Yes." Judith made a face. "Eight tiny pink flamingos pulling Santa's sleigh didn't strike the right Yuletide note. Neither did Santa wearing a bikini. And I certainly could have done without the scratch-'n'-sniff martini inside that smelled like gin."

Joe shrugged. "You have to admit, it was all very Vivian." He emptied another bag that contained a cordless screwdriver. "This one bends," he explained. "My other one has only one position."

"Just like your first wife," Judith remarked. "As in facedown on the bar."

"Hey," Joe retorted, sorting different-sized nails, "lay off. Be honest. Since Vivian bought the house in the cul-de-sac, she hasn't lived there for more than a year or so off and on. She's a sun person, she hates the rain. That condo on the Florida gulf is her idea of paradise."

"I know that," Judith said, "but when she's here the whole tone of the neighborhood changes. I hate to say this, but her lifestyle doesn't fit in with the rest of us. Not with us or the Rankers, the Porters, the Steins, the Ericsons, and Mrs. Swanson. Herself," Judith went on using the nickname she'd given her rival years ago, "is a creature of the night, drinking and partying and having all sorts of strange men come and go."

Joe scowled at his wife. "Some people might say that you have too many guests who come and go—permanently."

"That's not fair," Judith snapped. "There have only been two guests in fifteen years who actually . . . passed away on the premises while they were guests. You're an ex-cop. You know better than anyone that I had absolutely no responsibility for their . . . bad luck."

Joe simply looked at Judith and said nothing.

Judith sighed. "Okay, okay. So I *have* gotten caught up in several homicides. But they just happened to occur in situations where I was involved." She came up to Joe and kissed his cheek. "That's not really the point. It's strange, but even after all these years, I feel a little jealous of Herself. Despite her . . . uh . . . flaws, she still retains some sort of glamour that I don't have."

"Yeah," Joe said, emptying yet another bag with an assortment of washers, screws, and electrical tape. "But you know damned well none of it's real." He put his arm around Judith. "I got what I wanted right here. I had it all along, but I blew it. Then I got a second chance." He hugged her tight. "Over forty years have gone by since I got drunk and eloped with Herself—I mean, Vivian. Isn't it about time we forgot it ever happened?"

Her head resting against Joe, Judith nodded. "I have. I mean,

I don't think about it very often, but seeing that van suddenly made me wonder if . . . well, you know."

"I do." Joe kissed his wife's lips and gave her another tight squeeze before letting her go. "Now—for the grand finale—" He gently shook a large brown paper bag. "Ta-da!" he exclaimed, catching a sealed item with his free hand. "The Nail Master 2 Heavy-Duty Electric Brad Nail Gun Kit!"

"Well." Folding her arms across her chest, Judith gazed at the device's packaging. "Frankly, it looks dangerous."

"It is," Joe said. "But oh so useful."

"If you say so." Judith looked at all the empty bags and all the acquisitions. "Where did you put the lightbulbs?"

"Lightbulbs?" Joe's round face was blank.

"That's what you went to the hardware store to buy," she pointed out in a quiet voice. "Remember?"

Joe clapped a hand to his head. "Damn! Okay, I'll go back up to the top of the hill."

As soon as Joe left, Judith began preparing her mother's lunch. She was placing an egg salad sandwich on a plate when the phone rang.

"I have a sudden and insatiable urge to eat curry," Cousin Renie announced. "You know how much Bill hates curry. Want to go to Taj Raj with me?"

Judith looked up at the old schoolhouse clock. It was ten minutes to twelve. "I suppose I could," she replied, "but I have to feed Mother and change clothes. Would twelve-thirty do?"

"Sure," Renie agreed. "It'll give me a head start. See you there."

After adding potato chips, fresh cherries, and three sugar cookies to the tray, Judith carried the repast out through the back door to the converted toolshed that served as her mother's apartment.

Gertrude Grover was in her usual place, seated in an armchair with a cluttered card table in front of her. "Well, dummy," she said in greeting, "what's in that sandwich? It looks like glop to me."

"Egg salad," Judith replied, placing the tray on the card table. "You like it."

"I do?" Gertrude glared at her daughter. "You're just saying that because you know I'm kind of forgetful."

"You remember the things you want to remember," Judith murmured.

"What? Speak up," the old lady rasped. "I'm deaf, too."

The complaints were so redundant that Judith was immune. "I baked those sugar cookies this morning after I made the guests' breakfast," she informed her mother. "I thought it might get too warm to turn the oven on later in the day."

Gertrude picked up one of the cookies and studied it with her magnifying glass. "Hunh. Yours never taste like Grandma Grover's. Now *there* was a sugar cookie."

"Grandma was an excellent baker," Judith allowed. "She had a special——"

"As for warm," Gertrude interrupted, "I don't know what you're talking about." She pulled at the sleeve of her wool cardigan. "I'm practically a popsicle in this icebox. Didn't you pay the heating bill?"

"It must be seventy-five degrees in here, Mother," Judith said patiently. "Later on today it'll feel like a greenhouse."

"Good," Gertrude snapped. "Maybe I can grow some new body parts. The originals don't work so good anymore."

"That's true of us all," Judith replied. "You seem to forget I've got an artificial hip."

Gertrude shot her daughter a quizzical look. "You do?"

Judith ignored the remark and gestured at some mail on the card table. "I see you got your new issue of *Reader's Digest* today. It's very nice of the postman to deliver your mail here instead of putting it in our box on the front porch."

"I live here, don't I?" Gertrude retorted. "If you can call it 'living' in this itty-bitty box."

There was no point in reminding Gertrude that she'd refused to live under the same roof as Joe Flynn. Judith's mother hadn't liked either of her sons-in-law who'd had the temerity to marry her only child.

"What else did you get?" Judith asked, pointing to a postcard and a couple of circulars.

"Don't touch that!" Gertrude cried, taking a swipe at Judith's hand. "That's personal stuff. You want me to report you for tampering with the U.S. mail?"

"Okay, okay," Judith said hastily. She'd check her mother's mail later. There had been previous occasions when Gertrude had forgotten to open important mail, or thrown it away. But it wasn't necessary to squabble over a postcard from somebody who, judging from what little Judith could see of it, had been to Hawaii or Mexico or some other place with a sandy beach. "I'm meeting Renie for lunch on top of the hill," she said to her mother. "I won't be gone long. Phyliss is still here, if you need anything."

"I don't need saving," Gertrude replied, yanking the stem off one of the cherries. "Save me from Phyliss is what I want. All that religious hooey gets me down." She removed the pit and put it on a paper napkin. "Where's Dumbcluck?"

"Joe went to the hardware store," Judith replied, heading for the door. "He'll be back soon."

"That's too bad," Gertrude said. "If he never came back, it'd be fine with me." Suddenly she smiled. A bit slyly, Judith thought. "It's a good thing I know people I actually like. They take me out of myself."

"Ah . . . I'm sure they do, Mother," Judith said, figuring that Gertrude was referring to Carl and Arlene Rankers, who doted on the old lady. "See you later."

Inside the house, Judith hurried as fast as her artificial hip would permit up the two flights of stairs that led to the family quarters. She changed clothes quickly, applied more makeup, and combed her newly frosted hair. After a brief word of parting to Phyliss, she got into her Subaru and was backing out of the driveway when someone called her name.

Braking, she rolled down the window and looked to her left. A blur of crimson and gold dazzled Judith's eyes. Rushing along the sidewalk in a colorful caftan and slave bracelets from wrist to elbow was Joe's ex-wife, Vivian Flynn.

Herself was back.

2

So lucky I caught you!" Vivian Flynn exclaimed, displaying considerable cleavage as she leaned down to talk to Judith through the car window. "I arrived fifteen minutes ago. Isn't this a gorgeous day?"

Judith felt like saying it *had* been until Herself appeared. Instead, she tried to smile. "I had no idea you were moving back here. Is this permanent?"

Vivian grimaced, displaying some cracks and creases in her overly made-up face. "I'm not sure. That depends on my husband."

Judith tried not to look surprised. "Your . . . husband?"

"Yes," Vivian replied, "Billy. Billy Buss. We were married last April on the beach by my condo. We had a Hawaiian theme, so we told all our guests to put their gifts for us on lei-away." She broke out into her too-familiar husky laugh. Vivian sobered suddenly. "Your darling mother didn't tell you about it?"

Judith recalled the postcard she'd seen on Gertrude's card table. "Um . . . I'm afraid she's getting rather forgetful."

"Of course. But she's such a sweet little dumpling," Vivian declared. "I can't wait to see her."

"She's having lunch right now," Judith said. "Go ahead, pay her a call. I'm on my way to meet my cousin at Taj Raj."

"Oooh! Curry! How wonderful! Why don't I join you? It'd be a giggle to see Roonie again."

"Renie," Judith corrected, "for Serena. Actually, Renie's not—"

"Wait," Vivian broke in, gesturing at a muscular young man in shorts and tank top who was standing in front of her house, waving his hand. "I must see if we've got a problem. I'll be back in a jiff."

As Vivian hurried back down the cul-de-sac, Judith's shoulders slumped. The moving van had left, so she assumed that the young man who had summoned Herself was some other workman. He led the way into the house while Judith tried to figure out a way to exclude her unwanted company from the lunch date. She could try to call Renie on her cell phone, but neither of the cousins turned their mobiles on unless they were out of town or operating in an emergency mode. Instead, she dialed the restaurant's number to ask if Mrs. Jones had arrived.

The manager, Feroze Bai, answered. "Yes, yes," he informed Judith. "Mrs. Jones is waiting for you to join her." He chuckled. "Hurry, hurry. She is *very* hungry, and tells me she is going to eat the menu."

"Could she come to the phone?" Judith asked.

"I shall see," Feroze replied. "She may want to eat that, too." He chuckled again.

Keeping one eye on Herself's house, Judith waited a full minute before hearing Renie's voice. "Where the hell are you?" she demanded. "It's twelve-thirty-six."

"We've got complications," Judith explained. "Herself is back and wants to have lunch with us."

"*What?*" Renie screamed into the phone. "Good God, do something! You're a genius at making up tall tales! Fake your own death, run over her, do anything to avoid having to sit down with that pain-in-the-butt! Where's Joe?"

"He had to go back to the hardware store," Judith said, her eyes on the rearview mirror. "Oh, no, here she comes!"

"Hit the gas! Reverse out onto the street! Just do what you have to! I'm not lunching with that ghastly woman!" Renie hung up.

The good-looking young man had followed Vivian out of the house. To Judith's amazement, he leaned down to kiss Joe's ex on the lips, then waved at Judith and started back toward the house.

"Isn't Billy a stud?" Vivian said as she got into the passenger seat, reeking of a heavy perfume that made Judith feel like sneezing. "So strong, so handsome, so good to me. He treats me like a queen."

"That's your . . . new . . . husband?" Judith asked, calculating that there must be at least a thirty-year age difference.

"Yes," Vivian replied, settling her leopard-print Prada handbag in her lap. "He's a former baseball player. Very athletic. Such moves he can make! If you get what I mean." She winked, false eyelashes fluttering like tiny bat wings.

"That's wonderful," Judith murmured, turning onto the through street that led to Heraldsgate Avenue.

"Billy's originally from Oklahoma," Vivian said, rearranging the gold bangles on her left arm. "He likes Florida, of course, but he has some unfortunate memories of living there. I told him we'd come back here for the rest of the summer, and if he really wanted to, I'd sell the condo on the gulf and make the move permanent. Naturally, we'd winter somewhere else— Hawaii, the Caribbean, whatever he'd enjoy."

The word *permanent* struck Judith's brain like a sharp nail. She made an effort to conceal her dismay and changed the subject. "The neighborhood has changed considerably since you were here last," she informed Herself. "It's gotten very upscale. The proximity to downtown has attracted all sorts of younger people, many of them with big money from high-tech ventures. We have lots of families, and most of them seem to be rich. Sometimes I feel out of place. The hill is no longer quite as comfortable for those of us who are getting older."

If Judith thought she could discourage Herself, she was wrong. "My goodness!" she exclaimed, raking long fingernails through her platinum curls. "It sounds perfect for us. And look at these new businesses and buildings," she went on as they reached the top of the hill and the terrain became flat. "Boutiques, restaurants, spas, and all sorts of specialty stores! Who wouldn't want to live here? I can't wait to go exploring with Billy."

"Mmm." Judith was at a loss for words. They were within a block of Taj Raj. The search was on for a parking spot. "It's getting overcrowded," she finally pointed out. "The population has more than doubled in the past few years. People who live on top of the hill have serious problems with water pressure. The sewers are on overload. A heavy rain causes backup that floods basements. And all these condos—not only do they attract more people, but the taller ones cut off views. Our county taxes have skyrocketed."

"A spice shop," Vivian noted. "French, Japanese, Mexican, Thai, and Italian restaurants. I can't wait until our cars arrive from Florida. That should happen late today or early tomorrow."

"Cars?" Judith said, going around the block for a second time after spotting Renie and Bill Jones's Toyota Camry parked in their insurance agent's small lot just a few doors down from Taj Raj.

"We each have one," Herself replied. "Mine's the prettiest lavender Bentley Continental GTC you ever could imagine. Billy has an Aston Martin DB9. We got rid of the Cadillac Escalade before we moved. Too bulky, especially for some of these narrow parking stalls."

Slowing down as a Mini Cooper appeared to be pulling away from the curb in front of the local tea shop, Judith silently marveled at the expensive vehicles Herself and Billy owned. Years ago, Vivian had made a decent living singing in nightspots around town, but none of her previous husbands—including Joe—had been wealthy. Yet somehow Herself never seemed to have financial woes. There always seemed to be a man in Vivian's life who was willing to pick up the tab in exchange for her overblown charms.

The Mini Cooper's driver apparently was trying to get his car closer to the curb rather than pulling away. The young man at the wheel got out and headed for Moonbeam's across the street. Judith kept driving.

"Haven't we gone by the restaurant a couple of times?" Herself inquired.

"Yes." Judith's eyes darted to both sides of the cross street and down past the intersection. "I told you, parking and traffic have gotten very difficult."

Vivian frowned. Or tried to, though Judith noticed that her companion had undergone so much cosmetic surgery that her skin was extremely taut. "This place has a full-service bar, doesn't it?"

"Yes." Judith began the fourth tour of the block. "Maybe I'll find a handicap space farther up the avenue. I have an official placard because of my artificial hip."

"Oh, poor baby!" Vivian cried. "Old age must be very unpleasant."

Given that Vivian was at least ten years her senior, Judith had to clamp her mouth shut to keep from saying anything.

"Aha!" Vivian exclaimed, pointing to a loading zone by the bagel shop. "There you go. Slide right in, as I always say to——"

"I can't park there even with my handicapped placard," Judith snapped. "Besides, there's a cop standing on the sidewalk."

"Stop the car," Herself ordered. "Let me handle this."

"I can't stop in the middle of the avenue," Judith argued. "There's a whole line of traffic behind us."

"Just do it." She uttered her throaty laugh. "You know I have a way with policemen."

Judith ignored the innuendo about Joe. She had started to refuse a second time when a trolley pulled away from a bus stop half a block away. She had to wait along with the rest of the vehicles. Vivian sprinted out of the car and sashayed over to the sidewalk, where she practically threw her caftan-clad body against the policeman. Judith recognized him as Darnell Hicks, who had been assigned to the Heraldsgate Hill area off and on for the past several years.

"Poor Darnell," she said under her breath as the bus continued down the avenue. There was no choice but to keep up with traffic and come back to collect Herself. Unless, Judith thought with uncharacteristic malice, Darnell arrested Vivian for soliciting.

It took almost five minutes to get back to where she'd dropped off Vivian. Joe's ex had drawn a crowd: two women pushing baby strollers, a middle-aged man with a greyhound on a leash, a young couple holding hands, and an elderly woman leaning on a cane had gathered around Vivian and Darnell. They all seemed to be having a good time as Herself gestured expansively and clapped her hands.

Judith honked just as the small crowd burst into gales of laughter. Apparently Herself hadn't heard the horn. She was pulling up her long skirt and exhibiting one of her still-shapely legs. A trio of young men stopped in their tracks and joined the rest of the onlookers. Judith honked again.

No one paid any attention, except for the produce truck

behind her car and the SUV behind the truck, whose drivers were now also honking their horns—at her. Flustered, Judith rolled down the passenger window and shouted.

"Vivian! Vivian! Here! Hurry!"

Joe's ex finally looked in Judith's direction, giggled, and motioned to pull the car into the loading zone. With a heavy sigh, Judith used all of her maneuvering skill to park the car. Darnell came to the sidewalk's edge, motioning for her to turn to the right, back up, turn a little more to the right, move forward, and reverse until her rear tire touched the curb.

At last, Judith turned off the engine and realized she was perspiring. "Why," she asked Darnell, who was standing next to the Subaru, "is it okay for me to park here?"

The policeman grinned at her. "It's your reward for not finding any dead bodies lately." He leaned closer and lowered his voice. "Besides, Mrs. Flynn—I mean, Mrs. *Buss*—volunteered to sing at the departmental picnic in August. She's even going to donate several kegs of beer."

"Wonderful," Judith muttered, opening the car door.

"Kisses on your face!" Herself exclaimed, making loud smacking noises on her fingertips. "Bye-bye, Darney. Bye-bye, all!" Hips swaying, she moved along the sidewalk at a faster pace than Judith could manage. "Oh, dear," Vivian murmured, stopping in front of Moonbeam's. "I forgot—you don't get around so well anymore. I'll pretend you're Potsy."

"What?" Judith asked, thinking that if Darnell wanted to find a body, he wouldn't have to look far if Vivian kept up her not-so-subtle digs.

"Potsy," Herself repeated as they waited to cross the street. "Porter, I should say. Billy's papa. I always called him Potsy. Such a dear, sweet man, but rather feeble in his final days."

"Did he live with you?" Judith asked, heading for Taj Raj's corner location.

"Of course." Vivian sounded puzzled. "Those were ten of the happiest months of my life."

Judith was reaching for the restaurant door when it practically flew straight at her. "Oh!" she cried, reeling back a step or two. "Look——"

"Look out yourself, you idiot," Renie snarled. "Do you realize it's almost one o'clock?"

"We got held up," Judith replied, catching her breath. "Where are you going?"

"Home," Renie yelled over her shoulder. "I already ate." She stalked off toward the insurance agency where her car was parked.

Herself breezed into the restaurant. "Roonie isn't in a very pleasant mood," she remarked, smiling at their host.

"We *were* quite late," Judith said, turning to the always-cheerful Feroze Bai. "Is Mrs. Jones's table still available, or did she eat that, too?"

"Ah," Feroze replied, "I enjoy watching a woman with a hearty appetite. Very enchanting. Come, ladies, I shall direct you to another table. We must tidy up where your charming cousin was seated."

All too aware of the mess Renie could make when she ate, Judith kept her eyes focused on Feroze's broad back. Fortunately, there were several vacant tables this late in the lunch hour. The owner settled Judith and Vivian by a window looking out onto Heraldsgate Avenue.

"Now, don't rush off," Herself said, wagging a finger that sported a long rose-colored nail. "I'm terribly thirsty. Do you have any George T. Stagg bourbon from last year?"

"Ah . . ." Feroze's smile froze. "Only this year's. Will that do?"

"It'll have to," Herself said resignedly, and then flashed her smile again. "Thank you. I do so love an attentive—as well as attractive—maître d'. And make it a double, hmm?"

Judith didn't know much about the brand Vivian had ordered except that the proof was well over one hundred. Slightly flummoxed, she asked for a Bloody Mary and began perusing the menu.

"The tiger prawns sound good," she noted.

Vivian waved a hand. "Oh, let's not rush to order food. I much prefer lingering over a cocktail or two before I make a decision about eating."

"You forgot," Judith said, trying to sound pleasant, "that I'm still a working girl."

"Aren't we all?" Vivian replied with a sly smile.

Judith ignored the remark. "I have to check on my cleaning woman." She looked at her watch. "I'll leave here at one-thirty."

"I'd think," Herself declared with a touch of asperity, "that if you still employ that religious fanatic, she could work without supervision."

"Of course," Judith replied, "but nothing is carved in stone when it comes to running a B&B. There are always changes I have to make to accommodate the different wishes of the guests who—"

"Ah!" Herself exclaimed. "Our drinks."

Judith handed the menu to Feroze. "I'll have the tiger prawns and mussels in the coconut and curry sauce, please."

Their host nodded. "And you, madam?" he said to Vivian.

She tapped her glass. "I'll have another one of these. And please call me Vi." She licked her crimson lips. "Everyone I'm intimate with does."

"Very good. *Vi.*" Feroze made a little bow and walked away.

"Really, Judith," Vivian said severely, "you should learn to relax. It's no wonder you have so many health problems. You're at an age when you simply cannot afford to take on so much responsibility."

For just a moment, Judith thought the warning might actually be motivated by consideration. But that didn't fit Herself's character. Joe's ex was rubbing another soupçon of salt into her rival's wounds.

With effort, Judith shrugged off the comment and changed the subject. "Have you heard from your daughter recently? Joe got an email about a week ago."

Herself took a deep drink of bourbon. "She's finally getting married."

"She *is* married," Judith said, wondering why Caitlin Flynn's mother wouldn't keep better track of the daughter she'd had by Joe. "The wedding was in April. Joe and I sent her a set of custom-made wineglasses."

"Oh." Herself bit her lip. "Yes, of course. I've been so busy with this move. I lost track of time. Anyway," she went on after another deep swallow of her cocktail, "Billy didn't want to go all the way to Switzerland. He says it's too cold there."

"They got married in Paris," Judith pointed out. "Caitlin's husband is French."

Vivian waved both hands. "Swiss, French, Italian—it's all the same these days. The European Union, you know. And travel is such a hassle." She narrowed her eyes at Judith after taking another swig of bourbon. "Why didn't you and Joe attend the wedding?"

"We couldn't afford it," Judith admitted. "We'd spent a couple of weeks in Scotland last March."

"Scotland!" Vivian shook her head in dismay. "How awfully dreary for you! All those bagpipes and whistles. Or do I mean thistles?"

"We actually had a good time," Judith said. "Bill and Renie went with us. The men fished most of the time, and Renie and I . . . managed to keep busy." It was best, Judith decided, not to mention the dead bodies they'd encountered at the castle in the Highlands. "How do you think Billy is going to like living here?"

"We'll see," Herself said with a hardening of her jaw. "I promised him a yacht."

"Why couldn't he have a yacht in Florida?" Judith asked innocently.

"The gulf can be dangerous," Vivian replied, polishing off her drink. "Sailing is much safer around here."

Judith couldn't argue. "That's very generous of you."

Vivian shrugged. "Potsy was a very generous man."

"Potsy?" Judith said, puzzled. "You mean Billy's father?"

Herself nodded but didn't say anything until after Feroze had brought her second double, along with a bread basket. "Potsy had piles of money, and despite his youthful . . . generosity when it came to the ladies, he was rather tightfisted as he grew older," she finally explained. "The money mostly came from a huge Oklahoma cattle ranch."

"I see," Judith said, not sure that she really did. "Then Billy could buy his own yacht."

Herself swallowed more bourbon. "No, no. He didn't inherit." She giggled slyly. "Potsy left everything to me."

Judith couldn't conceal her surprise. "You mean because Potsy lived with you and Billy before he passed away?"

Again, Vivian had to wait as Feroze brought Judith's food. The enticingly pungent odor of curry always evoked memories of Grandma Grover's mutton dinners as well as Judith's first trip to San Francisco's India House. "Wonderful," she said to Feroze. "The stir-fry vegetables look terrific, too."

The owner made another little bow. "It will delight your taste buds, Mrs. Flynn." He turned to Vivian. "Have you decided, madam?"

She pointed to her glass. "One more."

Feroze hesitated. "Along with perhaps an appetizer?"

Vivian shook her head. "Later, maybe." She sipped bourbon and softly hummed a few bars of "My Heart Belongs to Daddy."

"Potsy?" Judith reminded her companion. "Gratitude? Money?"

"Oh." Herself's eyes weren't quite focused. "Yes. All of it."

"All of . . . ?" Judith let the words dangle as she tasted a tiger prawn.

"Of course Potsy left me all his wealth," Vivian finally said, sounding a little defensive. "Why shouldn't he? I was his wife."

So," Judith said to Renie over the phone three hours later, "I couldn't do anything else except leave Herself at Taj Raj. She never did order lunch. I almost expected her to climb up on the table and burst into a torch song. I've no idea how she got home. *If* she got home."

"I forgive you," Renie said. "I should've known she'd screw you over. She always does. But let me get this straight—she married this rich old coot, he died ten months later, and then she married his son, Billy, less than a year after Potsy popped off."

"That's the gist of it," Judith replied. "Billy and his brother, Frankie, didn't get a dime."

"Not fair," Renie pointed out, "but what is? Did Herself mention if Billy has a job?"

"The only job he ever had was playing baseball," Judith said, going to the front door, where a taxi had just pulled up. "He wasn't very good at it and never made it past the minors, where he played for the Nowata Flycatchers, a team Potsy owned in Oklahoma. Billy's fielding wasn't very good, which is how he got the nickname 'Blunder' Buss. Hey, I've got guests arriving. Talk to you later."

Judith went out to the porch to greet a young couple from

British Columbia. By six-thirty, Hillside Manor's guest rooms were all occupied. The social hour was in full swing, with appetizers of fresh vegetables, three kinds of dip, mini-bagels with lox, cream cheese, red onion, and capers, as well as the usual choices of sherry, lemonade, and sodas.

The day ended on a quiet note. After Joe's initial shock at the news that Vivian had returned, he wavered back and forth about whether he should go see his ex-wife.

"Damned if you do," Judith said, as she and Joe got ready for bed, "and damned if you don't. For all I know, she passed out after she finally got home."

Joe agreed. "She's not going anywhere for a while." His tone was rueful. "Unfortunately."

"She hasn't changed except that she must be really rich," Judith mused. "You'd think she'd want to move to a bigger house. That bungalow is hardly the style of a wealthy widow."

"You're just hoping she feels that way," Joe said, putting an arm around Judith's waist after they'd gotten under the covers. "Like it or not, I should go over there tomorrow and make a courtesy call."

"That," Judith pointed out, snuggling closer to her husband, "doesn't sound like you."

"What I really mean," Joe said, pausing to yawn, "is that I'd like to kick her butt from here to Florida for being a lousy mother. I can't believe she didn't know that Caitlin got married. That's a new low, even for Herself."

"After all these years living abroad, Caitlin must be used to being neglected," Judith said. "She's carved out a very nice life, given the poor example set by her mother. I've always insisted she takes after you, not Herself." She paused. "Do you ever wish you could see her more often?"

"Caitlin?" Joe yawned again. "Oh, sure, but given the crappy state of the marriage she grew up in, I figure she wanted to put all that behind her, maybe even me. It was no picnic for Caitlin. Most of the time Vivian's daughter Terri lived with her dad, husband number one. But the two half-brothers Vivian had by her other husbands were a real piece of work. I'm surprised they didn't end up in jail."

"How do you know they didn't?"

"I don't," Joe replied. "And I don't want to. They never liked me, and the feeling was mutual. The word *discipline* wasn't part of their vocabulary."

"Do you suppose they know that Herself is stinking rich?"

"I don't even know if they're still alive," Joe said in a drowsy voice. "They were headed for trouble from the day they were born."

A sudden, unsettling thought came to Judith, but she didn't give it voice. Instead, she silently hoped that Vivian's sons weren't headed for Hillside Manor.

3

In the weeks that followed, Judith mercifully saw little of Vivian Flynn Buss. Her nemesis had called on Gertrude at least twice, but never stopped to see Judith—or Joe. The summer was flying by, with Judith caught up in the busy tourist season and Joe working on a couple of private investigations for corporate clients seeking deep background checks on prospective employees.

The weather had turned almost too warm, with little rain and a prognosis of drought for the usually moist region. When Judith had any spare time off from running the B&B, she was busy in the garden, trying to prevent her flowers, shrubs, and trees from dying for lack of water.

On the last Friday of July, a For Sale sign went up at the corner house where Miko Swanson lived. When Judith returned from Falstaff's grocery that afternoon she stopped to talk to Mrs. Swanson, who was picking dead leaves from some pansies in a planter on her front porch.

"We're going to miss you," Judith said to the elderly Japanese widow. "I hope you'll always feel free to drop by."

Mrs. Swanson smiled warmly. "I shall miss all of you, too. So many years, yet I know it's time to be sensible and accept my daughter's kind offer to live with her and her family. It's not so far away, after all, only over on the bluff." She motioned at the house next door. "I must admit, I don't miss that violinist. Oh, I was a bit . . . *anxious* when I learned that Mrs. Flynn had come back." Mrs. Swanson made a dismissive gesture. "That is, Mrs. *Buss*. But all has been quiet there. They go sailing often, I think."

"Vivian—Mrs. Buss—was going to buy her husband a yacht," Judith said. "Dare I ask the price of your house?"

Mrs. Swanson pointed to the box below the For Sale sign. "Oh, please take one of those flyers. They list all the details. The real estate agent says he can sell it for seven hundred thousand dollars. Imagine! My husband and I paid twelve thousand for this house almost fifty years ago."

"Typical," Judith murmured. "My grandparents paid four thousand for ours back in the nineteen-thirties."

Mrs. Swanson shook her head. "I don't know how young couples can afford to live around here. That is, the ones who don't make those big whatever-you-call-them salaries."

"Dot-com millionaires, mostly," Judith said. "Some are even billionaires." She paused as a plump, pretty, dark-haired young woman came out of Vivian's house next door. "Who's that?" Judith murmured.

Mrs. Swanson moved closer to the sidewalk for a better view. The woman was heading their way. "The maid," she whispered. "Or secretary. Hello, Adelita," she said in a much louder voice.

Adelita smiled. "Hello, Mrs. Swanson." She had a slight accent and large, limpid black eyes. "How are you today?"

"Reasonably well," Mrs. Swanson replied. "I do not believe you've met one of our neighbors. This is Mrs. Flynn, who owns the bed-and-breakfast."

"Oh, yes," Adelita said. "I have heard much about you."

I'll bet you have, Judith thought. "Mrs. Buss and I go way back," she said, shaking the young woman's hand. "I understand you work for her. Or is it for Mr. Buss?"

"I work for both," she said. "I am what they call an assistant."

Judith nodded. "Did you come with them from Florida?"

"Yes." Adelita made an expansive gesture. "This is very different. I was born in Mexico. Here is . . . very northern. Not so hot, not so sweating."

"Do you live nearby?" Judith inquired.

Adelita's smile widened. "Oh, very! I live with Mr. and Mrs. Buss."

"Really?" Judith recalled that the owners before Vivian had raised two children in the small bungalow. "That's convenient."

Adelita nodded. "Now I must go. I walk up Heraldsgate Avenue to the hilltop. It makes for good exercise." She said good-bye before continuing on her way.

"Adelita seems very sweet," Mrs. Swanson remarked. "I've visited with her over the fence. Sometimes she gardens." The older woman sighed. "I cannot do what I used to. It makes me sad, even angry, but that is part of getting old. I shall miss very much my own garden."

"It's always been lovely," Judith said. "Your dahlias are especially gorgeous this year."

"Yes," Mrs. Swanson agreed. "I've had good fortune with them. I hope the new owner will enjoy my plantings." She blinked a couple of times, perhaps, Judith thought, to ward off tears.

"I'd better put my groceries away," Judith said. "It's quite warm today."

Mrs. Swanson nodded. "The heat is good for my old bones."

"For my mother, too." Impulsively, Judith hugged Mrs. Swanson. "We really will miss you. You're a wonderful neighbor."

"And so are you, my dear," Mrs. Swanson said as Judith released her. "But I doubt I'll be leaving soon." She gestured at the big maple tree that grew out of her parking strip. "I'd rather not be here in the fall to rake all those leaves, but you never know how long it takes to sell a house. To be honest, I think mine is overpriced."

"I'm not sure," Judith admitted. "Cathy Rankers would know. I see that she's not the realtor handling the sale, though."

Mrs. Swanson looked apologetic. "My husband never thought it was wise to mix business with friends or relatives. He said that often you might make a profit, but you could lose someone you love. People are far more important than money."

"How true," Judith agreed, thinking how much she'd miss the old lady's kindness and understanding. With a bitter-sweet smile, she got into the Subaru and drove on to her own driveway.

Two days later when Judith and Joe were returning from ten o'clock Mass at Our Lady, Star of the Sea, they noticed a Sold sign in front of Mrs. Swanson's house.

"That was quick," Judith said. "The realtor hasn't even held an open house yet."

"Maybe the realtor had a private viewing for other agents," Joe suggested.

"Maybe," Judith said, but sounded skeptical. "Whatever happened, the buyer must have agreed to the asking price."

Less than five minutes after the Flynns had gone inside, Arlene Rankers arrived via the back door, the entrance that was always used by family and friends.

"You left church so fast I couldn't catch you," she said to Judith in reproach. "We were sitting on the other side of the altar."

"You know we always have to get back for the eleven-thirty checkout time on Sundays," Judith replied, and held out the mug of coffee she'd just poured herself. "Want some?"

"No, thanks." Arlene sidled closer to Judith and lowered her voice. "You've heard?"

"Heard what?"

"Mrs. Swanson. Her house sold for seven-fifty."

"That's more than was asked," Judith said, surprised. "Who bought it?"

Arlene began to pace the length of the long kitchen. "I don't know. I simply *don't know*." She whirled around as she reached the swinging half-doors that led to the dining room. "But I'll find out. You can be sure of that."

"I'm sure," Judith asserted with a little smile. "Cathy, right?"

"Either my daughter or Mrs. Swanson," Arlene said, frowning. "I don't like it."

"How come?" Judith inquired as Joe came into the kitchen from the back stairs.

Arlene glanced at Joe. "I'm not sure. There's something fishy about this."

"About what?" Joe asked.

Arlene explained. "You're a detective, Joe. You must have some ideas. Something's afoot."

He shrugged. "This whole real estate boom on Heraldsgate Hill is no mystery. Except for some older mansions on the south slope, the neighborhood was blue-collar. Suddenly everybody got the idea that instead of rushing off to the suburbs, they could live five minutes from downtown and virtually walk to work. This became the in place, and with all that dot-com money, the sky was the limit. Old houses are torn down, big new ones go up. Longtime apartment buildings are turned into condos. Every possible commercial property is converting to retail on the bottom and residential on top. Meanwhile, the rest of the area is catching up with us. We're going to become the first city where being poor means you can only afford to have your cleaning service come once a month. It's ridiculous. I liked it better in the old days."

Arlene looked thoughtful. "I didn't realize Carl and I were poor."

Judith shot Arlene a quizzical look. "What do you mean?"

"I don't have a cleaning service," Arlene replied in a woeful voice. "I like doing the work myself. I know it gets done right. But maybe I should hire someone before people start to . . . talk."

Judith put an arm around Arlene. "You are not poor. My goodness, look at all that money you put into your elegant new driveway last summer. It's gorgeous!"

Arlene was silent for a long moment. "Then maybe we should sell the Mercedes or the SUV and park something more expensive there." She shook her head. "Goodness, I never realized—" She broke away from Judith and hurried past Joe. "I've got to talk to Carl. We're going to have to sort this out."

"Fortunately," Joe said after Arlene had rushed out the back door, "she'll forget about it in the next five minutes. Or Carl will tell her she's crazy."

"She's not," Judith said in a distracted voice.

"I don't mean literally, I mean . . . " Joe paused, studying his wife's worried expression. "Now what?"

"Arlene's right. There *is* something fishy about Mrs. Swanson's house sale. I don't like it, either."

"Don't even think about telling me to sell my old MG and buy a Lamborghini," Joe said, only half serious.

"No, of course not." Hearing guests coming into the entry hall, Judith tried to shake off her sudden bothersome mood. "Never mind. I've got work to do. Maybe Arlene and I are both a little unhinged. It must be the weather. It's supposed to get into the high eighties later today." She set her coffee mug on the counter and went to see to her departing guests.

An hour later, Renie called Judith. "Want some clams?" she asked.

"Clams?" Judith echoed. "I suppose so. Where did you get them?"

"Auntie Vance and Uncle Vince came down from the island this morning," Renie replied. "They were on their way to visit those old friends of theirs who live on the bluff. Since our house is the closest to where they were headed, they dumped off a big bucket of clams they dug this morning at low tide."

"What kind?" Judith inquired. "Not gooey ducks or horse clams, I hope."

"No, the usual—Manila, native, butter clams. Auntie Vance already cleaned them. Have you got time to come over here and collect some? Bill took our car over to Shell Shoal Marina to take his Sunday constitutional walk."

"Sure," Judith said. "I'll be there in a few minutes."

After telling both Joe and Gertrude where she was going, Judith got into her Subaru and started out of the cul-de-sac. She braked at the corner, checking to see if there was any activity at the Swanson house. All appeared quiet. She considered asking Mrs. Swanson about the buyer, but decided to wait. Arlene would find out in due time.

The front door to the Joneses' Dutch Colonial was open. Judith called to Renie. "Coz? Where are you?"

Renie appeared in the kitchen doorway at the end of the entry hall, a banana peel in her hand. "Sorry. I was just making sure you didn't have a nasty fall. Oscar tried to play his favorite trick on you again."

Judith glanced into the living room, where Bill and Renie's stuffed dwarf ape sat in his usual place of honor on the sofa. *"Please,"* Judith begged, following Renie into the kitchen, "no more of your family's Oscar-Is-a-Real-Creature fantasies. You know that annoys me."

"Not as annoyed as you'd be if you slipped on this banana peel," Renie responded as she tossed the peel into the garbage under the sink. "Want some lemonade?"

"Sure," Judith said.

Renie took out two glasses from the cupboard and went to the refrigerator. "We'll go out on the deck. That's where the clams are. Auntie Vance told me to divvy them up with you. It's a good thing Oscar doesn't like clams, or there wouldn't be enough for——"

"Stop!" Judith put her hands over her ears. "I warned you!"

Renie shrugged. "Fine. When it comes to quirks, I can't even begin to rival you with your penchant for tripping over dead bodies instead of banana peels."

"Don't remind me," Judith murmured as her cousin led the way through the back door to the deck. "By the way, Mrs. Swanson's house has already been sold for fifty grand above the asking price."

"No kidding!" Renie exclaimed. "That was quick."

"Too quick, maybe," Judith said, settling into one of the matching green patio chairs.

"Not really." Renie placed her lemonade glass on the small table between the two chairs. "This is such a hot real estate market. Remember back in late April when I was redesigning Grasmere Realty's Web site? They had to keep changing the copy every couple of days because the properties were selling so fast."

"That's so," Judith allowed. "But there's something about this deal that bothers me. I can't think why, but it does. Arlene feels the same way."

"Look," Renie pointed out, "if these people can afford to shell out that much money, they can't be a bunch of bums. Think how nice it is for Mrs. Swanson to make such a profit on——" She stopped speaking as the phone rang from somewhere in the kitchen. "Drat. I'll be right back," Renie said, getting up and hurrying inside.

Even if Judith had tried not to eavesdrop, she couldn't help but hear Renie screech into the phone.

"What? You're kidding? Why?"

Judith got up and moved to the doorway, taking in her cousin's incredulous expression from across the island counter. Pointing to the receiver, Renie mouthed a one-syllable word. Judith couldn't figure out what it was.

"Okay, Joe," Renie said, emphasizing his name for Judith's benefit. "She's right here. I'll tell her." Clicking the phone off, she leaned her elbow on the counter and gazed in bewilderment at Judith. "Arlene told Joe who bought the Swanson house." Renie paused, either for dramatic effect or because she was stupefied. "The new owner is Herself."

Judith groaned. "That's crazy!"

Renie, however, shook her head. "Apparently, Herself and Billy Bob Buford Bud—or whatever his name is—want to do a big remodel and need more space. I suppose Mrs. Swanson's house is a teardown. Let's face it, people are doing that all the time around here, with even million-dollar homes falling under the wrecking ball for some new mega-mansion."

"I know." Judith sighed. "I suddenly have visions of a Mediterranean villa complete with palm trees and pink flamingos in the cul-de-sac. All flash and dash. Herself has no taste."

"Oh, I don't know," Renie said with a little smirk as the cousins went back out to the deck. "She married Joe, didn't she?"

Judith ignored the remark. "Even if they build something decent," she said after taking a sip of lemonade, "think of all the construction. That's going to turn everything upside-down at the B&B. Guests don't come to Hillside Manor to be awakened at seven in the morning by heavy trucks and concrete mixers. And don't start me on parking places or peaceful neighborhood strolls, or the wretched eyesore that will be right outside our front door. Damn!" She banged her fist hard on the patio chair's arm. "I knew Herself would bring nothing but trouble!"

"You may be exaggerating," Renie said, trying to sound reasonable. "Both Herself and Mrs. Swanson's houses are small, and so are their yards. They look as if they were constructed by the same builder. Is my memory failing even more than I thought, or wasn't there a third house just like the other two?"

"You mean next to Herself's place, where the Ericsons live?" Judith nodded. "Yes. They tore that one down about the same time I moved back home after Dan died. But Ted Ericson is an architect, and although their home is more modern, he was able to hurry along the builders and the rest of the workmen. Our house and the Rankerses' are the two oldest ones in the cul-de-sac. They were put up about the same time, almost a hundred years ago. As I recall, the homes where the Porters and the Steins live were built in the mid-twenties, or even a little later. But none of our houses seem out of place, at least now that I've gotten used to the Ericsons' sharp angles and so much glass. They've fenced in their front yard, and all their plantings have matured to soften the appearance."

"Yes," Renie agreed. "The exterior has weathered well, too."

The cousins sat in silence for a couple of minutes, watching a hummingbird zip from the camellia bush to the cedar tree and taking in the view to the east, where the mountains were silhouetted against the bright blue sky. The Joneses' lot was a block wide, with their garage on the street that ran past the back of the house.

"Someday," Renie said ruefully, "this house will be a teardown, too. The double lot is probably worth more than the house. Worse yet, I assume this block is zoned for condos, since we've already got them across the street out front."

"But they're rather modest in size," Judith pointed out. "I'll bet Herself will put in a swimming pool."

"And fill it with gin?" Renie grimaced. "Don't look for trouble, Coz."

"I try not to," Judith said in woeful tone, "but I have a feeling it's coming my way."

Renie didn't argue.

When Judith got home later that afternoon, she went over to see Arlene and Carl. They were in the backyard, sitting under an old pear tree and watching their Boston terrier, Tulip, chase a tennis ball.

"Well?" Judith said. "Do you know anything more than what Joe passed on to me?"

Arlene shook her head. "I went to see Mrs. Swanson after Cathy called me about the house sale. Unfortunately, Mrs. Swanson was on her way to her daughter's to make plans about the move. Then I tried to call on Vivian. We'd gotten a letter for someone at that address. A substitute carrier left it in our mailbox." She frowned. "Is that Spanish girl's last name Agra?"

"She's not Spanish," Judith replied, "she's Hispanic, and her last name is Vasquez. Nobody named Agra ever lived at that address."

Arlene shrugged. "With the post office, who knows? Anyway, this girl who *looks* like she *might* be *Spanish* told me that her employers had gone to an appointment about the sale. I don't understand what all the rush is about. It's a Sunday, after all."

Carl took the tennis ball from Tulip and threw it in the direction of the hedge. "If they're going to remodel, they probably want to start while the weather's still good."

"I suppose," Judith said. "No matter when they start working, it'll have an impact on Hillside Manor. I wouldn't feel right about taking reservations without telling potential guests that there's major construction going on just two doors away. I'm already getting requests for the Thanksgiving and Christmas holiday seasons."

Tulip came tearing out from under the hedge. Sweetums was in pursuit, his big plume of a tail waving like a battle banner. The dog leaped into Carl's lap. The cat stopped just short of where Judith was standing.

"Knock it off," she shouted at Sweetums. "Sorry," she murmured to Carl and Arlene. "You know what this wretched cat is like. He has no manners."

"We're used to him," Carl said dryly. "Like my lovely wife," he added with a twinkle in his blue eyes, "he doesn't show his age."

"No," Judith agreed as Sweetums engaged in a stare-down with Tulip. "He's certainly old enough." She sighed. "I'd better take him home. Let me know as soon as you find out anything more about what's going on with Vivian and Company."

Arlene nodded vaguely, distracted by the cowering Tulip. "You know I will. Find out. And let you know."

But July turned into August before there was news from Arlene or anyone else. And when the new development occurred, it came via Judith's computer.

"I got a reservation request just now from someone named Marva Lou Buss in Broken Bow, Oklahoma," she informed Joe as he returned late Wednesday afternoon from reporting to one of his corporate clients. "That can't be a coincidence, can it?"

Joe grimaced. "Probably not. When does Marva Lou Buss plan to come to town?"

"Next Monday, with an open-ended departure," Judith said, pointing at the computer screen. "Two people. I can fit them in until Friday. We're already full for the weekends in August and the first two weeks of September. What do you think?"

Joe loosened the royal blue tie he'd worn to his meeting. "About what?"

"About whether or not this Marva Lou is married to Frankie, Billy Buss's brother," Judith explained. "Remember, I told you that Vivian inherited all of Potsy Buss's money. Billy and Frankie were left out of the will."

Joe unbuttoned his pale blue short-sleeved shirt. "So? What does that have to do with them paying a visit? The B&B would be a logical place for them to stay."

Judith frowned. "I don't like it. It makes me nervous."

"It shouldn't," Joe said, taking a can of beer out of the fridge. "Do you want me to ask Vivian about Marva Lou?"

Judith turned pleading dark eyes on her husband. "Would you?"

"Sure," he replied. "I'll do it after dinner. Right now I'm going to drink this beer, take a shower, and change. It must be close to ninety outside. Did you ever get a quote on air-conditioning this place?"

Judith looked rueful. "No. I meant to, but I keep hoping it'll cool off. It seems like such a big expense for our usually short bouts of hot weather. The fans you installed in all the bedroom windows help."

Help, however, was not coming from Herself. Joe went to see his ex a little after seven but returned almost immediately. "Adelita Vasquez told me that Mr. and Mrs. Buss have gone on an evening cruise to try out Mr. B's new yacht. I wonder if it's bigger than the *QE2*." He cocked his head, listening for any guest activity following the six o'clock social hour. All was quiet. "What are you going to do about the Buss reservation?"

Judith pondered her options. "I don't like turning away

guests, no matter who they are. You're right——it's a perfectly logical request."

"And *you* are always perfectly logical," Joe said, kissing his wife's cheek.

"I'll warn them that they can't stay past Thursday night," Judith said, as much to herself as to Joe. "I'll do it now."

An hour later when Judith checked her email, Marva Lou Buss had responded: "Confirm Monday, Aug. 9 through Thursday, Aug. 12. Please advise convenient location for weekend of Friday the 13th."

"Friday the thirteenth," Judith murmured. "I don't like that, either."

4

Judith was sweeping up dead leaves from under the camellia bush at the corner of the house early Wednesday afternoon and praying for rain when Herself, wearing a glittering gold lamé kimono, came outside to get the mail. Setting her broom aside, Judith hurried across the cul-de-sac.

"Joe and I have been trying to talk to you," she said, making an effort to put on her friendliest smile. "We heard you bought Mrs. Swanson's house. Are you expanding?"

Herself uttered a throaty laugh. "Expanding? How quaint!"

"Well . . . " Judith paused, mesmerized by the sun glinting off of all that gold lamé and platinum curls. "I assume that with adjoining properties, you might want to add on to your original house."

Clutching a thick batch of mail to her bosom, Vivian regarded Judith with amusement. "That would be the case with some people. But Billy and I have other plans." She winked. "Check your own mail, Judith. You'll find an invitation to our coming-out party next week. All of the neighbors in the cul-de-sac are invited. It'll be *very* exciting." With a flip of gold folds, Herself went back inside.

"I don't like this," Judith declared to Joe after he got home around five, and she showed him the gold-edged invitation.

Joe looked bemused. "There's a lot of things you don't seem to like these days. This seems like a perfectly ordinary neighborhood bash to me. Six-thirty Monday evening, which happens to coincide with the annual citywide Block Watch get-togethers. Have you talked to Carl and Arlene? They usually host it, since he's our neighborhood captain."

"They're still on the other side of the mountains at that time-share their daughter, Cathy, owns," Judith replied, sounding cross. "If it's hot here, it must be a hundred degrees on the lake over there. For all I know, they've melted. Besides, Carl dropped the flyers off last week. I've already notified the guests who'll be staying here that night about how the city puts out sawhorses to partially block off the areas where the potlucks are being held."

Joe waved the Busses' invitation at Judith. "This isn't a potluck. It says food and beverages provided."

"Herself had better clear this with Arlene and Carl," Judith snapped. "We've been doing the Block Watch thing for years."

"Maybe it's a party to welcome Billy's brother and his wife," Joe said, putting the invitation on the kitchen counter.

Judith clapped a hand to her cheek. "Oh! I forgot that's when the other Busses get here!"

A woman's voice called out from the back porch. "Judith? Joe?"

Judith glanced down the hall that led from the kitchen. Naomi Stein was standing at the screen door.

"Come in," Judith called to her neighbor. "I see you're back from California."

"Last night," Naomi said, a worried expression on her usually serene face and Vivian's invitation in her hand. "What's going on around here? Did Mrs. Swanson move out while we were gone?"

Judith nodded. "Over the weekend. I guess she had to be out of the house by August first."

"I hate to see her go," Naomi said with feeling. "Mrs. Swanson was like an anchor in this neighborhood, always the calm in the eye of any storm. I'll certainly miss seeing her working in the garden across the cul-de-sac."

"I know," Judith agreed. "I see you got the Busses' invitation."

"Yes." Naomi looked at Joe. "I realize that you were married to her, but I'll be blunt. Hamish and I are concerned about what she and that muscle-bound husband of hers are up to." She waved the invitation. "Is there going to be some kind of dreadful announcement that comes along with the free food and drink?"

"It's possible," Joe admitted in his mellow voice. "Judith figures they're going to add on to their own house."

Naomi frowned. "That could be a nuisance, especially for your B&B. I wonder if they'll move out while the construction is under way."

"That'd be the only good part," Judith murmured.

"True," Naomi agreed. "I'm not crazy about the kind of people that show up there at all hours, either."

Judith stared at Naomi. "Such as . . . who? When?"

"Ham was up late last night unpacking and getting organized for work today," Naomi explained. "About one in the morning, a car pulled up in front of the Buss house. Nobody got out right away, and the house was dark. Ham wondered if someone was . . . you know, casing the joint, as they say. Finally a man got out and walked all around the house. The lights never went on as far as Ham could see, and after a few minutes the man came back and drove away. It seemed odd. Ham thought about calling the police, but he decided against it. He didn't get a good look at the car or the driver, let alone the license plates."

"Could Ham describe the man?" Judith asked.

Naomi frowned. "Not really. Medium height, probably older, ordinary clothes, some kind of cap. Ham said it was a sedan, dark color, probably. I hate to say it, but that house has been bad luck for years."

Joe held up his hands. "Hold it. No offense, Naomi, but you and Rochelle and Arlene and," he added, glancing at Judith, "my wife are all looking for trouble where there may not be any. Is this some kind of guilt trip on me for having made a big mistake thirty-odd years ago in marrying the wrong woman?"

Naomi looked embarrassed. Judith, however, was annoyed. "You don't need to defend yourself, Joe," she declared. "Or to defend Herself."

Naomi bit her lip. "I'm sorry. I didn't mean to cause trouble." She looked away from both Flynns. "Jeanne Ericson feels the same way."

"Women," Joe muttered. "I'm going upstairs to change."

As he went through the hall to the back stairs, Naomi heaved a heavy sigh. "I had no intention of upsetting your husband, Judith."

"I know," Judith responded kindly. "But Joe *does* feel guilty. He somehow feels responsible for Vivian. Or Vi, as she wants to be called these days. Don't you remember when he got her to join AA, but she flunked out? He even went to meetings with her."

"Yes, I do." Naomi put a hand on Judith's arm. "I'd better go before I make an utter fool of myself. It might turn out to be a lovely neighborhood party. I hope," she added softly, "it's kosher."

"I do, too," Judith agreed. "In every way."

✳ ✳ ✳

"A re you nuts?" Renie demanded a couple of days later when she stopped at the B&B to drop off a couple of hard-boiled detective novels Bill was passing on to Joe. "Why would we come to your neighborhood get-together Monday? We have our own. I'm bringing fried chickens."

"*Chickens?* How many?" Judith asked, wiping perspiration off of her forehead.

"Three," Renie replied. "Everybody laps up those fryers since I finally learned how to cook them right after forty years of marriage. How come Carl and Arlene Rankers aren't doing their usual thing?"

"They are," Judith replied, sitting down at the kitchen table, across from Renie. "They'd already made arrangements with the city to hold their annual Block Watch party. So we'll end up with two shindigs going on at the same time in the cul-de-sac. Arlene asked Herself to change their event, but she refused. It should be quite a mob, since all the Dooleys will be coming, too."

"How many at this point?" Renie inquired, referring to the large family that lived in back of the Flynn and Ericson properties.

"I've lost track," Judith admitted. "With so many children and grandchildren and various others relatives in and out, I just know a Dooley when I see one. They all kind of look alike."

"Nice people, though," Renie remarked, lifting the lid on Judith's sheep-shaped cookie jar. "Hey, Coz, this thing's empty!"

"I don't bake in this heat," Judith said. "I won't turn on the oven."

Renie looked forlorn. "Store-bought is fine with me."

"None here." Judith slumped in the chair. "I hate summer."

"Me, too," Renie agreed. "Worst season of the year. Bring on the rain." She sipped from the Pepsi Judith had given her. "I'm going to dread seeing our water bill. I can't *not* try to keep all of our flowers and shrubs and trees from dying of thirst. In the long run, it'd cost more money to——" She stopped and reached into her enormous purse, which was on the vacant chair next to her. "I almost forgot. Your mailman must be suffering from heat exhaustion with all our steep hills. He dropped these in your driveway." She handed over the latest issues of *Country Life, National Geographic,* and *Architectural Digest,* along with a couple of ads, the cable bill, and two letters.

Judith scanned the stack of mail. "*Architectural Digest* belongs to Ted Ericson. We've had a sub on the route the past week or so. Cecil's on vacation." She tossed the ads aside and looked at the first letter. "It's a thank-you, I think, from that nice South Dakota couple who stayed here last month. I'll read it later." The other letter brought a scowl to her face. "This is addressed to J. C. Agra at Herself's address. Damn. I suppose I'll have to take it over there."

"Her last name isn't Agra," Renie pointed out.

Judith shrugged. "I know, but the letter's intended for that address. Maybe Billy has an alias."

"That sounds right," Renie said, and yawned. "This heat also makes me sleepy. I should finish up my errands before I nod off." She stared at Judith. "What is it? You look weird."

"That name—Agra. Somebody else in the cul-de-sac got a letter for a person by that name. It was also misdelivered."

Renie took a last swig of Pepsi and stood up. "Who knows? Every so often we get a religious newsletter for a family who lived in our house fifty years ago. Last week I got something in the mail for my dad, and he's been dead for thirty years. They wanted to sell him life insurance. I almost signed up, figuring maybe I could cash in by waiting a couple of months and sending them his death certificate."

"You'd actually do that," Judith murmured.

"But I didn't," Renie said, not without regret. "See you Sunday for Joe and Mike's birthdays."

In previous years, Judith often hosted a small party for her husband and son, who shared the same birthday. Usually she invited some of Joe's former police coworkers, a few of Mike's current colleagues, and various family members and friends. But on this eighth day of August, Mike was turning forty. It didn't seem possible to Judith. Where had all the years gone? It seemed like only yesterday that she was pushing his stroller along the ill-maintained sidewalks by the McMonigles' seedy rental in the city's south end. Or kissing him good-bye before she headed for work at the local library. She'd been an often-absent mother, working two jobs, and forced to leave most of the routine parenting to the frequently unemployed Dan McMonigle. Judith had always acknowledged Dan as a decent father—despite the fact that he knew Mike wasn't his son. Ironic, of course, because Joe didn't know Judith had borne him a child until he showed up as the primary detective in a murder that had occurred at Hillside Manor. Even after Judith and Joe had finally married, it had taken her a long time to work up the courage to tell Mike. More irony there, Judith recalled. Her son had figured out his biological identity long before she revealed the truth.

Paternity issues aside, Mike was traumatized by the thought of turning forty. He'd get over it, his parents agreed, if only because he had no choice. When he'd told her he didn't want to make a big deal out of reaching the threshold of middle age, she was bemused as well as relieved. Joe had stepped in, pointing out that the relentlessly hot, dry weather was taking its toll on Judith, and suggested an intimate buffet supper with their son's family, Gertrude, and the Joneses. Neither Judith nor Mike protested. In addition to Mike's confrontation with growing older and the debilitating heat wave, it was never easy for Judith to juggle private parties as well as full occupancy at the B&B.

"That was great," Joe declared Sunday night after the last present had been unwrapped, the remains of the ice cream had been devoured by the two grandsons, the small chunk of left-over cake had been sent home with Mike and Kristin, and the attendees had gone. Caitlin's gift to her father was a handsome wool sweater made in Switzerland. Joe's brothers, who lived in far-flung places around the world, had chipped in to buy their sibling what appeared to be a complete DVD collection of John Wayne's movies, from Westerns to WWII and several in between. Judith and Joe had presented Mike with a check for two thousand dollars, to be spent on a getaway with Kristin to Hawaii.

"Thanks again for the sport coat," Joe said to his wife. "It's a really nifty color of green."

"I tried to match your eyes," Judith said, smiling.

Joe leaned to kiss her, but was interrupted by a knock at the back door. "Who's that? Did some of our gang forget something?"

"I don't think so," Judith said, glancing at the schoolhouse clock as Joe started down the hall to open the door. "It's not quite ten, so the front door is still unlocked for guests."

"Happy birthday, baby!" Vivian shouted. "Here's a little something to celebrate with on your special day!"

Judith stayed put, but could see Herself handing over what looked like a big bottle wrapped in gold foil.

"Thanks, Vivian," Joe said, not quite able to keep the surprise out of his voice.

"Go ahead, unwrap it," his ex urged, swaying slightly on the threshold. "Judith! Come see what I got for Joe!"

Reluctantly, Judith joined Joe and his former spouse in the narrow hallway. As he removed the gold foil, a magnum of

Dom Perignon 1998 was exposed. "Wow," Joe said softly. "This is really nice of you . . . Vi."

She lurched forward and kissed him soundly on the lips. "You deserve it, doll face! Drink it up at your party today!"

"Today?" Judith said, puzzled.

"I meant to bring it yesterday," Vivian explained, leaning against Joe, "but I didn't have time. So I woke up early this morning, and here I am. I know, I'm usually one for sleeping in. I can't believe it's not even ten o'clock!"

"Ah . . . ," Joe began, gently trying to move away from Herself. "It's ten o'clock at *night.*"

Vivian looked startled. "It is? Hunh." She stumbled a bit as she turned to look outside. "No wonder it's so dark. I just thought it was one of those typical gloomy days in this part of the world."

"Be careful going home," Judith said, starting to close the door.

"Home." Herself looked blank. "Oh, yes, *home.*" She giggled. "Show me the way to go . . ." Singing softly, she managed to go down the stairs and turn in the direction of the driveway.

"Good Lord," Judith murmured, locking the door. "I hope she's relatively sober for her party tomorrow night."

Joe was admiring the magnum of champagne. "I'll bet this bottle of bubbly cost at least five bills."

"Are you impressed?" Judith's tone was caustic.

"What?" Joe looked up from reading the label. "Well . . . it *was* thoughtful."

"I suppose," Judith mumbled. She went back into the kitchen to empty the dishwasher.

"I gather," Joe said wryly as he set the magnum on the counter, "you don't want to pop the top and have a toast?"

"The only thing I'd like to toast right now is Herself," Judith retorted. "It's been a long day. I'm tired. I'm too pooped to pop. Anything," she added, darting her husband a pointed glance.

"You're being petty," Joe said, forced to raise his voice over the clatter of plates that his wife was stacking in the cupboard. "You don't have anything to be jealous about."

Face frozen, Judith clamped her mouth shut. Joe regarded her with reproachful eyes. "Okay," she finally admitted, "that's probably true. But I still don't like having Vivian around here all the time. I always sense trouble in the making."

"Come on, get real," Joe said, exasperated. "I keep trying to tell you, stop fussing. Don't look for trouble."

Judith grimaced. "I'll try not to."

Joe's expression softened. "Try harder," he said, putting an arm around her waist.

Looking into those magic green eyes, Judith managed a small smile. "Okay. I will. I'll think of positive things, like"——her smile grew wider——"you."

But as they went upstairs to the third floor family quarters, Judith could have sworn she heard footsteps. Not real, not audible, not visible, but something tangible, as if trouble lurked in the shadows.

5

"Should I get all gussied up?" Gertrude asked Judith late Monday afternoon. "Where's my good dress? Did you find my rouge?"

"Your good dress," Judith said patiently, "is wool. It's ninety-three degrees outside. Why don't you wear that new housecoat Renie and Bill gave you for Christmas last year? You've never taken it out of the box."

Gertrude scowled. "I was saving it for something special—like my funeral. But I'll bet Vivian's going to put on a real good party. The housecoat's in the bottom drawer of my bureau."

Dutifully, Judith went into the small bedroom next to the small living room and the even smaller kitchenette. The gift box wasn't in the bottom drawer—or anywhere in the bureau. She finally found it under the bed. Collecting rouge, lipstick, and a pair of blue rhinestone earrings that would go well with the blue, green, and yellow floral housecoat, she asked her mother if she needed help getting dressed.

"I can still do that myself, you nitwit," Gertrude rasped. "It might take me an hour or so, but I can manage just fine. You look like you better spend a while getting yourself together.

Where'd you find that ugly sundress? It looks like it fell off the back of a garbage truck."

Judith had bought the simple red-and-white cotton sheath at Nordquist's on sale, a relative bargain at ninety dollars. Ignoring her mother's barb, she told her to be ready by six-thirty, smiled thinly, and left the toolshed.

The schoolhouse clock's hands stood at five-thirty. The appetizers were ready for the B&B's social hour, but one party of guests had yet to arrive. Ironically, it was the Oklahoma Busses. Judith wondered if they'd stopped first at Herself's house.

Forty-five minutes later, she was checking on the three-bean salad she'd made for the Block Watch potluck when the doorbell rang. A tall, lean, gray-haired man and a short, plump dumpling of a woman with six pieces of luggage awaited her welcome.

"We're the Busses," the woman announced in a soft, slightly southern voice somewhere between a drawl and a twang.

Judith introduced herself and ushered the couple inside. "Welcome to Hillside Manor. You're in Room Five. You share a bathroom with Room Six, though there is another bathroom you can use off the hallway between your room and Room Four. The social hour has already begun, but I'm sure you want to get settled. Here's the registration. . . . " She paused, realizing that the Busses had left their luggage on the porch. "Uh . . . wouldn't you like to bring your suitcases inside?"

Marva Lou Buss frowned. "Is there a lot of crime around here?"

"No," Judith replied, unwilling to admit to the occasional corpse she found in or around the premises. "This neighborhood is very quiet." A sharp noise not unlike a gunshot suddenly rang out. "Usually," she added, going to the open front door. Billy Buss was standing on the curb in front of his house, holding aloft what looked like a six-shooter.

"Ya-*ha*!" he shouted. "It's party time!"

"Sounds like Billy," Frankie Buss murmured to Marva Lou. "We'd best hightail it over there to howdy-do him." He loped out of the house.

"Frankie's all het up to have a sit-down with Billy," Marva Lou said to Judith. "I'll leave the bags on the porch till he gets back."

Judith was still looking outside. The sawhorses were in place at the entrance to the cul-de-sac, the Rankers had set up their trestle table and folding chairs, Jeanne Ericson was unloading paper plates and plastic tableware from a big carton, Naomi Stein carefully placed slices of corned beef and pastrami on a platter, Rochelle Porter was putting the final touches to a lazy Susan loaded with fresh fruits and vegetables that her husband, Gabe, had brought from his produce company, and Hamish Stein was helping Ted Ericson set up the beverages. Just a few yards away, on the other side of the open area, Judith saw Vivian in a slithery silver gown with a slit skirt. She was supervising two white-coated waiters and three nubile young women in abbreviated maids' costumes. Billy and Frankie Buss stood off to one side, where a small bandstand had been set up. Judith felt as if she were watching a war zone with the enemies preparing for battle.

"What the hell was that?" Joe shouted, coming through the dining room into the entry hall. He saw Marva Lou and stopped short. "Oh! Sorry." He gave an imitation of his most engaging grin to the newly arrived guest. "That sounded like a shot, but of course it must have been . . . ?" He transferred his questioning gaze to Judith.

"Billy Buss," Judith said, speaking rapidly lest Joe interrupt with a tactless remark in front of Billy's sister-in-law as well as a couple from Iowa who'd left the social gathering in the living room, apparently to ask about the loud noise. "This is Billy's brother's wife, Marva Lou. They just arrived." Judith smiled at the curious Iowans under the archway between the living room and the entrance hall. "The neighbors are celebrating their recent move from Florida. No need for alarm."

Marva Lou waved a plump hand. "Oh, pay no notice to Billy. He likes to think he's a cowboy. You got to see him do tricks with his lasso."

The Iowa guests returned to the living room. Joe, however, went out into the cul-de-sac. Judith had a feeling he was going to speak to Billy about discharging firearms in an urban setting.

Judith turned her attention back to the registration form. "Fill this out, and I'll give you your keys," she said to Marva Lou. "One is to your room, the other is to the front door. We lock up at ten every night. When my husband gets back, I'll have him move your luggage upstairs."

"That's real nice of him," Marva Lou said, scribbling down the required guest information. "I sure hope you enjoy having Billy around. Isn't he a hoot?"

"I haven't met him," Judith said, watching Marva Lou sign the registration with a flourish. "He and . . . his wife are gone quite a lot."

Marva Lou nodded, as Judith handed her the keys. "Sounds right to me. Billy never was one to stay put. Restless, that's Billy. Frankie's just the opposite. Hard to get him out of the house. Funny how kids in the same family turn out so different. The roving kind, the stay-at-homes, and the in-betweens. My own sister's another gadabout. A good thing she went to work for Amtrak. After fifteen years, you'd figure she'd have her fill of traveling, but she still loves it." Marva Lou paused, frowning. "We wouldn't have made this trip if it wasn't for . . ." She paused again. "Well, let's say family matters. I suppose I ought to go freshen up. Or at least comb my hair." She patted her short, honey-colored curls. "I'll bet the party's already started."

"Both parties," Judith said, glancing at her watch. It was twenty minutes to seven. "Our Block Watch is having its annual get-together. It's a citywide event."

Marva Lou nodded. "We have those in Oklahoma. A good idea." She clasped the B&B keys in her hand. "I'll go up to the room now. See you at the party. Or parties."

As Marva Lou disappeared up the stairs, Joe returned. "My first meeting with Billy Buss was a bust. He didn't appreciate my words of wisdom about shooting off a gun on Heraldsgate Hill."

"I assume he didn't do that in Florida," Judith remarked. "Maybe it would be different in the wide-open spaces of Oklahoma." She started down the entry hall. "I'm going to take Mother to the Block Watch party. She's probably chomping at the bit. I'm almost fifteen minutes late."

"Skip it," Joe called after her. "She's already there."

Judith turned around. "She is?"

"Vivian came to escort her," Joe said wryly. "Your mother's at the Buss party."

Judith sighed. "Oh, well. I suppose that's okay. It's awkward, though. I refuse to abandon our neighbors. I'll stay on the potluck side of the cul-de-sac." Seeing a faintly sheepish expression on Joe's face, she took a couple of steps toward him. "Well? What about you?"

Joe grimaced. "I thought I'd do both."

Judith glared at him. "Have fun. You and Mother make a cute couple." She continued on through the dining room to the kitchen.

Joe didn't follow her. Five minutes later, carrying her big glass bowl of three-bean salad through the front door, she spotted him on Vivian's side of the cul-de-sac, talking to one of the two men who appeared to be waiters. At least two dozen people Judith didn't recognize were gathered around Herself's lavish buffet and equally opulent bar.

"I've never seen so many bags of ice in my life," Arlene remarked as Judith set the salad bowl on the trestle table. "It's going to melt all over the place. How much are they going to drink? And who are they?"

"Hangers-on," Judith replied bitterly. "Probably some of the barflies Vivian knew in the old days. I'd have assumed most of them had been permanently pickled by now."

"They're certainly not from around here," Arlene huffed. "Except," she added, lowering her voice, "for your husband."

"Don't rub it in," Judith shot back. "He probably knows some of those creeps from the cop bars. That's how he met Vivian. She was the lounge singer in a seedy dive downtown."

Arlene looked sympathetic. "A moment's madness," she murmured. "And years of sorrow." She paused as Joe slapped one of the waiters on the back and broke into an uncharacteristically boisterous laugh. "Or maybe not," Arlene said under her breath.

Judith turned her back on Herself's gathering. "Remind me to kill Joe when he gets over here."

Arlene brightened. "Would you like help? I can practice on Carl."

Judith shuddered. "I shouldn't have said that. About killing Joe. Just saying that out loud scares me."

"Yes," Arlene said, putting a hand on Judith's arm. "You do seem to attract dead people. That is, people who——"

She was interrupted by the sudden sound of a snare drum. A half-dozen musicians had set up on the bandstand across the cul-de-sac. Ragtime music blared from speakers, almost deafening Judith. "Oh, no!" she cried, putting her fingers in her ears. "This is awful!"

"Worse than that," Arlene shouted. "Here come some of your B&B guests."

The couple who had been startled by the gunshot and two

young women from Boston stood on Hillside Manor's front steps, staring in surprise at the commotion. The lean and lanky Iowa husband spotted Judith and marched in her direction.

"Is this your evening entertainment?" he demanded, his florid face almost purple. "You didn't mention that in your brochure."

"It has nothing to do with me," Judith declared. "I'm angry, too."

The man from Iowa jerked a thumb in the direction of Herself's gathering. "Then why is the man I thought was your husband dancing with that blond hussy in the silver dress?"

Judith stared. Sure enough, Joe and Vivian were doing a foxtrot to the music. Several others had joined in. Gertrude sat in her motorized wheelchair, tapping her foot in time to the beat.

"I apologize," Judith finally said, shoulders slumping. "Let me treat you and your wife to dinner. I have some gift certificates inside."

She hurried back into the house, the man and his wife—as well as the two Bostonians—following. She unlocked the drawer of the small desk in the entry hall and removed a hundred-dollar gift certificate for the Manhattan Grill Steak House. Aware that the two young women were about to pounce, she took out a second gift card, this one for Ugeto's, an upscale Italian restaurant. The foursome grudgingly thanked her and withdrew to the living room just as the two older couples traveling together from Bakersfield, California, came down the stairs.

"Here," she said, grabbing the only remaining pair of certificates, which were for Papaya Pete's expensive Polynesian eatery in one of the city's big hotels. "Enjoy."

Judith retreated into the kitchen, where the music was muted. Her nerves were frazzled. Impulsively, she took a bottle of Glenlivet from the top kitchen shelf and poured a generous inch into a glass. Adding ice, she sipped deeply, savoring the liquor's golden glow. The whisky was from the Scottish Highlands, brought back by Judith and Joe when they returned in March from their stay at a castle on the North Sea.

She was swirling the drink in her hands when the last of her guests—newlyweds from Anchorage—poked their heads in the kitchen.

"Hey," said the red-haired bride whose first name Judith recalled as Ashley, "what's going on outside?"

Judith kept both hands on the cocktail glass, preferring not to let her guests think she stood around the kitchen getting snockered. "The neighbors are having a Block Watch potluck," she explained. "But some people who recently moved here are giving their own party as well. I'm sorry about the noise. Look," she went on, hoping to forestall another complaint, "I keep restaurant gift certificates on hand for certain kinds of emergencies, such as visitors who lose their travelers' checks or credit cards. I've run out, but if you want to enjoy a pleasant, quiet dinner, go ahead and I'll credit your bill here for the cost of your evening out."

Ashley looked at her fair-haired groom. "Dare we?" she said.

"It's not a dare," Judith began. "I'm perfectly willing to—"

"No, no," the young man broke in. "We were wondering if we could join that party with the band. They sound like they're having fun."

"Be my guest," Judith responded. "I mean . . . well, you already are. But I'm sure Mr. and Mrs. Buss won't mind one bit."

Ashley clapped. "Let's go, Jake! A live band! Way cool!"

The couple hurried off through the dining room. Judith finished her drink and reluctantly went back outside.

At least a dozen Dooleys had arrived. The matriarch,

Corinne, was setting out homemade pies. Judith was about to commend her for baking in such warm weather, but Rochelle Porter intervened, shouting to make herself heard above the band's rendition of "Caramba, It's the Samba!"

"I hate that kind of music," Rochelle declared, wincing. She removed her half-glasses to stare across the cul-de-sac. "Where's that black sedan? It was parked where the bar's set up."

"What sedan?" Judith asked in a loud voice.

Rochelle put her glasses back on. "Ham said it was the same car he saw the other night, and probably the same man who went around the back of the house and then left." She shrugged. "Maybe he was delivering something for this shindig. I hear there's going to be a big announcement after the band takes a break."

"Hopefully," Judith said, "it'll be soon."

Jeanne Ericson poked Judith in the arm. "We have noise ordinances in this city," she shouted. "Can't we report this?"

Seeing Joe doing the samba with Marva Lou Buss, Judith grimaced. "It depends on the time of day, I think, like after ten at night. Let's wait. I wouldn't want to see my husband busted by one of his former cop buddies."

Jeanne followed Judith's gaze. "Oh. I keep forgetting—Joe used to be married to Whatever-Her-Name-Is-Now. Sorry."

"So am I," Judith murmured, feeling a headache coming on. "Excuse me, I'm going to get some aspirin."

Rochelle and Jeanne both nodded. The samba ended, providing a moment of relative quiet. But as Judith went up Hillside Manor's front steps, she saw Herself appear on the bandstand.

"Don't forget," Vivian said into the microphone that was pinned to the deep vee of her cleavage, "our big news is coming up in just a few minutes. Meanwhile, I'm going to serenade you with one of my old favorites, 'I Ain't Got Nobody.'" She swiveled her hips and patted her bosom. "Not true, of course. As

my darling Billy Boy will tell you, I still have plenty of body."
Her guests broke into gusts of laughter and scattered applause.
Judith felt like throwing up.

"How much," Jeanne Ericson murmured, "of that body is
plastic?"

Rochelle snickered. "I may have too much body, but it's all
mine."

"Only my hip is artificial," Judith asserted. "I can't stand
listening to this." She fled into the house as Herself began to
sing.

Downing two aspirin, she leaned against the kitchen counter, wondering if she could endure going back outside. Hunger
pangs were gnawing at her stomach. The neighbors always provided delicious food, though it suddenly occurred to Judith that
they'd all miss Miko Swanson's Japanese delicacies this time
around. They'd also miss the older woman's gentle kindness.
At least, Judith thought with a pang, Mrs. Swanson had been
spared the raucous party in the cul-de-sac.

Finally, a few minutes before eight o'clock, she worked up
the courage to rejoin the Block Watch potluck. The aspirin was
easing her headache, though she was still annoyed with both
Joe and Gertrude for blatantly joining Herself's shindig.

To Judith's relief, the music had stopped. The bandstand
had been vacated. Joe had been talking to an older man who
looked vaguely familiar and might have been one of the cop-bar
habitués, judging from his somewhat drunken gestures. Judith
watched her husband leave the Buss celebration and walk across
the cul-de-sac to join Gabe Porter, Hamish Stein, and one of
the Dooleys' grown daughters. The newlyweds from Anchorage remained on the other side of the cul-de-sac, engaged in an
animated conversation with one of the waiters.

Judith ignored Joe. She filled a paper plate with pastrami,

Russian rye bread, macaroni salad, and several of Gabe's vegetables with sides of Rochelle's creamy herbed dip and Naomi's zesty horseradish.

Arlene sidled up to Judith. "If you want to give Joe a few good whacks, I've got my wooden spoon in the potato salad."

Judith sighed. "Why can't men understand what upsets women?"

"Probably because they're men," Arlene said. "There's not much we can do about that. Unfortunately."

Judith took a bite of the pastrami, which was excellent. She was about to taste Jeanne's macaroni salad when Herself again ascended the bandstand to the accompaniment of a drum roll. Conversations died away; guests on both sides of the cul-de-sac stopped in their tracks; only Sweetums seemed uninterested, prowling toward the Rankerses' hedge, possibly in search of Tulip.

"Old friends, new friends, buddies, and neighbors," Vivian began, "this might as well be New Year's Eve. This is the start of a new era, looking forward to the future. We know you'll want to join us as we ring out the old and bring in the new."

"What's she talking about?" Jeanne whispered to Judith.

"I've no idea," Judith replied. "She doesn't seem drunk. But she probably is."

". . . Good enough for the last century, but not for this one," Herself continued, though Judith had missed the first part of the sentence. "Most of you know we recently purchased the house next door on the corner." She raised a languid arm in the direction of Mrs. Swanson's bungalow. "That little house and the one I already own are outmoded on Heraldsgate Hill. They're the past, we're the future. Right after Labor Day, both of these little cracker boxes will be razed . . ." She paused and beamed at her audience. "And in their place, like a phoenix rising from the ashes, will stand a six-story, twelve-unit, glorious, beautiful, stunning condominium!"

"My God!" Jeanne gasped.

"Lordy, Lordy," Rochelle muttered.

"Mad as a hatter," Arlene declared angrily. "Where's my wooden spoon? I'm going to beat some sense into that woman!"

"So," Herself went on as her guests applauded enthusiastically, "hop on the Twenty-first Century Express for the ride of your life!" The band began to play; Vivian chimed in with a lusty, if rusty, version of "Chattanooga Choo Choo."

The neighbors had begun talking at once. Judith marched up to Joe, who appeared to be under attack from Ted Ericson and three of the Dooleys.

"Did you know about this?" Judith demanded of her husband, dispensing with good manners for interrupting an irate Ted.

"Hell, no!" Joe retorted. "That's just what I was trying to tell—"

A commotion broke out by the bandstand. Arlene hadn't been kidding. She was trying to get at Vivian, wielding her wooden spoon as if it were a mace. Billy Buss was trying to restrain her. The band kept playing, but Herself stopped singing and stepped backward, falling into the bass drum.

Billy's muscle finally overcame Arlene's rage. She shrieked as he hauled her away from the bandstand, where the musicians had abruptly stopped the music while the drummer helped Vivian stand up. Halfway across the cul-de-sac, Billy released Arlene. Still clutching the wooden spoon, she whacked her enemy on the head. He reeled slightly just as Carl Rankers hurried to the site of the melee.

"Don't," the usually unflappable Carl warned Billy, "ever lay a hand on my wife again! If my darling wants to whack somebody with her spoon, let her do it. That spoon belonged to her grandmother, and it's whacked plenty of people better than you in the last hundred years!"

Billy shot Carl a menacing look. Frankie Buss put a hand on his brother's shoulder. "C'mon, Billy, have another drink."

Judith glared at Joe. "And you told me to stop looking for trouble! Now what have you got to say for yourself about Herself?"

"Okay, okay," Joe said, holding his hands in front of him as if he expected either his wife or Arlene to go on the attack. "But how the hell would I know Vivian intended to build a condo?"

"You might've guessed she'd do something disruptive," Judith asserted. "I just had that feeling——" She stopped, seeing Gertrude hurtling across the cul-de-sac in her wheelchair. "Mother? Have you defected from the enemy camp?" Judith asked.

Gertrude ignored her daughter, heading for Arlene. "You okay, kiddo?" Judith heard her mother ask.

"Oh, great!" Clapping her hands to her temples, Judith whirled around—and bumped into Naomi Stein. "Sorry," she apologized. "My mother must be having a loyalty crisis. All her sympathy is for Arlene, but being so ornery, she likes Vivian, too. I'm the one left out in the cold. Or the heat, in this case. Oh, damn, I'm going inside to mope!"

"Poor you!" Naomi exclaimed, but her sympathy was lost on Judith, who fled toward the B&B. Shutting the front door to muffle the noise from outside, she went into the living room, grabbed the phone from the cherrywood table, and called her cousin on the other side of the hill.

"We just got back from our Block Watch party," Renie said, answering on the second ring and sounding chipper. "They ate all of my chickens. How'd your potluck turn out?"

"A disaster," Judith said, collapsing onto one of the matching sofas. "You won't believe what I'm going to tell you."

Five minutes later, Renie got a word in edgewise. "But I *do* believe it," she insisted. "It's just the kind of stunt Herself would pull. Maybe she can't carry it off. Zoning and permits and all that stuff. I'm not sure their property is zoned for multifamily dwellings."

"I had to apply for a permit when I opened the B&B," Judith said. "I got it," she added glumly.

"A condo's a different matter," Renie responded, "especially if the neighbors put up a fuss. You're going to have to band together. It sounds as if they're as upset as you are."

"They are," Judith assured her cousin. "Arlene was at her most combative, and everybody else in the cul-de-sac probably would've joined her if Billy hadn't backed off."

"That's good," Renie declared. "You've got momentum. March on City Hall tomorrow. Launch whatever's the best offensive. Maybe you should start with the Heraldsgate Hill Community Association."

"Good idea," Judith said. "Now I'm going to have another shot of Glenlivet and try to relax. Talk to you tomorrow."

Thirty minutes later, Judith was still on the sofa, having fallen asleep after downing her second drink of the evening. She was awakened by Joe, calling her name from what sounded like the dining room.

"Wha'?" Her body jerked at the sound of his voice. Disoriented, she tried to sit up. "Joe?" she finally said after he'd repeated her name a couple of times.

"There you are," he said, looking sheepish as he entered the living room. "Are you still mad at me?"

Judith held her head. "I don't know. I feel groggy."

He sat down next to her on the sofa. "Go to bed. You're beat. It's after nine o'clock. I did our share of cleanup from the potluck. Your glass bowl's in the dishwasher."

Judith yawned and stretched. "No. I should stay up at least

until ten, when we officially lock the doors." She paused, suddenly aware that except for the ticking of the grandfather clock, there was an absence of noise in or out of the house. "What happened to that awful music? Did Arlene actually break up the big party?"

"Not exactly," Joe said, wincing. "The band played for a little while after . . . after you left, but by that time some of Vivian's partygoers were kind of sloshed. The stripper that Billy hired refused to . . . perform. Then everybody started arguing and some fights broke out and the band stopped playing and all the musicians decided to take advantage of the free booze and . . . well, Vivian passed out, so Billy carried her into the house and more fights broke out because, I guess, Billy didn't come back to pay the band and everything got out of hand and somebody called the cops. Gabe Porter, I think. By the time the patrol car got here, everybody had pretty much left. That's when Ted Ericson and Naomi Stein decided to press charges for disturbing the peace and littering private property." He winced again. "I'm afraid that side of the cul-de-sac is kind of a mess, but none of our gang will touch it with a ten-foot pole."

"Oh, good grief!" Judith was wide awake now. "A stripper! What next? No, don't tell me. It's bad enough already, especially since our guests will have to come back to the B&B through a disaster area!"

"That couple from Anchorage didn't seem to mind," Joe remarked. "They grabbed a couple of bottles from the bar and went off to the park up the street. I gave them directions on how to get there."

"What! You know it's illegal to drink alcohol in a public park! Are you crazy?"

"Probably." Joe sighed. "It's been that kind of evening."

Judith couldn't argue. "Yes," she said, and tried to curb her anger. It was pointless to keep berating Joe. She needed support, not hostility. "We're going to have to fight this dreadful condo project, you know."

Joe leaned forward on the sofa, head down, hands on his knees. "It sure as hell puts me on the spot."

Judith was taken aback. "What do you mean? Just because you were married to Herself shouldn't enter into the picture. If she were anybody else, you'd be the first one to file a protest."

"But she isn't anybody else," Joe murmured, staring at the glass-topped coffee table's collection of glossy magazines.

"That's it!" Judith cried, bracing herself to get her tired body off of the sofa. "I *am* going to bed! You check on Mother, you take care of the guests, you lock up, you apologize to them again for all this mess! I've had it!" She stomped out of the living room, taking the shorter route to the third floor via the front stairs.

Joe didn't try to stop her. In fact, he didn't even bother to look up. He remained motionless, still staring with unseeing eyes at the cover of the latest *House Beautiful* magazine.

Judith couldn't settle down after she got into bed. Maybe it was the change in routine, maybe it was the evening's unsettling events, maybe it was the quarrel with Joe—whatever the cause, it was going on midnight when she finally drifted into a restless slumber.

When she woke up, she thought it was because she heard Joe coming to bed. Still annoyed, Judith rolled over as far as she could to avoid any attempted gesture of affection. But after a couple of moments, she realized that the sound was caused not by her husband getting into bed, but by him getting out of it. He was moving hurriedly around the bedroom. Judith opened her eyes as she heard him go out into the hall. Glancing at the digital clock, she saw that it read 2:47 A.M.

Propping herself up in bed, she listened for any sound of a commotion. The two bedroom windows facing the Rankerses were open. The fans that Joe had put in whirred softly, muffling any but the loudest of noises coming from outside. She turned them off and peered through the window on Joe's side of the bed. Carl and Arlene's house was dark. After a moment or two, Judith heard voices. One of them belonged to Joe, though she couldn't make out what he was saying. The other belonged to a woman who sounded distraught. *Not Mother,* she thought, as anxiety replaced anger. *Not Arlene, either,* she decided, or the lights would be on at their house.

She turned on the bedside lamp, put on her lightweight summer robe, and slid her feet into a pair of sturdy slippers. Heading down the narrow stairway to the guest rooms, she noted that everything seemed quiet. When she reached the bottom of the back stairs, Judith noticed that the hallway and porch lights were on. The back door was wide open. Opening the screen door, she saw two figures on the sidewalk just off the porch.

Joe had his arms around Vivian. At first, Judith thought they were embracing, and her ire returned. Then, as she moved to the steps, she realized that Joe was holding on to Herself to keep her from falling. He turned slightly when he heard the screen door close behind Judith.

"Call nine-one-one," he said, keeping his voice down. "Get some brandy. I think Vivian fainted." With a grunt, Joe picked up his former wife and started for the porch steps.

Rattled, Judith stood aside as her husband and his burden squeezed through the narrow corridor. "Shall I ask for a medic?" she called after Joe.

"Yes," he answered, using his elbow to open the swinging half-door between the kitchen and dining room. "Call the cops, too."

Judith snatched up the phone from the counter and dialed 911. The answer was prompt. "We have a neighbor at our house," she said, giving the address, "who's collapsed. She needs medical attention."

As the emergency operator responded, Judith hurried to join Joe in the living room, where he was placing Vivian's limp body on one of the matching sofas. "Why," Judith whispered, a hand over the phone's mouthpiece, "do we need the cops?"

"Because," Joe said grimly, "Vivian's got a dead body in her backyard."

6

Judith was stunned. "No!" she cried. "I can't believe it!"

Pausing in his efforts to rally Vivian with gentle shakes, Joe scowled at his wife. "Just tell them to send the cops, and get the brandy."

As Judith headed for the guest bar in the dining room, she spoke again into the phone. "We need the police as well. There's been . . . an accident. It's . . ." She swallowed hard before finishing the sentence. ". . . a fatal one, I believe."

The female operator relayed the call, then spoke again to Judith. "Is this Mrs. Flynn at that B&B on Heraldsgate Hill?"

Judith still felt rattled. "Yes, Mrs. Flynn is unconscious in the living room. She found the body."

"Of course she did," the operator said dryly. "Who's calling?"

Judith suddenly realized the operator was confused. "Oh, my God! This is *Judith* Flynn. It's the *other* Mrs. Flynn who passed out. I mean, she's Mrs. Buss now, but I——"

"Forget it," the operator interrupted. "Help is on the way." She paused. "*Two* Mrs. Flynns? Man, the body count is really going to go up around here!" She abruptly rang off.

Resentment stiffened Judith's spine. She put the phone down

on the dining room table, got the brandy out of the antique washstand in the corner, and grabbed a small snifter. Before returning to the living room, she made sure the front porch light was turned on and opened the door. By the time she rejoined Joe, Vivian was starting to come around.

"Who's dead?" Judith asked, pouring brandy into the snifter.

"How the hell would I know?" Joe snapped. "Vivian!" He gave her a less gentle shake, dislodging one of her false eyelashes, which fluttered onto her red and green kimono. "Drink this," he said, holding the snifter to his ex-wife's lipstick-smeared mouth. "Come on, be a good girl."

"Ha!" Judith said under her breath.

Herself drained the brandy in one big gulp, choked, sputtered, and finally slumped back against the sofa. "Thanks," she said in an overwrought voice. "I needed that."

"You always do," Judith muttered, ignoring Joe's reproachful glance. "I think I hear the first of the emergency vehicles arriving."

Judith hadn't heard any such thing, but needed a few moments to collect her wits. By the time she reached the entry hall, however, headlights were coming into the cul-de-sac. Or trying to come in. For the first time, she saw the havoc that had been wreaked by the wild partygoers. The usually pristine area was littered with all sorts of debris, including an overturned table, broken bottles, dirty table linen, and a mangled saxophone. The lead vehicle, a medic van, had to slow down to maneuver its way through the mess. A fire engine followed for a few yards and stopped in front of the Steins' house on the corner. Apparently, there wasn't enough room to guide the big truck any farther.

Thankfully, Judith thought, the emergency crews hadn't had to use their sirens. The neighborhood was usually quiet at three in the morning. *Usually*, Judith thought, *except for Joe's wives finding corpses.*

"Hi," she said with a feeble smile for the lead EMT, known to Judith only as Medic Kinsella. "How've you been?"

"You mean since your last disaster?" The expression on Kinsella's long, horselike face was wry. "Where's this one?"

"The patient's in the living room," Judith said wearily. "You know the way. The body's in the patient's backyard."

"We can't do much about the dead ones," Kinsella said.

"Neither can I," Judith murmured, stepping back as the rest of the emergency crew followed Kinsella's lead. She recognized a couple of them who glanced in her direction as she stood next to the Duncan Phyfe desk by the stairs.

Judith knew it was best to keep out of the way while the medics treated Herself. She might as well wait for the police to show up. After a couple of minutes she wandered out onto the front porch. Her dark eyes traveled in the direction of the Buss house. Who, she wondered, was the corpse in their backyard? Billy? Frankie? Marva Lou? She assumed that the visiting Busses from Oklahoma were sound asleep in their room on the second floor. But maybe they weren't. Judith couldn't bear to think about another guest who had come to a violent end while staying at Hillside Manor.

At last, a patrol car drove slowly and carefully through the cul-de-sac. Would she know the officers on duty?

The two patrol officers who got out of the car were strangers. The tall, lean one was a woman; the short, stocky cop was a man. They both looked very young to Judith, probably fresh from the police academy. Their name tags identified them as Smith and Wesson. For a brief moment, Judith thought it must be a joke. But judging from their somber expressions, neither of them struck her as having been given the gift of laughter, let alone, she thought, borrowing a quote from Sabatini, a sense that the world was mad.

"You can skip the wisecracks," the female cop named Smith said somberly. "We've heard it all. Is the victim inside?"

"No," Judith replied. "The victim is in our neighbor's back-yard." She pointed to the Busses' bungalow. "I don't know who it is. Mrs. Buss collapsed and hasn't been able to tell us much."

"Are you sure this person is dead?" Wesson asked without any change in his solemn expression.

"You'll have to find that out from Mrs. Buss," Judith said. "Or by seeing for yourself."

Smith stood ramrod straight under the porch light. "Where is Mrs. Buss?"

"In our living room," Judith replied. "She's receiving medical treatment."

Wesson frowned. "Was she injured as well?"

Judith made a disparaging gesture. "Of course not. She's in shock from finding the corpse." *That happens to people who aren't used to stumbling over murder victims.*

Smith nodded once. "Is this death connected to the party that was held earlier? The patrol officers from the previous shift were called to a disturbance at an address in this cul-de-sac."

"I've no idea if the victim was involved," Judith declared testily. "Again, you'll have to ask Mrs. Buss. She and her husband hosted the party. The rest of us were involved in the Block Watch potluck." *Unless you count my idiot husband and my contrary mother.*

"Where is Mr. Buss?" Wesson asked, leaning across the threshold in an apparent attempt to look inside.

"He's not here," Judith snapped. "I assume he's at home."

The young officers exchanged glances, but didn't speak. As if they communicated with ESP, Smith and Wesson turned around and headed down the steps. Judith watched them pick their way through the cluttered cul-de-sac. As far as she could tell, there were no lights on in the Busses' house. She waited to see if anyone came to the door. After a few minutes, the cops gave up and walked in the direction of the backyard. Judith went back into the living room, where Herself was lying limply on the sofa. Joe, wearing his short summer pajamas and a pair of worn Romeo bedroom slippers, stood by the window seat, arms folded across his chest, a worried expression on his round face.

"Well?" Judith said, joining him.

Joe shrugged. "She's okay. But I still haven't had a chance to ask who the hell is dangling out there in her cherry tree."

"It's not Billy, I assume."

"I guess not. She would've said so before she passed out."

Judith watched Kinsella, who was kneeling next to the sofa and speaking quietly to Vivian. The other EMTs stood idly by, apparently finished with their duties.

"How," Judith asked Joe, keeping her voice down, "did Herself get hold of you? I didn't hear the phone ring."

Joe looked uncomfortable. "She has a whistle. She used to blow it when she wanted me to . . . um . . . well . . . you know."

"I see. Just like Lauren Bacall and Bogie. 'If you want me, Steve, just whistle,'" she quoted.

He didn't look at Judith. "Kind of, yes."

Judith cocked her head to one side. "So she whistled, and you rushed to her side?"

Joe expelled a rueful sigh. "It woke me up. She was under the bedroom window. I guess you were too tired to hear it."

"Probably."

Kinsella had stood up. "I think Mrs. Buss will be fine," he announced. "She's had a severe shock. Have the police arrived?"

Judith nodded. "About five minutes ago. They went over to her house to look for the . . . accident victim."

"Okay." The medic motioned to the other emergency personnel. "Let's hit it." He turned back to Judith and Joe. "You folks had better do something about that hazardous waste site out front. Didn't somebody already call in tonight about a disturbance around here?"

"Yes." Joe's tone was curt.

"Must've been some party," Kinsella murmured. "See you later. Unless I take early retirement."

The medics and firefighters trooped out of the house. Vivian called Joe's name in a pitiful voice.

"What can I do?" he asked, going over to the sofa.

"I could use a real drink," Herself said. "If you know what I mean." She winked—and the other eyelash fell off.

"Sure," Joe said. "I'll get it."

Judith sat down on the other sofa. "Would you mind telling us who's dead?"

"Really, Judith," Herself said sharply, "you sound very callous."

"I'm not," Judith retorted. "I'm just . . . tired. *Who is dead?*"

Heaving a huge sigh, Vivian shook her head. "I've no idea. It's a man. I've never seen him before in my life." She shuddered. "It was horrible!"

"I'm sure it was," Judith said, trying to exhibit some of her usual compassion. "Have you any idea how he died? Was he elderly?"

"No." Herself offered Joe a feeble smile as he handed her a stiff bourbon over ice. "Thanks, darling. You're a pet. As always."

Without looking at either his past or present wife, Joe sat down next to Judith. "You'd better tell us what happened, Vi, before the detectives get here. Why were you outside in the middle of the night?"

Vivian frowned. "Middle of the night? I suppose it is—to some."

"That doesn't tell me why you were outside." Joe sounded very much like the policeman that he'd been for so many years.

Herself took a big sip of bourbon and shrugged. "I wanted some fresh air. The house seemed very stuffy. It doesn't have AC like my condo on the gulf."

Judith could almost accept the explanation. But not quite. Maybe she didn't want to believe Herself.

"And?" Joe prodded as his ex took another sip.

"And there he was," Herself said with a helpless gesture. "Hanging from that cherry—or apple or whatever it is—tree. I didn't have to get close to tell he was dead."

"What did you do then?" Joe inquired.

"I . . ." Vivian frowned. "I'm not sure. Billy was asleep on the couch. He sort of . . . wore out after all the commotion. My first thought," she said somewhat coyly, "was you. After all, you *are* a detective."

If, Judith thought, *I have to listen to much more of this simpering old tart play games with my husband while some poor soul is hanging from a tree, I'll run away from home. Or at least go back to bed.*

Joe had another question for his ex. "How was he dressed?"

"Dressed?" Herself looked as if she needed a definition of the word. "Oh—I'm not sure. But he *was* dressed." She swallowed more bourbon and giggled. "You know me, I would've paid attention if he wasn't."

"That's it," Judith said, getting up and stomping out of the living room. As she reached the entry hall, Wesson appeared at the door. His stolid demeanor hadn't changed, but he looked pale. Judith wondered if this was the first corpse the young officer had ever seen.

Wesson removed his regulation hat. "My partner is with the body. We've sent for someone from the homicide unit."

He cleared his throat. "The deceased may have met with foul play."

"No kidding!"

Smith nodded solemnly. "It's a suspicious death. It might be an accident, but it could also be a suicide or a——"

"Homicide!" Judith broke in. "Ha-ha!"

At last, there was a reaction from Wesson. "Ma'am," he said, sounding alarmed, "are you okay?"

Judith willed herself to behave as if she were a perfectly normal citizen whose encounter with violent death was a shocking occurrence. "I'm stunned, that's all," she asserted. "Who is the victim?" She had almost added "this time."

"We don't know," Wesson replied, putting his hat back on as both officers stepped inside. "We followed procedure and didn't touch the body. Do you know who found him?"

"I certainly do." Judith grimaced. "Mrs. Buss is a . . . a neighbor, and she's in the living room. She's the one who collapsed."

"Thank you," Wesson said. "May I talk to her?"

"Be my . . . of course," Judith amended. "Go straight through the arch. She's with my husband." *Who used to be* her *husband,* Judith thought, *and who is also a retired homicide detective, and we both know more about homicide than you two kiddies could ever imagine.*

Wesson entered the living room very quietly. Judith heard Joe greet him and introduce Vivian. Not wanting to listen to a rerun of Herself's grisly discovery, Judith went into the kitchen, poured water into a glass, and added a couple of ice cubes. Standing by the sink, she gazed out into the darkness. It was going on four. Very soon, the first streaks of light would appear in the eastern sky beyond the Rankerses' house. It was Tuesday morning. In a little over two hours, some of the neighbors would be up and about. The detectives might still be working what was possibly a crime scene. Judith's only consolation was that at least this time she wasn't the Mrs. Flynn who had found a dead body.

After a few quiet moments marred only by the ticking of the schoolhouse clock and an occasional snatch of conversation from the living room, Judith took the glass of water with her and went upstairs to bed.

She fell asleep almost at once, waking only when the alarm rang at six. Still exhausted, she tried willing herself to get up, but went back to sleep and didn't awaken until twenty minutes after seven. Joe's side of the bed was empty. Maybe he'd gotten up when the alarm went off. Or else he hadn't come back to bed. As she brushed her teeth and showered, Judith hoped that Joe had already started the guests' breakfast in time to serve at eight o'clock. She dressed hurriedly, combed her hair, and applied lipstick. It was after seven-thirty when she reached the kitchen.

Joe was nowhere in sight, and the coffeemaker hadn't been turned on. Rushing around the kitchen to prepare a buffet of ham, bacon, sausages, eggs, toast, pancakes, fruit, and crois-sants, Judith wondered if Joe had slept on the sofa. After the meats had been put on the stove, she went into the living room. No one was there. The only signs of recent activity were the empty snifter and two cocktail glasses.

Judith opened the front door. A white unmarked car that might have been a police vehicle was parked near the entrance to the cul-de-sac. None of the debris had been removed. The area looked even more unsightly in the bright light of morning.

Ten minutes later, Judith had finished making the pancake batter and prepared the various fresh fruits for presentation. She was setting the bun warmer for the croissants on the oak buffet when Joe, wearing rumpled suntan pants and a T-shirt with a green shamrock and the imprint "Everyone Loves an Irish Boy," came through the front door.

"Where've you been?" Judith asked, surprised.

"At the crime scene," Joe retorted. "Where the hell else?" He hurried past her and went into the kitchen. "Coffee! Thank God!"

"Crime scene?" Judith echoed as she joined him by the counter. "Really?"

"As if you couldn't guess," he growled, sloshing coffee onto the floor—and his pants. "Goddamnit!" He started for the back stairs. "I'm going to take a shower."

"Hold it!" Judith shouted. "Who's dead?"

"Who knows?" Joe kept on going.

Judith put her mother's ham, eggs, toast, and coffee on a tray and took it out to the toolshed. Gertrude was just getting dressed.

"So I'm late this morning," she snapped. "I don't get much chance to party these days. Want to make something of it?"

Judith ignored her mother's pugnacious expression. "Of course not. I'm running late, too." She hesitated, wondering if she should tell Gertrude about the body in Herself's yard, but held off. Her mother might not be as deaf as she pretended, but she hadn't heard or seen any of the activity in the wee small hours of the night. The old lady would eventually find out, but Judith wanted to wait until she had more facts.

"You're a pickle-puss today," Gertrude declared. "What is it now?"

"Nothing," Judith lied. "I told you, I got off to a late start."

"Hunh," Gertrude said, zipping up her housecoat. "I suppose you're all green with envy because Vi had a better party."

"Not really," Judith said, resisting the urge to say that at least nobody had been murdered at the Block Watch venue. "I'll see you later, Mother." She headed back into the house.

The couple from Iowa had entered the dining room. He wore bib overalls over a T-shirt; she had on a plaid blouse and a denim skirt. They looked like the poster pair for the American Farm Couple. Judith recalled that their last name was Griggs. Or Greggs or Gruggs or possibly even Groggs. Her brain wasn't working at full bore.

"Good morning," she said, lugging the coffee urn to the buffet. "Would you like some grapefruit and juice?"

"Florida fresh-squeezed oranges," the husband said. "Pink grapefruit, and don't hold the sugar."

"The sugar's on the table," Judith said, a frozen smile in place. She turned to the wife, who was as lean and almost as lanky as her husband. "And you?"

"Toast." Mrs. Griggs——or whatever her name was——sat down. "I only eat toast for breakfast. Unless you have biscuits."

"Not this morning," Judith replied. "Tomorrow, perhaps. The weather's too warm to turn on the oven."

The husband gripped the back of the oak captain's chair that had always been reserved for Grandpa Grover. "Warm? You don't know what 'warm' is. If you lived in Iowa, you'd be wearing a couple of sweaters in this kind of so-called 'warm.' Hell's bells, try working out in the cornfields in August to make danged sure that every ear on every stalk is getting enough danged fertilizer to produce every danged kernel without any danged gaps. Then, if it's still hot—*danged* hot—in mid-September, that's when we start the harvest. Now, that can be danged miserable!"

"No doubt," Judith said. "Excuse me. I have to check the sausages."

"Tomato juice for me," the wife called after Judith. "Grapefruit gives me sour stomach."

The Iowans were souring Judith's disposition. Back in the kitchen, she brought up the couple's reservations to memorize their last name: It was Griggs. It should, she thought, have been Gripes.

Judith was removing the bacon from the skillet when she heard the foursome from Bakersfield enter the dining room. They were exchanging pleasantries—or trying to—with the Griggses. By the time Judith had brought out the rest of the buffet items, the young Bostonians arrived at the table. The only parties not yet up and about were the newlyweds and, more ominously, Marva Lou and Frankie Buss.

Just before nine, Joe came downstairs, dressed for the day but still in an edgy mood.

"I don't suppose," Judith said drily as she dished up scrambled eggs, sausage, and pancakes for both of them, "you'd care to let me know what's going on at Herself's house?"

Joe had refilled his coffee mug and took a big drink before answering. "According to what was found in his wallet, the vic was Charles Brooks, sixty-eight, from Henderson, Nevada. No emergency contact information on him, but there was an address and a phone number in the 702 area code."

Judith sat down across from Joe. "He really was murdered?"

"He was strangled." Joe popped a bite of sausage in his mouth.

"You mean hanged?"

Joe shook his head and finished chewing. "Despite Vivian's description of how she found the guy, he wasn't hanged. There was a long rope around his neck. The end of it had been tossed over a low-lying limb of the cherry tree, and the vic was propped up against the trunk. I suppose that in the dark it might have looked to Vivian as if he'd been hanged."

"Especially," Judith added wryly, "if she was crocked."

"Back off," Joe retorted. "Unlike you, Vivian isn't used to stumbling over corpses. She's damned upset."

Judith put her fork down and folded her arms across her chest. "You think I find bodies on purpose. Okay, so the discovery disturbed Vivian. I understand. I'll try to stop making cracks about her. But remember, I'm the one who worried about her return causing trouble. You can't say you weren't warned."

Joe didn't reply. Only a flicker of his green eyes indicated that he'd acknowledged his wife's words.

Judith waited a couple of minutes before she spoke. "Nobody knows this guy?"

Joe shook his head again. "He wasn't on their guest list. Vivian and Billy didn't recognize him. Neither did the assistant, Adelita. She wasn't there last night and only got back this morning just before I left."

"Why wasn't she at the party?"

"I gather she had some relatives in town and stayed with them at their motel," Joe said. "Oh, don't worry," he went on in a caustic tone, "the cops will check her out."

"Who's in charge of the investigation?" Judith asked.

"They're new to Homicide," Joe replied, "but they seem sharp. K. C. Griffin and Jay Almquist, female and male, respectively."

"Do they know you're a retired detective?"

A slight smile played at Joe's mouth. "It seems I'm a Legend in My Own Time." The smile faded. "So are you."

Judith frowned. "Are you ready to deliver the cautionary tale?"

"About keeping your nose out of this one?" Joe uttered what sounded like a grunt. "Why bother? You never listen."

It was useless for Judith to argue, as useless as it was for Joe to warn her of dire consequences. It was also useless for Judith to insist that she never searched for murder. It always found her first.

Wordlessly, she got up to check on the guests. The newly-weds had just come into the dining room, looking distinctly hung-over. The bride fumbled as she tried to pull out a chair;

the groom nodded absently at the others before gingerly sitting down.

"Can I get anyone anything?" Judith asked, trying to sound gracious.

"How 'bout a new head?" the groom murmured.

"Toast," said the bride. "Maybe I could eat some toast."

Mr. Griggs stood up. "Excess," he said, "is harmful to the body and the mind. Clean living, hard work, walk the straight and narrow. Come on, Trish, let's hitch up the wagon and go see some sights."

"Have a pleasant outing," Judith called after the couple. They kept going, heading out the front door. They'd arrived in a taxi, so Judith assumed that they'd either already called one or planned to take the bus. Maybe, she thought, being such hearty souls, they planned to walk.

"Has anyone seen Mr. and Mrs. Buss this morning?" she asked of the other guests.

The newlyweds looked blank. The Californians shook their heads. Judith shrugged and went back to the kitchen. It was a quarter after nine. Marva Lou and Frankie still had forty-five minutes before the breakfast service would be cleared away.

Judith had finished pouring more coffee into her mug when her cleaning woman, Phyliss Rackley, came through the back door.

"Armageddon!" she exclaimed. "Repent! The end is near!"

"If," Judith said wearily, all too familiar with Phyliss's religious mania, "you're referring to the mess in the cul-de-sac, it's left over from the neighbors' party."

Phyliss shook her head, the gray sausage curls bobbing up and down. "Not just that. I saw the Grim Reaper out there. Two of them, in fact, male and female, all gaunt and spooky." She put a hand to her flat bosom. "If they aren't a sign of doom, I don't know what is!"

"They're guests," Judith said. "Farmers from Iowa. Stop fussing."

Phyliss was unconvinced. "You can't fool me. I'll swear on a stack of Holy Bibles that I smelled the stench of death out there."

Judith grimaced. "Okay, you might as well know. Somebody did die last night, over at the Buss house."

"Aha!" Phyliss brightened and squared her shoulders. "Do I or do I not know the Hounds of Hell when I see them? Was it that Jezebel who flaunts her body all over the place?"

"No," Judith answered. "It was a stranger. Nobody seems to know who he was. I'm afraid that he may have been murdered."

The cleaning woman's eyes widened. "Well! Just deserts, maybe. I can only imagine the wickedness that goes on with that shameless hussy! I've often marveled at the thought of Mr. Flynn being married to that harlot. He must have been drugged."

"Perhaps," Judith murmured. Joe had, in fact, been drunk. His first encounter with dead bodies had occurred when two teenagers overdosed on cocaine. To cope with the tragedy of young lives needlessly cut short, he'd gone to the bar where Herself sang and somehow ended up being hijacked to Las Vegas for a quickie wedding that was only a blur in his memory.

"By the way," Judith said, changing the subject, "the couple in Room Four haven't come down yet. The other guests are still at breakfast, except for Room One. They're the ones you saw heading out for the day."

Phyliss shuddered. "I'll make a sign to ward off the Evil Eye when I do that room," she muttered, heading for the back stairs. "I'm off."

"In more ways than one," Judith said under her breath.

By five to ten, the rest of the B&B's visitors had also left the premises. The young women from Boston had checked out, moving on to British Columbia. Their room would be occupied that night by two single men from Virginia.

Joe, who had joined Carl Rankers in the cul-de-sac to start cleaning up, came back inside. "Carl ordered a Dumpster," he said, refilling his coffee mug. "I wasn't sure we should get rid of all that crap until we cleared it with K.C. and Jay, but they had some uniforms go through it earlier, just in case there might be something that'd tie in to the Brooks homicide." He shrugged. "If they found anything, they bagged and tagged it."

"I assume Vivian and Billy will pay for the Dumpster," Judith said.

"Probably." Joe started toward the back door.

"Hey," Judith called after him, "Frankie Buss and his wife haven't shown up for breakfast. Do you think we should check on them?"

"They aren't here," Joe replied. "They went over to Vivian and Billy's at the crack of dawn, offering cold comfort."

"Cold comfort or Southern Comfort?" Judith asked wryly.

Joe narrowed his eyes at his wife. "You've been warned."

"Okay, okay," Judith said testily, "but how did Frankie and Marva Lou know about the dead man?"

"Billy called his brother on his cell phone," Joe replied. "You're too damned suspicious. I'm going back to work with Carl."

When Phyliss came downstairs with a load of linen for the washer, she paused at the top of the basement stairs. "Those Grim Reapers in Room One are pulling a fast one, if you ask me."

Judith, who had cleared off the buffet and was putting some of the uneaten fruit in the fridge, took a few steps into the hallway. "What do you mean?" she asked.

"Farmers, you say," Phyliss huffed. "Ha! Since when do farmers and their wives wear fancy Eye-talian clothes?"

Judith was puzzled. "I don't understand."

"Neither do I," Phyliss declared. "I may be a poor God-fearing cleaning woman, but I know Harmony when I see it. It says so, right on the labels in their closet. His and her suits, of all things."

"Harmony?" Judith repeated. "Honestly, Phyliss, I don't know what you're talking about."

"See for yourself," she said, continuing on to the basement.

Judith finished putting the fruit away, grabbed the cordless phone, and went up the back stairs. It was after ten o'clock. Never a morning person and rarely crawling out of bed before ten, Renie might be up and semi-conscious. She dialed her cousin's number as soon as she reached the second floor.

"Yeah?" Renie said, sounding surly. "What?"

"Hold it," Judith said. "I'm doing two things at once." She used her master key to get into Room One. "I suppose you haven't heard about our latest corpse," she said, opening the guest room door.

"I sure haven't, and I don't want to," Renie snapped. "I haven't had breakfast yet. I'm not dressed. I just poured my first cup of—*Corpse?*"

"Yes, in Herself's backyard." Judith went to the closet, where at least half a dozen men's and women's suits had been hung. "Strangled. An older guy from Henderson, Nevada. Nobody seems to know him."

"Good Lord! You *are* serious?"

"Do I ever kid about dead bodies?" Judith asked, unzipping the first of the garment bags and wishing in vain that Phyliss wouldn't snoop in the guests' belongings.

"Of course you're not kidding about corpses." Renie paused. "Do you want me to come over after I get myself together?"

"You don't have to," Judith said, checking the labels on the suits. "Armani!"

"What?"

"Armani suits owned by a farmer and his wife from Iowa."

"What?"

"You heard me."

"I'm going to pretend I didn't. I'll see you in about an hour. You're obviously unhinged." Renie hung up.

Judith stood still for a few moments. She knew that many farmers were wealthy and could well afford to buy Armani or any other expensive designer's clothing. But the Griggses didn't seem like the type. The wardrobe they'd worn since their arrival had been typical of midwestern farm folks—maybe *too* typical, Judith realized, stereotypes of what urbanites thought a farmer and his wife were expected to wear.

She looked around the room, seeking any other signs of an upscale lifestyle. Their luggage, which consisted of two large and very shabby matching suitcases and an equally well-worn fold-over, didn't exude prosperity. The bureau drawers revealed nothing of interest, although the couples' underwear looked new.

Judith checked the closet again. There were six shoe bags. Two of the woman's pumps were Manolo Blahnik; the third was by a designer Judith had never heard of, Christian Louboutin. All three pairs of the man's lace-up shoes were from Dolce & Gabbana.

The only item she hadn't checked was a black leather attaché case propped up next to the room's only chair, an armless rocker that had belonged to Gertrude's mother.

The case was locked. Judith was tempted to use her skills at picking locks, but the sound of voices in front of the house diverted her attention. Looking out the window, she saw Joe standing just off the front porch with Arlene and Carl. Arlene was screaming at both men. Judith opened the window as far as it would go and called down to the trio. "What's wrong?"

Arlene was yelling so loud that Judith couldn't be heard. She raised her voice and called again—twice. Finally, Joe looked up.

"Never mind," he shouted. "Everything's fine."

Arlene pushed at Joe and looked up to the window. "It's not fine! The police think I murdered that man in the tree! Help me, Judith! I can't be arrested and have to wear one of those orange jumpsuits! It's not my color!"

7

Judith hurried down the front stairs as fast as her artificial hip would permit. Arlene was railing at Joe. Carl had edged away in the direction of the huge laurel hedge. Sweetums sat on the porch steps, watching the human drama with apparent interest—until he yawned, stretched, and slipped back inside before the screen door closed behind Judith.

"Arlene!" Judith exclaimed. "Talk to me!"

"Police brutality!" Arlene cried, hurrying to Judith, who was standing at the bottom of the steps. "And after all the times we've called in about suspicious doings in the neighborhood! Don't they realize I'm the wife of a Block Watch captain? Doesn't rank mean anything to these monsters? Why can't Joe make them stop tormenting me?"

Joe had walked away to join Carl. The two men exchanged quick, helpless glances, but didn't speak.

"Come inside," Judith urged, noting that the husbands had cleared up most of the junk and filled what looked like all of the neighbors' garbage cans and bins. "Have some coffee. It's getting too warm standing here in the sun."

Arlene stomped up the stairs and into the house. "Am I being followed?" she asked, looking over her shoulder as she continued down the entry hall to the kitchen.

"Not yet," Judith said. "Have a seat." She poured Arlene a mug of coffee and one for herself. "Now tell me what happened."

Arlene sighed. "Someone—I suppose it was the Busses—told those two detectives that I'd tried to attack Vivian. And Billy. And . . . " She paused, an anxious expression on her pretty face. "Was there anybody else? It was such a muddle. I don't recall it very clearly."

"I don't think so," Judith said. "Carl stepped in about that time."

"Oh, yes. Carl. He's so protective of me. Unless we have an argument and are attacking each other." She sighed again. "Anyway, the young woman detective came to talk to us a while ago. She was very aggressive, asking all kinds of ridiculous questions about my wooden spoon. It's a wonder she didn't take it away from me."

Judith tried to maintain a noncommittal facade. "You didn't . . . ah . . . threaten her with it, did you?"

"Of course not!" Arlene was indignant. "I was taking it out of the dishwasher when she arrived. What does she think I am? A hooligan?"

"So then what?" Judith inquired.

"She started asking all these questions about how I got along with the neighbors," Arlene said, her blue eyes snapping at the mere thought of such impertinence. "I told her that everyone in the cul-de-sac liked each other very much, thank you, *Ms. Nosey Parker*. But," she went on, wagging a finger, "the Busses do not fit in. They simply aren't our kind of people."

An outsider might have thought that Arlene was being a snob, but Judith understood. "I know. Too much flash and dash.

And now that Vivian is rich, she intends to ruin our comfy little nest."

"I shouldn't say this," Arlene said, lowering her voice, "but if someone had to get murdered, why wasn't it her?"

Judith grimaced. "That thought crossed my mind, but I tried to put it aside." She paused to take a sip of coffee. "That's a very good question, though."

Arlene's blue eyes widened. "You think she may be next?"

"No, no, of course not," Judith said emphatically. "Let's hope and pray there is no 'next.'"

"Really?" Arlene looked disappointed. "Don't you usually find your dead people in bunches?"

Judith winced. "Not always. What's odd is that the dead man seems to be a stranger. Strangers rarely come into the cul-de-sac. There's no reason for them to do that."

"Your guests are usually strangers," Arlene pointed out.

"That's different." Judith frowned. "It's not my guests that I'm thinking of in terms of a connection to the corpse. It's Herself's guests. Somebody in that crowd may have known him."

Arlene nodded. "Joe told me he was from out of town. Las Vegas, was it?"

"Henderson," Judith said. "It's a suburb, I think." She smiled at Arlene. "You seem to be recovering from the police brutality."

"What?" Arlene looked surprised. "Oh, that. I overreacted. I've been subject to more grueling questions by our kids at Christmastime when they wanted to find out what they were getting as presents. The year they tied me up to the telephone pole on the corner really annoyed me, especially since it was snowing." She shrugged. "Still, I very much resent the way that young woman detective spoke to me. It was almost as if she thought I knew everything about everybody in this neighborhood. Cheeky, I thought."

Judith suppressed a smile. "You do keep an eye out on what goes on around here. Which," she added quickly, "is good."

"That's part of being a Block Watch captain's wife," Arlene said. "Surely the detectives will speak to those awful people the Busses had at their party."

"Oh, yes," Judith assured her. "I wouldn't mind having a look at that guest list myself."

"Neither would I." Arlene leaned forward, an eager expression on her face. "How do we do it?"

"Maybe Joe can get it," Judith said, "either from the cops or Vivian."

Arlene shook her head. "That sounds too simple. Wouldn't it be more exciting to break into the Busses' house?"

Judith burst out laughing. "Arlene! That's a crime!"

"I suppose," Arlene said after heaving a resigned sigh. "It sounds like fun, though."

"It's not," Judith said, having broken into one or more residences in the course of her checkered career as an amateur sleuth. "It's also dangerous. We could get shot. Billy has a gun, remember?"

"True." Arlene looked thoughtful. "Do we eliminate Billy as the killer because the victim wasn't shot?"

"Not necessarily," Judith replied. "Damn. I wish I knew Billy better. I've never really talked to him."

Arlene stood up. "Why not now?"

"I don't know what's going on over at their house," Judith admitted. "It's still a crime scene."

"That white car is gone," Arlene said, heading out of the kitchen. "It belonged to those detectives. Let's pay a call on the Busses."

"Well . . ." Judith wasn't anxious to see Herself, but decided to humor Arlene. "Okay. I suppose that's the considerate thing to do."

As the two women went out onto the front porch, a flatbed truck with a large green Dumpster was pulling into the cul-de-sac. Apparently the driver was honking his horn to warn any bystanders of his approach. When the truck stopped just after clearing the cross street, the driver got out, but the horn kept blaring.

"That horn must be stuck," Arlene said, wincing at the noise. "Why doesn't the driver fix it?"

"I don't know," Judith said. "It's really annoying."

Joe and Carl moved away from the hedge to meet the driver. As Judith and Arlene hesitated on the porch, a car appeared from behind the truck, its right wheels precariously on the sidewalk and the left ones in the street.

"What on earth . . . ?" Judith began as the horn kept beeping. "Oh, no! It's Renie!"

The Toyota Camry came to an abrupt halt just inches short of ramming the Porters' recycling bin. "Who's the idiot blocking my way?" Renie demanded, lurching out of her car.

"Coz!" Judith cried. "I wasn't expecting you so soon. Would you mind parking in our driveway?"

"I wouldn't mind," Renie retorted, "if I could *see* your driveway. That big clunk of a truck blocked my view."

"I'll guide you," Judith said.

Renie got back in the car. Rochelle Porter had come out of her house and was watching the Camry reverse just enough to avoid hitting her recycling bin.

"Your cousin isn't much of a driver, is she?" a bemused Rochelle remarked to Judith.

"Let's say she's inclined to occasional lapses," Judith allowed. "By the way, have the police talked to you and Gabe yet?"

Rochelle shook her head. "Gabe's at work. You know he always leaves before six to make sure all the produce orders are ready to go. If the police came to see me, I wasn't home. I had a dentist appointment earlier." She nodded in the direction of the Buss house. "Nasty doings over there. Too much Demon Rum makes for trouble."

"Absolutely," Arlene agreed. "There's a devil in every glass. Except, of course, for the wine at Holy Communion. The devil wouldn't dare try something with that."

Rochelle smiled. "To think I always thought that's why you Catholics called yourselves SOTS!"

"No, no," Arlene insisted. "That's the nickname for this parish, Our Lady, Star of the Sea. You should know——" She stopped as Renie hurried toward the trio.

"Where's the stiff?" Renie asked matter-of-factly.

"Gone," Judith said. "Or so I assume. The detectives left. They wouldn't leave the body in the Busses' backyard."

Renie looked around the cul-de-sac at the collection of garbage cans and recycling bins. "I thought maybe they just stuffed him into one of those."

"You are sometimes truly callous," Judith admonished her cousin, though she noticed that Rochelle had chuckled and Arlene was staring at her own yard waste bin as if wondering if she should check it out.

"So," Renie said, forced to shout as the big green Dumpster was being unloaded under the supervision of Joe and Carl, "what are we doing?"

"Doing?" Judith glanced at Arlene. "Well, we were thinking about paying a condolence call on Vivian and Billy."

"Right." Renie's brown eyes danced. "Hey, Rochelle, want to make it a foursome?"

Rochelle shrugged. "Why not? There's safety in numbers."

The women took the longer route along the sidewalk, not wanting to get in the way of the Dumpster project. As they reached the Busses' bungalow, Frankie and Marva Lou came out through the front door.

"Are we too late for breakfast?" Marva Lou inquired.

"I'm afraid so," Judith replied. "It's almost eleven. I stop serving at ten."

"Mind if we fix ourselves some eggs?" Frankie asked. "I'm starved. Billy's wife isn't much of a cook."

"Surprise!" Judith said under her breath.

"What?" Marva Lou asked, standing at the edge of the sidewalk.

"Her eyes," Judith fibbed. "She . . . um . . . needs glasses. Vivian has trouble reading recipes."

"What," Frankie demanded, "does she need to read to fry an egg? I thought she used to be in the restaurant business."

"She was," Judith said, "in a way. One of her former husbands owned a bar and grill downtown. Vivian worked there." That much was true. It wasn't necessary to elaborate about how Herself had provided the entertainment, both at the piano in the bar and, so the rumors ran, in other, less musical parts of the establishment.

"Johnny Agra," Renie murmured. "Wasn't that the name of Husband Number One? It suddenly came to me that he was an old pal of Uncle Al's."

"I think you're right," Judith said quietly, but kept her attention fixed on the visitors. "Mrs. Rackley, my cleaning woman, can show you where the skillets are stored. The eggs, of course, are in the fridge, the bread is in the breadbox."

"Got it," Frankie said, leading the way to the B&B.

Renie poked Judith. "You never let guests cook. How come?"

"Because," she said as Arlene and Rochelle started for the front door, "I want to finally meet Billy. Phyliss will watch them like a hawk."

Arlene rang the doorbell, which played the all-too-familiar notes of "How Dry I Am." The violinist who had rented the house from Vivian had mercifully changed the chimes to a half-dozen bars of Beethoven's Pastoral Symphony. Apparently, Herself had preferred reverting to the tasteless original.

Adelita opened the front door. She seemed surprised to see the four women on the small porch. "Yes?" she said, her brown eyes wary.

Arlene took over as designated spokesperson. "We've come to offer our condolences to Mr. and Mrs. Buss for their sad situation. That is, it's not exactly *sad,* but then again it's not *happy,* either. If they didn't know the dead man, they shouldn't be *too* sad." She didn't wait for a response, but barged through the doorway, the others following her lead.

Stepping into the living room, Judith saw Billy Buss lying on the sofa, attired only in a pair of boxer shorts featuring the logo for XXX Tequila. He turned away from the NASCAR channel to gaze blearily at his visitors. "Whassup?" he asked, sounding as if he didn't much care.

"Mr. Buss," Arlene said, undaunted, "may we offer our sympathy for your misfortune." She had moved to the sofa and put out her hand.

Billy looked puzzled. "It's Vi who's got the fortune." He moved slightly and shook Arlene's hand in an apathetic manner. "Yeah," he went on, "I guess you could say I missed Pa's fortune. So did my brother and——" His gaze returned to the TV screen, which was showing a six-car pile-up with flames spurting from the wrecked vehicles. "Wow," he said softly. "Now, that *is* bad luck."

Adelita had left the house as soon as the visitors entered. She hadn't closed the front door behind her, which, Judith thought, was a good thing since the small, gaudily decorated living room not only felt crowded and airless, but smelled faintly rank.

"Is Mrs. Buss here?" Judith inquired.

Billy didn't look away from the TV. "Which one?"

"Vivian," Judith said. "Your wife."

"In the can, maybe," he said, running a hand over his blond hair, which was beginning to thin on top. "Or in the cellar. She says it's cooler there. May well be." He chuckled. "We got a bunch of coolers down there." Billy picked up a Miller High Life beer can that was sitting on the floor. "Damn. This sucker's empty. We'd better not be out of Millers. Those guests really guzzled them down. Where's Adelita?"

"Adelita ran off with Mr. Dumpster," Renie said. "She's got a thing for garbage. Looking around this dump, I can see why."

Billy eyed Renie curiously. "Who's Mr. Dumpster? Who are *you?*"

"Enough's enough," Rochelle declared. "I'm getting out of here. This place smells like the disposal bins at Gabe's warehouse." She stomped out of the house but left the door open.

"That makes two of us," Renie said, and followed Rochelle.

Arlene, however, persevered. "As I recall, your basement entrance is off the back porch. Come, Judith, we'll go through the kitchen."

The kitchen was even a sorrier sight than the living room. Leftover food from the party was strewn all over the counters, the table, the chairs, and the floor. Dirty dishes, glassware, and a couple of broken bottles were scattered around the small area. Judith and Arlene had to pick their way through the mess to reach the back door.

"Pigs," Arlene said in disgust as they went down the half-dozen steps to the basement. "Is Adelita an assistant or the maid? Whatever she is, she isn't doing much to earn her money around here."

"That depends," Judith murmured as Arlene rapped loudly on the basement door, "what she has to do to earn it."

Arlene stared at Judith. "You mean . . . ?"

Judith shrugged. "Who knows, with this bunch."

The women waited for over a full minute. Arlene knocked again. "Vivian? Yoo-hoo!"

"Maybe," Judith suggested, "she'd rather not face you after last night. It might be just as well if we went——"

"Nonsense!" Arlene interrupted. "I don't hold a grudge. Why should she? Exchanging an occasional blow with someone doesn't mean you don't care for them." She turned the knob. The door opened easily.

Judith followed Arlene inside. The basement looked far different than it had when Rudi and Taryn occupied the house. Gone was the piano where Taryn had given lessons. The music books, the carpet, the bench, the bust of Chopin, and all the other trappings of a piano teacher had been replaced by cartons of liquor, unmarked boxes, coolers, an ugly pole-lamp, and a big freezer.

"No Vivian," Arlene murmured.

Judith pointed to a small hallway. "There are a couple of rooms off of that. Mostly storage, I think, but maybe used for something else now."

Arlene went over to the freezer. "What would Vivian keep in here?" She tugged at the latch and lifted the lid. "Nothing. How wasteful!"

"Let's face it," Judith said, shaking her head at the vast quantity of liquor, "vodka's the only booze I know of that you can freeze. Maybe they're waiting for some of those specialty meats from the Midwest that you can put in your freezer. Billy strikes me as a steak man. Besides," she went on, pointing to the wall by the freezer, "the thing's not even plugged in yet."

Arlene started toward the hall. "Where *is* Vivian?"

"Forget it," Judith said, moving to the door. "I really don't want to see her, especially if she's drunk."

"But," Arlene protested, "won't she be talkative? We might learn all kinds of lurid secrets."

Judith made a face. "I already know some of them. I wish I didn't." She led the way up the stairs. "I doubt that she'd be able to tell us much, since she insists she doesn't know the man who was killed."

Arlene was right behind Judith. "Do you believe her?"

"I suppose so," Judith said grudgingly, reaching the walkway. "There's the cherry tree. See the yellow tape cordoning off most of the yard? I was so focused on watching my step going into the basement that I didn't notice."

"That's gruesome," Arlene remarked. "But intriguing. What do you think? You must have some ideas about what went on."

"I don't," Judith said, "although I have to wonder where the victim was killed. In the house, outside, or somewhere else?"

Arlene tapped her fingers against her cheek. "If the murder didn't happen here, it must have taken some strength to haul the body over to the tree and make it look as if he'd been hanged."

"Maybe," Judith said. "But we don't know how big the victim was."

Arlene shot Judith a quizzical look. "You mean small and easy to carry? Maybe a jockey?"

Despite the grim subject matter, Judith grinned. "Anything's possible, but I doubt it. Joe can find out."

"Yes," Arlene said. "You must make him do his part. He certainly knows how to go about it. Or does he?"

"Of course," Judith replied. "It's not a skill he'd forget."

"You never know," Arlene said darkly. "Men forget so many things, like birthdays and anniversaries, and where they put their shoes."

"True." Judith gazed around the small garden. Vivian didn't enjoy yard work, and neither had her former tenants. The previous owner, however, had been an avid gardener. Little was left of his efforts. Small patches of grass had turned brown in the summer heat, the rosebushes had reverted to their original wild state, and weeds had choked out most of the once lovingly cultivated perennials.

"Clues," Arlene said. "Shouldn't we search for some?"

Judith shook her head. "The police are very thorough. If there was anything to find, they'd have taken it with them."

"Drat. No matchbooks, no cigarette butts, no cocktail napkins with scribbled phone numbers?" Arlene looked disgusted. "What kind of a murder *is* this?"

"A wasteful one," Judith responded. "They all are. Killing creates more problems than it ever solves. I've never understood that sinister place in the human heart."

Arlene nodded. "Murder makes such a mess. Blood to clean up—a serious problem, because it leaves stains, as hard to get out as red wine. Breakage, if you hit someone over the head with heavy china. As for poison, what do you do with the leftovers? It seems so wasteful. Not to mention moving the body off the carpet because it's in the way of foot traffic. And the noise if you use a gun! I suppose that's why I've never killed Carl. It'd just make for more housework."

Judith shot Arlene a bemused sidelong glance. "You wouldn't want that. I've never known anyone who kept a tidier home."

Arlene shrugged. "I rather enjoy it. Gardening, too. Obviously, Vivian doesn't do either one."

Judith paused at the garden gate. "I wonder . . ."

"What?"

"If I should believe Vivian about not knowing the victim."

Arlene's face lit up. "Then let's grill her! Isn't that police talk?"

"I'd like to grill her—on a spit over the barbecue in our backyard," Judith muttered, lifting the latch on the gate. "Oh, damn! I shouldn't say things like that. Anyway, my misgivings are probably off base. Sometimes I——" She stopped, staring down at two pale pink rose petals just inside the fence. "Hold on," she said. "Where did these come from?"

Arlene examined the petals. "Not here. All the roses have returned to their natural red color." She beamed with excitement. "A clue?"

"I don't know," Judith said. "It *could* be the kind of thing the police would overlook if they weren't into gardening." She carefully picked up the petals and cupped them in her hand. "Our roses are orange and white and yellow and red. You don't have any pink ones, do you?"

Arlene shook her head. "Carl and I have never been rose fanciers. Oh, they're lovely, but they require so much care. Years ago, Mrs. Swanson tried to teach me how to grow and prune the rosebushes we had then, but they never turned out right. I just didn't have the knack, and Carl didn't have the patience."

"Mrs. Swanson," Judith murmured. "She had gorgeous roses in her backyard. We have some, but none of them are this color. Who else around here has pink roses?"

"The Ericsons?" Arlene suggested. "Not the Porters. They grow only a couple of climbers on trellises. One is orange, and the other is yellow. The Steins lost all of theirs to some disease a few years ago and never put in new ones."

They had strolled as far as the Ericson house. "I suppose Jeanne and Ted are at work," Judith said. "Do you think they'd mind if we took a look at their garden?"

"No. They like to show it off," Arlene said, opening the gate with its rustic iron trellis covered by deep purple clematis blossoms. "I think they have some roses in back." She gestured at the drought-resistant plants and grasses spaced between concrete stepping stones and tiny pebble fillers. "Ted designed all this, too."

"Smart people," Judith remarked, admiring a large reflecting globe on a stone pedestal. "An architect and a lawyer, but no kids."

"As you said," Arlene agreed, "smart people."

Judith smiled. "I defer to you. I only had one. You've had five."

Arlene shrugged. "It seemed like a good idea at the time."

"Your kids have turned out very well," Judith declared as they went into the backyard. The enclosed garden was more traditional, with a small fishpond, a lilac tree, gladioli, dahlias, pansies—and roses. But none of the half-dozen bushes had pale pink blooms. "We've struck out." She gazed over the wooden fence, studying the Dooleys' white Colonial. "I don't think the Dooleys raise roses. Only children. Besides, they're a bit off the beaten track."

Arlene looked disappointed. "You don't think the petals are clues?"

"Probably not," Judith replied as they walked back to the front of the Ericson house. "Still, it's odd to find them by the Busses' gate. Maybe somebody wore a corsage or stuck a rose in her hair."

Out on the sidewalk, the women noticed that their husbands had finished filling the Dumpster. The truck and its driver had left after dropping off the Dumpster, but Renie's car was still parked in the Flynns' driveway. Joe and Carl were nowhere in sight.

"I wonder," Arlene said, "how long that ugly green thing is going to sit there."

"I wonder if Ted and Naomi actually went ahead and pressed charges against the Busses," Judith remarked.

"If they did, I'd like to sign the complaint, too," Arlene said.

Judith smiled wryly. "Isn't that kind of . . . ironic? I mean, we just paid a condolence call."

"So? We can be sorry about one thing and angry about the other. That's what makes life interesting."

"I guess," Judith responded in an uncertain voice. "I'd better find Renie. Maybe she went with Rochelle to the Porters' house."

"I suppose Carl and Joe are taking a nap," Arlene said as they walked toward Hillside Manor. "All that exertion probably did them in. Men have no stamina."

Judith saw Joe's red MG parked in front of Renie's Camry. "I guess Joe's taking the day off from his latest investigation."

"He could investigate this murder right here if he'd bother himself," Arlene said, moving on to her own house.

"He'll leave that to the cops who haven't retired," Judith said, starting up the front steps. "See you later."

As soon as she got inside the house, she heard voices in the dining room. The loudest belonged to Renie.

"I don't give a damn if you want a three-and-a-half-minute egg," she said harshly. "What do I look like—a Swiss watch? If you won't eat it, breakfast's over."

To avoid confronting Renie duking it out with the Busses, Judith backtracked, went up the front stairs, through the hallway on the second floor, and came down the back stairs. By the time she reached the kitchen, Renie was picking up pieces of what looked like a dinner plate.

"Hey!" Renie shouted. "Watch out! The Oklahomans broke an egg on the floor, busted a plate, and boiled water all over your stove. I exiled them to the dining room and finished making their breakfast myself."

"That was nice of you," Judith said, leaning against the refrigerator. "I think."

Renie glared at Judith. "Not really. I was defending your premises. After I yakked it up with Rochelle, I came in here to use your downstairs bathroom. I heard those Busses banging around in the kitchen, and Marva Lou was fiddling with your computer while Frankie was dropping everything but his pants."

Judith put a finger to her lips. "Keep it down," she murmured. "They can hear you."

"So?" Renie was wiping up the rest of the broken egg. "I don't care. They made a mess. They're idiots."

"Well, I care," Judith said crossly. "They're my guests. It wasn't their fault that their relatives got involved in a murder."

Renie stood up. "Whose relatives don't? Not ours, that's for sure. Are you going to start defending Herself? Sheesh!" She tossed the dirty dishcloth into the sink.

The only way Judith could shut Renie up—short of throttling her—was to keep quiet. The schoolhouse clock indicated it was almost noon. Ignoring her cousin, Judith opened the fridge and took out baloney, mayonnaise, and a cube of butter.

"What are you doing?" Renie asked.

"Making Mother's lunch."

Renie's temper, which was quick to ignite and quick to dissolve, was already on the wane. "I'll take it out to her. I should pay a duty call. Mom is next on my list. I have to cut her toenails. I'd rather work out under a hot sun on a Georgia chain gang. Breaking up rocks can't be any harder than cutting Mom's nails. They're so thick I practically need a saw. And she squirms."

"I understand," Judith said. "All too well."

The phone rang. Judith picked up the receiver from the counter.

"The media is here," Rochelle Porter said. "Do you want to hide?"

"Oh, drat!" Judith cried. "I was hoping they wouldn't show up. Thanks for the alert. Yes, I'll seek refuge in the toolshed with Mother."

"Who was that?" Renie asked after Judith disconnected the call. "What's wrong?"

"Rochelle says the media has arrived. I want to avoid them.

You know what it's like if Mavis Lean-Brodie is here from KINE-TV."

"Mavis has sometimes been your ally," Renie pointed out. "She's only doing her job."

"I don't care," Judith asserted. "That is, I don't want any more exposure about my reputation as FATSO."

Renie was obviously trying not to smile. "That Web site your admirers set up should be good for business."

"It's not," Judith snapped. "I've made darned sure that they don't mention the name of my B&B. That would only bring in the ghouls and thrill-seekers."

"It annoys you because the acronym got screwed up," Renie said. "I know, I know—Female Amateur Sleuth Tracking Offenders should be FASTO, but FATSO is easier to remember. Good Lord, you haven't been fat since you were a kid. Get over it."

Judith scowled at Renie. "You know I've always had to watch my weight. You, on the other hand, could eat your way through six aisles at Falstaff's Grocery and never put on an ounce."

Renie shrugged. "So? It's my metabolism. How many times do I have to tell you—you're five-nine, you've got a good-sized frame. You can gain or lose twenty pounds, and most people don't notice the difference."

Judith's expression remained sour. "Look outside and see if Mavis is there. I'll finish fixing Mother's lunch."

With a resigned sigh, Renie went out the back way, apparently also wanting to avoid the Busses. Judith tiptoed to the swinging half-doors between the kitchen and dining room and peeked in on her guests. The couple looked as if they were almost finished eating their late breakfast.

"What now?" she heard Marva Lou ask softly.

"We wait," Frankie replied, also in a low voice. "We can't risk anything else."

Judith moved out of sight, but continued to listen. The Busses, however, remained silent. A couple of minutes passed before they wordlessly left the dining room and headed for the front stairs.

Renie came hurrying in through the back door. "No Mavis," she announced. "KINE sent a young man I don't recognize. But I almost never watch the TV news. Both the daily papers are here, and a couple of other television vans. I couldn't make out the logos. That Dumpster blocked my view, and I didn't want to be seen." She stared closely at Judith. "You look weird. What's wrong?"

"The Busses," she said. "They're up to something. I wish I knew what it is. I hope it doesn't involve murder."

8

Judith related the brief exchange between Marva Lou and Frankie. "I wonder what their real reason was for visiting Billy and Vivian. Could it be about Herself inheriting all that money?"

"That's a good guess," Renie replied. "As far as Billy's concerned, he married his father's fortune. But Frankie's left out in the cold."

"True," Judith agreed, "but Vivian's marital track record isn't very good. If she runs true to form, Billy could find himself dumped after a few years." She placed some apple slices on Gertrude's tray. "Do you still want to take this out to Mother?"

"Sure. You stay inside, away from prying eyes." Renie picked up the tray and headed out through the back door.

Joe came into the house a couple of minutes later. "Have you seen the news vultures?"

"No," Judith said. "And I don't want to."

"Good thinking." He picked up the remaining chunk of apple and took a bite. "I crawled through the hedge from the Rankerses to elude the press."

Judith studied her husband's appearance. "No wonder you've got leaves in your hair." *At least, the hair that you still have,* she thought, realizing that Joe's forehead was growing higher and higher at a rather rapid rate. "There's a ladybug on your pants, and some of those little cedar cones on your shoulder."

Joe brushed himself off. Judith saw the insect drop to the floor. "I'm taking this outside. It's bad luck to kill a ladybug." She went to the back door and down the steps, gently putting the ladybug in the dirt. As she watched the little creature scurry under a maidenhair fern, Renie came out of the toolshed.

Judith eyed her cousin with curiosity. "That was a quick visit. Did you and Mother get into a row?"

"No," Renie replied testily. "She has a visitor—Herself."

"Ah. That's why Arlene and I couldn't get her to come to the basement door." Judith's gaze took in the little building where her mother had retreated rather than live under the same roof as her son-in-law. "What sort of bunk was Vivian telling Mother? Not about the murder, I hope."

"I didn't stay long enough to find out," Renie replied. "They were laughing their heads off. Maybe Aunt Gert and Vivian enjoy an occasional body in a fruit tree." She folded her arms across her chest and looked disgusted. "Everywhere I go since I got here, I run into somebody or something that annoys me. I'd go home and get some work done on that design project for the city parks brochure, but I don't want to get stopped by the media. I'm trapped. Who shows up next? Osama bin Laden?"

"If you leave now," Judith pointed out, leading the way into the house, "you're going to have to climb up the hill from our backyard or crawl through the Rankerses' hedge. Which, I might add, Joe just did."

"I could tunnel." Renie gazed around the kitchen. "Where *is* Joe?"

"He was here a minute ago. Maybe he went down to the basement. Or up to the family quarters." Judith opened a can of tuna. "Lunch?"

Renie had sat down on the counter, swinging her feet above the golden oak Pergo flooring. "I finished breakfast at ten-thirty. I'm really not hungry now."

Judith stared at her cousin in mock amazement. "You? Not hungry? Maybe you should see a doctor."

"Not funny." Renie was looking unusually serious. "Why are you making tuna salad when you should be trying to figure out who killed the man nobody knows?"

"Because," Judith said matter-of-factly, "that's Vivian's problem. I have faith in the police." She removed the lid from a jar of mayonnaise and scooped out a heaping tablespoon, shaking it vigorously into the bowl where she'd already added the tuna and salt and pepper. "If you think I want to get mixed up with that woman and her awful problems, you're crazy. I knew she'd be trouble when she moved back here. I'm not going to touch this homicide with a ten-foot pole."

"Okay." Renie hopped off of the counter. "Got any sweet pickles?"

"Look in the fridge." Judith added relish and stirred the ingredients with more force than necessary.

"I suppose," Renie remarked, opening a jar of gherkins, "Joe will be up to his ears in this one."

"I don't think so."

"You ought to know." Renie ate a pickle before she spoke again. "So why did you go to Herself's house?"

"To be polite," Judith replied. "Arlene wanted to go, too. So did Rochelle."

"Neighborly of you." Renie watched Sweetums enter from the hallway. "Too bad Jeanne Ericson and Naomi Stein weren't on hand. Sorry I wasn't a better sub for them, but I couldn't stand looking at all that repulsive stuff in the living room—including Billy."

Sweetums leaped up onto the counter. Judith whisked the

bowl of tuna salad out of the cat's reach. "What's with you?" she demanded of Renie. "Are you suggesting I'm getting involved in this mess?"

"Coz." Renie regarded Judith with serious brown eyes. "This is one time you *should* get involved. Whatever else you think about Herself, she's still—sad to say—a neighbor. The body was found only a hundred feet away from your B&B. Besides," she added with a sly expression, "if you finger her as the killer, she'll have to go to prison. End of annoying situation and vulgar decor."

"Maybe Billy would go back to Florida or Oklahoma or somewhere else far, far away," Judith muttered, trying to shake off Sweetums, who was clawing her tan slacks.

Renie popped another gherkin into her mouth before leaning down to grab the cat. "You are a greedy menace," she declared. "I'm turning you over to the Kitty Kops."

Sweetums squirmed and hissed as Renie carted him out to the back porch. Just as she was setting him down, he scratched her wrist.

"Damn you!" Renie cried as the cat raced off toward the garage and out of sight. "You'll pay for that!"

"Band-Aids are in the guest bathroom," Judith said wearily. "You know where to find them. That was a dumb stunt," she added as Renie went through the dining room to the half-bath off the entry hall. "Sweetums doesn't like to be touched."

Phyliss Rackley came up from the basement, carrying a big wicker basket full of clean laundry. "Is that heathen cousin of yours still here?"

"Serena's in the guest bathroom," Judith replied. "And she's not a heathen. She's Catholic, like me."

"I don't get you people." Phyliss set the laundry on the counter by the computer. "How come your kind worships skunks?"

"Skunks?" Judith was only mildly surprised at the question.

The cleaning woman had some very peculiar ideas about Catholicism. "I don't know what you're talking about."

"Your mother dropped her prayer book this morning when I was cleaning her place," Phyliss said. "I picked it up for her and saw all those pictures of people with circles around their heads. I handed those to her, then she insisted I didn't give her the one of what she called 'The Little Flower.' Now, I've seen that movie *Bambi*—it's a clean, wholesome show, not a bit of filth in it—and I know that Little Flower's the skunk in the forest. So what kind of religion is it that people worship a skunk, no matter how cute it might be in the moving picture?"

Judith sighed. "The Little Flower is a name for Saint Thérèse of Lisieux," she explained. "That's because she promised to send down miracles from heaven like rose petals."

"Rose petals are a miracle? You people are really crazy! What next? Praying to a heifer so somebody drops a rib roast on your head?"

"No, Phyliss," Judith said, seeing Renie coming back through the dining room. "I'll explain it to you later."

"People in India won't even eat a cow," Phyliss muttered, putting clean dish towels into a drawer under the counter. "No wonder they all starve to death!"

"Hi, Phyliss," Renie said with forced enthusiasm. "My, but you're looking well today. Great tan!"

"Tan?" Phyliss looked startled. "What do you mean, 'tan'?"

Renie came closer to the cleaning woman. "Oh—maybe not. Your color is more like jaundice. You'd better have that seen to." She proffered the gherkin jar. "Want a pickle?"

"Not from you," Phyliss huffed. She turned to Judith. "Do I look jaundiced to you? It wouldn't be the first time."

Judith made a show of studying her cleaning woman's appearance. "Well . . . not really. Maybe it's a trick of the light."

Phyliss shot Renie an ominous look. "I can't trust either of you. I'm going to call my doctor as soon as I put the rest of this laundry away." She picked up the half-empty wicker basket and stomped off down the hallway. "Why," she called over her shoulder, "don't you two go pray to one of your skunks?"

"Wacko," Renie muttered.

"You should never comment on Phyliss's health," Judith admonished. "You know she's a hypochondriac."

Renie shrugged and put the gherkin jar back in the fridge. "That's why I enjoy needling her. It's payback for all those idiotic questions about Catholics. Skunks, my butt!"

"That reminds me," Judith said, reaching into the pocket of her slacks and taking out the rose petals she'd found by the Busses' gate. "I found these when Arlene and I went out the back way at Herself's."

Renie looked at the petals. "So?"

"Nobody around here has pink roses."

Renie laughed. "And you're not sleuthing!"

Judith shot her cousin a withering glance. "It just seems odd."

"Does it?" Renie shrugged. "They had a party. Somebody brought flowers as a hostess gift. How many times has that happened here?"

"Did you see any flowers in Herself's living room?"

Renie pondered the question. "I don't think so. All I saw was a muscle-bound lump on the sofa watching what looked like a demolition derby. Not to mention some hideous furniture that insulted my artistic eye. But," she added, "I wasn't there very long."

"Arlene and I went through the kitchen to reach the basement door," Judith recalled. "We didn't see any flowers—let alone roses—there, either. Oh, I know that a bouquet might have been trashed during the various melees, but why did I find these petals——" She stopped speaking as a sudden thought came to her. "The Dumpster! If a bouquet was thrown away, it'd be in there."

Renie held up a hand. "If you think I'm going Dumpster-diving, you're really out of your mind."

Judith shook her head. "Not us. The cops. They should check all that trash anyway. Just in case."

"Don't you think they already did that?"

"Yes," Judith replied, buttering four slices of bread. "But they wouldn't consider flowers as evidence."

"And you do? Hmm."

Exasperated, Judith waved the butter knife at Renie. "Not necessarily, but the petals seemed out of place. I can't help it if I'm . . . curious."

"Okay." Renie kept a straight face. "So who asks the cops to look for the pretty pink roses?"

"Ah . . ." Judith paused, frowning. "Joe."

"Tell him to do it before the garbage is collected," Renie said.

"We've got the Dumpster until next Tuesday," Judith pointed out, putting the sandwiches on separate plates. "I'm going to let him know lunch is ready." She went into the hall by the pantry door and pressed the recently installed intercom to the third-floor family quarters. "Lunch is ready," she announced and waited for a response. The intercom was silent. "Joe?" Judith said, frowning. She pushed the switch on and off. Not only had it been working properly, but the device was saving her from going up and down two flights of steps when one of them was in the private area and the other was downstairs. Judith repeated the message about lunch. There was still no answer. Shaking her head, she went back into the kitchen.

"Maybe he went outside again," she said to Renie.

"Um."

"Coz!" Judith exclaimed. "You're eating Joe's sandwich! I thought you weren't hungry."

"I wasn't," Renie said after swallowing. "Then. I am now. Let's say I'm eating *your* sandwich. You can make yourself another one with the rest of the tuna salad."

"Oooh . . ." Judith sighed and took out two more slices of bread. "I suppose you want potato chips, too."

"Right." Renie gestured with what was left of the sandwich. "I wouldn't mind some lettuce on this."

"Get it yourself," Judith snapped.

"Okay." Renie ripped off half of a romaine leaf and haphazardly stuck it into her sandwich. "I'm going to peek outside and see what the press is doing."

"I don't care as long as they aren't on our front porch," Judith asserted, making another sandwich.

By the time she finished, Renie was already back in the kitchen, munching on potato chips.

"Well?" Judith said.

"Well what?" Renie responded.

"What's going on out there?"

"You told me you didn't care."

Judith sighed. "I care about whether they're still here."

"They are."

"But not coming our way?"

"They don't have to." Renie paused as she polished off the sandwich. "Joe's talking to them."

"Joe?" Judith looked appalled. "Damn him! Why's he doing that?"

Renie shrugged. "Maybe he's trying to get equal time. You've certainly been in the news more often than he has over the years."

"That's ridiculous," Judith said angrily, shoving Joe's sandwich into the fridge.

"As long as your husband's distracting the media," Renie said, licking some mayo off of her thumb, "I'm going home.

Color trends of the future—that's my next project after the parks brochure. How do you like Banana Peel? Oscar loves it. He's also crazy about Jungle Green."

"You can leave immediately," Judith retorted. "I refuse to listen to you jabber about a stuffed animal."

"That's it!" Renie cried. "Oscar Ocher!"

Judith glared at Renie as her cousin strolled nonchalantly out the back door. Less than a minute later the phone rang. To her astonishment, it was Renie.

"I just saw Herself returning to her cozy, yet deadly, bungalow," Renie said. "Luckily, she didn't see me in the driveway. The coast is clear for me to pay a quick call on Aunt Gert before I rent a chain saw to cut my mother's toenails. G'bye."

Ten minutes later, Joe returned from outside. Judith regarded him with reproachful eyes. "So," she said, "you caved in to the media."

"Caved in?" Joe looked puzzled. "What do you mean?"

"We don't need that kind of publicity for the B&B. You better not have mentioned Hillside Manor, and I sure hope you didn't stand in front of the B&B sign on the lawn."

"Oh, for——" Joe noticed that Judith was putting an empty plate into the dishwasher. "Did you already eat?"

"Yes. Your sandwich is in the fridge." Her stern gaze didn't waver. "Well?"

Plate in hand, Joe sat down at the table. "There was no mention of the B&B, and sure as hell no reference to you. The only reason I talked to the media was because they'd spotted me with the homicide detectives, and thought maybe I had some knowledge that the tecs were interested in. I explained that I was retired from the force and just being friendly, checking up on some of the other old-timers."

"Oh." Judith was somewhat placated. "Sorry." She finally lowered her eyes. "It's just that . . . you know."

"Yeah, yeah," Joe retorted. "I don't need reminding. Your track record speaks for itself."

Judith ignored the comment. "Tell me about the detectives."

"Newcomers, young, white male and black female, Almquist and Griffin. They seem sharp, if inexperienced."

Before Judith could probe further, the phone rang. Once again it was Renie, calling from her cell. "I'm at Mother's," she said. "I wanted to let you know that I didn't visit Aunt Gert because . . ." Renie's voice faded slightly. "Yes, I'm sure she isn't dead."

Judith heard Aunt Deb's faint voice in the background but couldn't make out the words. "No, Mother, if she has germs, I never got close enough to catch them." Another pause. "But it's eighty-two degrees and I don't need a damned coat! And never mind the sandals, I will *not* wear socks with them!"

"Coz," Judith said, putting aside her earlier annoyance with Renie, "you'd better tend to your mom. But why wouldn't my mother let you in?"

"I don't know," Renie said crossly. "She told me to beat it, that's all. Yes, Mom, I'll help you with your shoes. What? So how can I cut your toenails if you're too chilly to take off—" Renie hung up.

Judith set the phone down on the counter. "I'm going to collect Mother's lunch things," she said. "Do you have any other plans except hobnobbing with the media?"

Joe shot her a vexed look. "They're leaving. Forget it. You're being a pain. I'll be on the computer upstairs this afternoon, working on those corporate background checks."

Judith started for the back door, but stopped. "Uh . . ." She realized it was time for a bite of humble pie. "Really, I am sorry," she said, turning back. "Too much confusion, not enough sleep, weather still hot, and another murder. I'm frazzled." She stopped just short of the kitchen table. "If you get a chance," she said, "that is, when you have a spare moment, could you . . . ah . . . ask the police if they found any roses in all the stuff they went through before it was chucked in the Dumpster?"

Joe wiped his mouth with a paper napkin and gazed at Judith with an ironic expression. "Did you lose some roses?"

"No. It's just that . . ." She involuntarily put a hand on the pocket where the petals were stashed. "Never mind. It's not important." She started again for the back door. Joe didn't comment on his wife's request. That, Judith thought, was just as well. Her idea was probably an exercise in futility.

To her surprise, the toolshed door was locked. "Mother?" Judith called, and knocked again. "Mother?"

"Go away!" Gertrude's voice was more raspy than usual.

"What's wrong?" Judith shouted.

"Nothing! Take a hike!"

Baffled, Judith stared at the locked door. The toolshed's small windows were not only closed, but the linen curtains were drawn. Like Aunt Deb, Gertrude's circulation was poor. Summer's heat didn't bother either of the cousins' mothers.

"Why," Judith shouted, "won't you open the door?"

"I can't hear you!" Gertrude yelled back. "I'm deaf, you know!"

Judith surrendered. As long as the old lady's lungs sounded strong, she obviously wasn't in any danger or pain. By the time Judith got back inside the house, Joe had gone upstairs to work on his research assignment. Phyliss was vacuuming the living room. The honeymoon couple had just returned from the public market downtown, where they'd apparently made several purchases, judging from the bags and boxes they carried up to their room.

As Phyliss shut off the vacuum, Judith asked if she knew if any of the other guests were in their quarters.

"Nobody home up there the last time I looked," Phyliss replied, caressing the handle of the vacuum, which she'd dubbed Moses. "I think someday the two of us are going all the way up to Mount Sinai. Hallelujah!"

"Good for you," Judith murmured. "When did the Busses leave?"

Phyliss made a face. "The ones with the fancy duds?"

"No. The designer clothes belong to the people from Iowa," Judith clarified. "Mr. and Mrs. Buss are the couple visiting the other Busses in the cul-de-sac."

The cleaning woman nodded. "You can put all of 'em in a sack, shake 'em out, and I wouldn't know the difference. Too many Busses, if you ask me. Anyways, the Buss people left, came back, and left again." She shrugged. "Could be anywhere. Try Hades."

Judith went into the front parlor, where she looked out the window into the cul-de-sac. Sure enough, the media vans were leaving. Wistfully, she gazed at the former home of Mrs. Swanson. *If only,* she thought, *Herself's grandiose plans to build a condo would come to naught.* Surely the city wouldn't allow a multifamily dwelling in such a quiet area. "Wishful thinking," she said aloud and went into the entry hall.

A voice called to her from the kitchen. Judith hurried through the dining room to find Arlene wearing an expression of triumph and waving a sheet of paper.

"Look what I found in the hedge!"

"Elvis?" Judith answered, only half facetiously. It wouldn't have been the first time that a person had managed to get lost among the laurel leaves.

"No, no," Arlene said, handing the paper over to Judith. "I think it's Vivian's guest list. Do you know any of these people?"

"I hope not," Judith replied, studying the handwritten

names. "This looks like Vivian's horrible penmanship," she said, recalling the erratic and overblown style from the infrequent postcards Herself had sent from the Florida gulf. "There must be thirty names here."

"No addresses or phone numbers, though," Arlene pointed out.

"The only names I recognize are Frankie and Marva Lou Buss," Judith said. "Was there another page?"

"This is all I found when I was looking for Tulip's favorite ball," Arlene replied. "Why? Do you think there were more guests at the party?"

"I never counted them," Judith said. "But look at this double space toward the bottom of the page. At the top Vivian's written 'VIPs,' so I'm assuming that's her pretentious way of identifying her friends and relations. Then, after skipping a couple of lines, she's put in 'HH' but there are only three names. What do you think that stands for? And since the neighbors were invited, where are we listed as guests?"

"You're right," Arlene agreed. "This must be only the first page. I'll go back into the hedge and see if I can find more."

For Judith, the task of crawling around in the hedge was just short of attacking an Afghani terrorist camp. Arlene, however, was unperturbed.

"How did this get into the hedge in the first place?" Judith asked her neighbor.

Arlene's face puckered as she considered the question. "I assumed it was with everything else that ended up in the cul-de-sac. Maybe Vivian or Billy had the list to keep track of who came and who didn't."

"Maybe," Judith said. "I wonder if . . . oh, never mind." She smiled at Arlene. "Good luck in the hedge. Do you want me to help?"

Arlene was aghast. "With your artificial hip? Goodness, we don't want more ambulances and medics around here, do we?"

Judith sobered quickly. "No. We do not."

✳ ✳ ✳

An hour later, Arlene returned. Judith marveled at her tidy appearance. "How do you manage not to get leaves and twigs and all that other stuff on you?"

Arlene shrugged. "I bonded with the hedge years ago. It's like part of the family." She sighed. "But I didn't find the rest of the list, only Carl's bedroom slippers and one of our kids' pacifiers."

"You mean your grandkids?"

"No. That pacifier's been there for going on forty years," Arlene said. "Carl's slippers have only been missing since 1994."

Judith pointed to the original guest list that Arlene had left on the counter by the computer. "Do you want this back?"

"I've no use for it. Maybe you can figure something out. You are," she added with a gleam in her blue eyes, "the sleuth, after all."

"Not this time," Judith asserted. "I'm staying out of it."

"Of course you aren't," Arlene said indulgently. "See you later." She left via the back door.

Judith stared at the wrinkled and slightly soiled piece of paper for almost a full minute. *Useless,* she thought. The only names she knew belonged to two of her B&B guests. A couple of others seemed vaguely familiar, perhaps people Joe had mentioned either from the police department or the cop bars. Maybe he'd recognize some of the invitees if they'd crawled out of whatever place they'd occupied in Vivian's past. But asking him would only reinforce her husband's conviction that she wanted to get involved. Judith picked up the sheet of paper, walked over to the stainless steel trash can by the hallway door, stepped on the pedal to open the lid—and paused.

"You in some kind of trance?" Phyliss asked as she came into the hall from the basement. "Pastor Goodheal stands like that when he's about to lay hands on our sick brethren."

"He does?" Judith said vaguely. "I mean . . ." She went to the counter and slipped the alleged guest list in a drawer. "Does he cure anyone?"

"That depends on what you mean by 'cure,'" Phyliss replied. "Two weeks ago Wilma Wallup came to Pastor Goodheal with a terrible rash. He told her—and rightly so—that she couldn't expect an instant miracle. Her faith was too weak for that. But he sold her some of his Saintly Salve, and last Sunday she showed up looking much better and hardly itching and scratching and wiggling around like she usually does during the sermons."

Judith tried to keep her expression blank. "He sells medicine?"

"Oh, yes, and it works wonders! I use his Heavenly Heat Liniment for my bursitis all the time."

"That's . . . good," Judith says. "I assume he doesn't charge much for his remedies."

"Cheap enough," Phyliss replied, taking off her apron. "He's a real fine Christian businessman. Incorporated, too. His company is called Prophet and Loss."

"Nice," Judith murmured. "I take it you're done for the day?"

"Everything's slick as a whistle," Phyliss assured her employer. "I can just make the two-twenty-two bus over on the avenue. That'll get me to my chiropractor in time." She put a bony hand to her gaunt cheek. "About this jaundice—what do you think?"

"Ask Pastor Goodheal," Judith said. "Frankly, you look fine to me."

"You never know," Phyliss said darkly. "Your cousin didn't think so. Of course, she *is* evil."

On that note, the cleaning woman departed. Judith decided

to try to get Gertrude to open the toolshed door. Respecting her mother's privacy—and ornery whims—could only go so far. The afternoon was growing warmer. Poor circulation or not, the old lady could still succumb to heat prostration in her closed-up, airless quarters. If she had to, Judith would use her own key to get in.

To her surprise—and relief—the toolshed door was ajar. "Mother?" Judith said, going inside.

"What?" Gertrude's tone was sharp, though she didn't look up from the jumble puzzle she was doing.

Judith sat down on the arm of the small divan. "How come you wouldn't let me in earlier?"

"I was busy."

"Doing what?"

"None of your beeswax," Gertrude shot back. "Is c-l-e-v-e a word?"

"I don't think so," Judith replied. "Is there an 'r' at the end of it?"

The old lady finally looked at her daughter. "If there was, I'd circle it, squirrel-bait. You're not as *clever* as you think you are."

"Probably not," Judith allowed. "That being so, can you explain why you wouldn't let me—or Renie—come inside this afternoon?"

"Renie came when Vi was here," Judith's mother said. "How many people can I entertain at once in this packing crate of an apartment?"

"I meant later," Judith clarified. "Renie came back, remember?"

"Maybe." Gertrude seemed absorbed in her puzzle.

"Then I knocked on your door to see if you were okay."

"I was. I am." Gertrude scowled. "What's a l-a-t-h?"

Judith frowned. "I think a lath is a wood strip."

Gertrude snorted. "Showing off because you used to be a librarian. Okay, I'll take your word for it."

"You should open at least one window," Judith advised. "It's going to be very hot later on this afternoon."

Gertrude, who was wearing a sweater over her housecoat, cast a withering glance in her daughter's direction. "Hot?" She tapped her pencil on the card table. "It doesn't feel hot to— Oops!" The lead broke off. "Drat! This needs sharpening." She tossed the pencil to Judith, but the old lady's aim was short; the pencil fell on the floor and rolled under the divan. "Well?" Gertrude said. "Can't you pick it up?"

"You know I can't bend that way with my artificial hip," Judith retorted. "I'll get your broom." She went into the kitchenette and grabbed an old broom that looked as if a goat had chewed off half of the straw. "You need a new one," Judith said. "This thing's a wreck."

"So am I," Gertrude snapped. "Don't spend money on some fancy new thingamabob with wheels or whatever they put on brooms nowadays. It works just fine. Ask your loony cleaning woman."

"No," Judith said, angling the broom under the divan, "Phyliss brings a decent broom from the house." After several swipes, the pencil rolled into sight. To Judith's astonishment, so did three pink rose petals. "Where'd these come from?" she asked her mother.

Gertrude stared at the floor. "I don't know." She kept staring.

With great care, Judith retrieved the pencil—and the rose petals. "Where's your little sharpener?" she inquired, putting the petals into her pocket along with the first two she'd found by Vivian's gate.

Gertrude fumbled through the clutter of magazines, playing cards, the morning newspaper, and the other items on the card table, including a dish of candy and the tray with her lunch dishes. The old lady's hands seemed to shake more than usual. "It's by the icebox," she murmured.

"Okay." Judith went back into the kitchenette. The pencil sharpener was nowhere in sight. But there were three empty juice glasses in the small sink. Judith picked one of them up and sniffed. She immediately recognized the odor of whisky.

Judith returned to the sitting room. "The sharpener must be here somewhere," she said, gesturing at the card table.

"I don't see it," Gertrude responded somewhat truculently.

"Did you and Vivian have a drink?" Judith asked, sorting through her mother's muddle.

"She did. I didn't." Gertrude removed a cigarette from the pack she kept in her housecoat pocket. "So what?"

"How come there are three glasses in the sink?"

Gertrude was having trouble lighting her cigarette. She finally put the slim lighter down and took the cigarette out of her mouth. "How do I know? That goofy Phyliss probably drank some of my juice."

"If she did, she'd wash the glass," Judith pointed out. "You know she always leaves everything spick-and-span."

"So she forgot." Gertrude kept her eyes on her lap.

"I don't think so," Judith snapped. "Mother, why won't you tell me who came to see you today? Besides Vivian, I mean."

Gertrude glared at her daughter. "You don't need to know everything I do around here. Beat it." Her fingers still shaking, she knocked over the candy bowl. Several pieces of candy scattered all over the card table—along with the pencil sharpener. "Ha! There it is! I knew I put it someplace."

With a resigned sigh, Judith picked up the sharpener and whittled the pencil into a fine point. "Here. Finish your puzzle. I can't believe you won't tell me who visited you. What's the big secret?"

None too steadily, Gertrude unwrapped some kind of

chocolate ball. "I'm too old to do a lot of things," she rasped, "but I can still keep a secret. Now go away and forget about what I do when you're not watching me like a hawk."

Judith had no choice. She left the toolshed and walked out into the bright sunlight. It wasn't unbearably hot, but the rose petals felt as if they were burning a hole in her pocket.

9

Joe was in the kitchen when Judith came back into the house. "Got to leave town," he announced, turning away from the phone directory he'd been studying.

Judith hoped he was kidding. "Why? Are you afraid of being hounded by the paparazzi now that you're a media star?"

"No," Joe responded in a calm voice. "Wirehoser Timber wants me to talk to some of the people who've worked with one of their CFO candidates. This guy lives and works in Atlanta." He shot his wife a mocking glance. "You really think I *want* to go to Atlanta in August?"

"Well . . . no," Judith said, "but the timing seems peculiar."

Joe set down the can of beer he'd been drinking. "Earning big bucks is peculiar this time of year?"

"How long will you be gone?" Judith asked.

"That's what I'm trying to figure out by checking airline and hotel reservations," he murmured. "Two-three days, probably. Got to figure out where this BOD is located."

"Bod?" Judith echoed. "What do you mean?"

"Bank of Dixie, where this guy works now." He moved to the computer and started a search. "Ah, perfect. There's a non-stop Delta flight leaving this evening at nine-fifty. I'll see if the shuttle can pick me up around seven." He hurried out of the kitchen and went back upstairs.

The phone rang. "This," Renie said, "is Bill Jones's underpaid and underappreciated secretary making a call for He Who Wishes Alexander Graham Bell Had Never Been Born. Ask Joe if he wants to go to the ocean tomorrow and fish for salmon. My phonophobic husband just found out the Kings are in."

"King Joe here is going to Atlanta tonight," Judith said in a resigned voice.

"King Joe, or are you Joe King?" Renie uttered a lame little laugh. "Sorry. Couldn't resist. How come he's going south?"

"Business," Judith replied. "Something to do with a potential CFO for Wirehoser."

"That beats having him stay out all night on surveillance waiting for Mr. Cheater to leave the motel after making whoopee with Mrs. Slut," Renie said. "It pays better, too, I'll bet. I've designed quite a few things for Wirehoser. They don't stint on spending money for consultants."

"I suppose that's a consolation," Judith said, pacing back and forth from the dining room's half-door to the hallway off the kitchen. "I just wish he didn't have to go away now with a murderer on the loose."

"Do you want me to stay with you while he's away?" Renie asked. "Bill's going tomorrow and won't get back until Friday. Of course I wouldn't want to leave Clarence by himself. Or Oscar. He gets agitated when Bill's not around to watch that X-rated TV channel with him."

"Coz," Judith said in a warning voice, "no more nonsense about your stupid stuffed animal. At least Clarence is a real bunny."

"And oh so soft," Renie murmured. "You should see him in his new swim trunks."

"Good grief. I'm hanging up now. Stay home. I'm fine. It isn't as if the house will be empty."

After disconnecting, Judith removed Herself's guest list from the drawer. A second reading of the invitees brought no further enlightenment. But there was something familiar about two of the three names listed under "HH": Barry Henckel and Doug Campbell. What, she wondered, did "HH" stand for? And why did she care?

Judith jumped when the doorbell rang. She assumed it might be the young men from Virginia, but Adelita Vasquez stood on the front porch, smiling brightly. "Señora Buss wishes to speak with Señor Flynn," she said. "It is very important."

"Mr. Flynn is about to leave town," Judith replied. "Tell Mrs. Buss to check in with him when he gets back."

Adelita's smile fled. "But he must talk to Señora Buss! She is very upset! She requires his . . . how do you say? Counsel?"

Judith glanced at her watch. It was almost three-thirty. Joe had plenty of time to prepare for his trip, but Judith was reluctant to give Vivian the satisfaction of having her ex do her bidding. "I'll see if he has time before he leaves for the airport, okay?"

Adelita looked downcast. "Oh, I so hope he can help! Señora Buss wishes to leave town, too."

"She does?" Judith stared at the young woman. "Why?"

"So much tragedy," Adelita replied, wringing her hands. "The man in the tree. *Pobre hombre!* Señora Buss thinks it is a warning."

"I'm sorry," Judith said, "I don't get it. I thought she didn't know the man. Why would she consider his murder a warning for her?"

"Fate," Adelita replied somberly. "Karma, she calls it. Maybe because of her plans to build the condominiums. She has received threats. And Señora Rankers tried to kill her."

"No, she didn't," Judith asserted. "Mrs. Rankers was just . . . upset. That's her way of expressing strong emotion."

"It is a very frightening way," Adelita said, her dark eyes narrowing. "Could she not simply say how she feels instead of hitting Señor Buss over the head?"

"Mrs. Rankers only whacked Mr. Buss after he tackled her," Judith stated firmly.

Adelita stood her ground. "It is still a very bad thing for her to do." Before Judith could further defend her neighbor, the young woman shifted gears, her expression humble. "Please, please. Ask Señor Flynn to call on Señora Buss as soon as possible. She is in much distress."

"Maybe she's sober," Judith muttered under her breath.

Adelita looked puzzled. "Pardon?"

"Ah . . . I said that . . . may bees see over." Judith forced a smile. "It's an old family saying. About bees in the garden, going from flower to . . . never mind. I'll tell Mr. Flynn that Mrs. Buss wants to see him. I can't promise he'll have time before he leaves, though."

"Thank you, thank you." Adelita made a little bow and left.

Judith went into the kitchen to use the intercom and pass on the request. Joe's response was a reluctant grunt.

"Does that mean you will or you won't?" Judith asked.

"I'll do it after I finish making the travel arrangements," Joe answered after a pause. "It's too late to take the shuttle— they're all booked. Can you drive me to the airport?"

Annoyed, Judith leaned against the wall and fought the urge to say no. "I can if you don't mind waiting until after the social hour. I'm not abandoning the guests. If you're only going to be gone for two or three days, why can't you take your car and leave it at the airport?"

Joe was aghast. "Leave my classic MG in a public garage? Are you nuts?"

"Okay," Judith said, "but don't blame me if I can't get you there on time. Why don't you call a cab?"

"A cab?" Joe practically shouted into the intercom. "Do you know what that'd cost?"

"I thought this Wirehoser job was bringing us great wealth," Judith said quietly. "Won't they pay for a cab?"

"Not until I submit my expenses," Joe replied. "Hey, I can't argue right now. I've still got some loose ends to tie up." He switched off just as the doorbell rang again.

This time it was the guests from Virginia, two polite young men in their mid-twenties. One wore a blue tee that read VIRGINIA; the other wore a white tee that read CAVALIERS. It didn't require Judith's sleuthing skills to figure out that they were students from the University of Virginia.

"I see you're from Charlottesville," she said, smiling. "Welcome to Hillside Manor."

The two young men turned out to be fraternal twins, Jesse and Jason Manning, both seeking graduate degrees in chemical engineering. They seemed pleasant, normal, and straightforward. Judith wondered how they'd react if—and when—they discovered that a murder had occurred two doors away from the B&B.

After checking in the Manning brothers and showing them to their room, Judith went into the kitchen to prepare the appetizers for the social hour. She had just opened a package of cream cheese for her crab dip when Vivian rushed in through the open back door.

"Where's Joe?" she asked, her voice quivering with distress. "Didn't Adelita tell him to come see me right away?"

"Joe's busy," Judith said calmly. "He's going away for a few days."

"He can't!" Vivian stamped her foot, showing off the gold sandals under her scarlet, green, and yellow caftan. "I need him!"

"Sorry," Judith said, removing the lid from a plastic container of Dungeness crab. "It's business."

"Where is he?" She gazed around the kitchen as if she expected Joe to pop out of the fridge like the Pillsbury Doughboy.

Judith dumped the crab into a bowl with the cream cheese. "Making arrangements to leave town. I wouldn't bother him if I were you. He's not in a good mood."

Vivian scowled at Judith. "You think I don't know how to handle his moods?"

"If you did, you'd still be Mrs. Flynn," Judith snapped. "What's so important that you have to pester him when he's busy?"

"Why should I tell you?" Vivian looked indignant. "You haven't been married to him as long as I was. Are you playing control freak?"

"I'm not playing anything," Judith retorted angrily. "I'm simply trying to keep him from being bothered by your latest disaster. He has other things on his mind."

To Judith's amazement, Herself burst into tears. "Oh, everyone's against me! Nobody knows what I've suffered! Nobody understands I have feelings, too!"

"Oh, dear," Judith said under her breath as she tried to fight off her natural compassion—and failed. "Vivian, it's nothing personal." *The hell it isn't,* her voice of conscience asserted. "I'm sorry." *No, you're not.* "I realize how upset you must be about finding a body." *I ought to know—get used to it.* "Tell me what's bothering you, and I'll pass it on to Joe to see if he can help."

Vivian stopped crying. She tried unsuccessfully to wipe away the eyeliner and mascara streaks from her cheeks. "Well . . . it's awkward."

Judith indicated the nearest chair. "Sit. You're a little wobbly."

Vivian's glance was sharp. "Nonsense! I'm in excellent shape. I'm just . . . upset."

It was fruitless to argue. Judith sat down on the other side of the table. Vivian hesitated, but finally eased herself into a chair. "That dead man was misidentified," she began. "The real Charles Brooks lost his wallet at a Vegas casino a few weeks ago. The police found that out when they tried to reach his home in Henderson, Nevada. Mr. Brooks answered the phone. The detectives checked his story with the local authorities. The missing wallet was reported July eighteenth."

"Was the wallet reported as lost or stolen?"

Vivian made a disparaging gesture. "I don't know. It sounded as if Mr. Brooks wasn't sure. What difference does it make? Charles Brooks isn't the man I found in the tree."

"So what do you want Joe to do?"

"I want to hire him as a bodyguard. If some stranger was killed on our property, he was probably mistaken for someone else. Billy, maybe, or one of the guests. I also want Joe to use his clout with the police to get them to close this case as soon as possible. I feel as if we're living with a death threat over our heads," Vivian said, sitting up very straight and looking self-righteous.

Judith grimaced. "He can't do anything about it until he gets back from Atlanta. Why do you think the police have to be pressured to move the investigation along? They'll want to close it as quickly as you do."

Vivian sighed impatiently. "It'll take them forever. I know. It's always a slow process, so much foot-dragging and ongoing cases and playing games with superiors. Have you forgotten that I was married to a cop for eighteen years?"

Oh, no, Judith thought, *I'm not likely to forget how miserable those years were for me. You stole a huge chunk of my life.* She shrugged. "It'll have to wait. Joe's leaving this evening."

"No!" Vivian slammed her hand on the table and stood up so fast that the sheep-shaped cookie jar rattled. "He can't do this to me!"

Judith leaned back in the chair, unable to resist enjoying her rival's distress. "He can, and he will. Talk to the cops. Or hire another P.I."

"You—and Joe—haven't heard the last of this!" Herself shouted, wagging a finger at Judith. "You'll both be sorry by the time I finish with the two of you!" She yanked her flowing skirt away from the chair and flounced out of the house.

Twenty minutes later, Joe came downstairs. "I'm all set," he declared, rubbing his hands together. "What's the deal with Vivian?"

"Forget it," Judith snapped. "She seems to think you're her errand boy. She came over after Adelita had failed to get you to jump on command. You're supposed to drop everything and help her."

"Help her do what?" Joe asked, puzzled.

"Be her bodyguard." Judith's tone was scathing. "She also wants you to exert your influence with the cops and make the case go away."

Joe frowned. "She lacks confidence in the detectives?"

"I guess so." Judith cocked an ear as she heard someone enter through the front door. The California foursome, she thought, hearing their voices on their way upstairs to the guest rooms. "By the way, Joe," she said softly, "I should be able to drive you to the airport. I'm sorry I was so crabby. It was a short night, and it seems like a long day."

"I know." He kissed her forehead. "I'm not crazy about leaving you here with this mess."

Judith shrugged. "I promise not to get involved."

"Good." He smiled at his wife.

She smiled back.

Neither of them believed Judith could keep her word.

10

The rest of the day played out uneventfully. All of the guests, including Marva Lou and Frankie Buss, seemed involved with their own comings and goings. Judith had been able to drive Joe to the airport drop-off. Gertrude seemed to be in fine fettle, though she still refused to say anything more about her unknown visitor. Hillside Manor was quiet that night. So was the rest of the cul-de-sac. Judith couldn't help but wonder if the peaceful evening was the lull before the storm.

The next morning she took Gertrude's breakfast out to the toolshed just after eight o'clock. The old lady was up and dressed, watching the *Today* show. She ignored her daughter's presence, eyes fixed firmly on the TV screen.

"Are you okay?" Judith inquired, setting the tray on the card table.

Gertrude didn't even blink.

"What is it?" Judith demanded. "Don't you feel well?"

Gertrude's eyes flashed in her daughter's direction. "I feel with my fingers," she snapped, her customary reply to the question, which was usually followed by a litany of complaints about the state of her health. This time, however, she stopped speaking and held out her left hand.

Judith stared. "What? Did you hurt yourself?"

"Keep looking, dummy," Gertrude ordered. "Where's my diamond ring?"

The old lady's wedding band was in place, but not her engagement ring. "Did you lose it?" Judith asked.

Gertrude's expression was exasperated. "If it wasn't missing, I'd be wearing it."

"When did you take it off?"

"Night before last," Gertrude answered, some of the hostility ebbing from her voice. "Sometimes my joints swell in the summer. You know that. I never, ever, take off my wedding band, no matter how tight it gets. But I won't wear the diamond ring when my fingers are puffy. I put it on the nightstand next to my bed. I didn't try to put it back on yesterday, but I decided to see how it felt this morning. It's gone."

"I'll look for it," Judith said and went into the bedroom.

The room with its single bed, nightstand, bureau, and closet was so small that Judith could scarcely turn around. Prevented by her artificial hip from kneeling on the floor, she got the tattered broom from the kitchenette and ran it under the bed and the nightstand several times. Judith looked in the closet, opened the drawers, and pulled back the bedclothes. The ring was nowhere to be found—nor was it in the tiny bathroom.

"I'll ask Phyliss to look when she arrives later this morning," Judith said after announcing the futility of her search. "It has to be somewhere. You haven't worn it outside, have you?"

Gertrude's chin jutted. "I wore it to Vi's party, but I took it off after I got back to my shipping crate of an apartment. It's insured, you know, but that's not the point. Your father paid five hundred dollars for that ring back in 1939. I don't want the money, I want that ring. It means . . ." Her wrinkled face crumpled.

"I know, Mother." Judith put a hand on Gertrude's shoulder.

"We'll find it. Don't get upset." She pointed to the tray. "I made you scrambled eggs with bits of ham the way you like it, and there's toast and a poached egg. Eat while it's still warm."

Leaving Gertrude mumbling to herself, Judith returned to the house, where the California foursome had arrived in the dining room. The grad students from Virginia came next, followed by Marva Lou and Frankie Buss. By ten o'clock the first round of guests had finished breakfast and gone off for the day. The honeymooners appeared a few minutes later.

Phyliss hadn't gotten to Hillside Manor until nine-thirty. "My bunions were killing me this morning. I had to pare 'em down before I could put on my shoes." She jabbed a finger at her sturdy black orthopedic oxfords. "Even with this deerskin lining, some days I can hardly manage to get to the bus. Today was one of 'em."

Trying to look sympathetic, Judith nodded. "That's a shame, Phyliss. By the way, you didn't see Mother's engagement ring in her apartment yesterday, did you?"

Phyliss frowned. "You mean on her finger?"

"No," Judith said, and explained that her mother had removed the ring the night before. "Could you go out and look for it? I can't get down to see under the bed."

Phyliss made a face. "I don't know about that. Is she in there praying to those skunks again? That gives me the willies."

Judith started to reiterate what "The Little Flower" meant to Catholics, but shut up before the first word came out. "Just see if you can find the ring. Mother's sometimes a little . . . um . . . confused, and she may have put it somewhere and forgotten about it."

"Mrs. Grover better not accuse me of stealing it," Phyliss declared. "She always watches me like I'm going to run off with her candy. Twice lately she yanked that glass dish of hers away from me before I could even look at it, let alone take a piece.

I never would—with my borderline diabetes and all. But your mother's the suspicious type. Not that I blame her, with the Prince of Darkness loose everywhere these days. Now body snatchers! What next?"

Judith, who was checking the computer for new reservation requests, had heard only part of the cleaning woman's latest rant. "Body snatchers? What do you mean?"

"On the news this morning before I left to take the bus," Phyliss replied. "Somebody stole a body out of the morgue."

"Really? That's awful," Judith responded. "I never have time to listen or watch the morning news. Joe reads the paper with his breakfast, and sometimes I'll skim through it if I have a spare minute."

"Creepy," Phyliss remarked, heading for the pantry. "God-less, too."

Judith went back to the reservation requests—three more, two in late September, one for the Thanksgiving weekend. The would-be November guest asked for two rooms, one for herself and her husband, and the other for her children. "I am aware," the woman named Anna Lindstrom had written, "that it's your policy not to allow anyone under eighteen. However, one of my sons is twenty and the other will be eighteen in early December. They are coming with us not only to share Thanksgiving with my sister who lives only half a mile from your B&B, but with their father, who owns a one-bedroom condo across the lake from the city. Neither he nor my sister has room to accommodate them, so I was hoping you could make an exception in this case. My husband and I stayed at Hillside Manor on our honeymoon six years ago, and we really enjoyed your congenial atmosphere as well as the convenient location."

Mulling over the request, Judith checked her database of previous guests. Kenneth and Anna Lindstrom of Minneapolis had indeed visited Hillside Manor for three days six years earlier. Now she remembered them quite well. They were close to middle age then, both taking a second chance on love, very much like her own situation. Now they wanted to come back to the B&B with her sons. The husband's stepsons, of course. Joe had taken on Herself's two boys by her ex-husbands. The youngsters had faded from his life after his marriage to Judith.

Recalling the Lindstroms, Judith made her decision. She never liked bending the rules and seldom did, but she'd make an exception. While typing in her response, something suddenly clicked in her brain. After hurrying through the confirmation, she opened the drawer by the computer and took out the guest list that Arlene had found in the hedge. Under the mysterious "HH" heading she stared again at two of the three names: Barry Henckel and Doug Campbell. Barry and Doug. Doug and Barry. Judith wondered if they might be Joe's stepsons. She cursed herself for not showing him the list.

An hour later, Phyliss came downstairs with a load of laundry. "You didn't tell me those farmers from Iowa in Room One checked out."

Judith looked up from the cooking magazine she'd been studying for new appetizer ideas. "What?"

The cleaning woman nodded. "Cleared out, fancy duds and all."

Judith realized that the Griggses had never showed up for breakfast. That wasn't unusual in itself. Sometimes guests wanted to explore recommended restaurants instead of eating at the B&B. Or, more rarely, some visitors didn't eat a morning meal.

"They were supposed to stay through tomorrow night," Judith said. "Did they leave their keys?"

"Yep." Phyliss took the keys out of her apron pocket. "Did they gyp you?"

"No. They used a credit card." Judith paused for a few moments. "An emergency might've come up."

"Good riddance, I say." Phyliss moved on to the basement.

Judith was looking over the Griggses' credit card information when the phone rang.

"I just waved Bill off on his fishing trip," Renie said. "Is your other half in Atlanta?"

"As far as I know," Judith replied, and realized she'd forgotten to tell Joe about Bill's invitation to go salmon fishing. Not that it would have changed his plans, Judith thought. But it struck her that in the past day or two there had been several things she should have told her husband, all of which she'd kept locked inside her head. "Joe told me he wouldn't call until this evening because of the time difference. He had a meeting this morning. Have you got time to stop by later on?"

Renie hesitated. "It's still morning, and my brain is foggy. I won't start work until one, so I could come by in a bit. Are you in trouble?"

"No," Judith replied, "but I need to bounce some ideas off of you."

"Rubber Renie can help, but I'm not as resilient as I used to be."

"Who is? See you soon." Judith hung up.

Half an hour later, she was making a marinade for London broil when the doorbell rang. A FedEx delivery man stood on the porch. "Overnight for a Franklin Buss," he said, holding out a letter-sized envelope and a small carton. "Do you want to sign for this?"

"Sure," Judith said, and accepted the pen the FedEx man offered.

She was about to go inside when Arlene called to her from the sidewalk by the Rankerses' house. "I'm heading to the grocery store," Arlene said as Judith came down the porch steps. "Unless," she added, "you've got an extra can of tomato paste."

"I do," Judith replied. "Come in. What size?"

"Small," Arlene replied. "I'm making my spaghetti recipe."

"Sounds delicious," Judith remarked as they went into the pantry. "Take your pick. I keep half a dozen on hand."

Arlene selected the nearest can. "Isn't it wonderful to have tomato paste in cans that aren't dented? I used to get so annoyed when our kids used them as croquet balls. Or weapons."

Judith nodded. "Mike used soup cans for bowling pins and cantaloupe for a ball. I suppose it showed imagination."

Arlene nodded. "Raising five kids was very expensive."

"Just one kept us broke," Judith said as they went back into the kitchen. "It would've helped if Dan had worked more often."

"Poor you." Arlene patted Judith's shoulder. "Thanks. Now I won't have to go to the store. I'll pay you back."

"You don't have to," Judith said, although Arlene always did.

They reached the entry hall just as Carl came up onto the porch. "Ah! There you are," he said to his wife. "I wondered where you went. The painters are on the way to give us an estimate on the exterior job."

Judith was surprised. "You're going to paint the house?"

Arlene nodded her head. Standing behind her, Carl mouthed the word "No." Obviously, the Rankerses were at odds about the project.

"It's been twenty years," Arlene said.

"Eight," Carl corrected.

"He's confused," Arlene said.

"She can't count," Carl asserted.

Judith didn't want to get into one of Arlene and Carl's complicated arguments. "Say, Carl, did Joe tell you anything about the people he talked to at Vivian's party?"

Carl hesitated, looking thoughtful. "He mentioned a couple of old pals from way back. One was a fishing partner. The other . . ." Ruefully, he shook his head. "I don't remember. It was getting pretty loud on the other side of the cul-de-sac."

"Were they cops or just drinking buddies?"

Carl grimaced. "Did you recognize somebody he worked with?"

"No," Judith said. "During the years we were . . . apart, I didn't know his colleagues. When we got married, his partner was Woody Price. I know Woody wouldn't come to Vivian's party. He has too much good sense. I've met some others along the way, but only one older man seemed familiar."

"Maybe," Arlene suggested, "he's someone Joe arrested."

"That," Judith said dryly as Renie pulled into the cul-de-sac, "is entirely possible."

Saying good-bye to Carl and Arlene, Judith walked over to the driveway, where Renie was parking the Camry. She watched her cousin with growing curiosity as she opened the trunk, hauled out a suitcase, a laptop computer, a small carton—and a wire cage containing Clarence, the Holland dwarf lop-eared bunny.

"The toilet blew up," Renie announced. "I'm moving in."

Judith gaped at her cousin. "You have two bathrooms."

"It's the pipes," Renie said. "That damned willow tree on the corner apparently has sent its roots way up into the main line. It affects the whole house. I can't get a plumber out until Friday. Six of the houses around the intersection are affected. We have to take a number to get an appointment. Do I get to sleep with you or your mother?"

"We've got the guest room on the third floor, as you well know," Judith said, carrying the carton in through the back door while Renie brought along the rest of her belongings. "I've cleaned and changed everything since the last time Mike and his family stayed over." She gestured at Clarence's cage. "How are you going to keep him away from Sweetums? Doesn't Clarence roam free in your basement?"

"During the day," Renie said. "Every night at eight-thirty he goes into his cage and waits for us to tuck him in."

"Gack."

Renie glared at her cousin. "You know it's true."

"Yes. That's why I said 'gack,'" Judith retorted. "You and Bill are idiots."

"You just don't get it," Renie muttered, setting the cage on the kitchen counter and putting a finger between the wires to touch the bunny's soft gray fur. "I figured we could let Clarence roam in your garage during the day. Joe's MG is locked up in there, isn't it?"

Judith sighed. "Okay, that might work. I'll admit, Sweetums never goes in there unless the garage door is open." She placed the envelope and box she'd been carrying on the kitchen table. "I'll give you the key so you can take him out there now."

"Good." Renie glanced at the table. "Is that yours?"

"No," Judith said, taking the garage key off of her chain. "It's for Frankie Buss. He's not here at the moment." She handed the key to Renie before studying the return address. "This is from somebody named Loren Ellsworth in Tushka, Oklahoma. Ever heard of the place?"

Renie had picked up the cage. "Nope. But then I've never been to Oklahoma. I've only flown over it. I think it was Oklahoma. Maybe it was Okinawa. I was kind of bleary from drinking a pint of Wild Turkey."

"Of course you were," Judith murmured, well aware of her cousin's need to get blotto before boarding an airplane. Shaking her head at Renie's folly—or follies, including Clarence's pampered existence—Judith went into the entry hall to put the FedEx deliveries in the old-fashioned bronze mailbox reserved for guests.

Ten minutes later, Renie returned to the kitchen. "Clarence

is settled, and I took everything else except for my purse upstairs."

"Good." Judith shot her cousin a caustic glance. "Does your bunny like the garage?"

"He's exploring," Renie replied, getting a can of Pepsi out of the fridge. "Or will be when he makes up his mind if it's safe to come out of the cage."

"At least you didn't bring Oscar," Judith said.

"I couldn't," Renie responded. "He went fishing with Bill. It's a bad idea. Oscar gets seasick. The last time—Oh, shoot! I almost forgot!" Renie grabbed her huge purse from the counter and rushed out of the kitchen.

Judith called after her. "What are you doing?" Not getting an answer, she followed her cousin into the living room. Renie was putting a framed photograph of Bill—and Oscar—on the mantel.

"Oh, for heaven's sake!" Judith cried. "Take that down!"

Renie gazed innocently at her cousin. "Why? I've always thought you were fond of family treasures."

"I am," Judith snapped, "but I'm not fond of you being an idiot! I have guests using this room. They'll think I'm unhinged."

"No, they won't," Renie said calmly. "They'll be intrigued."

"How? By trying to figure who is who in that damned picture?"

"Bill's the one wearing the suit and tie," Renie replied.

"Oh, good grief!" Judith shook herself and leaned a hand on the back of the nearest sofa. "If you must, put it in the guest bedroom, where nobody else can see it."

"Don't be so sensitive." Renie was beginning to sound testy. "This is a studio portrait."

Judith glowered at Renie. "What studio? Metro-Goldwyn-Moron?"

Sadly, Renie shook her head. "You seem to have lost your sense of whimsy."

"You seem to have lost your mind." Judith studied Renie's mulish expression. It was a bad sign, as well as a bad start to her cousin's visit. "Okay, leave it there for now. Come on, I want to show you something."

Back in the kitchen, Judith explained how Arlene had found the sheet of paper in the hedge. "What do you think 'HH' at the bottom stands for?" she asked after handing the guest list to Renie.

"Hubert Humphrey?"

"Get serious. *Please.*"

"Okay." Renie pointed to the top of the page. "I take it these are the guests?"

Judith nodded. "You'll notice, though, that the neighbors in the cul-de-sac aren't listed. I suspect we were an afterthought."

"Not necessarily," Renie said. "If this paper was floating around at the party, it may have been used to indicate who was or wasn't attending. All the neighbors would be here—if not actually at the party—because this is where you live. Herself sent you the invitations because she wanted to be darned sure you all heard her big announcement about the condo project."

"You may be right," Judith allowed. "Back to 'HH.'"

"There are only three names," Renie murmured. "Maybe there was another page."

"Yes, I wondered about that, too. It may've been tossed in all the mayhem and confusion. Do the first two names sound familiar?"

Renie shook her head. "No. Neither does the third one, the woman. What kind of a name is . . . this is hard to read. The bottom of the page is wrinkled. Flora Something-or-other."

"Bando or Bundy, maybe?"

"I can't tell." Renie propped her chin on her hand and looked thoughtful. "Where's your famous logic? This is for a party, with guests listed first. Who are these other people? Potential party crashers?"

"Maybe," Judith conceded. "I think the two men *might* be Herself's sons. Joe lost track of them after the divorce. He's always said they were headed for trouble. They'd be in their forties by now."

Renie shook her head. "I don't recall anything about them. Wasn't there a stepdaughter, too?"

"Yes. She spent most of her time with her father, Vivian's first husband. I can't remember her name." Judith grimaced. "I should've shown this list to Joe."

"You can ask him when he calls," Renie pointed out.

"The problem is," Judith said slowly, "I don't want him to think I'm getting embroiled in this murder."

"Oh, Coz," Renie said, leaning back in the chair, "you already are, and he knows it. You can't help yourself. You're an addict. There's no rehab to cure your urge to solve a crime. Unfortunately, your addiction can be just as dangerous as mainlining heroin."

"It's not as if I don't have faith in the police," Judith asserted, on the defensive. "I do. Why wouldn't I? Joe was—still is—an excellent detective, so's Woody Price, and several other cops I got to know over the years. They're professionals. I'm only an amateur. They get paid for what they do. I don't. But I still have to—" She stopped. "'HH,'" she said softly. "Could it stand for Hired Help?"

Renie grinned. "Ah. Your logic just kicked in. I'll bet you're right."

Judith ticked off the possibilities on her fingers. "The band, the waiters, the caterer, a trio of skimpily clad waitresses. Who else?"

"Mercifully," Renie said, "I wouldn't know because I wasn't there. The florist? The bouncer?"

Judith shook her head. "There weren't any flowers. That's why finding the rose petals by Vivian's gate seemed odd. If there was a bouncer, I didn't see him. I figure that job was left to Billy because he looks as if he works out."

"On the sofa watching car crashes?"

"Downtime?" Judith said sarcastically. "Billy does have muscles, if no brains." She paused. "There was supposed to be a stripper. Luckily, I missed her. Maybe she's Flora Dora or whatever."

Renie gestured at the list. "If you're right, the stepsons— Barry and Doug?—could have been waiters."

Judith nodded. "Yes. I saw Joe talking to them. I guess they're not in jail after all." She got up to consult the phone directory. "Let's see if they're listed."

Renie snickered. "Listed by the phone company or wanted by the police?"

"Both maybe," Judith murmured. "Hunh. No Henckel inside the city." She flipped back to the C listings. "A bunch of Campbells with names that start with D, including two Douglases."

"What was the stepdaughter's name?" Renie asked. "Was that old chum of Uncle Al's her father?"

"I think so, but I vaguely recall that she moved away or got married," Judith said, closing the directory. "Joe lost track of her years ago. I wonder if Johnny is still around."

"Ask Uncle Al," Renie suggested. "He keeps up with a lot of his old cronies from his restaurant days."

"You know that restaurant was only a front for an illegal gambling operation," Judith said. "The real action was in the back room."

"Right," Renie responded. "We were too young to go back there. Instead, we got free malts at the counter. I fell off the stool twice."

The doorbell rang. Judith stood up. "Now what?" She headed out of the kitchen, followed by a curious Renie.

To Judith's chagrin, Mavis Lean-Brodie stood on the front porch. The rest of her crew was getting out of a KINE-TV van parked at the curb.

"You're at it again," Mavis said, faintly amused. "Who-dunit?"

"Mavis——" Judith stopped. "You can come in if you don't bring your creatures with you."

"Thanks." Mavis, impeccably coiffed and attired as always, turned to her cohorts. "Go over to the second house from the corner and see if you can get any good shots. Try for the tree where the stiff was found."

Judith led the way into the parlor. "How come you weren't here yesterday?" she asked as Mavis sat down in one of the two matching high-backed chairs in front of the stone fireplace.

"I was on vacation," Mavis replied in her usual brittle manner. "I'd just come back from hiking up to Machu Picchu in Peru when I got a call from KINE telling me to get my butt back here. I didn't get in until nine o'clock this morning."

"How was Machu Picchu?" Renie asked from the narrow window seat that looked out onto the driveway.

"I wouldn't know," Mavis replied. "Too damned much cloud cover. For all I know, it's made out of Legos."

Judith had sat down in the other high-backed chair. "Let me warn you, Mavis," she said sternly, "I don't want to get involved in this one. Forget about the FATSO site, forget about some of the other murders I've gotten roped into, forget that I exist."

Mavis burst out laughing. "Yeah, right, sure. Don't con me, Judith. This one's a natural. Somebody told me the woman who owns the house where the body was found used to be married to your husband. How can I resist?"

"If I can, you can," Judith declared with a straight face.

Mavis smirked. "That's crap. If you want to play 'Let's Pretend,' I've got a game of my own—'To Tell the Truth.' Let's hear about the party."

Judith sighed. "I wasn't there. We had our own Block Watch party that night. I was in and out of our house."

Mavis winced and leaned her head against the back of the chair. Remarkably, every hair of her perfect blond pageboy stayed in place. "I can't stand it! You'd know more about what was going on at the Buss party even if you were ten miles away."

Judith remained silent.

"Want a Pepsi?" Renie asked Mavis, holding out the can she'd brought with her into the parlor.

Mavis shot Renie a sharp glance. "Only if you put truth serum in it and I could make your obstinate cousin drink it down." She leaned forward in the chair. "Come on," she coaxed Judith, "give me the good stuff that I can't find in the official police report."

Judith stared straight ahead at the fireplace. "No."

"Okay." Mavis straightened up. "How's this? I'll tell you something you don't know."

Judith's eyelids flickered in Mavis's direction. "No deal."

Mavis shrugged. "Fine. I'll tell your cousin." She smiled thinly at Renie. "Have you heard the one about the body stolen from the morgue?"

Renie looked blank. "Whatever happened to the one about the priest, the rabbi, and the minister going into the bar?"

"This one's better," Mavis said, looking smug. "The body stolen out of the morgue last night was your cousin's latest murder victim."

11

I t's not *my* body!" Judith cried. "Damnit, I'm not on the case!"

"Maybe you should be," Mavis said calmly. "If it's occurred to me, it's also occurred to the police that stealing a body out of the city morgue could only be accomplished with help from a city employee. Like . . . oh, let's say . . . a retired police detective with a vested interest in a corpse found on his ex-wife's premises?"

"That's outrageous!" Judith got to her feet. "Joe's not even here. He left town last night."

Mavis eyed Judith with a complacent expression. "Left town, huh? That's convenient. The body was snatched sometime between eight and ten. What time did Joe leave?"

Judith's strong features expressed righteous indignation. "We left for the airport at seven-thirty, a couple of hours before his scheduled flight around nine-thirty."

Mavis's etched mauve lips curled upward. "Flight? How fitting!"

"Oh, for heaven's sake!" Judith exclaimed. "You know Joe wouldn't get mixed up in this!"

"I may know it," Mavis said, "but those newbie cops don't.

This is their first homicide. Not smart of the higher-ups to put a couple of rookies on the case." She reached out a hand in appeal. "Come on, Judith, stop being a pain in the butt. Was I or was I not a guest at your B&B when you got mixed up in your very first murder? Not to mention the music guy who got killed last year. We cooperated pretty damned well on that one. We make a good team. Why not go for the sequel?"

Judith sighed heavily and sat down. "The problem is, I promised Joe not to get involved. I promised *myself* not to get involved."

Renie threw her hands up in the air. "Stop! How many times have I heard that one? Just do what you always do and find the wretched killer. You know perfectly well you've already started your sleuthing thing. These lengthy preludes to your adventures drive me nuts."

"Serena's right," Mavis said. "Now, let's start with the neighbors' reaction to this big project Vivian Buss announced at her party."

Judith wished she didn't feel she had to defend herself as well as Joe. "We hated the idea," she admitted, and stopped right there.

Mavis looked reproachful. "There was more to it than that. Didn't the party break up because it turned violent?"

"The party ended somewhat later," Judith said, grateful for the chance to omit Arlene's wooden spoon attack. "The Busses' guests got drunk and unruly. Yes, I understand there was some brawling, but I honestly wasn't there."

"Too bad," Mavis murmured. "Was Joe on hand for the fisticuffs?"

"He took no part in them," Judith asserted, "and as far as I know, none of the neighbors did, either. In fact, the next day Mrs. Rankers and Mrs. Porter and I went over to offer our condolences for the tragedy."

"Hey," Renie yelped, "I went, too."

Mavis turned in her direction. "You aren't a neighbor. Keep it down, Jonesy."

"Don't call me Jonesy," Renie warned, looking pugnacious, "or I'll call you Leansy."

Mavis ignored the threat and turned back to Judith. "According to the nine-one-one records, you made the call about the dead guy. How come?"

Judith explained about Herself's frantic arrival in the middle of the night at Hillside Manor. Upon conclusion, she pointed a finger at Mavis. "I've given you everything you want. Now tell me more about this body-snatching."

"Fair enough," Mavis agreed. "Tuesdays are usually quiet at the morgue, unlike the weekends or holidays. Oh, people croak, but they're usually solid citizens dying from natural causes, so they get shipped off to their favorite funeral home. The backyard victim—whose identity is still unknown, according to the cops—was the only newcomer. The preliminary autopsy was performed yesterday, but the complete results won't be ready for at least a week. The coroner's office is short-staffed right now because of vacations." She made a face. "I guess they don't get called back to the job like TV anchors. Anyway, the initial findings were released late yesterday. Cause of death was strangulation, time of death was somewhere between ten and midnight. He'd been put in cold storage, awaiting identification. This morning a member of the custodial crew noticed somebody hadn't closed the corpse's drawer all the way. He took a look and discovered Mr. Nameless was the man who wasn't there."

Judith shuddered. "That's awful. Why, I wonder?"

Mavis smiled slyly. "Isn't that where you come in?"

Judith shook her head. "I certainly can't explain it."

"Maybe not," Mavis allowed, "but you can figure out who, and why this guy ended up on the property of your nemesis."

Judith looked bleakly at Mavis. "Let's start with how he was strangled. Was it with the rope that was found in the garden?"

"The cops haven't given out that information yet," Mavis replied. "Why don't you tell me how Mrs. Buss got so rich?"

"She married well," Judith replied, paying no attention to Renie's groan. "Her wealthy husband died and left everything to her."

"That is *so* unworthy of you!" Mavis cried. "Don't waste time. I can still get something on the noon news if you start dishing the real dirt."

Judith glanced at her watch. It was ten to twelve. "All I have is hearsay. Do you want to get both of us sued?"

Mavis hesitated. "No. Let's call it deep background. Give, Judith."

"Okay. I'll keep it simple. Vivian married a rich old coot who owned a big ranch in Oklahoma. He died about a year later. She inherited everything, and then married his son, Billy, a former minor-league baseball player. Billy didn't want to live in Florida or Oklahoma, so they moved back here to her house in the cul-de-sac. Billy and his brother, Frankie, got zip from their dad. Frankie and his wife, Marva Lou, are staying here at my B&B for a few days. That's all I know."

"That's quite a bit," Mavis said. "God, you've got it all! Money, sex, violence—now put it together and we'll both be geniuses."

Judith shook her head. "I can't begin to figure it out until I know who got killed."

"Do you know who was at the party?" Mavis inquired.

Judith could hardly refrain from smiling. "Well—I do have the guest list. I think. What's it worth to you?"

Mavis grinned. "Dinner at the Manhattan Grill?"

Renie slid off the window seat. "For that, *I'll* get the list." She shot both women a dirty look. "I'm getting really bored sitting here like a stuffed dummy. I *knew* I should've brought Oscar. At least he's amusing." She stalked out of the parlor.

"Oscar?" Mavis said with a curious expression.

"Please." Judith spoke through tight lips. "Don't ask."

"Nothing to do with the murder?"

"A long-standing bone of contention," Judith replied. "Ignore my cousin. You don't want to get sidetracked."

Mavis didn't pursue the subject. "Have you been questioned by the police?"

"No."

"That's odd. Aren't they canvassing the neighborhood?"

"I assume so," Judith said, "but Joe had already talked to them. I never saw the body. I don't know what the man looked like."

"Caucasian, five-eleven, a hundred and eighty pounds, late sixties to mid-seventies, balding, black hair gone gray, brown eyes, small scars on left cheek and right arm, and seemingly in good health," Mavis recited from memory. "No defensive wounds or signs of a struggle."

"In other words," Judith said dryly, "he could be anybody."

"Exactly," Mavis agreed as Renie returned to the parlor.

"Here," she said, handing Mavis a sheet of paper. "I scanned the list and made copies." She gave the original to Judith and kept a copy for herself. "Do you want me to make your mother's lunch?" she asked. "Or should I go help Phyliss clean the guest toilets?"

Judith started to apologize, but stopped. "Yes, Mother will be annoyed if lunch isn't on time. Thanks."

Taken aback, Renie glowered at her cousin—and then nodded. "Will do." She made her exit without another word.

"Hmm," Mavis murmured. "I don't remember Serena as docile."

"It's an act," Judith said. "She must have her reasons."

"No doubt." Mavis studied the list. "Do you know these people?"

"Only Frankie and Marva Lou Buss," she replied. "I think the HH stands for hired help. I also think there was another page. It ends abruptly, especially since the band had at least half a dozen musicians."

Mavis shook her head. "This doesn't mean squat to me. Have you checked out anybody on this list?"

"No," Judith admitted, "though I wondered if Doug and Barry might be Vivian's sons. They're listed under that HH. There were two waiters in their forties, which would be the right age."

Mavis looked incredulous. "You can't ask?"

"Of course," Judith responded. "Joe's calling me around three our time. I suppose," she continued, her eyes scanning the other names on the list, "I could ask one of the Busses."

"You'd better," Mavis said, getting out of the chair. "You're dragging your feet on this one, FATSO."

"Don't use that nickname," Judith snapped. "You know I hate it, and you also know it's an incorrect acronym."

"So what? You think that as a kid I liked being called Slats and Skinny?" Mavis shot back. "I'd have dropped my maiden name of Lean long ago if I hadn't already become well known in TV before I married Lance Brodie. See you later . . . *FASTO*."

The anchorwoman was down the front porch steps before Judith could catch up with her. The KINE-TV technical crew members were by the van, apparently having finished filming anything that might be worth five seconds of viewing time.

"Let's hit it," Mavis called to her colleagues and pointed to Vivian's house. "We're going to see the Busses."

Good luck, Judith thought as Arlene slipped out from around the end of the hedge. "What's happening?" she asked, standing at the bottom of the steps.

"Just routine," Judith said. "KINE's anchorwoman was out of town yesterday. Mavis Lean-Brodie's making up for lost time."

"Ah." Arlene watched the TV group head across the cul-de-sac. "Tell me," she said, lowering her voice, "is that her real hair?"

"I think so," Judith replied.

"It's too perfect," Arlene contended. "It's got to be a wig. What about her eyes? Are those colored contacts? Is it true that when she's sitting at that desk giving the TV news she doesn't wear any pants?"

"She wears jeans," Judith said, noticing there was no response to Herself's doorbell or Mavis's imperious knock.

Arlene was also looking in the direction of the Buss house. "Isn't anyone home over there?"

"I can't tell," Judith said. "I don't think Billy's car has arrived yet from Florida. It's an Aston Martin."

Arlene scowled. "A what?"

"Expensive, that's all I know. They sold their Cadillac Escalade before they moved." She paused, watching one of KINE's crew go around to the side of the house, presumably to try the back door.

"Show-offs," Arlene sniffed. "I'd never buy a car I hadn't heard of."

"No," Judith agreed, though she wasn't sure what her neighbor meant. Seeing Mavis and her minions return to the sidewalk, Judith turned back to Arlene. "I'm going inside before Mavis nails me again."

She hurried into the house. There was no sign of Renie in the kitchen. A strange smell and a dirty saucepan in the sink were evidence that she'd cooked something on the stove. From the back door, Judith saw her cousin carrying a tray into the toolshed. She decided to tend to business, using the phone in the living room to inform Ingrid Heffelman at the state B&B association that a sudden vacancy had opened up.

"Oh, dear God!" Ingrid howled after Judith identified herself. "I've been praying that I wouldn't hear from you! If that man who got murdered near Hillside Manor was another one of your doomed guests, you're getting your innkeeper's license stripped ASAP!"

"I don't even know who got killed," Judith said indignantly. "This time, I had nothing to do with what happened. It's only a coincidence that the body was found in a neighbor's yard."

"When it comes to you," Ingrid snarled, "there is no such thing as a coincidence. Some people collect stamps. You collect corpses. I mean it. Another one of your homicidal adventures will shut you down for good. You won't pass muster with the review board like you did last time after that music guy who was staying at your B&B got whacked."

"That's not what I'm calling about," Judith said in her most self-righteous voice. "Two guests checked out early, and I wanted to—"

"Checked out in what way?" Ingrid demanded. "Were they carrying luggage or stuffed into body bags?"

Judith forced herself to stay calm. "They left in perfect health. I simply wanted to let you know that I have a vacancy, in case anyone asks. That's what you want innkeepers to do during the busy summer season. How much more professional can I be?"

"I get all shivery when I'm forced to recommend your House of Horrors," Ingrid asserted. "I feel as if I'm sending visitors to Iraq."

"Knock it off," Judith snapped. "Your point is made. I'm hanging up now." Putting the receiver back into its cradle on

the cherrywood table, she entered the kitchen as Renie arrived
via the back door.

"Oh," Renie said innocently, "you've finished your gig as a
media star. Shall we TiVo the five o'clock news for posterity?"

"Don't be a smart-ass," Judith retorted. "I've just gone a
couple of rounds with Ingrid Heffelman."

"She didn't ask for your autograph?"

"Drop it." Judith opened the fridge. "What did you feed
Mother?"

"My special shrimp dump," Renie replied. "You had a hard-
boiled egg and some shrimp in the refrigerator. She loves it."

"She would," Judith muttered. "My mother may be the
only person in the world besides you who can stand to eat that
crap."

Renie hopped up onto the counter. "Then it's a good thing I
didn't make enough for us, too."

"Thank God. I'm having a BLT. You're on your own."

"I'd like a BLT. Make one for me, and I'll tell you who your
mother's visitor was yesterday."

Holding a package of bacon, Judith stared at her cousin.
"How did you get that out of her?"

"By putting a big dose of vodka in her ice tea," Renie replied.
"How else do you think I could get her to eat shrimp dump?"

Judith couldn't help but grin at Renie. "Clever, if sneaky. I
should've guessed you had a reason for being so mild-mannered
when I asked you to fix Mother's lunch. So who was her mystery caller?"

"A woman named Flora Bunda," Renie replied, "fleeing the
cops."

"You're kidding!"

Renie shook her head. "Oh, no. She was the stripper at Vivian's party. She never got the chance to take it off because of
the brawl."

"Why," Judith asked, setting a tomato and some lettuce on the drain board, "was Flora avoiding the . . . *Flora Bunda?*"

Renie smirked. "Yes, as in floribunda roses. I wondered when you'd twig to that. So to speak."

"I don't suppose," Judith said dryly, "you know her real name?"

"No," Renie replied ruefully. "I don't think your mother knows it, either. But at least you know where those rose petals came from. They were a big part of her act, and hence the stage name of Flora Bunda."

Judith grimaced. "I don't recall seeing anybody at the party covered in rose petals."

"*Partially* covered," Renie corrected. "Your mother said the stripper was no spring chicken. Flora changed into her costume after Herself's condo shocker. By the time for her act, the band got into it with the guests. She was told to wait until the dust settled, but it never did. She was stuck in the basement because she was to come out that way, bumping and grinding through the garden gate. Her clothes were upstairs."

Judith frowned. "So?"

"Your mother didn't know why she couldn't go upstairs to get them," Renie said. "It sounds as if she spent the night in the basement and didn't emerge until after the cops showed up."

"It makes no sense," Judith murmured, putting bacon slices into a skillet. "If time of death was between ten and midnight, this Flora person must have been in the basement when the murder occurred. Did she hear anything? See anything? Or was the murder committed off the premises? I'd certainly like to talk to her."

"You could call No Nudes R Good Nudes and ask for her."

"Funny, Coz," Judith muttered. "I wonder if Flora stole Mother's engagement ring."

"Her ring is missing?"

Judith nodded. "Flora couldn't have come to the toolshed until after I served Mother's breakfast. The cops showed up long before that. I searched everywhere for the ring, but couldn't find it. And I certainly didn't see Flora anywhere. Did Mother say if the stripper was still wearing her costume when she arrived?"

"Your mother seemed a little confused about that," Renie replied. "Flora had a blanket over whatever she was or wasn't wearing."

"We'll have to find out who she is," Judith said, tearing off lettuce leaves. "Put some bread in the toaster."

Renie hopped off of the counter and crossed the kitchen to Grandma Grover's breadbox. After eighty years, the painted cherries-on-a-stem décor had faded and a faint line of rust showed around the edges. Judith was too sentimental to replace the metal heirloom.

"Why," she asked, "did Mother take pity on Flora?"

Renie sighed. "I suppose Vivian set her up. She'd already been to see your mother. Flora claimed she was avoiding police persecution for taking part in a pro-bingo rally. She gushed about Vivian's affection and esteem for your good-hearted mother because . . . blah-blah-blah."

"Good grief," Judith muttered, flipping the bacon. "The bingo bit sounds like something Herself would use to gain Mother's sympathy."

"If Flora swiped your mother's ring, Aunt Gert may not think so highly of her," Renie pointed out.

"True," Judith agreed. "*If* she believes Flora took it. If, in fact, Mother simply hasn't mislaid it." She finished making the sandwiches. The cousins sat at the kitchen table, temporarily lost in thought. "I feel stymied until I talk to Joe," Judith finally said. "He can at least tell me who he knew at the party."

Renie's expression was ironic. "And if he pitches a five-star fit because you're trying to solve the case?"

"That's a chance I have to take," Judith said. "I can't get anywhere if I don't know who's who. And nobody knows who the victim is."

"Not true," Renie remarked. "The killer knows."

Judith didn't argue.

Three o'clock passed with no word from Joe. Judith was tempted to call his hotel, but she waited. Finally, at three-thirty the phone rang just as Frankie and Marva Lou came through the door. "You have mail," Judith called before pressing the receiver's ON button.

"Muggy, hot, humid," Joe said without preamble. "Do not complain about our local weather. It's not that bad by comparison."

"I'm sure it isn't," Judith said, and paused. "I hate to, but I must ask a question." She paused again.

"Well?" Joe finally said when his wife remained silent. "What?"

Judith took a deep breath and summoned up her courage. "How many people did you actually know at Herself's party?"

"Oh, for—" Joe stopped. "Okay, I knew you couldn't resist. There's not a damned thing I can do about it from here in Atlanta, so I might as well cooperate. I suppose I could hire a bodyguard for you."

"Renie's staying with me," Judith said.

"Renie's a little squirt with a bad shoulder and—" Joe hesitated. "Is she in a good mood?"

"Temporarily," Judith replied, "but that won't last. It never does. I rest my case."

"Don't feed her," Joe urged. "Then I know she'll be ready for war."

"I'll *have* to feed her," Judith said, sitting down at the kitchen table. "I don't want her going to war with *me*."

"Right. Okay," Joe went on, resigned, "what's your question?"

"Which partygoers did you know?"

"The waiters," Joe replied. "Vivian's boys by a couple of husbands before me. They're not boys anymore, must be in their forties. Barry Henckel and Doug Campbell. I didn't recognize them at first. It's been fifteen years since I've seen them. Vivian says they've been a lot of help since she moved back. They both work in the restaurant industry."

"Their names were familiar," Judith said. "Do they live nearby?"

"They do now, though they've been all over in the food industry—Paris, Rio, New York, New—"

"Spare me the details," Judith broke in.

"Fine." Joe's tone was faintly sarcastic. "Barry lives in town, not far from the zoo."

"How appropriate."

"*Spare me* the editorial comments," Joe grumbled. "I really wish you weren't—Oh, skip it. There were a couple of cops I knew from way back, Carney Mitchell and Andy Pruitt. Both retired. Andy spends half of the year out north and winters in Arizona. Carney lives east of the lake. I saw some other familiar faces, but couldn't place them. They may've been city or county workers. Some of those guys were regulars at the cop bars back then because we were all headquartered in the same part of town. Vivian had quite a few fans in those days. She was a pretty good torch singer. Maybe she kept in touch with some of them."

Judith refrained from making a scathing comeback, focusing

instead on making notes. "I don't recall meeting either Carney Mitchell or Andy Pruitt, although there was one older guy who looked familiar. Fairly tall, thatch of white hair, a slight paunch, gestured a lot."

"Carney. We used to go lake fishing together. Andy's shorter, and when he had hair, it was kind of red. He's bow-legged. You may've met them at a departmental party. Both transferred out of Homicide later."

Judith heard voices from the entry hall, followed by the closing of the front door. *The Busses,* she thought, wondering if their FedEx delivery had spurred them into action. "That's it?" she asked Joe.

"That's it." His words had a ring of finality. "Any news on the vic?"

"You mean who he is? No, but . . ." Judith winced. "His body was stolen from the morgue last night."

"Oh, for—" Joe stopped. Judith could hear him sigh. "I won't ask if you're kidding," he finally said, "because I know you're not. I think I'll just head for the bar and try to forget I called you."

"It's not my fault the body got snatched," Judith snapped. "I'm keeping a low profile. What *can* I do if nobody knows who got killed?"

"A blessing in disguise," Joe murmured. "It sounds as if somebody doesn't want the vic identified. I'm not mad at you, just worried. How come Renie's at our house?"

Judith had hoped that Joe wouldn't ask. "Well . . . Bill went fishing."

"He did?" Joe sounded surprised. "Where?"

"Down to the coast," Judith said. "The salmon are in. He invited you, but that was after you were getting ready to go to Atlanta."

"Damn! Why the hell didn't you tell me?"

"I . . . ah . . . I assumed this was a trip you couldn't postpone."

"I could postpone dying if I thought the salmon were in," Joe retorted, practically shouting.

"You couldn't postpone this trip to find a killer in our own neighborhood, not to mention the victim was in your ex-wife's backyard? How will you explain that to Caitlin?" Judith wasn't finished, despite Joe's protests. "If nothing else, Vivian is your daughter's mother."

"Keep Caitlin out of this," Joe shot back. "I've spent most of Caitlin's life trying to keep her from getting sucked into Vivian's decadent adventures, and I've done a damned good job of it. Caitlin's got a nice life in Switzerland, a great job, and a good husband. She's never followed in her mother's tawdry footsteps. I don't want her getting mixed up in this sordid mess. I'm damned glad she's not near her mother."

"You're right," Judith conceded, hearing the doorbell and moving out of the kitchen. "I've always admired the way you've handled——" She stopped, halfway through the dining room.

"Coz," Renie called from the entry hall, "you have a visitor. It's Caitlin Flynn, just in from Switzerland."

12

Judith froze by the dining room table. "Joe," she said, lowering her voice almost to a whisper, "Caitlin's here."

"What?"

"Caitlin. She's here, talking to Renie. Got to go."

"Hey, wait a—"

Judith ended the call before Joe could finish. She left the receiver on the dining room table and hurried to meet her husband's daughter.

"Judith!" Caitlin exclaimed, long legs taking big strides to embrace her stepmother in an enthusiastic hug. "How wonderful to see you!"

"I'm stunned," Judith admitted when Caitlin let go. "You look terrific. But you're not Caitlin Flynn anymore. Or did you keep your maiden name?"

"Only at work. Otherwise, I go by Claude's name, Rouget."

"Come into the living room," Judith urged, leading the way. "I was just talking to your father. I can't believe you're here."

Caitlin settled onto one of the dark blue sofas. "I can't, either," she said, her expression suddenly grim. "My mother sent for me. I was shocked. I hadn't talked to her, let alone seen her, in at least a year."

Judith had sat down on the matching sofa. Renie leaned against the arm. "You two chat. Can I get you something to drink?" She darted a quick look at her cousin. "No, I'm not playing docile dogsbody this time. I'm trying to be thoughtful."

"Thanks, Coz," Judith said, turning to Caitlin. "Go ahead. I'm going to have Scotch-rocks. I feel a bit wobbly."

"Any white wine will do," Caitlin said to Renie. She smiled, exhibiting her father's Irish charm. "I've never cared much for the stronger stuff. It always reminds me of my mother, mixed with a heavy whiff of My Sin perfume."

As Renie headed for the kitchen, Judith shook her head in wonder. "I still can't believe you're here. Have you seen your mother?"

"Oh, yes," Caitlin replied in a bittersweet voice. "I spent the last hour listening to her carry on about the strange man she found dead in the backyard. It *is* true, I suppose. You're never sure with Mom."

"That's why she sent for you?" Judith asked.

Caitlin's green eyes flashed with what Judith thought was anger. "Yes. In fact, it wasn't me she really wanted. It was my husband, Claude, who's a lawyer. She thought he could help her with this latest mess—for free, of course. That's ridiculous. He can't practice law in this country. Anyway, he's preparing for a big case in Marseilles. By the way," she said, gazing around the living room, "where *is* Dad?"

"Atlanta." Judith looked apologetic. "On business. He left last night. I told him you were here. Feel free to call him from our phone."

"I can use my own." Caitlin's expression grew wistful. "I didn't realize that after retirement from the force, he accepted outside jobs that required travel. I thought he was kicking back."

"He is, generally." Judith shifted around on the sofa for a

more comfortable position. *Maybe,* she thought, *my discomfort isn't physical; maybe I'm embarrassed defending Joe's absence at such a crucial time in Vivian's life; maybe I should've kept my big mouth shut.* "This client is very important," Judith explained. "Usually, he doesn't travel much."

"I should've called ahead," Caitlin said ruefully. "I left in such a hurry. Since it's vacation time all over Europe, the chemical company I work for in Geneva is relatively quiet."

Renie's voice resounded from the dining room. "Keep your trap shut, Phyliss! This isn't an orgy, it's an early cocktail hour. And stop making the sign to ward off the evil eye whenever you see me."

There was no audible response from the cleaning woman. Renie appeared, carrying three glasses on a tray. "Someday I'll clobber that old bat," she declared, setting the tray on the coffee table. "I know zilch about wine, but this is white, even if it says pinot grigio on the label."

"That's fine," Caitlin said. "Thanks."

Judith picked up her Scotch-rocks and raised the glass. "To you, Caitlin. You do plan to stay for a few days, don't you?"

"Yes," Caitlin replied, lifting her slim wineglass in response to the toast. "I have an open-ended return ticket. The only problem is, I don't want to stay with Mom. In fact, there isn't room for me with her assistant living there. What would you recommend?"

"How about here?" Judith responded. "I've got an unex-pected vacancy tonight. After that, I'm not sure. . . ." Her glance strayed to Renie, who had sat down next to her on the sofa.

"Don't even think about me giving up the third-floor guest room," Renie said, looking daggers at her cousin. "I'm not sleep-ing with you. Not only do you talk and sing in your sleep, one time you hit me and shoved me out of bed. I got stuck between the wall and the headboard."

"I was twelve at the time," Judith retorted. "Joe never complains."

Renie turned a less hostile face to Caitlin. "Ordinarily, you could stay at our house. We have plenty of room with all our kids living so far away. Except," she added, grimacing, "the toilets are out of commission for a couple days. That's why I'm staying here."

Caitlin smiled. "You have your own problems. Mom said I could get a sleeping bag and put it in the vacant house she bought next door."

"We'll work out something here," Judith assured her. "Forget a hotel or motel. You can use your dad's MG. It's in the garage."

Caitlin laughed. "Of course! He'll drive it until the wheels fall off."

"The car's," Renie said, "or his?"

"Coz . . ." Judith glared at Renie. "Why don't you take your drink out to the garage and play with Clarence?"

"Damned if I won't," Renie said, getting up with glass in hand. She stalked out of the living room.

Caitlin looked puzzled. "Clarence?"

"Renie and Bill's bunny," Judith explained. "Bill went fishing."

Caitlin pointed to the mantel. "That's Renie's husband, isn't it? Why do you have a picture on the mantel of him with a stuffed monkey?"

"He's not a monkey, he's an ape," Judith said, and wanted to bite her tongue. She refused to play into Renie and Bill's ridiculous fantasy. "Never mind," she continued. "I'll explain that some other time. If you're really lucky, I'll forget you asked. So will you."

"Okay." Caitlin settled back on the sofa just as the doorbell rang.

"I have to get that," Judith said. "Excuse me."

✻ ✻ ✻

The two men who stood on the porch looked vaguely familiar. "How may I help you?" Judith asked, wondering if they'd been B&B guests at some time and had heard about the vacancy.

"We came to see Sis," the shorter of the two replied. "Is she here?"

"Sis?" Judith's jaw dropped. "You're the waiters!"

Both men laughed. "Sometimes," the short one said. "Mom told us Caitlin came to see her dad."

Caitlin had, in fact, come into the entry hall. "Doug! Barry!" she exclaimed, though her enthusiasm struck Judith as forced even as she allowed each of the men to give her a hug. "Have you met my half-brothers?" Caitlin asked Judith.

"No." She held out her hand to the shorter of the pair.

"Doug Campbell," he said, practically squeezing Judith's fingers to the point of pain. "This is Barry, Barry Henckel, my kid brother. Half-brother, half-wit. Ha-ha."

Barry's handshake wasn't as strong. Judith tried to find a resemblance between the two, but only their brown hair and brown eyes indicated a family relationship. Doug was not only short and stocky, but apparently hadn't shaved for a couple of days. Barry was much thinner, a few inches taller, and his scraggly hair was going gray. In their well-worn jeans and T-shirts, the half-brothers struck Judith as scruffy.

Barry and Doug were edging their way into the living room. "Hey," Doug cried, espying the drinking glasses, "it looks like you've already started to party! Awwwright!" He punched his fist into the palm of his other hand. "Let's get it on!"

"Actually," Caitlin said quietly, "I was about to leave to collect my luggage from Mom's house. Maybe you two could get it for me."

Barry, who Judith decided was the silent partner in the sibling relationship, spoke in a deep, rumbling voice. "No rush."

"Awesome!" Doug cried, slapping Barry's back. "Who's buying?"

Before Caitlin—or Judith—could protest, voices could be heard coming from the front porch, where the door had been left open. A moment later, Marva Lou and Frankie Buss appeared in the archway between the living room and the entry hall.

"What are you two doing here?" Frankie demanded.

"Seeing our sis," Doug retorted, fists clenching and unclenching at his side. "You got a problem with that?"

"Your sis?" Marva Lou said with a sour expression on her puddinglike face. "I thought you were waiters. Which one is your so-called sis?"

"Her," Barry replied, pointing to Caitlin, who looked to Judith as if she'd rather be just about anywhere but Hillside Manor.

"How many pups did your mother whelp?" Marva Lou said harshly. "Or is this one hers?" she added, gesturing at Judith.

"Hey!" Judith cried. "That's enough!" She put a hand on Caitlin's arm. "We're going to see . . . Clarence. Let's go before he . . . um . . . hops off."

Judith hustled Caitlin out through the French doors at the far end of the living room.

"Should we leave them in there?" Caitlin asked, looking over her shoulder. "It sounds as if big trouble is brewing."

"I'm insured," Judith said grimly.

"I'm so sorry Barry and Doug showed up," Caitlin said as they went down the back steps. "Who are those other two people?"

"Billy's brother and his wife," Judith replied, heading for the garage. "I take it you didn't meet them at your mother's."

Caitlin shook her head. "Are they staying here?"

"I'm afraid so," Judith answered. "They've been out all day. I assumed they might have been at your mom's house."

"Not while I was there, but Mom mentioned some visiting relatives from Oklahoma." Caitlin cringed as the sound of shattered glass reverberated from inside the house. "Oh, no! Should we call the police?"

Judith grimaced. "Maybe." Before she could make up her mind, Barry and Frankie hurtled through the French doors, seemingly engaged in mortal combat. The two men grappled with each other until Barry threw Frankie over the porch rail and into a pyracantha shrub.

Renie came out of the garage, holding Clarence in her arms. "What the hell's going on?" she cried, and stopped abruptly when she spotted Frankie rolling onto the sidewalk. "Yikes! Come on, Clarence, we're going back to your cage!"

Barry dusted off his hands and went inside the house. Frankie was cussing his head off and trying to stand up. "I've been wounded!" he finally shouted. "Help! Get a doctor!"

Judith came closer, scrutinizing the stricken man. Trickles of blood ran down his face and hands. "It's just thorn scratches from that bush you fell into," she said, putting out a hand to help him get up. "You'll be fine."

Refusing Judith's offer, Frankie made a weak but futile attempt to stand. Caitlin moved behind him and gripped his elbows with her hands. "Give it another try," she urged.

Slowly but surely, Frankie managed to get on his feet. Caitlin was as tall as Judith and sturdily built. "Regular workouts," she murmured, keeping one hand on Frankie's back. "I try to stay fit."

"You are," Judith said admiringly. "Let's put him in one of the patio chairs for now."

Caitlin steered Frankie along the walk and over to the small patio. "Nothing seems to be broken," she said to Frankie. "How do you feel?"

"Like crap," he mumbled. "I'm prething chargeths."

"What?" Caitlin asked.

"I thaid," Frankie practically shouted and then paused to run a finger inside his mouth, "*I'm prething chargeth.* I've lotht a tooth." He curled his upper lip under to show that the left incisor was missing.

Judith bent down to take a look and made a face. "That's terrible. Do you want me to look for it?"

"Why?" Frankie demanded. "I'm not a dentith. Are you?"

"Of course not." Judith offered a sympathetic smile. "I'll get some antiseptic and Band-Aids for those scratches. Caitlin will stay with you. I'll tell Mrs. Buss what's happened."

She hurried to the back door, wondering how Marva Lou Buss was faring with the half-brothers. Before going into the guest bathroom, Judith peeked into the living room. No one was there. Her cocktail glass was empty, and so was Caitlin's wineglass. She guessed that Barry and Doug had drained them before taking off.

Glancing out through the open front door, Judith spotted Marva Lou standing by the curb. "Mrs. Buss," she called. "Could you help me care for your husband?"

Marva Lou turned around slowly. "Why?" she asked wearily.

Judith stepped onto the porch. "He lost a tooth and has some scratches from a pyracantha shrub. Or maybe you call it firethorn."

"Serves him right," Marva Lou snapped, coming up the steps. "This trip's a disaster. Where's that bozo now?"

"In the backyard," Judith replied as the two women went inside. "What happened to Doug and Barry?"

"They chugalugged those drinks and took off in a pickup parked in front of Billy's house," Marva Lou replied. "Good riddance, I say. I could use a stiff drink myself. Where's the booze?"

"In the antique washstand by the dining room window," Judith said. "I'll get Mr. Buss."

"You can keep him, for all I care," Marva Lou muttered, barging in front of Judith and heading for the liquor stash. "Men are idiots. Why did Frankie think he could talk Billy into sharing the money? It's not Billy's money, it belongs to that wretched woman he married. She'd steal from a beggar. Why didn't she get killed instead of that guy in the tree?"

"I've wondered that myself," Judith murmured, recalling the dozens of times that she'd wished Herself would fall off a cliff.

Marva Lou, who was holding a bottle of bourbon by the neck, stared at Judith. "You have? How come? You mean that condo deal that's got the neighbors all riled up? Sounds like a crock to me. She's over at the house drawing up plans for a creek and a waterfall and God knows what else to show off her money."

"Ostentatious," Judith said and left to go back outside. "All clear," she announced from the porch. "Come on in, Mr. Buss."

With Caitlin's help, Frankie got out of the chair. Before he could take another step, the toolshed door opened.

"What's all this racket?" Gertrude demanded. "I'm trying to watch *Oprah*." She jabbed a finger at Caitlin. "I know you." Suddenly she stood stock-still and bit her lip. "Or maybe I don't." The old lady stepped back and slammed the door.

"Mrs. Grover," Caitlin murmured. "I haven't seen her since your wedding. She must be really getting up there."

"She's getting . . . older," Judith conceded, allowing Caitlin and Frankie to walk ahead of her. "She's sometimes forgetful. I'll take you to visit her at a more . . . ah . . . convenient time."

Marva Lou wasn't anywhere on the main floor. Judith

assumed she'd taken the bottle up to her room. Frankie didn't ask after his wife's whereabouts, but collapsed on one of the sofas.

"I could uthe a drink," he murmured. "Got any brandy?"

"Yes, I'll get it after I tend to your scratches," Judith replied. "They look superficial."

"Call a dentith," Frankie yelped as Judith headed for the guest bathroom. "I got to thee one today."

Judith paused under the arch between the living room and entry hall. "It's almost five o'clock. You'll have to wait until morning." She kept going, ignoring a few choice cuss words from Frankie.

After Judith had quickly assembled the necessary first-aid items, she went into the dining room. Caitlin was already there.

"Maybe I should go," she murmured. "Or do you need help? You must have other guests staying here."

"Yes," Judith replied, pouring an inch of brandy into a snifter, "except for the unexpected vacancy, I'm full up. Why don't you get your things from your mother's house and come back? I'm okay as long as I can get Renie out of the garage."

Caitlin looked uncertain. "Are you sure you're all right?" She hesitated. "Is *she* all right?"

"Renie?" Judith was surprised by the question. "Yes. That is, as all right as she ever was."

"I didn't mean——" Caitlin's fair skin flushed slightly. "It's the rabbit and the ape and . . . Bill. It seems a . . . little . . . odd."

"It may strike some people that way," Judith said, forcing a smile.

"Of course." But Caitlin didn't sound convinced. "With your mother in the toolshed and your cousin in the garage . . . Never mind. I'll collect my luggage now."

Great, Judith thought, trudging into the living room. *Caitlin*

*probably figures her father married into a bunch of lunatics. I hope she
doesn't pass that along to Vivian.*

"Here you are," Judith said, handing the snifter to Frankie.
She set the antiseptic, cotton balls, and some Band-Aids on the
coffee table. "Shall I take care of those scratches, or will you?"

Frankie sipped brandy and shook his head. "Go away."

"Sure." Judith was only too glad to comply. Out of the corner
of her eye she saw a scattering of glass near the baby grand
piano. "My Lalique mermaid vase!" she cried, and remembered
the sound of glass breaking just before Frankie and Doug had
erupted through the French doors. "That was a Christmas present from Renie and Bill!"

Frankie just kept sipping.

Judith shot him a dirty look, snatched up a copy of the *Wall
Street Journal* from the coffee table, and hurried over to the
piano. She was gingerly picking up pieces of precious glass and
placing them on the newspaper when Renie came through the
French doors.

"What now?" she asked.

"Your vase," Judith said between clenched teeth. "Those idiots
broke it." She didn't care whether Frankie heard her or not.

"No!" Renie grabbed a bronze bookend shaped like a buffalo
from the shelf near the piano. "Let me at 'em!" she yelled.

Judith blocked her path. "*Please.* Not now. I'm really upset."

Renie sighed heavily and put the bookend back on the shelf.
"Okay. But only for your sake will I forgo violence." She bent
down and gathered up the three purple gladioli that had reposed
in the vase. "The carpet's wet. I'll get some rags. How much are
the Busses paying for their stay?" she asked, raising her voice.

"What?" Judith looked at Renie. "So far, not including
tonight, three hundred and twenty dollars."

"That vase cost three-sixty plus tax," Renie said loudly,
marching past Frankie. "Charge them double."

"I'm thuing!" Frankie shrieked. "I'm calling the polithe!" He struggled to his feet, rammed against the coffee table, and knocked over the brandy snifter. It fell to the floor and rolled onto the hearth, where it smashed into a hundred pieces. Frankie paid no attention and staggered to the phone on the cherrywood table.

"Hold it!" Judith yelled, moving as fast as she could to prevent Frankie from making the call. "Okay, I won't charge you double. I won't charge you at all if you don't sue me instead of the jerks who knocked you around. Sit down. I'll see if I can get you in at our dentist's tomorrow."

To Judith's surprise, Frankie backed off. "Okay," he mumbled. "Thorry about the thnifter. Got another one? I could uthe more brandy."

"Wait until I talk to the dentist's office," Judith said, dialing the number from memory. "They're about to close for the day."

Renie returned while Judith was arranging for a nine-thirty appointment. "What the hell," Renie demanded of Frankie when she saw the glass on the hearth, "did you bust up now? You're a one-man weapon of mass destruction. Or should I say glass destruction?" Shaking her head, she went over to the piano and used the rag to soak up the spilled water.

"You're set," Judith said, hanging up the phone and turning to Frankie. "I'll give you Dr. Fortuna's address. His office is on top of Heraldsgate Hill, across from Falstaff's Grocery."

"Done," Renie announced, standing up. "Don't go barefoot here, though. I'll take care of the hearth. You tend to the patient."

Reluctantly, Judith went back to the dining room to get more brandy. The California foursome had just returned from wherever they'd been all day and were heading upstairs.

"Now," Judith said, after handing Frankie his refill and sitting down on the other sofa, "why don't you tell me about the bad blood between you and Vivian Buss's sons?"

"Why do you think?" Frankie retorted, with a hostile look. "They want their greedy mother to give them thome of her money. It ought to belong to Billy and me. I don't figure Pappy made that new will without thome kind of . . . whath the word? Coerthion?"

"Coercion," Judith murmured, watching out of the corner of her eye to see how Renie was faring with the hearth cleanup. "Why do you think that?"

"Why do you think Vi married an old guy like Pappy?" he snarled.

Judith nodded halfheartedly. "I understand, although Vivian isn't as young as she claims."

Renie got up from the hearth, holding the pieces of shattered glass in a rag. "She sure isn't. A long time ago, I was ten years younger than she was. Now I'm ten years older. I'm no good at math, but that doesn't make sense even to me." She edged past Judith and left the room.

"I got *fifteen* years older," Judith said under her breath. "Surely," she went on, looking at Frankie, who was drinking his brandy rather fast, "your father's wealth provided for you and Billy over the years."

"Pappy wath kind of tightfithted," Frankie replied. "He did get me a hardware buthineth." He shrugged. "I done okay, no matter what Marva Lou might tell you. Billy wath a ballplayer, but not very good. Played on the team Pappy owned. Couldn't field a ball for thour owl thweat. Nickname was 'Blunderbuth.' Tried out in thpring training with the Tampa Bay Devil Rayth in Florida and got cut right off the bat—tho to thpeak. Thath why he hated Florida. Pappy got him a thporting goodth thtore back home. It went broke. Maybe Billy could've handled the farm. Or not."

"Was your father a widower?" Judith asked.

Frankie nodded. "Yep. Ma died ten yearth ago. Wonderful woman. Never thought Pappy'd get married again. But he did, dangit." His eyes filled with tears. "Never been the same after Ma went."

Despite the damage Frankie had contributed to, Judith's natural sympathy welled up inside. His thin hands were trembling slightly as he held the brandy snifter, and a tear rolled down each cheek. Maybe he was crying because he missed his mother—and his father. Or, she thought, his lost inheritance.

"Excuse me," she said, getting up. "I have to prepare the appetizers for the social hour."

Frankie merely snuffled. Judith joined Renie in the kitchen.

"Now what?" Renie inquired, making drinks for herself and Judith. "Is Frankie moved to tears, or is this the Age of Snivelry? After two sentences of that lisp, I thought I'd go nuts."

"Don't be so harsh," Judith said. "Frankie has gotten a raw deal. So has Billy, though as long as he can put up with Vivian, he'll be okay. It does make me wonder, though."

"About what?" Renie asked, handing Judith her Scotch.

After taking a sip of her drink, Judith set her glass on the counter and removed a block of sharp cheddar from the fridge. "First, we don't know the victim's identity. That's crucial, and yet it strikes me as some kind of . . . oh, I hate to use the word, but it's a clue. The dead man had to be known to somebody at the party."

"Or known to the neighbors in the cul-de-sac?" Renie suggested.

"I doubt it," she said, grating cheese into a bowl. "Can you think of anybody in this close-knit neighborhood who'd kill someone?"

"It did happen once," Renie reminded Judith, referring to

the previous murder in the cul-de-sac. "All human beings are said to have the capacity to kill in certain situations."

"I don't think this murder was caused by desperation or in self-defense." Judith used the back of her hand to wipe perspiration off her forehead. The temperature had risen, inching toward ninety. "Hey, get me two cans of Dungeness crab from the pantry. Thanks."

"Keep talking," Renie said, moving down the hall. "I can hear you."

But Judith didn't respond. The young men from Virginia had entered the house and were going upstairs. Not wanting to raise her voice lest they hear their innkeeper discussing motives for murder, she waited until her cousin was back in the kitchen.

"Go on," Renie urged.

"We'll keep the neighbors out of this," Judith said. "A couple of people have mentioned that Vivian was a more likely victim. On the surface, that makes sense. But who would benefit from her death?"

"You," Renie responded with a grin.

"Get serious." Judith opened the cans of crab.

"Billy?" Renie offered, her expression serious. "This is a community property state. He'd get everything unless Vivian's made some other arrangements or they signed a prenup."

Judith shook her head. "The point is, she's not the victim. Still, her sudden wealth must be tied into the motive for killing Mr. Mystery. The killer—let's assume it was the killer who snatched the body from the morgue—didn't want the victim IDed. Why? If I knew that, I might understand the motive and have a better chance to figure out whodunit."

Renie sipped her bourbon and looked thoughtful. "That angle makes sense. What about blackmail? What if Herself killed—what was the old coot's name? Poopsy?"

"Potsy," Judith corrected her cousin. "No. Vivian's got a lot of faults, but she wouldn't kill an old guy whose number was coming up anyway. Unless," she went on, "she . . . um . . . wore him out."

"So he died happy," Renie mused. "Thus, my blackmail theory is kaput. Okay, what do we know for certain about the victim?"

"He was late sixties, early seventies, and in good health," Judith replied. "Average height, weight, brown hair going gray. Nothing extraordinary—unfortunately."

"Was he at the party?"

"No," Judith said. "Joe would've mentioned that if he had been. The cops obviously came up empty."

"So he shows up after the party," Renie murmured. "When? You told me it broke up early. The murder took place between ten and midnight. Who stayed on besides Flora Bunda? The two half-brothers?"

"I've no idea," Judith said.

"If," Renie said slowly, "the victim had stolen ID from a guy in Nevada, maybe he came from there. If so, he had a purpose."

Judith nodded. "Yes." She stopped in the middle of peeling a ripe avocado. "Herself never lived in Vegas or anywhere else in Nevada. She hauled Joe there for the quickie wedding. But that doesn't mean that some of the men she's known—and the list is long—haven't a Nevada connection. Maybe," she continued, lowering her voice as she heard the honeymooners in the entry hall, "it's time to call Uncle Al."

"Why?"

"Because," Judith replied, "I just remembered that some mail came for a J. C. Agra a while ago. The substitute carrier left one letter at the Rankerses' and the other one here."

"You told me about that," Renie said. "You think those letters were for Herself's first husband? Is Johnny Agra still around?"

Judith's expression turned grim. "I think maybe he's not. At least, not as of the last few days. I'm wondering if he's the murdered mystery man."

13

Uncle Al answered the phone on the fifth ring. "What's the score?" he asked in his typical fashion. "I see somebody else cashed in his chips by your place the other night. What's the morning line on whether or not you'll nail the killer? I'll take five-to-one. It's money in the bank."

Judith was accustomed to Uncle Al's sporting attitude. "How come," she asked, "you're not at the track today?"

"Bunch of nickel nags running," Uncle Al replied. "No big stakes races on a Wednesday. Maidens, claiming, glue-factory futures. Why? You want a tip? I've got one for tomorrow in the sixth. Little Juice, probably going off at eight-to-one."

"No, thanks, Uncle Al," Judith said. "I'm calling about an old pal of yours, Johnny Agra. Is he still . . . around?"

"Johnny Agra," Uncle Al said in a musing tone. "No, Johnny's long gone. After his restaurant folded years ago, I heard he died or moved out of town. L.A., maybe. Same thing, as far as I'm concerned. Wasn't he married to Joe's ex at one time?"

"The very same," Judith said, watching Renie finish preparing the guests' vegetable platter. "The dead body was found in her backyard."

"No kidding!" Uncle Al chuckled. "The TV news left out

the name of the owners. They just said a corpse had been found outside of a home on Heraldsgate Hill, and then the body was stolen out of the morgue. Helluva note. You're not even safe after you're dead these days." He chortled. "It wasn't Johnny, was it?"

"Not if he's been dead for years," Judith replied. "You're sure about that?"

"You mean, would I bet on it?" Uncle Al paused. "Depends on the odds. Could be he had a reason to disappear. Still, if he was alive, I might've heard something about him. I've got connections."

"Oh, yes," Judith said, glancing at Renie. "You have connections."

"Not to mention," Renie murmured, "a hotline to every gambling site on- and offshore on the planet."

"I was just curious," Judith went on. "Thanks. And good luck with that hot tip tomorrow."

She hung up. "Uncle Al thinks Johnny may be dead. He'd bet on it, if the odds were good."

"Uncle Al would bet on anything," Renie pointed out. "He put a hunsky on how long Cousin Trixie's third marriage would last. And won. Four years, seven months, a record for her at the time."

"I know. It was a family pool. I missed by two years."

"So," Renie said, adding one more radish to the vegetable platter, "you're at a dead end—so to speak—with Johnny Agra."

"Apparently." Judith put the crab, cheddar, and mayonnaise mixture into puff pastry shells.

Looking pensive, Renie sipped her bourbon. "If Johnny died here, the local papers would've run his obit. He was well known in the restaurant trade. Want me to check him out to see if he checked out?"

"You mean on the computer?" Judith hesitated. "Go ahead. But if he died years ago, won't you have to pay to get into the archives?"

"It's a business expense, and therefore tax deductible," Renie pointed out. "I can give it a try." She went to the computer.

Judith started to turn on the oven, but decided that was a bad idea. The temperature felt as if it already must be ninety in the kitchen. Instead, she put the crab puffs in the microwave. "Any luck?" she asked.

"No. I can only go back a year, and I'm too inept to figure out this site." Renie signed off. "We could go to the courthouse tomorrow."

"It's not worth it," Judith said, then clapped a hand to her head. "I forgot to call Joe back about Caitlin! My mind's turned to mush!" She snatched up the receiver from the counter and dialed Joe's cell.

Drink in hand, Renie wandered out of the kitchen. Judith held her breath while the phone rang four times. Just when she thought Joe wasn't picking up, she heard his voice—barely.

"I can't hear you very well," she all but shouted. "Where are you?"

"I'm eating in . . ." He faded away.

"Call me back!" Judith said loudly, and clicked off.

Renie returned to the kitchen. "Frankie passed out," she announced. "Or else he's dead."

"Don't say things like that!" Judith snapped. "Wake him up, get him moving before the other guests come down to socialize."

"Can't," Renie replied. "A visitor is approaching."

Judith stared at Renie. "Who?"

"A middle-aged man dressed in a courtly manner." She paused as the doorbell sounded. "Shall I let him in?"

"I'll do it," Judith retorted, wondering what her cousin meant by *a courtly manner*. "If Joe calls back, tell him to hang on."

At the front door, Judith realized Renie's description was apt. The handsome, silver-haired man with a neatly trimmed Van Dyke wore a cream-colored summer suit, a navy blue tie with a crisp white shirt, and, upon seeing Judith, doffed his navy blue straw fedora. "Mrs. Flynn?" he inquired softly.

"Yes." Judith smiled. "Are you here about the vacancy?"

"Vacancy?" He turned to look out into the cul-de-sac. "Oh! Of course." He gestured with a well-manicured hand. "May I come in?"

"Well . . . yes," Judith said, stepping aside. "I'd like to help you if I can. Did you talk to someone at the state association?"

Entering the house, the man chuckled richly, if quietly. "No, but I will if that's necessary. My name's Mandrake Stokes."

Judith paused in the entry hall to shake her visitor's hand. "The parlor would be best," she said. "Here, this door. You must tell me how you found our place."

"Of course." Mr. Stokes gazed around the cozy parlor. "A delightful setting," he remarked, with a touch of the South in his melodious voice.

Judith indicated one of the two matching chairs. "You'll have to forgive me," she said, puzzled. "I didn't realize you were coming."

Mr. Stokes frowned. "You didn't? The letter was sent last week."

"We had a substitute postman," Judith said, sitting in the other chair. "I'm afraid some of our mail went astray."

"Ah! I see." He smiled warmly. "I have the entire presentation in my car. When would you like to study it?"

"Presentation?" Judith frowned. "I'm sorry, I don't understand."

Renie stood in the parlor doorway. "It's Joe," she said, holding the receiver. "Can you talk to him?"

Judith stood up. "Excuse me, Mr. Stokes. I must take this call." Hurrying out of the parlor, she shoved Renie into the dining room. "If this guy's a salesman," she said in a low voice, "get rid of him. If he's involved in Vivian's condo project, stall him." She spoke to Joe as she moved into the kitchen. "Caitlin is here because Vivian wanted her help," she said. "Where are you?"

"I was having dinner in the bar," he replied, sounding cross. "I'm back in my room. Where did you think I was, out on Peachtree Street looking for hookers?"

"Of course not," Judith asserted. "Anyway, Caitlin will probably call you later. She's staying here tonight. I had an early departure. The Griggses from Iowa simply walked out."

"It happens," Joe remarked. "Where's Caitlin now?"

"Collecting her luggage from Vivian's," Judith replied. "You'll never guess who showed up to see her."

"No guessing games," Joe grumbled. "It's been a long day after a short night."

"Her half-brothers, Doug and Barry," Judith informed him.

"Right, I told you they were waiters at the party. She got on with them okay. Got to go. The light on my phone just went on. It's probably a call-back from one of the bank guys I met today. Talk to you later." Joe hung up.

The abrupt conclusion rankled, but Judith shrugged it off. She hurried back to the parlor, anxious to find out why her unexpected visitor had come to Hillside Manor.

Renie was by the hearth, chatting with Mr. Stokes. "Hey, Coz," she said, "Manny here wants to know what you intend to do with your cows."

"My——" Judith stopped in her tracks. "Sorry. Did you say *cows*?"

Renie nodded. "You two sort that out while I finish the appetizers."

Staring at her cousin as she left the parlor, Judith felt as if she was having a bad dream. "Excuse me," she said to Mr. Stokes, "but I don't own any cows."

Mandrake Stokes looked equally mystified. "Surely you haven't sold them off?"

"No," Judith replied, leaning on the back of the empty chair. "Where would I keep cows around here?"

Mr. Stokes stroked his short silver beard. "There must be some confusion. I understood that following your move here, you intended to sell the Double UB Ranch in order to build condominiums. I was informed by the university that the livestock would be included."

Enlightenment dawned. "Ah! I'm not *Vivian* Flynn. I'm *Judith* Flynn. Mrs. Flynn—that is, Vivian—is now Mrs. Buss. She lives a couple of doors away."

"Well!" Mr. Stokes seemed embarrassed. "I must beg forgiveness for my error," he said, standing up. "Not to mention wasting your valuable time. I assume Mrs. Flynn—that is, Mrs. *Buss?*—used her maiden name instead of her husband's."

The concept of Vivian as any sort of "maiden" in the true sense almost triggered a derisive outburst from Judith, but she managed to maintain a relatively sober expression. "That's possible. She married two Busses." The straight face became more difficult to keep. "The first Buss crashed——I mean, *died*. The other one——" Judith couldn't help it. She started to laugh, leaning on the chair for support.

"Yes, well . . ." Mr. Stokes backed away toward the door. "If you could point me in the proper direction, I'll call on her now."

But Judith couldn't stop laughing. "Or perhaps not," Mr. Stokes murmured. "I'll check my notes for the correct address." He all but ran into the entry hall and out the door.

Renie strolled into the parlor. "What *did* you do with all

those cows?" she asked with a puckish expression. "It must have been pretty damned funny. Or are you hysterical?"

Judith tried to stop laughing. Gasping for breath, she began to sputter. "I . . . can't . . . help . . . it."

"I was eavesdropping by the other parlor door off of the living room," Renie explained. "I gather that Herself inherited a cattle ranch from Potsy. That must be worth a lot of moo-lah."

"Don't!" Judith cried, and finally caught her breath. "Yes." She paused, a hand to her breast. "This murder case is so crazy. Or is it because Vivian's involved? Is she what's sending me over the edge?"

"She usually does," Renie replied, turning to glance out into the hall. "Here come some of the guests for the social hour. Do you want me to pretend Frankie is a stuffed animal decorating your sofa, or shall I feign ignorance?"

Judith narrowed her eyes at Renie. "Stuffed like Oscar?"

"Of course not!" Renie shook her head in disbelief. "Oscar is real!"

Shaking her head in disbelief, Judith went through the parlor door that led into the living room. The two older couples from Bakersfield had gathered by the buffet, where Renie had set out the appetizers, a pitcher of pink lemonade, and a bottle of sherry. As Judith entered, they stared at her with unconcealed curiosity.

"Excuse me," the taller of the two men said, "but is that fellow on the couch asleep?"

"He's not well," Judith replied. "He . . . fell down. I told him to rest until he felt like walking up the stairs to his room. Poor man," she added, trying to look sympathetic.

"Oh, my!" the tall man's wife exclaimed, and poked her husband's arm. "Maybe you should have a look at him, Bob." She turned to Judith. "My husband was an army medic during the Korean War."

Bob tweaked his wife's cheek and chuckled. "You don't think I've lost my touch? Sure, why not? I always did okay by our kids when they were young and took a tumble."

Judith had qualms. "I'm not sure that's a good idea. I'm responsible for what happens in my B&B. Mr. Buss wasn't badly hurt."

The other man pointed a pudgy finger at the brandy snifter. "Maybe he passed out. Looks to me as if he's been drinking, Bob."

"Aha!" Bob chuckled again. "Guess you're right," he said to Judith. "Let sleeping dogs lie, and all that."

The pudgy man's wife disagreed. "He doesn't seem to be breathing. What if he's . . . dead?"

Bob considered the question. "I suppose I could take his pulse." He looked at Judith. "That okay?"

Anxiety rising, Judith had to make a decision. "I can take his pulse," she said. "I've had medical experience, too." *If,* she thought unhappily, *that includes determining if a putative corpse is really dead.*

"Sure," Bob agreed. "Go ahead. It's your B&B."

Judith was walking over to the sofa when the honeymooners came into the living room. Renie was right behind them.

"Guess what?" she said. "The groom here is a doctor."

Judith stared at the young man. "You are?"

"A resident," he replied, "at Alaska Regional Hospital in Anchorage. I'm a cardiologist."

"That's good enough for me," Judith said, and backpedaled away from the sofa to stand by Renie under the archway. "How'd you know?" she whispered.

"How do you think?" Renie shot back. "I overheard you in here and when the lovebirds came downstairs I took a wild shot and asked if either of them had any medical expertise. You got lucky."

"Maybe," Judith allowed.

"His pulse is faint," the groom announced. "He should be hospitalized. Call nine-one-one."

Judith jabbed Renie in the ribs. "You call," she whispered. "Use your cell. I refuse to get into it with one of those snotty operators."

"I'll give the Rankerses' address," Renie murmured. "Then I'll divert them here." She hurried into the kitchen to make the call.

"Hallo!" called a voice from the entry hall. Judith swerved around to see who was there.

"Adelita," she said, keeping her composure. "Can I help you?"

"Yes," the young woman replied. "Mrs. Buss would like very much to borrow your blender. Hers is broken."

Judith had a feeling that if she loaned her blender to Vivian, it would never be returned. "Oh, darn!" she exclaimed, standing directly in front of Adelita to prevent her from seeing what was going on in the living room. "Mine broke, too. It must be contagious."

Adelita's expression was skeptical. "Pardon?"

Judith lifted her hands in a helpless gesture. "My blender's motor must've gone out. It doesn't work. I'm so sorry."

"Do you have a mixer?" Adelita inquired.

"You mean an electric one?" Judith saw Adelita nod. "Oddly enough, that went out on me, too. Both the hand mixer and the big freestanding one. Maybe it's a fuse."

Adelita was inching her way forward. "An eggbeater, perhaps?"

Renie had come into the entry hall. Judith turned to her cousin and winked. "Did you ever bring back my eggbeater?"

"Your eggbeater?" For a brief moment, Renie looked blank. "Oh! *That* eggbeater! No, I forgot. Sorry."

Adelita had managed to worm her way almost to the living room's arched entrance. "Isn't there more than one eggbeater?"

Behind Adelita, a medic van was arriving. Mercifully, the EMTs hadn't turned on their siren or flashing lights.

"Yes," Judith said, taking Adelita by the arm. "Let's see if we can find it." She hustled her visitor into the kitchen while Renie went outside to direct the emergency personnel. "Let me see," Judith murmured, tapping her cheek and gazing every which way. Voices could be heard from the entry hall. The only one she recognized belonged to Renie.

"The pantry, maybe. Let's look." Judith led Adelita down the hall. "Now, where would I have put that older one?"

Adelita's attention seemed distracted by the sounds coming from the front part of the house. "What is happening? Is there trouble here?"

"Trouble?" Judith purposefully turned around so fast that she knocked several cans off of the shelf. "Oh, drat! Could you help me pick up these cans? I have an artificial hip and can't bend over."

Adelita's dark eyes flashed. "I am not a maid! I am an assistant!" She whirled around and ran off down the hall.

Frustrated, Judith gently nudged the cans with her foot to keep them from rolling toward the basement stairs. A century of earthquakes had taken their toll on the old house. Floors sloped, doorways were uneven, and windows were crooked. At the moment, Judith felt she, too, was damaged by time and circumstances.

When she reached the entry hall, Renie was shoving Adelita out through the front door. "Nothing to see here!" Renie shouted, with one last push, and slammed the door behind Adelita before turning to Judith. "What was that all about?"

"I'm not sure," Judith replied. "Adelita wasn't really interested in blenders or eggbeaters. What's going on with Frankie?"

"I don't know," Renie replied. "They're working on him. As usual, the emergency folks seemed to be parked close by."

Judith sighed. "I guess that's to be expected. Would you mind going upstairs to Room Five and telling Marva Lou about her husband?"

"Sure." Renie hurried up the stairs. Judith went into the living room, where the brothers from Virginia had joined the rest of the guests—and the EMTs. For once, Judith didn't recognize any of the medical personnel. Somehow, that was a relief. She didn't need any more snide comments about her propensity for disasters.

A woman with short blond hair seemed to be in charge. Judith noted that her name tag identified her as Roxanne Sundberg. She was talking to the groom as his bride sidled up to Judith.

"It may be an allergic reaction," she said. "They're taking him to the hospital. I wonder if Jake should go with them."

"That's up to the EMTs," Judith said, watching as Frankie was placed on a gurney. "I'm sure that Mr. Buss will receive excellent care. If anybody should go along, it ought to be his wife."

"Where is she?" Ashley inquired.

"My cousin is getting her now," Judith said. "Mrs. Buss has been . . . resting in their room."

"Oh." Ashley nodded. "Yes, you're right. That'd be best."

Judith and Ashley moved out of the way as two male EMTs pushed the gurney through the living room and into the entry hall. Roxanne Sundberg followed, but stopped when she reached Judith. "Dr. Kerr just told me you own this B&B. Mrs. Flynn, I believe?"

"Yes. You think it's allergies?"

"We can't be sure," Roxanne replied, "but it's possible. I understand his wife is here. Does she know what's happened?"

"My cousin is bringing her downstairs right now," Judith replied. "In fact, here she comes."

Roxanne turned toward the staircase. "Mrs. Buss?"

"No," Renie replied. "I can't wake up Frankie's wife. Have you got a gurney for two?"

14

What?" Judith cried.

"You heard me," Renie said, reaching the entry hall. "Marva Lou's passed out, just like Frankie. It's a good thing she didn't lock the door."

Roxanne was already on her cell, summoning more help. "I've got an ambulance on the way," she announced, clicking off the phone. "They should be here in less than five minutes. I'll take a quick look while Mr. Buss is being put into the van. Show me the way."

Renie started back up the stairs. "Stay put," she called to Judith. "You look worn out."

"I am," Judith muttered, "but I have to see what's going on." She followed Roxanne, but didn't force herself to hurry. Her brain was full of questions, none of them pleasant. Allergies? Food poisoning? Some weird strain of virus? Or . . . Judith didn't want to consider another possibility. Not yet, anyway.

Marva Lou Buss was lying motionless on the bed. The liquor bottle she'd taken from the washstand in the dining room was almost half empty. Judith and Renie both remained in the doorway to Room Five while Roxanne checked Marva Lou's vital signs.

"You're right," she said grimly. "Her condition seems similar to her husband's. Do you know what they ate or drank in the last few hours?"

"He had brandy, and Mrs. Buss had bourbon," Judith replied, pointing to the bottle on the nightstand. "The bourbon hadn't yet been opened. The brandy bottle was over half full. I have no idea what or where they ate after they had breakfast."

Roxanne's expression was somber. "Are you sure?"

"Yes," Judith insisted. "Mr. and Mrs. Buss were gone most of the day. They have relatives two doors down on the west side of the cul-de-sac, a Mr. and Mrs. Billy Buss. I know they were there at some time today because Mrs. Buss mentioned it."

"All right." Roxanne started toward the stairs. "Stay here until the ambulance arrives. I'll alert Dr. Kerr before I leave with Mr. Buss. Both of the victims will be taken to Bayview Hospital."

"I know the drill," Judith murmured. "Roxanne's new around here," she said to Renie. "She avoided calling me a herald of doom."

"True," Renie conceded, "but she's smart. I get the impression that Roxanne figures this isn't an ordinary emergency. She's suspicious."

"Not of me, I hope," Judith said, glancing at her watch. "Good grief! I forgot to feed Mother! Can you wait here while I fix something before she pitches a five-star fit?"

"Sure," Renie said, motioning for Judith to go.

Taking the back stairs, Judith went into the kitchen, took a frozen TV dinner out of the fridge, and popped it in the microwave. Fortunately, Gertrude liked some of the ready-made entrees, often insisting they tasted better than her daughter's home cooking.

While Judith waited for the food to cook, she went out to the entry hall. There was no sign of the ambulance yet, but the medic van was pulling away. From the living room, she heard the sounds of animated chatter from her guests.

"Excuse me," she said loudly, standing under the arch. "Mr. and Mrs. Buss are suffering from an illness with similar symptoms, possibly an allergic reaction or even food poisoning. Did any of you speak to them today about their plans? It might be helpful if we knew where they'd spent their time after leaving here this morning."

The twins looked blank. The honeymooners shook their heads. The Californians exchanged glances.

"Just saw them briefly this morning," Bob, the former Army medic, said. "Asked if they were enjoying their visit. They acted grumpy."

"Not a very friendly couple," his wife put in. "I thought she mentioned something about this not being a vacation so much as work."

Judith nodded. "They have family nearby. Sometimes visiting relatives can be stressful." *And deadly,* she thought. "I assure all of you that whatever caused their illness didn't occur here at Hillside Manor. They ate the same breakfast that you had, and I assume none of you are ill." Judith paused for a response. The little group agreed that they felt fine. "Good," Judith said with a smile. "I'm sorry for this disruption."

"Oh, no," the other California wife said with a big smile. "It's kind of exciting, a real icebreaker." She beamed at the other guests. "Isn't that so, folks? It gives us something to talk about. Especially," she added, winking at the newlyweds, "the dead body in the neighbors' yard."

"Uh . . . yes," Judith said, feeling the need to fib a bit. "Very unfortunate, very unusual around here." She glanced over her shoulder. "I think the ambulance is here for Mrs. Buss. Excuse me."

Not only had the ambulance arrived, but so had Caitlin, complete with three pieces of luggage.

"What's happening?" she asked. "Is someone sick?"

"I'm afraid so," Judith admitted, ushering Caitlin inside and away from the ambulance attendants' path. "Billy's brother and his wife are quite ill."

"Oh, no!" Caitlin exclaimed. "Should I tell Mom and Billy?"

"Yes." Judith paused as a gurney was brought up the front steps. "They'll have to know. Did your mother mention if Frankie and Marva Lou had anything to eat or drink at their house today?"

Caitlin shook her head. "Mom just said that Marva Lou had a nasty tongue, and Frankie whined all the time. Where shall I put my luggage? After I do that, I'll go back to Mom's."

"It's Room One," Judith said, hurriedly giving Caitlin her keys.

Unfortunately, Judith recognized one of the ambulance attendants from a previous disaster. The burly man with the blond buzz cut snickered as he passed her in the entry hall. "You got a twofer this time, Mrs. Flynn. Maybe someday we can fix up an old bus just for your guests and haul away a couple of dozen victims all at once. You're not thinking about opening a hotel, are you? If you do, give us some advance warning, okay?"

Judith glared at him before going out to the kitchen to rescue her mother's TV dinner. The timer had just gone off. Renie could handle any details concerning the latest catastrophe.

Opening the toolshed's door and seeing Gertrude sitting at the card table playing solitaire somehow comforted Judith. "You're late," the old lady snapped.

Even the reprimand felt reassuring. The world around her might be going to hell in a handcart, but Gertrude Grover remained a fixture, a human lighthouse promising some kind of safe harbor—no matter how rough her tongue might be.

"A couple of guests got sick," Judith said. "You have Salisbury steak, mashed potatoes, and green beans. There's pudding for dessert."

Gertrude studied the food. "Good. You didn't cook it your-self. Did those guests get sick from your egg mess with the pieces of dried-up fish and toadstools in it?"

"That omelet recipe has smoked salmon and portobello mushrooms," Judith said. "My guests love it, but I didn't make it today."

"Maybe it was your French toast," Gertrude said, cutting her Salisbury steak. "You could use it as carpeting, and then the waffles with fruit—"

"Mother," Judith broke in, "I'm kind of tired this evening. And it's still hot. You didn't find your ring, by any chance, did you?"

"No." Gertrude made a face. "Maybe you cooked it in one of your conglomerations. Whoever ate it wouldn't know the difference."

"If it was stolen," Judith said, "I should call our insurance agent."

"It wasn't," Gertrude replied stubbornly. "I lost it, that's all."

Judith scrutinized the old lady's mulish expression as she added salt and pepper to her mashed potatoes. "Did your visitor take it?"

Gertrude looked up. "Vivian? Don't be so dumb. She's rich now. Done real well for herself. She can buy all the rings she wants and wear 'em in her nose if she feels like it."

"Okay, so it wasn't Vivian," Judith agreed. "But what about Flora Bunda? Who is she?"

"Who she said she is," Gertrude said, stabbing a couple of green beans with her fork. "Now beat it, and leave me in peace."

Judith sat on the davenport's arm. "Please. A man has been killed. Nobody knows who he is or who killed him. You're fond of Vivian, and since the body was found in her backyard, she's bound to be a suspect. You'd be glad to help her, wouldn't you?"

"I *am* helping her," Gertrude replied, darting her daughter an obdurate look. "Let me enjoy my supper."

It was useless to badger Gertrude. Once her mother's mind was made up, the devil himself couldn't change it. It was only after she got back inside the house that Judith wondered what Gertrude had meant about helping Vivian.

"The second patient has been carted off," Renie announced when Judith entered the kitchen. "The guests are having such a good time yakking about the calamities that the social hour is being extended."

"Great," Judith muttered. "They'll go home and tell everybody they know that I'm a magnet for death and near-death experiences."

"You are, actually," Renie replied. "But they don't seem scared or upset. Californians are very resilient. So are Alaskans, in a different way. Those twins from Virginia are engineers. They're taking the situation as a puzzle they could solve."

"Good," Judith retorted, picking up her glass of Scotch and noting that the ice had melted. "They can take over the case so I can back off."

"That won't work," Renie said, searching through Judith's freezer compartment. "Mavis called. She wants breaking news for her eleven o'clock broadcast. What are we eating? Steak? Chicken? Oh—you've got those big prawns. Yummy! Want me to do tempura?"

"Whoa!" Judith cried. "What does Mavis mean? I don't know anything."

"Neither does she," Renie replied, unwrapping the prawns. "That's the problem. According to her, the detectives are slow but not necessarily sure. They don't know you're FATSO, by the way. I mean," Renie said hastily, "*FASTO*. No sign of the missing body, nothing new to report. The five o'clock anchor had to bury the story with some mumbo-jumbo about the police continuing their investigation and following up leads. Mavis says that's guff. They don't have any leads."

Judith sighed. "Neither do I. In fact, I think Mother knows more about what's going on than I do."

Holding an onion in one hand, a yellow bell pepper in the other, Renie stared at her cousin. "You're serious."

"I am. She told me she was helping Vivian—maybe an allusion to the stripper." Judith opened the cupboard to take out a box of tempura mix and a jar of cooking oil. "Why would Herself protect Flora Bunda?"

"I can tell you that," said a voice from the dining room. Caitlin walked into the kitchen. "That's the name my half-sister, Terri, went by in her days as an exotic dancer."

"Terri?" Judith frowned. "Oh!" Her memory kicked into high gear. "Johnny Agra's daughter! She was a . . . whatever?"

Caitlin nodded. "She's much older. I lost track of her long ago. As a kid, I was impressed when Mom talked about Terri's show business career—until I found out it involved taking off her clothes."

"So," Judith said in a thoughtful tone, "Terri must be—how old?"

Caitlin considered the question. "Mid to late forties?"

"A little long in the tooth and droopy in the whatevers," Renie murmured. She held up her cocktail glass. "Want a refill on that wine?"

"Yes," Caitlin said. "I never finished the original." She turned back to Judith. "I told Mom about Frankie and Marva Lou."

"And?" Judith inquired.

Caitlin shrugged. "Mom's kind of foggy this time of day. Billy seemed more upset. He mentioned checking with the hospital later on to see if they're okay." She paused to accept a fresh glass of wine from Renie. "I asked what they'd had to eat or drink while they were at Mom's. The only thing, according to

Billy, was a drink or two. Marva Lou had some bourbon, and Frankie had a couple of beers straight from the can." Caitlin regarded Judith with an incredulous expression. "Do you really think someone poisoned them?"

"I don't know," Judith admitted. "We'll have to wait to hear what the doctors say. Maybe I should go upstairs to their room and see if I can find anything of interest."

"Let me," Renie volunteered. "You've climbed enough steps for one day." She set her glass on the counter and headed for the back stairs.

Judith scanned the tempura mix directions and got some ice from the fridge to make sure the water for the batter was chilled. "Your mother didn't mention Terri, I take it."

Caitlin shook her head. "She hasn't mentioned Terri in years. They were never close. Terri was Daddy's girl. Oddly enough, even though Terri and I had different fathers, we kind of look alike."

Judith smiled. "Interesting. When my mother saw you today, she said she knew you—and then changed her mind. That's because Terri was hiding out in the toolshed yesterday."

Caitlin's green eyes widened. "You're kidding! Why?"

"I'm not sure," Judith replied, adding more ice to her cocktail and topping it with a half inch of Scotch. "My mother's explanation to Renie was convoluted. It had to do with Flora— I mean, Terri—getting trapped in your mom's basement. It doesn't make much sense."

Caitlin sighed. "Not making sense is a way of life with Mom."

Judith nodded. "That reminds me, did a man named Stokes call on your mother in the last hour or so?"

"Stokes?" Caitlin looked puzzled. "Not that I know of. Mom was lying down in her bedroom when I talked to her."

"*Her* bedroom?" Judith said.

"I got the impression she and Billy have separate bedrooms," Caitlin replied. "That was why I couldn't stay there. Mom keeps such odd hours, and when she does sleep, she has to go through a big rigmarole with an eye mask and earplugs and a chin strap and I don't know what all before she actually settles down. Adelita must sleep in the basement. I assume there's a bedroom down there."

Judith recalled that the previous owner had two bedrooms on the main floor and another in the basement that the violinist had converted into a piano studio for his girlfriend, who gave lessons. But there had been no sign of a bed or any other furnishings when Judith and Arlene had been in the basement. "Maybe," she hedged, and changed the subject. "Can you get in touch with Terri?"

Caitlin shook her head. "I haven't had any contact with her for . . . oh, I don't know how long. Fifteen years, maybe."

Renie returned from Frankie and Marva Lou's room. "Item one," she began, raising her index finger. "The letter that arrived via FedEx from Loren Ellsworth in Tushka, Oklahoma, who is on the faculty of Southeastern Agricultural College near Tulsa. Item two," she went on, raising her middle finger, "another letter dated a week ago from somebody named Jim Dickson who works at the Double UB Ranch and was mailed to Frankie and Marva Lou's home in Broken Bow. Item three, a box of chocolates with only two left. Number five, a handwritten note that said 'Could Potsy help?' and last but most ghastly, the ugliest purple polyester pantsuit I've ever seen in my life, size 46 petite. I assume it belongs to Marva Lou."

Judith frowned. "Where are the letters?"

"You think I handled them?" Renie eyed her cousin with reproach. "I know better than that. As for the chocolates, the box was open, and you're thinking poison. Don't worry, I didn't sample the few that were left. I wasn't wearing my glasses, so I couldn't read the ingredients to see if they might contain nuts or peanuts and send me into a severe allergy attack. Heck, I wouldn't even touch that pantsuit. I might contract a disease that would rob me of my fashion sense."

"I don't know how you ever see out of your glasses," Judith said, "the lenses are always filthy. As for your current attire," she went on, studying her cousin's baggy summer slacks and rumpled T-shirt bearing the logo from a Native American casino, "it looks like you already misplaced any notion of fashionable clothes."

Renie made a face. "You know I don't wear my good—and very chic—clothes for every day."

"The note about Potsy," Judith murmured. "How could he help, being dead? Unless Frankie and his wife figured he wasn't in his right mind when he made the new will."

"That's possible," Renie allowed. "I would've thought they'd already taken that route, though."

"True," Judith conceded. "I wonder if we should tell the cops about the chocolates. Any idea where they came from?"

Renie shook her head. "They're a fairly high-end national brand. They could've been bought anywhere."

"Or sent from anywhere," Judith murmured. "The FedEx guy dropped off a package along with the letter. I forgot to look at the return address on the box. The letter was on top. I wonder if the FedEx labels are still in the room."

"I didn't see them," Renie replied. "Phyliss must have thrown them out. I'll check the recycling bin." She paused, looking at the unopened box of tempura mix. "You haven't made much progress with dinner. I'm wasting away."

"You were going to fix dinner," Judith reminded her cousin.

"So I was. I'll be right back." Renie exited through the back door.

Judith turned to Caitlin. "You'll join us, of course."

"I can't," she said apologetically. "I'm meeting an old high school friend for dinner downtown at eight. In fact, I should change and get ready now. Do you really think it's okay to use Dad's MG?"

"Call him," Judith said, handing over the Atlanta hotel's number. "He's probably still up. It's ten-thirty back there."

"Thanks," Caitlin said. "I'll do that right now." She took her wineglass with her and headed for the front stairs.

Renie came back into the house looking annoyed. "No FedEx packaging. I checked all the bins, in case Phyliss was having a heavenly vision and dumped the wastebasket trash into the wrong receptacle."

"That's strange," Judith murmured. "It suggests that somebody got rid of it. We don't have a tracking number, but maybe FedEx can tell us who sent the box. Assuming, of course, that it contained the chocolates. We don't know if the Busses were poisoned, and even if they were, we don't know if the chocolates were the cause."

Before Renie could respond, the phone rang. "You didn't return my call," Mavis Lean-Brodie rebuked Judith. "The clock's ticking. It's almost seven-thirty. Give me your latest bulletin ASAP."

"I really don't—"

Mavis broke into Judith's response. "You had two people named Buss hauled off from your B&B to Bayview Hospital. You think we don't keep track of nine-one-one calls at KINE? If that isn't news, what is?"

"So call the police," Judith said. "The Busses were sick. That's all I know. They weren't stabbed, shot, bludgeoned, or pushed off a cliff. It could be flu. I'm not a doctor."

"Flu!" Mavis guffawed. "That's good, Judith. Flu!" She repeated the word with scorn. "Since when did anybody con-

nected to you and a murder investigation merely get anything
as mundane as the flu?"

"I've no idea why they got sick," Judith insisted. "If you find
anything out from the cops or the hospital, *you* call *me*." She
hung up.

"That's telling her," Renie said mildly. "How many prawns
can you eat? I'm good for at least five."

"There are only eight in the package, Petunia Pig."

Renie stared at the prawns. "Hmm. You're right. I was never
good at math. Guess I'll have to share."

Judith ignored her cousin. She wondered if it would be
better to wait to contact the police until she heard from the
hospital. Maybe it *was* the flu that had struck down Frankie
and Marva Lou. Viral illnesses kept getting stronger and more
varied. Most people would never consider poison as the cause
of illness. But experience with unnatural death had made Judith
inordinately—and often justifiably—suspicious.

"I wonder why the cops haven't been around here today," she
said. "I also wonder if they've made any progress."

"They should've already checked with you," Renie said,
mixing the batter with the ice water. "They must not know
your reputation."

"That's just as well if they don't." Judith began slicing the
bell pepper, but was interrupted by Arlene's voice coming from
the back porch.

"Yoo-hoo," Arlene called, moving briskly down the hall. "I
just got home from helping Cathy stage a house for sale over on
the bluff. Carl told me that you had emergency personnel here
a while ago. I can't believe he didn't come over to find out why.
I've never let a broken leg stop me from doing what needs to
be done."

Judith gaped at Arlene. "Carl broke his leg? How?"

"He was up on a ladder on the other side of the house after

lunch this afternoon and fell when he stepped back to see how the old paint looked in the sunlight," Arlene explained. "Apparently, he forgot he was ten feet off the ground. I took him to the ER at Norway General, and it's only a slight fracture. The least he could've done was to pick up the phone and call you to find out what was going on here."

Renie looked up from the prawns she was dipping into the batter. "How *did* the paint look?"

"Carl insists it looks fine," Arlene retorted. "How would he know? He probably got a concussion, too. Men!" She shook her head in disgust. "Now tell me about your ambulances. If they'd come sooner they might have saved me a trip to the ER."

Judith related the sudden illnesses and ensuing emergency runs to the hospital. "I've no idea why they both got sick," she concluded.

"Oh, Judith," Arlene said after a slight pause, "surely someone around here is trying to kill them."

"It isn't me," Judith said wryly. "If they did eat something that made them sick, I'll be Suspect Number One."

Arlene stood by the refrigerator, looking thoughtful. "Was there a fracas here this afternoon? Carl told me he heard some odd noises before the emergency people arrived."

Judith nodded. "Herself's sons got into it with Frankie. Those sons, by the way, were the waiters at Vivian's party."

"Why were they mad at Frankie?" Arlene asked.

"Self-serving and stupid," Judith said. "That's my guess. They probably see Frankie and Marva Lou as a threat to whatever money they can worm out of Vivian. Or Billy. The Oklahoma Busses came here to get at least a portion of the late Mr. Buss's estate. I figure Frankie presumed that Billy must feel some guilt for marrying his father's money. Judging from Marva Lou's attitude, they've failed."

Arlene seemed taken aback. "Did the sons poison the disinherited Busses? Why not poison Vivian? She holds the purse strings."

"She *is* their mother, though her maternal instincts are dubious. We don't know if Frankie and Marva Lou were poisoned." Judith sighed wearily. "It always comes back to Vivian as the most likely victim."

Renie smirked. "You wish," she murmured.

"No." Judith's expression hardened. "I'd never wish that on anybody, including her. I'm simply trying to see the logic in this case."

Renie nodded. "Ah, yes." She glanced at Arlene. "My cousin's famous logic. It usually works, but this time the cards are being dealt from a short deck. The people involved are all jokers."

"True enough," Judith agreed. "By the way," she went on, turning to Arlene, "Joe's daughter, Caitlin, is staying with us."

"Oh, that's good," Arlene said. "I guess."

"Caitlin's the one rose among Vivian's other thorns," Judith explained. "Speaking of which, those rose petals came off of the stripper, who happens to be Vivian's elder daughter."

Arlene threw her hands up in the air. "Holy Mother of God! How . . . fitting." She paused, then snapped her fingers. "I almost forgot. Speaking of daughters, Cathy told me Vivian has filed for some kind of building permits. I ran into Mrs. Swanson this afternoon while I was on the bluff with Cathy. She said she wishes she hadn't sold the house. I told her it wasn't her fault that Vivian is a selfish, greedy woman. It's sad. The only good that can come out of all this is that Vivian and Billy will have to move out while the construction is under way. Oh," she added, starting for the back door, "how I'd love to wring Vivian's neck!"

Renie looked up from the deep fryer, where she was tending to the vegetables. "Don't say that too loud, Arlene. You may still be a suspect."

"I don't kill people I don't know," Arlene retorted. "There are too many I *do* know that I'd like to strangle." On that ominous note, she left.

Judith turned to Renie. "Speaking of strangling, we still don't know what was used to kill our mysterious corpse."

"I thought you said there was rope around his neck."

"The cops hadn't yet determined if the rope was the actual method," Judith replied. "I'd like to know if it was Billy's lasso."

Renie stared at Judith. "What lasso?"

"The one that Billy is good at using." Judith frowned. "What if he used it for something other than showing off his roping skills?"

"I suppose," Renie said thoughtfully, "that would depend on what he was wrangling."

"Wrangling?" Judith repeated. "Or strangling?"

Renie shot her cousin an ironic glance. "Maybe both."

15

After the cousins had finished their meal of tempura and udon, Judith called FedEx to find out who had sent a parcel to Marva Lou and Frankie. "I signed for two deliveries today for guests at Hillside Manor," she explained to a real person after answering a raft of recorded queries. "The recipients got the packages, but both fell ill and were hospitalized. I need the package sender's name in case an urgent reply is necessary."

"I'm sorry," the female voice said, "but I can give that information only to the recipient. If inquiries are made, I'm sure you can explain that your guests are ill and temporarily unable to respond."

Faced with a stone wall, Judith blurted the first thing that came into her head. "What if it was a bomb?"

"A bomb?" The voice sounded composed. "Our labels require the sender to state information about hazardous materials. I assume you looked at that section when you signed for the package."

"I never thought about it," Judith replied.

"Did you hear an explosion?" the voice inquired. "Were these guests hospitalized because they'd been injured by explosives?"

"I hardly think that anyone sending a bomb would note that on a packing label," Judith huffed. "I don't see why it matters if you tell me . . . oh, forget it!" She slammed the phone down on the kitchen counter.

"What now?" Renie asked as she came in from the toolshed with Gertrude's tray.

"FedEx won't tell me who sent the package," Judith said, still vexed. "Where could the box have gone if not into the trash?"

"Don't ask me," Renie said. "Your mother's on the warpath again. This time somebody stole the candy that Auntie Vance and Uncle Vince brought her last week. She blames Phyliss."

"That's the least of my problems," Judith grumbled. "She has tons of goodies stashed away. I'm calling the hospital to see what's going on with the Busses."

The phone rang before she could look up Bayview's number. "Now what?" she muttered, grabbing the receiver and saying hello. No one responded. "It must've been a wrong number." She disconnected. The phone rang again.

"Oh!" Renie exclaimed. "It's my cell." She reached into her purse and hurriedly took out her own phone, dumping several items on the floor in the process, including two rolls of breath mints, her checkbook, a plastic compact, and what looked like a small piece of bone. "Oh, hi, Mom. I was just going to call you." Renie shot Judith a resigned look and wandered into the hallway. "No, I didn't say I'd call as soon as I got to Judith's. I told you I'd call later. . . . Yes, I'm fine. No, I didn't pack extra sweaters. . . . Mom, it's sweltering outside. . . . Hey, I don't even *own* a sun hat. . . . Look, it's not Judith's fault that some guy got whacked down the street. . . . Gun? No, I didn't bring one with me. . . ." Renie continued walking and talking until she was outside and beyond Judith's hearing range.

Before calling Bayview, Judith went into the living room to clear away the dregs of the social hour. The guests had vacated the B&B, going their separate ways. Back in the kitchen, she dialed the hospital, but the staff was uncooperative. After five transfers, Judith couldn't find out the Busses' current status, or even if they were still alive. Frustrated, she wondered if she should ask Billy if he knew anything about his brother and sister-in-law's condition. She was still mulling when Renie, shoulders slumped and slow of step, came back into the house.

"Under fifteen minutes," she murmured, tossing the cell into her purse. "It could've been worse."

"It can be," Judith said. "I'm going to see Billy. Want to join me?"

Renie recoiled. "Oh, my God! I promised Mom I wouldn't put myself in harm's way. But for you, I'll risk it." She bent down to pick up the items that had fallen out of her purse.

"What's that thing that looks like a bone?" Judith asked.

"One of Clarence's chew toys," Renie replied. "I'll take it to him when I put the little guy to bed. He needs to chew it more. The vet says it helps with his overbite. Maybe we should've gotten him braces when he was a baby, but it seemed so expensive at the time."

"He's a rabbit!" Judith virtually shouted. "His teeth are supposed to stick out!"

Renie shook her head. "Not *that* far. We think he's self-conscious. It's bad for Clarence's self-esteem. Bill knows a colleague who specializes in animal psychology. We're considering therapy."

"For you and Bill?"

"Neener-neener." Renie made a face. "Of course not. For Clarence."

"Let's go before I decide to kill you." Judith led the way out through the back.

"Care to tell me why we're visiting Billy?" Renie asked as they walked down the driveway.

"To find out if he's heard anything about his relatives," Judith replied. "The hospital staff wouldn't tell me how they're doing."

"You can't phone Billy?"

Judith shot Renie a derisive glance. "You've obviously never had to listen to Herself's voice mail. She sings Cole Porter's 'Make It Another Old-Fashioned, Please.' Three verses."

"From *Panama Hattie,*" Renie said. "That takes me way back, though I was a little young to see Broadway shows in those days."

"Maybe Herself wasn't," Judith remarked. "She's gotten to the point where she claims to be about the same age as her eldest child, Terri." She paused at Vivian's property line next to the Ericson house. "What would you do with a dead body if you stole it from the morgue?"

"That depends on why I stole it in the first place," Renie replied. "If our mothers needed a fourth for their bridge club, a corpse wouldn't be much different than having Agnes O'Toole or Tina Gianelli as a partner."

."Get serious."

Renie thought for a moment. "Dump the body in the bay?"

"When?"

"Before it started to smell bad? Or right after it bid four no-trump with a really weak hand?"

Judith ignored the remark. "Why take it in the first place? It had to be because somebody—such as the killer—didn't want it identified. Since the corpse was first IDed as someone who isn't dead, we don't know if fingerprints were taken."

"Didn't they know about the guy in Henderson before they put Mr. No Name into cold storage?"

"I think so," Judith said, "but it was late in the day. For once, I wish the cops would interview me. Then I might be able to squeeze something out of them." She used a paper towel to wipe perspiration from her forehead. "I don't think clearly in this kind of weather."

"Neither do I," Renie said. "What's your theory?"

"I don't have one," Judith admitted. "I'm trying to figure out what the body snatcher would do. The dead man was taken from the morgue sometime between eight and ten, remember? It's summer, it stays light until after nine. People are outside much later. Teenagers aren't in school, so they party at public beaches or more private spots to avoid the cops. Everything's so built up, especially waterfront property." She gestured at the Buss house. "Single dwellings on virtually every city lot, condos being built all over the place, restaurants and shops springing up in all the neighborhoods. Would you drive the body thirty miles out of town to ditch it some place where you'd be assured of absolute privacy?"

Renie nodded. "All too true. Burying it takes time. A Dumpster's convenient, but only temporary. Where would *you* ditch a body?"

"That," Judith said, "is what I'm trying to figure out. I only drove the last body I had in my car for three miles."

"You didn't know it was in your trunk, though," Renie responded, trying to keep a straight face.

"Don't remind me," Judith shot back. "Honestly, I don't know why all these weird things happen to me!"

"And here comes one of the weirdest," Renie murmured as Vivian came out onto her front porch, cocktail shaker in hand.

"Judith!" she cried. "Beanie! Come in, have a drink!"

"Okay," Judith called out, walking up to the porch steps.

"It's awfully warm for this time of day," Vivian said, fanning herself with the hand that wasn't holding the cocktail shaker. "I decided a tall, cool one would taste rather good."

"Actually," Judith said, "I'd just as soon have some ice water. What about you, Coz?" She turned around, but Renie had disappeared. "Did you see where my cousin went?" Judith asked Vivian.

"No," Herself replied, removing her huge sunglasses. "It's so bright this time of day. These lenses blur things a bit."

So does a hundred-and-fifty-proof whatever, Judith thought. "Maybe Renie was called away by . . . Oscar." She almost gagged on the ape's name.

"Oscar is welcome to join us," Vivian said. "Does he like to party?"

"Ah . . . yes, but he's . . . stuffed. From dinner," Judith added as Vivian ushered her into the house. *Ohmigod, I'm falling into the Joneses' fantasy trap. What next? Teaching Clarence to ride a bicycle?*

The living room was dark and faintly dank, though this time Billy wasn't lounging on the sofa. Instead, an older, roly-poly man Judith didn't recognize had dozed off in front of the blaring TV, where a game show was in progress.

"I'll turn that down," Vivian said, going over to the set. "Ray's a bit deaf. Ooops!" Apparently, she poked the wrong button. The increased volume made Judith wince. "Sorry." After several seconds, Vivian managed to shut off the sound. "Here," she said, indicating a red-and-green-striped armchair piled high with newspapers and magazines. "Move those things and sit. I'll fix our drinks." In a swish of her orange, gold, and chartreuse caftan, Herself exited the living room.

"Just water," Judith called after her hostess. With a sigh, she began to remove the stack of periodicals, putting them on the floor next to the chair. The man named Ray snored a couple of times, but otherwise didn't budge.

Judith could hear a clink of glasses and a clatter of something else, but almost five minutes passed before Vivian emerged with two martini glasses, each accompanied by a large olive.

"You mustn't tease me about not wanting a real drinkie-poo," Vivian said. "Who ever drinks just water?"

"I do," Judith said quietly.

"Tsk-tsk." Vivian giggled and sat down on the arm of the sofa. "How nice of you to drop by. Would you like to see the plans I'm drawing up for the condos?"

"Not just now," Judith said. "I came to ask Billy how his brother and sister-in-law are doing at the hospital."

Vivian waved a careless hand. "How like them to get sick while on vacation! They don't know how to have fun. Spoilsports, I call them."

Judith persevered. "Are Frankie and Marva Lou okay?"

Vivian sipped her martini and shook her head. "Goodness, no." She glanced at the sleeping man. "Did you ever meet Ray?"

"I don't think so," Judith replied. "Who is he?"

Herself burst into peals of high-pitched laughter. "Number Two Husband. Ray Campbell. He was at the party the other night." Suddenly she frowned. "I think he was. Or was it Number Four?"

"Joe was Number Four," Judith said grimly. "Yes, he stopped by."

"Oh, of course!" She leaned over and tugged at Ray's ear. "Wake up, darling. Meet the secondhand Mrs. Flynn."

Ray groaned softly and kept on sleeping.

"What about Husband Number One?" Judith asked, trying to remain civil. "Johnny Agra, right?"

"Johnny." Herself gazed up at the ceiling. "Yes, Johnny. He was such fun. I'm afraid he died ages ago."

Judith evinced surprise. "He must have been quite young. What happened to him?"

Vivian gulped down a good quarter-inch of her martini. "Heart attack, I think. He drank." She took another big swallow of gin.

"You and he had a son," Judith remarked, feigning ignorance. "Or was it a daughter?"

"Terri," Herself said, eyes still fixed on the ceiling. "Terri Lynn."

"A girl?"

Vivian nodded. "Terri with an *i*, not a *y*."

"I don't think I ever met her," Judith said.

"She moved away years ago. California, I think."

"That's odd," Judith murmured. "I heard she was at your party." Catching the slip of the tongue as soon as it came out of her mouth, Judith hastily clarified her remark lest Vivian think Gertrude had betrayed her trust. "I mean, someone mentioned that your eldest child was there. I assumed it was Terry with a *y*."

Vivian's eyes flickered in Judith's direction. "Who said that?"

Judith pretended to consider the question. "Joe, maybe? It's strange, really. In all the time you've lived in this neighborhood, I don't ever recall meeting any of your children except Caitlin."

Vivian waved a hand. "Oh, these young people! Always on the go! No time for parents unless they——" She broke off, disgusted. "I'm sure you know all about that. Kids!"

Ray suddenly jerked a couple of times and opened his eyes. "Kids? Wha' kids? Wha' time's it?" he mumbled.

Vivian held up her glass. "Cocktail time. Isn't it always?"

Ray sat up, scratching at various parts of his chubby body. He wore Bermuda shorts and a khaki tank top over a hairy chest. A pair of flip-flops lay by the sofa. Squeezing his eyes shut, he slowly opened them and stared at Judith. "Hiya," he said without much interest.

Vivian giggled. "Ray, this is Joe Flynn's latest wife, Judith. You remember Joe, don't you?"

Ray scratched his head with its fringe of graying curly dark hair. "Was he at the party?"

"Yes." Herself smiled benignly at Ray. "Joe used to be a cop."

"Oh." Ray stretched and yawned. "He the one I punched out?"

"No." Vivian's face hardened. "Let's forget about all that. I prefer remembering the good times." She leaned closer, a hand on Ray's hairy arm. "Why don't you go shower and see if Doug can take you home?"

Ray grunted. "Want to get rid of me, huh?" He hauled himself off of the sofa and tried to put his feet into the flip-flops, but couldn't quite manage. "To hell with it," he muttered, kicking at one of the rubber slip-ons before wobbling out of the room.

"I think," Vivian said to Judith, "you met Ray's son, Doug, earlier. And Barry. His dad was Lou Henckel, Husband Number Three. He didn't come to the party." She tapped her chin. "I wonder if Lou's dead. I forgot to ask Barry. How's your drink? Shall I top it for you?"

"No," Judith replied, trying not to sound as aggravated as she felt, "you can drink it for me. I had some Scotch earlier. I never mix grains."

"Very wise." Herself nodded several times. "Shall I bring you a bottle of Johnny Walker?"

Judith stood up. "No, I really should be——"

Ray poked his head around the kitchen door. "H-e-e-e-r-e's Johnny! Wh-e-e-e-r-e's Johnny?" he shouted hoarsely before coming back into the living room, "Hey, I remember your husband now. He looks like the guy from the old Johnny Carson show, Ed McMahon."

Judith stared at Ray. "Joe? No, he doesn't."

Ray's little eyes squinted at Judith. "He doesn't? Then who did?"

"Forget it, Ray," Vivian said sharply. "Take your shower, okay?"

Judith had gotten as far as the front door. "Vivian, please let me know what you hear about Frankie and Marva Lou. If Billy talks to someone at the hospital, I'd really like to find out how they're doing."

"Will do." Vivian put her big sunglasses back on. "Toodles," she called, lifting her glass once more.

Judith found Renie in the B&B's living room, flipping through a volume of Tiffany lamp reproductions. "If we ever get our plumbing fixed," she said, "we're going to put some of these pendant lights in the kitchen."

"Where the hell did you go?" Judith demanded, ignoring her cousin's statement.

"I refuse to be called Beanie. I fled in horror. Why can't that imbecile remember my name?"

"She's lucky she remembers her own," Judith retorted, sitting down opposite Renie. "Especially her current last name. I never saw Billy, and Herself had no news of the in-laws. Husband Number Two, Ray Campbell, had taken Billy's place on the sofa."

Renie closed the Tiffany volume. "Anywhere else?"

"Like in bed?" Judith's tone was derisive. "Who knows? Vivian seemed anxious to get rid of him, though." She put both hands to her head in a gesture of frustration. "I don't recall ever dealing with such a bunch of . . . what should I call them? Superficial?"

"Hollow," Renie said. "Nothing inside. Just a shell. No soul."

Judith nodded. "After spending ten minutes with that bunch, I get off track and derail all over the place." She sat up straight. "It's not just because Herself is Herself. Let's put aside any personal feelings, and focus on the murder. Which, I must add, wasn't even alluded to during my brief and gruesome visit. It's as if it never happened. Is that because Vivian is in a permanent alcoholic haze or . . . what?"

"That's part of it," Renie agreed. "It's ego, too, and lack of a moral compass. Vivian—or 'Vi,' as she now prefers—is interested only in Vi and whatever pleasure she can get out of life. She's always on the run, from place to place, from husband to husband. I often marvel at how long she and Joe stayed together. In fact, I've always assumed it was because Joe was committed to the marriage and provided a decent income. Not to mention that he had no idea how miserable you were without him."

"It wasn't always horrible with Dan," Judith pointed out. "It just was never . . . right."

"No," Renie said. "Neither of your first marriages was 'right' because you both entered them under false pretenses. You and Joe didn't realize what was going on with each other. So you stayed put, two honorable people who made one hell of a sacrifice to keep your vows."

"Most people do that," Judith pointed out, "in one way or another."

Renie shook her head. "Not as much as you and Joe did. You both went beyond the call, but I'd never criticize you for it. Your forbearance was noble—if tragic."

"Okay," Judith said, and sighed. "But rehashing our marital woes doesn't help figure out who killed the guy hanging in the tree." She paused. "You trust my instincts?"

"Usually." Renie looked curious. "Try me."

Judith sat back on the sofa, her dark eyes roaming around the long, comfortable living room. A slight breeze coming through the open French doors stirred the lace curtains and jacquard drapes. The fresh air seemed to shift Judith's brain into high gear.

"I'm guessing," she admitted. "I believe in Uncle Al's hunches, but even he hedged his imaginary bet about Johnny being dead. Call me crazy, but I'm more and more convinced that the murdered man is—was—Johnny Agra."

16

Renie looked skeptical. "Didn't Vivian tell you he was dead? What did they do, dig him up and put him in her backyard? Wouldn't it have been easier to make a scarecrow?"

"I'm serious," Judith responded. "We only have Herself's word for it, and she's not very reliable. Uncle Al had heard Johnny was dead or had moved to L.A. I suggest we run his name through the computer and see if anything comes up."

"Okay." Renie got up from the sofa. "Shall I do the dirty work?"

"Well . . . yes." Judith followed her cousin out to the kitchen. "While you're looking, I can get tomorrow's breakfast organized. By the way, where's Caitlin?"

"She came back from dinner with her old chums and said she was making an early night of it," Renie replied. "Jet lag and all that."

"Of course. It's going on ten. It must be seven A.M. Swiss time."

"Which is always accurate," Renie murmured, sitting on the stool in front of the computer. "What makes you think Johnny's alive—or was, until a couple of days ago?"

"Vivian's vague reaction about Johnny, for one thing," Judith replied, slicing a ham she'd gotten out of the fridge. "She wouldn't look me in the eye. Then Ray Campbell made an odd remark, imitating Ed McMahon introducing Johnny Carson. Apparently, someone at the party reminded him of McMahon on the old *Tonight* show."

Renie cast Judith a doubtful look. "Isn't that a bit thin?"

Judith put the ham slices in a plastic wrap. "You have to trust my instincts, Coz."

"Okay." But Renie sounded unconvinced. "Here we go . . ." She made several attempts before finding a reference to Johnny Agra. "This information is ancient, going back to the fifties. It's about his restaurant and bar businesses with nothing later than forty years ago."

"That's about the time Johnny closed the Rumpus Room downtown," Judith said.

"But not where Joe met Vivian, right?"

"No," Judith said, breaking eggs into a big bowl. "Herself and Johnny split ten years earlier. While they were married, he owned Risky Business Bar & Grill. Its clientele called it The Risqué." She paused. "Vivian got it as part of the divorce settlement. Ray and Vivian were married soon after she and Johnny broke up. Ray ran the place while Herself warbled and wobbled in the bar. When Joe met her she was a fixture at the Silver Slipper, next door to the porn theater that closed twenty-odd years ago."

Renie looked befuddled. "I don't know how you remember all this restaurant stuff. You weren't old enough to drink in the fifties."

"I know the history because Dan was in the business, too," Judith explained. "Now that I remember who Ray is, I recall that he wasn't very successful. Joe thought Ray took on the business for Vivian's sake so she could have a place in the spotlight and sing for a bunch of drunks."

"I need a family tree," Renie muttered, taking a lined tablet out of the drawer under the counter. "List husbands and kids. I know about Johnny Agra and Terri the Stripper. Which son belongs to Ray?"

"Doug," Judith replied. "Barry is Lou Henckel's boy. I don't recall much about Lou, but the marriage was brief. Vivian was vague about Lou. I guess she hadn't asked Barry if he was dead or alive."

"Doesn't know, doesn't care," Renie murmured, scribbling notes. "Joe's next, followed by two Busses. Does Vivian know a guy named Yellow Cab?"

Judith was getting exasperated. "Coz, can you at least *pretend* to take this seriously?"

Renie shook her head. "You know I can't take serious things seriously. If I did, I'd be so sick at heart that I couldn't function. I especially can't handle violent deaths without being flippant. Not," she added, gazing meaningfully at her cousin, "when you keep encountering corpses. Anybody else would've fled your company years ago."

Judith pulled out a chair from the kitchen table and sat down. "I'm sorry. I understand, because the only way I can deal with these tragedies is by trying to make sense of them. I put the pieces together the way I make a jigsaw puzzle. It's not only truth and justice I seek, but it's turning the world's chaos into some kind of order. If I focus on finding a solution, I can try to detach myself from the horror."

"I know." Renie looked unusually solemn. "The world's a chaotic place. Human beings are such a combination of good and evil."

Judith nodded. "Sometimes it's hard to tell which is which. A senseless killing, like serial murderers or somebody who goes off the rails and shoots up a shopping mall, is almost impossible for ordinary—dare I say normal?—people like us to understand because the reason is hidden under a camouflage of seemingly acceptable behavior. I don't try to figure out how or why those things happen. The fatal flaw is beyond me. But all the murders I've come across have had a motive, and there aren't that many reasons for seemingly rational people to kill someone else. I think this one has to do with greed."

"I agree," Renie said. "Despite the sex angle, which Herself's image always conjures up, money must be the root of this particular evil."

"So," Judith said, leaning forward enough to see the monitor screen, "no obit for Johnny Agra?"

"Nothing local," Renie replied.

"Try L.A.," Judith suggested.

"Hoo boy. This could take a while."

Half an hour later, Judith realized her cousin wasn't exaggerating. "No luck," Renie said, coming into the living room where Judith was reading a book. "L.A. is so spread out and made up of so many entities that even searching the whole county, I flunked. Either Johnny didn't die there, or I don't know how to find the right search method."

"No mention of him at all?" Judith asked.

"Nary a one," Renie replied, flopping down on the opposite sofa. "That's odd, because if he stayed in the restaurant business, you'd think I'd get some kind of hit, even in a city as huge as L.A."

"That *is* strange," Judith said. "Restaurants were his métier."

"Maybe he never went to California," Renie said.

Hearing some of the guests return, Judith glanced at her watch. "It's one A.M. in Atlanta, too late to call Joe. He knew some of the other partygoers, including a couple of retired cops. I'm trying to remember their names. They hung out at those same bars. I never really knew them." She pressed her fist against her lips and concentrated.

Renie sat quietly, waiting for Judith's memory to spring into action. "Hey," she finally said, "call Woody. He'd know those guys.".

"You're right," Judith said. "It's kind of late, though."

"Ten's not so late," Renie pointed out. "Oh, no!" she shrieked, jumping up and racing to the French doors. "I didn't put Clarence to bed! He always gets tucked in at eight-thirty! What's wrong with me?"

"I've wondered that for years," Judith murmured, going over to get the phone from the cherrywood table. When she dialed the number of Joe's longtime partner, Woody Price, his wife, Sondra, answered.

"Judith!" she cried. "I've been meaning to call you ever since we found out about the body at Joe's ex-wife's house."

"Unfortunately," Judith replied, "that's why I called. I could use some help from Woody."

"So could the police," Sondra said, lowering her voice. "Woody was asked to handle that case, but he turned it down. Conflict of interest, he told his captain. I understand the two tecs assigned to the investigation aren't making much headway."

"You mean Woody had a conflict because of Vivian?"

"Yes." Sondra paused. "He knew her too well from the old days, and felt he'd be prejudiced from the get-go. Do you think she did it?"

Judith was startled. "I don't know," she managed to respond. "Vivian's . . . difficult, but I've never considered her dangerous or violent."

Sondra laughed. "Dangerous to herself more than to others. That's my guess. Oh, I know, a policeman's wife isn't supposed to talk about cases—any cases, whether their spouse is involved or not. But this one really hit home. I didn't realize Vivian was back in town."

"She is," Judith said grimly, "and arrived with a vengeance. She's rich now, courtesy of her previous husband, and now she's married to—— Hey, we've got to get together. It's been too long. As soon as Labor Day is over, things will slow down at the B&B. We'll set a dinner date."

"That'd be great," Sondra said. "Do you want to talk to Woody?"

"If he's available," Judith said.

"He's half asleep in his recliner." Sondra's tone was wry. "It's getting to the point that I have to wake him up so he can go to bed. Getting older is kind of a pain."

"Don't I know it," Judith agreed. "Joe and I are several years ahead of you and Woody on that road." An image of Joe's former partner appeared in her mind's eye, not the young, stolid, good-looking black man with a full head of hair and walrus mustache, but the Woody of middle age, receding dark hair dusted with gray, dark skin lined around the eyes and mouth, still fit, though carrying maybe an extra ten pounds—but as stolid as ever. She was smiling to herself when Woody's deep, soft voice reached her ear.

"You have questions," he said to Judith, "but I don't have answers. I realize you have a special interest because of Vivian, not to mention your—— Well, let's be candid, you have a genuine knack for solving murder cases. Did Sondra tell you I'm giving this case a wide berth?"

"She did," Judith said, "and I understand." After explaining that Joe was out of town, she asked Woody to take a stroll down memory lane. "Joe said two of the guests were retired cops. He worked closely with one of them before your time. They both later transferred out of Homicide. Any ideas?"

"Retired," Woody repeated. "Transferred." He grew silent, obviously thinking. "At the party, so they knew Vivian from years ago," he said. "Was one of them kind of tall with gray hair?"

"Yes," Judith replied, beginning to remember some of the details Joe had related. "White hair, actually, and he talked with his hands."

"I haven't seen him in a long time," Woody said. "That could be Carney Mitchell. He lives over here on the Eastside. I ran into him once about four years ago at the local Gutbusters flagship store."

"That's one of the names," Judith said. "The other man is bowlegged and used to have red hair, but he's balding and going gray."

"Andy Truitt," Woody said. "No, *Pruitt*. I never really knew him. Both of them hit the bars after work."

"Joe didn't know him very well, either. Maybe I shouldn't ask, but was either of them . . . bent?"

"Bent?" Woody sounded shocked. "Not that I know of. Did Joe suggest they weren't straight arrows?"

"No," Judith assured Woody. "It's that body-snatching thing. Wouldn't you have to be with the city or county to pull that off?"

"Well . . ." Woody paused. "It's embarrassing."

"But it happened," Judith said as Renie came back inside through the French doors. "Can you explain how?"

Woody remained silent for so long that Judith wondered if he'd gone back to sleep. She shot Renie a puzzled look.

"Say hi for me," Renie whispered. "Tell him Clarence was hopping mad, but he's settled down for the night, despite my neglect."

Judith made a disparaging face. "Woody?" she finally said.

"I'm here." He sounded apologetic. "The media may have screwed up. It's not a case of body-snatching, though. . . . Look, Judith, I'm not sure what it is. Honestly, I'm trying to stay away from this thing. I've worked for the city a long time, and I know when we have to close ranks. All I can tell you is that somebody claimed the corpse after the initial autopsy, and it was released. It shouldn't have been, but it was."

"Released to whom?"

"I don't know." He sighed, or maybe, Judith thought, it was more of a groan. "Do you want me to do some checking?"

"Not if it causes you big problems," Judith said. "Maybe the media will get it straightened out. Let's wait and see, okay?"

"That sounds . . . like the thing to do. Hey, I feel bad about not being more help. You have to understand that when I started working with Joe, he was still married to Vivian. He didn't gripe that much, but I knew he was miserable. I'm afraid I developed a very negative attitude toward her. Once they separated, Joe was a changed man. It was like a miracle." He paused again. "*You* were the miracle."

Judith couldn't be upset about Woody's reluctance. Instead, she started to cry. "Thank you, Woody," she finally managed to say in a tearful voice. "I feel better already."

"Now what?" Renie demanded after Judith hung up. "You're upset because you didn't tell Woody about Clarence?"

"Shut up!" Judith snapped, the tender moment broken by Renie's remark. "It's something Woody said. He's kind and good-hearted, unlike some people I know, *and will you stop rearranging Oscar's picture?*"

"The light doesn't strike it properly after dark," Renie replied. "You can't see his ever-engaging smile very well."

"Oh, shut up!" Judith dabbed at her eyes with a tissue. "Sit down, I'll tell you what Woody said about the so-called body-snatching."

"That's more like it." Renie smiled sardonically and resumed her place on the sofa. "Let's hear it."

After Judith finished telling her cousin about the former

cops at the party and the foul-up at the morgue, Renie looked puzzled. "Odd," she said. "A release form had to be signed by the claimant and the person who released the body." She glanced at the grandfather clock. "It's twenty to eleven. We should watch Mavis on the news."

"All right. Let's get ready for bed first and watch the TV in the family quarters." Judith got up from the sofa.

"Dibs on the bathtub," Renie said.

Five minutes later, Judith had finished her nightly rounds on the main floor. All seemed quiet in the guest area, though she hadn't heard the newlyweds or the university students return yet. When she reached the third floor, she saw that the master bathroom door was closed and heard Renie running the water.

"We don't own stock in the public utilities company," Judith shouted through the closed door. "And you can't swim, remember?"

"I'm floating," Renie yelled back before turning off the tap. "Damn the summer surcharge! We just get it paid off, and then they stick us with the winter surcharge. And don't get me started on the light bill!"

It was almost eleven before both cousins were ready for the night. The window fans whirred softly, cooling off the otherwise hot and stuffy former attic. Judith climbed into bed and turned on the TV. Renie propped herself up with a couple of pillows and lounged against the headboard. Following a car dealership commercial, Mavis and her coanchor, a young and earnest Hispanic man whose first name Judith recalled was Hector, appeared behind their news desk, smiling as if there couldn't possibly be any bad news to report.

"Permanent state of denial," Renie declared. "Those phony smiles are intended to assure you that the world isn't full of mayhem and misery. I'd like it better if they did some weeping and wailing."

Judith scowled. "*Please.* I can't hear with you babbling away."

The Wednesday-night gloom and doom began with a five-car pileup on one of the floating bridges, which had killed two people and sent five more to local hospitals. A forest fire on the eastern side of the mountains was threatening not just trees and wildlife, but a small town near the Canadian border. A child predator had escaped from jail, and viewers were asked to call authorities if they'd seen him.

"I don't want to see him," Renie murmured as the man's picture was shown. "He's uglier than a pig's hind end."

Before going to a commercial break, Mavis also urged citizens to call KINE's hotline with any tips or breaking news stories. "They fired all their reporters?" Renie asked in disgust. "Why haven't they been paying you for solving so many murder cases? The cops should chip in, too."

"I don't do it for the money, as you damned well know," Judith snapped. "Nothing so far on our current death. No news to report?"

"No big news." Renie yawned as the parade of advertisers marched across the screen. "How many August sales? Blowouts, blockbusters, clearance sales, inventory with prices so low they'll pay you to lug a bunch of crap out of their stores. Cars, mattresses, bedding, loan sharks, friendly bankers who might—but don't—recognize you even if you've been a customer for almost forty years. The last time I went to our bank and they asked for ID, I wouldn't show it to the teller until he showed me *his* ID first. Good grief, he wasn't even born by the time I wrote my umpteenth rubber check!"

"Now I remember why I don't like watching TV with you," Judith said. "Will you shut up? Mavis is back."

"Yippee." Renie sank lower onto the pillows, muttering to herself during a series of minor events, including a temporarily lost helicopter, a new arthritis drug under development at a local biotech company, a real estate scam in which the sellers were offering nonexistent lots to out-of-state buyers on a public golf course, and a rash of phony fifty-dollar bills being passed around on the Eastside.

"I'm bored," Renie finally announced out loud. "This is why I never watch TV news."

"I don't care," Judith asserted. "Go to bed. In the other room."

Before Renie could react, Hector, looking faintly sheepish, caught both of the cousins' attention: "The body of a man who was found in a Heraldsgate Hill backyard early Tuesday morning wasn't illegally removed from the city morgue but claimed by next of kin. We apologize for the misinformation, but there had been an error in the paperwork. Meanwhile, the police continue their investigation."

Mavis, who had been staring tight-lipped into the camera while her colleague spoke, forced a small smile. "We'll be right back after messages from our sponsors. Stay tuned for the latest sports news and weather forecast."

"That's . . . odd," Judith said. "*What* investigation? Did you hear the word 'homicide' anywhere in that segment?"

"No," Renie replied, getting off the bed. "Apparently the police had an August clearance sale on murders, and they don't have any cases left to solve. Or could it have been an accident?"

Judith considered the question. "It *could* be, given the drunken nature of the people involved. Some kind of freak accident, maybe inspiring one of those idiots who surround Vivian to play a prank and put the guy in the tree. But wouldn't the police state that it was an accidental death?"

"Maybe they will," Renie replied, standing by the bedroom door. "It's not official yet, so the media can't say so. Still, you know what some people say—there's no such thing as an accident."

"I don't believe that," Judith countered. "I'd like to, though, at least this time."

But she couldn't. If there was one thing Judith knew for certain, it was that any dead body she'd come across had been no accident.

17

That night, Judith had strange dreams. They weren't exactly nightmares, but disjointed incidents, a few of which she remembered upon awakening. A waterfall had plunged from a tall building at the end of the cul-de-sac, threatening to flood Hillside Manor. Gertrude displayed her engagement ring, but instead of a diamond, a large chocolate bonbon rested in the setting. Clarence the bunny showed up wearing a cowboy outfit, singing "Happy Trails" while twirling a lariat. Maybe, Judith thought as she showered, the peculiar dreams had been caused by the deep-fried tempura.

Judith knew Renie wouldn't wake before ten. There were only eight guests to feed instead of the usual full summer occupancy of up to twelve. Judith figured Caitlin would prefer eating in the kitchen.

Just before eight, Judith carried her mother's tray out to the toolshed. Gertrude was up, dressed, and looking vexed. "You shake down your goofy cleaning woman," she told her daughter. "I know she took my candy. She has her eye on it whenever she comes to tidy up."

Judith glanced at the glass dish on the card table. "You seem to have plenty of sweets there now."

Gertrude waved an impatient hand. "Not *that* candy. The new box I hadn't opened. Granny Goodness, a whole pound of it." She licked her lips. "The best chocolates anywhere. And anywhere is where they've gone, because they're not here. See for yourself. My idiot niece couldn't find 'em. You think you can do better?"

"If Renie couldn't, I probably couldn't, either." Seeing her mother's face pucker before uttering a stinging retort, Judith put up a hand. "I'll look later. Now I have to serve my guests."

"Don't serve those morons any of my candy," Gertrude rasped as Judith went out the door.

The four Californians had arrived in the dining room even earlier than usual. They were going on a sightseeing tour in one of several amphibious World War II vessels, called Ducks, that offered land and water views of the city. While consuming hearty portions of ham, sausage patties, scrambled eggs, coddled eggs, toast, muffins, and fresh fruit, the quartet chattered in happy anticipation of their adventure. Just before nine, as they went upstairs to finish getting ready for the tour, the front doorbell rang. A white man and a black woman stood on the front porch. Although they wore street clothes, they had "police" oozing from their pores. They also looked as if they hadn't yet hit thirty.

"We'd like to talk to you," the female detective said in a flat, expressionless voice. "May we come in?"

"Yes," Judith said, though she was irked by their arrival so early in the day and so late in the investigation. "We'll go into the parlor. I have to keep track of my guests. Not all of them have had breakfast."

"No problem," the male partner said. "Breakfast, huh?"

"Can I get you something?" Judith asked, opening the parlor door.

"Well . . ." He glanced at the woman, who stared straight ahead. "Such as what?"

Judith reeled off the morning menu.

"Sounds good," the man responded. "I'm Jay Almquist, by the way. Homicide. This is K. C. Griffin, my partner."

Judith smiled, and asked the woman, "How about you?"

Griffin, who was short but sturdy, shook her head. "I'm good. I eat breakfast. Every day." She glanced up at her partner, who was almost a foot taller and thin as a sapling. "Some don't. Some eat twice."

Almquist's face registered eager anticipation.

Judith pointed toward the dining room. "Go ahead, get a plate and fill up. None of the guests are at breakfast right now."

Almquist didn't need coaxing. Judith led Griffin into the parlor and pointed to one of the matching chairs. "Have a seat. I'll sit in this other chair. Your partner will probably be better off on the window seat, since he'll be eating."

Griffin scowled. "He often is, as long as the food's free."

"He doesn't look as if he's able to mooch very often," Judith pointed out. "He's quite skinny."

Griffin sighed. "I know. One of the lucky ones."

"Yes," Judith said. "I have a cousin like that. Renie—Serena, I should say—has metabolism that burns up calories."

Griffin regarded Judith solemnly. "I'm not criticizing Jay. Detective Almquist, I ought to call him. Partners have to stick together."

It seemed to Judith as if Griffin was reminding herself of that concept. "Yes."

Griffin removed a notebook from her shoulder bag. "Mrs. Buss came here to tell you and your husband about the dead man she'd found in her yard. Why?"

Judith sensed that Griffin knew the answer, so there was no point in being coy. "First, she was married to my husband for many years. Second, my husband, Joe Flynn, is a retired police detective."

Griffin didn't write anything down, which confirmed Judith's suspicions about the detective's knowledge. "I understand," the detective continued, "Mrs. Buss was very agitated."

"Very."

"Did she tell you she didn't recognize the victim?"

"Yes."

"Was anyone else able to ID him?"

"I assume so." Judith paused. "Someone claimed the body as next of kin. Who?"

"That's privileged information," Griffin replied, eyes averted.

"It shouldn't be," Judith asserted, and for one brief moment was tempted to trot out her reputation as FATSO. "I mean," she went on, overcoming the impulse, "the city has an obligation to clarify what happened at the morgue after the media erroneously stated that the body had been stolen. Did their original information come from city officials?"

Griffin looked faintly chagrined. "Mistakes happen," she replied through taut lips. "That doesn't mean that the police can violate policy."

"Okay, how about this? I know who the victim is, or was. Tell me if I'm right. His name is Johnny Agra."

To Judith's surprise, the detective shook her head. "No."

Astonished, Judith stared at the other woman. "I think you're wrong. Prove to me he's not Johnny Agra."

"I don't have to," Griffin retorted, taking umbrage. "That's not my job, and even if it were, I see no need to question the deceased's identity."

"Then why was he murdered?"

Before the detective could answer, her partner came through the parlor door, juggling two plates heaped with food.

"Somebody's here to see you," Almquist announced. "She says she's your cleaning lady."

"She is," Judith murmured, with a sharp glance at Griffin. "Excuse me." Getting up from the chair, she left the room.

Phyliss was in the kitchen, already scouring a couple of pans left over from the breakfast preparations. "Who's the hog?" she asked. "Gluttony is one of the seven deadly sins, you know."

"Yes, yes," Judith said testily. "He's a cop. His partner is in the parlor." Hearing voices in the entry hall, she went back into the dining room to make sure that Almquist had left enough food for the guests. The sausage was gone, the fruit was depleted, and all that was left of the toast were some crumbs.

The Virginians entered, greeting their innkeeper with smiles.

"I'm getting more fruit," Judith informed them, "as well as sausages and toast. It'll take only a few minutes."

"No rush," one of the twins assured her.

In the kitchen, she found Caitlin introducing herself to Phyliss.

"Have you been saved?" the cleaning woman asked.

Caitlin looked nonplussed. "From what?"

Phyliss narrowed her eyes. "From leading a life that will put you in hell. Have you?"

"Ah . . ." Caitlin shot Judith a helpless glance. "I'll have to get back to you on that."

"Phyliss," Judith said, her tone strident, "start upstairs. Start now. Only the honeymooners haven't come down yet. Go."

"Go? I just got here. What kind of devilish doings are going on here now?" She slapped a dishrag against the sink's edge and stomped off down the hall.

Caitlin seemed bewildered. "Did I do something I shouldn't have?"

"No, of course not," Judith replied, taking a package of

sausage patties out of the fridge. "Phyliss is a religious fanatic. Ignore her. She's a very hard worker. Oops!" She dropped the unopened package on the floor.

"Let me get that," Caitlin said. "What *is* going on? You're upset."

"I am," Judith replied, and briefly explained why.

Caitlin was sympathetic. "Let me take over your breakfast cooking. Don't forget, I inherited my father's knack in the kitchen. I had to, since my mother rarely prepared anything that didn't come with ice cubes."

Judith patted Caitlin's arm. "Thanks. I appreciate your help."

"I'm glad to do it," Caitlin said. "Staying here is much better than being at Mom's."

"Your room's vacant again tonight," Judith said. "So is Frankie and Marva Lou's. I wish I could find out if they're okay."

"I'll call the hospital," Caitlin volunteered. "I can claim kinship, however tenuous. Telling them I'm a niece, which I suppose I am, since they're mother's in-laws. Bayview, right?"

"Yes." Judith pointed to the bulletin board next to the swinging doors. "I put the number there. I'm rejoining the cops."

The honeymooning Kerrs had come downstairs. Judith greeted them in the entry hall and told them her stepdaughter was temporarily in charge, in case they needed anything.

"Thanks," Jake Kerr said. "By the way, I called the hospital this morning. Mr. and Mrs. Buss are in satisfactory condition, but they may not be released today."

Judith was embarrassed. "Thank you! I had no luck. I didn't even think about you being a doctor and able to get information out of the medical staff. I struck out."

Jake smiled. "I find that a medical degree opens some doors."

"Would you mind telling my stepdaughter?" Judith said.

"She was going to call Bayview to find out what was going on. Were you told what made them so sick?"

"Some kind of food poisoning," he answered. "Without all the tests completed, they can't be specific."

"I understand." Thanking him again, she went into the parlor. Griffin was pacing the room; Almquist was stuffing his face. "Okay," Judith said, fists on hips, "what else do you want to ask me?"

Griffin stopped pacing just short of the hearth. "I'd like to know why you're acting as if you're the one in charge here. *We* ask the questions. *You* answer them. Got it?"

Judith made a sweeping gesture with one hand. "Go ahead."

Griffin nodded once. "Describe your relationship with Mrs. Buss."

Judith repressed an urge to blurt, *"I can't stand the woman, she almost ruined my life."* Instead, she said, "We're cordial," and wondered what the detective was getting at.

"Great sausage," Almquist said.

Griffin ignored her partner, keeping her eyes on Judith. "What about Mr. Flynn?"

"What about him?"

Griffin remained standing; Almquist was still eating.

"Does he get along with his ex-wife?"

"Yes." That much was true, Judith thought. Rancor wasn't one of Joe's traits.

"Terrific muffins," Almquist put in. "Not soggy or dry, like some." He darted his partner an accusing glance.

Again, Griffin's attention stayed focused on Judith. "We know that there was some kind of dispute earlier in the evening between the Busses and the neighbors. Mrs. Buss made an announcement about a construction project that didn't go down well with the people who live in the cul-de-sac. How did you feel about her plans?"

"I was upset," Judith replied, leaning on the back of the chair she'd vacated earlier. "A condo seems out of place in this area."

"This reaction was shared by all of the neighbors?"

"Yes."

"Have any of you discussed ways to contest Mrs. Buss's proposal?"

"You mean—formally? No."

Griffin's face hardened. "Are you certain about that?"

"Of course." A light began to dawn in Judith's mind. "Are you suggesting some kind of ecoterrorism plot?"

"It happens these days," Griffin said grimly.

Judith knew the statement was true. The media had featured several stories about outraged citizens who were willing to resort to arson and other illegal means in an effort to halt construction projects. She felt that their actions were misguided, despite sympathizing with their desire to preserve the environment.

"So," Judith said, "you think that . . . what? This man was murdered in an effort to frighten Mrs. Buss?"

"I didn't say that," Griffin said stiffly. "Another scenario would be that the victim was deeply involved in the project, and doing away with him would hamper Mrs. Buss's progress with the condo construction."

"Got any more of those scrambled eggs?" Almquist asked, wiping his mouth with a napkin.

"No," Judith snapped.

Both of Almquist's plates were empty. "I'll see if there's more fruit," he said, getting up and ambling out of the parlor.

Judith turned a severe expression on Griffin. "Does your partner always eat during an investigation?"

"Sometimes." Griffin's face was impassive. "Where's Mr. Flynn? We'd like to talk to him."

"'We'?" Judith echoed. "Why? Does Almquist want his egg recipe?"

"Sarcasm is counterproductive," Griffin declared. "Mr. Flynn is on our witness list."

"Mr. Flynn is in Atlanta," Judith replied with some satisfaction. Joe would be able to deal with the situation far better than she seemed to be doing. "In fact," she went on, "I understand you spoke with him earlier, on Tuesday morning, after you came to look at the body."

"That was brief and informal," Griffin said. "When will he return?"

Not soon enough, Judith thought. "Tomorrow night, maybe. Or Saturday. He's working."

Griffin made a note for the first time since the interview had begun. "Who else resides here?"

"You mean other than guests?"

"Of course."

At that moment, Caitlin stepped into the parlor. "Everything's ready. I'm going to——" She stopped, looking tense. "I have errands to run. 'Bye." She hurried off through the entry hall.

"Who's that?" Griffin inquired.

"My stepdaughter, visiting from Switzerland," Judith replied, hearing the college students coming out of the dining room. "No, she wasn't here when the murder occurred."

"No one else?" Griffin inquired.

"My mother has a separate apartment in back of the house."

Griffin looked thoughtful. "She's quite elderly, I assume."

"Yes."

"That's it?"

"Yes." Sensing that the interview was about to end, Judith

held up a hand. "I realize you find me . . . overly inquisitive, but did Adelita Vasquez attend the Buss party?"

Griffin scowled. "Vasquez? Oh, the young woman who works for Mr. and Mrs. Buss. No. She had the night off to visit relatives and didn't return until shortly before midnight. Why do you ask?"

The honeymooners' laughter could be heard as they headed out the front door. "You checked her alibi?" Judith inquired.

"Yes." Griffin's face had become impassive. "If your husband is a retired policeman, you should know how cops interact with witnesses. We ask, you answer. That's it." She closed her notebook with a vengeance. "We'll contact Mr. Flynn when he—" A loud crash and a shattering of glass startled both women. A male voice screamed in pain. A female voice shrieked obscenities.

"What," Griffin asked, finally showing some animation, "is that?"

Judith put a hand to her head. "My cousin. And probably your partner." She walked as fast as she could, heading for the kitchen. Griffin was right behind her.

Renie was clutching a plate close to her bosom and glaring at Almquist, who was cowering in front of the stove. "Get this freeloader out of here," she yelled, "or I'm calling the cops!"

"He *is* the cops," Judith said, trying to avoid stepping on the broken plate and shattered juice glass on the kitchen floor.

Renie snarled as she stared at Almquist. "A cop? So what? Does that give him the right to steal my breakfast? I'm filing a complaint!"

"She attacked me!" Almquist shouted. "She took my juice!"

"Ha!" Renie thrust out her chin. "He took my eggs!"

"Could we have a truce?" Judith demanded in disgust.

"Truce?" Renie looked shocked. "When did I ever give in?"

"Never," Judith shot back. "But that doesn't mean you're

right." She turned to Griffin. "You said you were done here. It'd be wise to leave and take your hungry partner with you."

"You offered me food!" Almquist cried in an offended voice.

"I did," Judith agreed, still calm. "But not all of it. Let's forget this incident happened." She shot Griffin a sharp glance. "None of this is a credit to anyone involved. I cannot imagine this kind of behavior by the police when my husband was on the force."

Griffin apparently decided to cut her losses, which was just as well, since Renie was still snarling. "Yes," the female detective agreed. "Let's go, Jay. Brush the egg off your sleeve."

Judith followed the pair to the front door. Griffin, however, wasn't quite finished. "That woman's your cousin? Does she live here?"

"No," Judith said emphatically. "And she wasn't around the night before the murder. She knows nothing."

"She knows how to make a scene," Griffin murmured and stalked out of the house.

In the kitchen, Renie was sweeping up the crockery and glass. "The breakage rate is climbing," she remarked in an ordinary voice. As usual, her temper was quick to ignite and almost as quick to extinguish. "Are you sure those are real cops?"

"I assume so," Judith said. "Like most of the younger set, they're a different breed. Not that cops or any other profession weren't flawed in the past. People are people. The difference, maybe, is style, not substance. Can you check some records on the computer?"

Using a dustpan, Renie dumped the broken pieces into a small garbage can. "What now?"

"Divorce records for Herself."

"Gee," Renie said, "I'm not sure there'd be room on your hard drive to download all of them."

"I only want one—the first, from Johnny Agra."

Renie got out a clean plate, filled it with some of the leftover food, and sat down at the computer. "I'll try to find a site where you don't have to pay for looking at the records."

Judith nodded absently as she opened the phone directory. "Ah! I found Carney Mitchell with an Eastside address. I'm calling him."

Renie looked up from the monitor. "Carney Mitchell? Who's that?"

"A retired cop who showed up at Vivian's party," Judith replied, dialing the number. "Carney?" she said as a male voice answered on the third ring. "This is Judith Flynn, Joe Flynn's wife. How are you?"

"Ah—fine," Carney replied, sounding startled. "What's up?"

"Joe's out of town," Judith said, "but he'll be back this afternoon." She ignored Renie's puzzled look. "He saw you at Vivian's party and wanted me to ask if you could have a drink with us around five. For old times' sake."

"Today?" Carney paused. "Heck, I can't make it today. In fact, I'm heading off for vacation in a couple of hours. Tell Joe I'll try to get together with him when I get back, okay?"

"Sure," Judith said. "By the way, have you got a number for Andy Pruitt? My phone book doesn't have listings for people who live as far north as he does."

"I'm not sure," Carney answered. "Andy spends most of the year in Arizona or someplace. Until Vi's bash, I hadn't seen him in six years. Got to run. Got to pack. For vacation."

"Have fun," Judith said, and clicked off. "Liar."

Renie turned to look at Judith. "Corny's a liar?"

"*Carney*. Yes. He says he's leaving on vacation. I don't believe him. He's avoiding me. Or Joe."

"If Carney came here, how would you explain Joe's absence?"

Judith shrugged. "That's easy. His flight home got canceled. How are you doing there, Coz?"

"Not so good," Renie said. "I can't find a divorce decree in this city or county for Vivian and Johnny Agra. What was her maiden name?"

"I don't think I ever knew," Judith admitted. "I doubt if she remembers."

Caitlin came through the back door. "Why," she demanded, looking frazzled, "did I decide to drop in on my mother? Why didn't I just go past her house and do my errands?"

"Your mother's up?" Judith said, surprised. "It's only ten o'clock."

"For all I know, she never went to bed." Caitlin pointed to the phone directory on the counter. "May I use that?"

Judith nodded. "Go ahead."

"I wish I'd never come," Caitlin grumbled, flipping through the yellow pages. "Living abroad is the smartest thing I ever did. Whenever I see my mother, I get trapped in her—— Ah! Here it is, The Travel Inn at the bottom of the hill." She got her cell phone out of her purse and dialed.

"Progress?" Judith asked her cousin in a low voice.

"I finished breakfast," Renie murmured. "That's about it."

"How far back do those records go?" Judith inquired.

"Quite a ways," Renie said.

"Maybe Caitlin can help us. She might know——" Judith stopped as Caitlin asked to be connected to a Mandrake Stokes.

"Yes," Caitlin said into the phone. "I think he wasn't checking out until tomorrow. Would you please have him call me? The number is . . ."

"The dapper guy who couldn't tell one Mrs. Flynn from another?" Renie whispered.

"It must be."

Caitlin thanked whoever was at the other end and hung

up. "I'm not calling my husband," she declared. "Mom thinks lawyers must be able to solve every legal problem. She has no understanding that many lawyers, like Claude, specialize. And she wants free advice."

"On what?" Judith asked.

Caitlin poured herself a mug of coffee. "She's trying to unload Potsy's ranch. It's huge, one of the biggest in Oklahoma. This Mr. Stokes came to see her yesterday to make an offer on behalf of a college near the ranch. They want to lease it as part of their agricultural curriculum. At least that's what I figured out from her garbled account. Now she insists that I meet with this Stokes and try to understand what's going on. Frankly, that sort of thing is out of my league."

"I met Mandrake Stokes," Judith said. "He got mixed up and came here first by mistake."

Caitlin's green eyes widened. "Really? He sounds addled, too. Not that I blame Mom for wanting to unload the property, but she has no head for business, and of course Billy doesn't, either."

"Would this sale involve Frankie and Marva Lou?" Judith asked.

Caitlin shrugged. "I've no idea. Mom claims she got everything in the will. What she needs is a competent local attorney."

Judith gazed at her cousin. "Bub?"

"No." Renie shook her head. "I'm too fond of my brother-in-law to let him get involved with Vivian."

"Good point," Judith murmured. "Caitlin, what's your mother's maiden name?"

Caitlin smiled. "Smith. Really. Vivian Smith. Why?"

Judith decided to be candid. "I'm trying to figure out when she got her first divorce decree. Renie can't find it under Johnny

Agra's name. Is it possible she didn't get the divorce in this city or county?"

"Anything is possible with Mom," Caitlin said dourly. "She could've gone to Nevada in those days for a quickie divorce. She always had ties there, which, I think, is why she hustled Dad to——" She grimaced. "I'm sorry. I know that's a sore point with you. But you see what I mean."

Judith dismissed the reference. "What kind of ties?"

"Her older brother, George, was a chef at one of the casinos," Caitlin explained. "I forget which one. I gather that many of the old landmarks have been demolished to make way for lavish new hotel-casinos. Anyway, George has been dead for a few years. I must dash." She grabbed her shoulder bag and went out the back way.

"I'm dashing, too," Renie said. "I have to get an estimate on the toilet damage so I can submit a claim to the city or our insurance company. And I'll have to visit my mother to prove I'm still alive."

After Renie left, Judith tried to focus on her daily tasks. She found a new bottle of furniture polish for Phyliss, who claimed she was losing her sight, but could be cured by putting mud packs on her eyes like the blind man in the Bible. Two more reservation requests came in for October, one from Maryland and the other from Ontario. It was almost lunchtime when Mavis Lean-Brodie called.

"Listen up, Judith," Mavis said in the less-than-cheery voice she often used on TV. "You're going to owe me for this one."

"Which is?" Judith asked warily.

"I found out who claimed the body from the morgue. Interested?"

Judith tensed in anticipation. "Yes."

"It was the vic's daughter," Mavis said, sounding smug. "Aileen

Rosenthal of Culver City, California. The vic is Carlo Giovanni Di Marco." She spelled the names slowly and precisely.

Judith was puzzled. "How'd you manage that?"

"Can't tell you," Mavis replied. "I'm a journalist, remember? I don't reveal my sources. In fact, I can't reveal what I just told you, at least not in public. This whole thing at the morgue was a screwup. A couple of people could get canned if I used this on the air."

"What if someone else in the media gets hold of it? They may not . . ." Judith paused. "I have a problem using your name and 'scruples' in the same sentence, but some journalists are unprincipled."

"Not a chance, and never mind why," Mavis said. "As for 'scruples,' what about you? How many lies have you told in the course of your career as FATSO?"

Judith sighed. "Okay, we're even. I'll try to pay you back eventually, but frankly, I don't see how this helps solve the murder."

"Neither do I," Mavis retorted. "That's how you can show your gratitude. I get the goods, you nail the killer. Good luck."

Mavis rang off.

18

The names Mavis had given Judith rang no bells. She couldn't think of any connection, unless the dead man had stolen Charles Brooks's wallet. But what was the link between Di Marco and Brooks? Logic eluded her. Judith stared out through the kitchen window, but her brain felt as thick, if not as vigorous, as the Rankerses' hedge.

She grabbed the receiver, hit the caller ID button, and retrieved Mavis's number. "You left something out," Judith said after Mavis answered on the second ring. "Where is this Di Marco from?"

Mavis groaned. "God, but you're a pain. How should I know? He didn't have any proper ID, or else the body wouldn't have been misidentified in the first place. Try Jupiter. I'm up against deadline." She severed the connection.

A few minutes later the phone rang just as Judith started making Gertrude's lunch.

"Just letting you know what's going on in Dixie," Joe said. "I'm heading out for a dinner meeting with a retiree in Kennesaw who worked with the Wirehoser candidate. Dare I ask how it's going with you?"

"It's not." Judith sat down at the kitchen table and considered giving Joe a detailed report, but thought better of it. Many of the bits and pieces she'd collected in her head were guesswork. That was anathema to Joe, a veteran detective who'd relied primarily on solid evidence. "When will you be home?"

"I don't know yet," he replied. "Tomorrow night? More likely Saturday. These southerners really do live at a more leisurely pace. I guess it's the heat and humidity."

"I don't blame them," she said. "It doesn't seem as hot here as it did yesterday. I have a question—why would Carney Mitchell avoid me?"

"Carney? What're you talking about?"

Judith wished she hadn't asked. "Well . . . it was something Ray Campbell said."

"Ray Campbell? You mean *that* Ray Campbell?" Joe's tone had become irritated. "When the hell did you talk to Ray?"

"He was at Vivian's the other day when I dropped by," Judith admitted. "He was at the party, right?"

"I saw him, but that was it," Joe replied, still annoyed. "I didn't really know Ray. The only thing we had in common was . . . you know."

"Yes, I do." It was Judith's turn to get riled. "Never mind. Here's Mother. Have a nice trip to Kennesaw." She banged down the phone.

Gertrude was sailing up the back porch ramp in her motorized wheelchair, announcing her arrival with the ga-goo-ga horn she'd attached to the controls. "I'm on a hunt," she announced. "I'm going to shake down your cleaning woman. Where is that crazy old bat?"

"Upstairs," Judith replied. "Are you still looking for your candy?"

"You bet," Gertrude retorted as Sweetums padded softly behind the wheelchair. "Did you ask her about it?"

"I forgot," Judith confessed. "It's been hectic here this morning."

"So?" The old lady glared at her daughter. Sweetums had leaped into Gertrude's lap, a habit he'd recently acquired, and he seemed to enjoy going along for the ride. "Between your crazy guests and those dead bodies you keep finding, how do you expect to run this house on a system? Remember what your Grandma Grover said—you have to have a system, or you don't get anything done. She never found any dead bodies, I can tell you that."

"Maybe not," Judith responded, "but Grandpa Grover found a severed head under his streetcar when he was a conductor for the city. He found one on the train tracks, too, when he worked in the sawmill."

"That's to be expected," Gertrude said. "Trolleys, trains, trucks—people are clumsy when they're going somewhere. What's for lunch?"

"Ham and cheese with fresh cherries and potato chips."

"Dessert?"

"Ice cream," Judith said. "It's too hot to bake."

"Not in the cold storage box where I live. It can't be over fifty degrees."

At that moment, Phyliss appeared from the back stairs. "What's going on with those people who got hauled off to the hospital? Are they coming back, or did they go to meet Jesus?"

"I'm not sure," Judith answered, noticing that Phyliss had a white-and-brown box in her hand. "They're still in the hospital. Just make sure the room is tidy. What are you holding?"

"A couple of chocolates are in this box, and they're half melted in this ungodly heat," Phyliss replied. "Do I toss them or what?"

Gertrude squirmed around to look at the cleaning woman, who was standing behind the wheelchair. "Let's see those!" she barked.

Phyliss dropped the box in Gertrude's lap. "You can have 'em," she said, heading for the basement. "I've got laundry to put in the dryer."

"I told you so!" Gertrude shouted. "This is my candy! Granny Goodness, my favorite! How come that greedy pig didn't eat all of them?"

Judith stared at the box her mother had opened. "Because she didn't eat any of them. These belonged to the guests who got sick."

"Serves them right," Gertrude declared. "Melted, my foot! Soft, maybe, but stick these last two in the icebox and they'll be fine." She replaced the lid and shoved the chocolates at Judith.

"I'm not sure anybody should eat them," Judith murmured.

"What's that? I'm deaf, you know."

"They may be poisoned," Judith said, putting the candy box into a plastic garbage liner bag.

Gertrude was aghast. "You think Auntie Vance and Uncle Vince are trying to kill me?" She waved an impatient hand. "Vance has got a mouth on her and doesn't know when to keep it shut, but she's good-hearted. You're talking through your hat!"

"No, Mother," Judith said defiantly, "I am *not* accusing Auntie Vance of anything. If these are the chocolates that she and Uncle Vince gave you, someone stole the box from your apartment and added poison to the chocolates. I think that's why Mr. and Mrs. Buss got sick."

Gertrude's wrinkled face was bewildered. "Who'd be dumb enough to ruin Granny Goodness chocolates? That takes a lot of gall. Granny Goodness makes the best ever."

Judith ignored her mother's dismissal of attempted murder. She realized that Gertrude, like many elderly people, lived in a constantly shrinking world as age and infirmity robbed her of mobility and control over even life's minor events. "I'll buy you a box of Granny Goodness the next time I go by their store at the bottom of the hill," Judith said. "Don't even think of accusing Auntie Vance of anything."

"Poisoning people doesn't sound like Vance," Gertrude muttered. "She'd just bash somebody in the head if they got her riled up."

Judith put the chocolate box in a drawer under the counter. "You haven't found your ring," she said matter-of-factly. "Whoever stole the ring probably took the candy. Unless there's something you're not telling me, Vivian or Terri swiped both."

"I told you, Vi wouldn't steal from me," Gertrude replied, indignant.

"Then it was her daughter," Judith said.

"She seemed okay," Gertrude insisted. "Is she really a stripper?"

"She was at one time, according to Caitlin." Judith buttered bread for Gertrude's sandwich. "Did she use the bathroom?"

"I don't remember," Gertrude said.

"If she did," Judith pointed out, "she could've gone into your bedroom and taken both the ring and the candy."

"Sounds goofy to me. Why? She didn't know what was in there."

"True." Pausing while she added a bit of mustard to the ham and cheese, Judith tried to figure out why Terri had cased Gertrude's bedroom. "The only thing I can think of is that she was looking for something valuable to steal. Vivian may be rich, but that doesn't mean she's handing out hundred-dollar bills to her daughter. I understand that Terri was always a daddy's girl. Johnny Agra actually raised her."

"Johnny Agra?" Gertrude looked curious. "Wasn't he Al's chum?"

"Yes," Judith said. "They were both in the same business."

"Monkey business," Gertrude remarked. "Your father and I

never approved of what Al was doing in the back of the restaurant. It's a wonder he didn't end up in the bay wearing cement shoes."

"Uncle Al knew whose palms to grease," Judith pointed out. "Or so I figured when I got older."

"Oh, you bet he did," Gertrude agreed. "Especially whoever was sheriff at the time. Al would get dressed up like a cowboy and ride a horse in parades as part of the posse. At least one of those sheriffs went to jail." The old lady sighed. "Oh, well. Al's a decent sort, always fun. I never met Johnny. Just as well. He left town and went to Hollywood and married that movie actress. I can imagine how that turned——"

"What?" Judith dropped one of the cherries she'd been putting on her mother's plate. "Who told you that?"

Gertrude frowned. "Vi? I think she mentioned it way back when I told her I'd sold my life story to the movies. What a bunch of guff *that* was after those Hollywood nitwits got done with it! I should've sued."

"You were well paid," Judith reminded her mother, but didn't want to get sidetracked discussing how little of the film paralleled Gertrude's life. "So Johnny married an actress? Are you sure?"

"I only know what Vi told me."

"Do you remember her name?"

Gertrude shook her head. "I don't know if I ever heard it. If I did, she wasn't anybody famous, like Joan Crawford or Greta Garbo."

"So Vivian told you this about . . ." Judith calculated Herself's comings and goings in her head. "At least three or four years ago?"

"More than that," Gertrude said. "It was around the time she bought the Goodrich house. Christmas, maybe."

Vivian had flown in from her Florida condo that year, dropping her bombshell during the family Christmas gathering. The announcement of her imminent and apparently permanent return hadn't quite ruined the spirit of the season, but it had definitely dropped some big rocks in Judith's usually deep well of charity.

"Goodness," Judith murmured, "that was almost ten years ago. Had Johnny just moved to California?"

Gertrude shook her head. "No. I think he'd been there a long time. Funny," she went on, fingering her chin, "I can't remember some particular things very well, but I can bring back how people acted when they were talking. The way Vi said it sounded as if she'd lost track of him and didn't care. If you know what I mean."

Judith smiled and nodded. "I do. It would be typical." She put some potato chips on Gertrude's plate. "Do you want to eat in here?"

"Why not?" Gertrude grimaced. "It's a change of pace. Just keep that religious goofball away from me."

Judith moved one of the chairs away from the table so that Gertrude could maneuver closer. "Want to play detective?" she asked, sitting down across from her mother.

The old lady looked suspicious. "What do you mean?"

"This murder," Judith said. "You could help both Vivian and me."

"How?" Gertrude asked, still wary.

"Well . . ." Judith searched for the right words to goad her mother into action. "Find out that actress's name."

Gertrude swallowed a bite of sandwich before responding. "Why?"

"I thought you liked Vivian," Judith said, feigning puzzlement. "You met her daughter. That is, her other daughter, Terri, who's also Johnny Agra's daughter. Not Caitlin. You like Caitlin, don't you?"

Gertrude bristled. "She hasn't come to see me."

"She hasn't had time, but she really wants to see you." A small fib wasn't amiss, Judith thought. "Caitlin's busy helping Vivian. Terri did pay you a call. That was very sweet of her. Wouldn't you like to know what happened to her father after he married the actress? Was she a kind stepmother? You've heard those horror stories about Hollywood mothers and stepmothers." Sadly, Judith shook her head. "Gruesome."

"That's so." Gertrude gazed off into space. "Vi should've stepped in," she finally said. "Mothers and daughters have to stick together. Though one time she told me boys were easier to raise than girls. I wouldn't know. Not," she added with a baleful glance at Judith, "that you were any picnic. Maybe Vi's right. She treats her boys pretty good. They were a big help being waiters at the party. Caitlin didn't show up for it, and poor Terri got stuck in the basement."

"Yes. Poor Terri." Judith feigned sympathy. "That's why you should help her. I suspect her life hasn't been happy."

"So what should I do?" Gertrude inquired.

"Ask Vivian to come see you," Judith said. "Tell her you want to . . . show her something."

Gertrude spat out a cherry pit. "Like what? My almost-empty candy box?"

Judith was scraping her brain for a reason that would pique Herself's interest. "Give her a copy of the DVD version of your movie."

Gertrude snorted. "*My* movie? That wasn't me. When did I ever take off all my clothes and do the Black Bottom on a tugboat?"

"For once and for all, we know *Dirty Gerty* wasn't about your real life," Judith explained reasonably, "but it's the kind of . . ." She paused, avoiding the word *raunchy*. "It's the kind of mischievous movie Vivian would enjoy. You know, a spunky heroine who's willing to take risks, even if they seem a bit . . . outlandish." She handed her mother the phone. "Tell Vivian you have something for her. A titillating surprise."

"Titillating? Don't use that kind of language," Gertrude admonished. "What's wrong with 'bosom'?"

"That's not what . . . Skip it." She took the phone from Gertrude and dialed Herself's number. "Just say it's naughty but nice."

Scowling at Judith, Gertrude grasped the receiver. "Vi?" The old lady paused. "You're addled? Who isn't?" She paused again. "Well, that's different. Yes, let me talk to Vivian." Gertrude put a hand over the mouthpiece. "Somebody called Addledita. What kind of a name is *that*? Why don't parents name their kids Maude or Joan or Hazel anymore?"

Judith shrugged. It wasn't the right time to explain Hispanic name diminutives.

"Vi?" Gertrude said. "How about stopping by this afternoon? I've got a present for you, kind of bawdy, but you'll like it. Fact is, I should've given it to you a long time ago."

Judith watched her mother's reaction, the scowl giving way to something akin to pleasure. "Swell. See you in half an hour." Gertrude clicked off and shoved the phone at Judith. "There. I did your dirty work with *Dirty Gerty*. Come to think of it, Vi might get a kick out of it."

Judith had gone to the fridge to get a quart of Razzle-Dazzle Raspberry ice cream. "While you eat dessert, I'll get one of the DVDs the producer sent you. They're in the basement."

"They should've been buried in the backyard," Gertrude muttered. "Don't be stingy with that ice cream, Toots."

"I won't," Judith promised, dishing three big spoonfuls into a bowl. "Okay, here's what you do. You give her the DVD, start talking about movies, and ask her the name of the actress Johnny married. Got it?"

"I guess so," Gertrude muttered as Judith set the ice cream on the table. "Do they call them BVDs because everybody's running around in their underwear? Or even less than that?"

"It's *DVD*," Judith said, "which stands for Digital Video Disc. Or maybe it's Digital Versatile Disc. Something like that, anyway."

"Too much crazy stuff these days," Gertrude grumbled, and dug into her ice cream.

By one o'clock, Renie still hadn't come back. Judith figured her cousin was probably being held prisoner by Aunt Deb. Caitlin returned a few minutes later, looking exasperated.

"The meeting with Mandrake Stokes was a fiasco," she declared. "He had all sorts of questions about the ranch that I couldn't answer. I guess he's legit, but I can't help him or my mother, who, by the way, wasn't home when I stopped by." She put her shoulder bag down on the credenza in the entry hall. "Adelita thought Mom was here. Is she?"

"Maybe," Judith replied. "She was supposed to call on my mother. Strangely enough, they seem to like each other."

"I've always wondered about that," Caitlin said. "Do you think their bond is a way of annoying you?"

"Probably," Judith said. "I figure that's part of it. Why can't Billy answer Mr. Stokes's questions? The ranch belonged to his father."

"I gather Billy hasn't spent much time at the ranch in the past ten years," Caitlin said. "More, maybe. Once he got out of baseball, he didn't hang around the old homestead. From what I can gather, he moved to Cancún in Mexico and was a beach bum. That's how he met Adelita. She wanted to come to the United States. Apparently, she had some family issues. Too overbearing or something, and she wanted to get out from under their strict surveillance. It's like pulling teeth to get anything straight out of Mom. Anyway, I think Adelita's affair with

Billy began in Cancún, so when he heard his dad was ailing, the two of them went to Florida, where Mr. Buss was taking in the sea air. Adelita came as a tourist and got Billy to sponsor her for a longer stay. And that's how Billy met Mom."

Judith was puzzled. "I thought he met her through Potsy."

Caitlin shook her head. "It was the other way around. Potsy was confined to a wheelchair. Billy wheeled him down to the beach where Mom was suntanning."

"I see."

Caitlin's green eyes danced with the same gold flecks inherited from her father. "I'm sure you do. Whatever was going on between Mom and Billy up to that point was out the window when she realized that Potsy was the one holding the purse strings."

Judith nodded. "Did your half-sister, Terri, ever mention who her father married after he and your mother divorced?"

Caitlin made a face. "No. Mom hardly ever mentioned him. Neither did Terri. She wasn't around much when I was a kid. The last time I saw Terri was when I was in my teens, and she'd just broken up with a guy she'd been living with in San Francisco."

"I'd like to talk to her," Judith said. "Your mom has an address or phone number, right?"

"I suppose so," Caitlin replied, picking up her shoulder bag. "Do you mind if I make myself a sandwich?"

"Go ahead. There's plenty of fixings in the fridge."

Caitlin went out to the kitchen. Judith checked her guest registry to see who would be coming to Hillside Manor over the weekend. She was making mental notes when Adelita appeared at the open front door.

"Mrs. Flynn? May I come in?" the young woman asked.

"Sure," Judith said. "What can I do for you?"

"I'm looking for Mrs. Buss. Is she here?"

"If she is, she's in my mother's apartment out back. Go down the driveway or through the kitchen to the back door."

"Thank you." Adelita headed for the dining room and the kitchen, but reappeared as Judith brought in the mail from the front porch.

"I go the other way," she murmured, and left the house.

Judith went to the porch to see if Adelita was, in fact, heading for the toolshed. Sure enough, the young woman had reached the driveway and was walking briskly toward the backyard. Returning inside, Judith went out to the kitchen.

"Is there a reason Adelita is avoiding you?" she asked Caitlin, who was sitting at the table eating a salami and cheese sandwich.

Caitlin shrugged. "I saw her peek in here over those swinging half-doors. She turned around and disappeared."

"Why did she do that?"

"Because I know about her and Billy."

Judith sat down at the table. "You mean they're still having an affair?"

Caitlin nodded. "That's why Mom and Billy have separate bedrooms."

"Does your mother know?"

"Probably." Caitlin stared glumly at the glass of milk next to her plate. "Maybe it's one of those ménage à trois situations. Mom likes her little sexual adventures." She looked up, her gaze fixed on Judith. "Do you know how often I've wished you'd been my real mother? Or is that too awful to even think, let alone say out loud?"

Judith was touched, if not flattered. "I never thought about it. I mean, I never knew you felt that way." Her smile was bittersweet. "Frankly, I haven't been a very attentive stepmother. Life on this side of the world has kept me too busy."

"It's not your fault," Caitlin asserted. "By the time you and my father got married, I was already living abroad. You never knew me until I was an adult."

"That's true," Judith conceded, "but I could have written or called or even emailed more often. On the other hand, I didn't want to overstep——" She stopped as the sound of loud, angry voices erupted from the backyard. "What's that?" she said, getting up.

"Let me look," Caitlin offered. "It sounds like Mom."

She hurried to the back porch, with Judith close behind. Vivian, Adelita, and a middle-aged woman were engaged in a shouting match. All of them were gesturing wildly. Judith started to go down the steps, but Caitlin put out a hand to stop her.

"Let them sort it out," she urged grimly. "You wanted to know where you could find Terri. There she is, in your own backyard."

19

From snatches of furious insults, the battle seemed to be waged mainly between mother and daughter. Adelita had backed off a few paces and was keeping her mouth shut. Beyond the volatile little group, Judith could see Gertrude inching her way out of the toolshed.

The woman Caitlin had identified as Terri was shaking a fist at Vivian. "You don't want me! You never cared about me! Don't think you can buy me off!"

Herself took a menacing step closer to Terri. "I can buy and sell you a hundred times over! You've sold yourself often enough!"

"And you haven't?" Terri shot back. "I learned plenty from you! A drunken slut for a mother is a real lesson in life!"

Vivian lunged at her daughter, grabbing her by the shoulders. Terri kicked her mother in the stomach, sending Vivian reeling onto the small patio, where she fell against the barbecue. Terri dove headfirst onto the older woman, grappling for a handhold. Adelita backed off from the fray, arms crossed and smirking with apparent pleasure.

"That's enough!" Caitlin shouted, rushing to the patio. Terri was pummeling Vivian, who was screaming like a madwoman.

Grasping a handful of her half-sister's dark hair, Caitlin yanked hard. Terri let out a painful shriek as she struggled to get free.

Judith went down the steps to help separate the women. Before she reached the patio, Gertrude had put her wheelchair into high gear, rolled down the toolshed ramp with the ga-goo-ga horn blaring, crashed into the family feud, and almost toppled the statue of Saint Francis. Vivian fell to the patio's flagstones; Terri staggered on the grass, trying to stay upright.

"Stop that!" the old lady growled. "That's no way to act!"

Judith smiled tremulously at Gertrude. "You saved the day."

The old lady's expression was stormy. "As Grandma Grover used to say, 'If you don't listen, you got to feel.'" She glowered at Terri, who was leaning on the birdbath, and breathing hard. "You behave yourself, girlie. I won't stand for a rumpus." On that note, she reversed the wheelchair and sped back into the toolshed.

Caitlin had managed to get Vivian on her feet. "Adelita," Caitlin said sharply, "please see to Terri."

Adelita's smirk disappeared, but she didn't budge. "I do not work for her. She can see to herself."

"I'll take care of her," Judith volunteered, with a tentative hand on Terri's arm. "Come inside. I'm Judith Flynn, Mrs. Grover's daughter."

Terri's dark eyes flashed insolently. "So?"

Judith's hand fell to her side. "I'm just trying to help." She paused. "I'd like to hear an explanation about how you and your mother got into such a fight on my turf."

"That's none of your business," Terri muttered, looking sullen.

"It is, actually," Judith asserted, noting that Adelita was saun-tering down the driveway, humming a faintly recognizable Latino song for lovers. "Especially when it involves *my* mother."

Terri looked uncertain. "You kind of have a point."

"Then why——" Judith was startled by the honk of a horn and the squeal of brakes. Her gaze swerved back to the driveway, where Renie's Camry had come to a halt with a screeching Adelita on the hood.

"Get the hell off of my car!" Renie yelled, jumping out into the driveway. "Put a dent in Cammy, and you're toast!"

Judith put both hands to her head. "Oh, God!"

Adelita slid off of the car, shaken but seemingly unharmed. She erupted into a stream of Spanish invective. Renie got out of the car and, with a hand on one hip, sneered. "I speak Spanish," she said. "Want to hear me cuss you out in French and Italian, too? Furthermore, I don't have a sister, so shut the hell up! *Comprende, chica?*"

Adelita's response was an obscene gesture as she stalked off down the driveway. For good measure, Renie leaned back inside the Camry and honked the horn four times. Adelita jumped slightly, but kept going.

"That twit's so annoying, she ought to work for our insurance company," Renie snarled. "I just finished Round One with State Crime." She stared at Terri. "Who are you, and how will you piss me off?"

"This," Judith said quickly, "is Terri Agra, Vivian's daughter."

"Not Agra," Terri asserted. "I go by my married name, Ostrom."

"Sorry," Judith said. "I didn't know."

Terri shrugged. "It doesn't matter. We're divorced."

"Surprise," Renie muttered. "I'm going inside. It's too hot in the sun." She stomped off, slamming the screen door behind her.

"Who," Terri inquired in a hostile tone, "is *she?*"

"My cousin, Serena," Judith replied. "Follow me. It *is* hot out here."

"Serena?" Terri's round face looked perplexed. "Not a very good description of her personality."

"No," Judith agreed, "not always, anyway."

"Then," Terri said, "I don't want to go into your house if she's there. I'm not wanted anywhere." Tears filled her dark eyes. "Typical. Nobody ever wanted me, except my dad, and even he——never mind."

Judith was shaken. Terri, a product of divorce, neglected by her amoral mother, shunted from pillar to post by her father, with at least one broken marriage, and earning a living as a stripper. Now, in middle age, Terri's sense of being unwanted and unloved seemed palpable to Judith.

"Come inside. Renie—Serena—isn't mad at you," Judith assured Terri. "She's having a bad day. She'll be fine."

Terri looked uncertain. "Well . . . I'd like a drink, even water."

"Okay." Judith gently steered her unexpected guest to the porch steps. A sidelong glance at Terri revealed a softly defined profile, though possibly her nose had undergone cosmetic surgery. The shoulder-length dark hair was probably dyed, but Judith couldn't criticize, having taken that route herself after prematurely going gray. She noticed the hint of a double chin, a large bust that might have been augmented, an orchid tattoo on her bare upper arm, and fake pink fingernails. Two were broken; one was chipped. To Judith, Terri's appearance added up to a lack of self-worth, an attempt to become someone else. Although they had just met, she felt as if she already knew Terri. When they reached the back door, Judith suppressed the urge to offer her a hug.

Renie wasn't in sight, though her voice could be faintly heard on the phone in either the entry hall or the living room. "Have a seat," Judith said. "What would you like? I've got plenty of choices. This is, as you may know, a B&B."

"Oh?" Terri looked as if that was news to her. She sat down

at the table, raking her disheveled hair with unsteady fingers. "Beer?"

"Sure." Judith reeled off the brands. Terri chose a Coors Light. Judith poured herself a glass of lemonade. "I gather you don't live here in town," she said, sitting down across from her guest.

"I don't live anywhere," Terri replied bitterly. "I lost my job in L.A. and came up here because I heard my so-called mother had moved back from Florida. I thought she might want to help instead of hinder me. We've never been close." She hung her head and bit her lips. "You really don't want to hear about my screwed-up life, do you?"

"Yes," Judith said. "I'm a people person. I'm interested in hearing life stories." *And have I ever heard some strange ones,* she thought.

Terri looked as if she didn't quite believe Judith. "Most people don't want to listen to anybody else."

Judith shrugged. "I guess I'm not one of those."

Terri studied her hostess for a moment. "You have a kind face. I suppose people trust you."

Judith nodded. "They seem to."

The hint of a smile played at Terri's wide mouth. "I'm not used to somebody who wants to hear me talk about myself."

"Give it a go," Judith responded, returning Terri's smile.

She sighed heavily. "Okay, I'll start at the beginning. After I was born, my mother thought she'd be the next Peggy Lee. Her so-called career as a singer came first. No time for her baby girl." Terri paused, nervously trying to scrape some of the pink polish from one of her artificial nails. "When my parents split, Mom insisted I'd be better off with Dad for a while. That turned out to be a long while, more like forever. I didn't know how she'd react to me coming here. At first, she seemed okay, but . . ." Shaking her head, Terri sipped some beer.

"I take it you're not staying with your mother."

"Right. I got here last Sunday. She said I'd have to stay at a motel, but she'd pay for it." Terri fondled the beer can, rubbing it as if it was a magic lamp and a genie might pop out. "She did. I mean, she gave them her credit card, but after I arrived, she asked me to take part in this big party she was giving. She told me," Terri added, sneering, "I could earn my keep doing my old stripper act. I hadn't done that in ages. Except," she added, dropping her voice, "for an occasional private party."

"But you didn't get to perform," Judith remarked.

"No." Terri's expression was ironic. "After my mother's big announcement, I was to make my entrance through the garden, so I waited in the basement. Then the fight broke out with the neighbors. I heard the commotion, but it quieted down. I figured everything was okay and waited for my cue. Suddenly there was more yelling and carrying on. Billy finally came down to say the party was over. I wanted to get my clothes from upstairs, but he said to hold off. The brawl had moved inside. I told Billy that Doug—my half-brother—was giving me a ride to the motel. When he was ready to leave, he'd bring my clothes with him." She paused to drink more beer.

"I heard Doug never showed up," Judith said, trying to ignore Renie, who was shouting into the phone from the living room.

"Oh, he showed up in the basement," Terri said in digust, "but he hadn't brought my clothes. Doug insisted I stay put. Barry would give me a ride when he sobered up. I just wanted to get out of there, but all this noise was going on upstairs." She shuddered. "It was awful."

"Did Barry ever come to get you?" Judith asked.

Terri shook her head. "Nobody came."

"Why didn't you call a cab and leave?"

Terri looked incredulous. "In the rig I was wearing? No way! I kept waiting." She lowered her head. "There was a bottle of bourbon in the basement. Oh, there's booze all over the house. God help my mother if she didn't have her next drink close enough. There was a blanket lying on a carton of Scotch, but the floor was wet, maybe from the ice for the party. I found a spare bedroom off a little hall and went to sleep. The next thing I knew, there were cops all over the place. I kept the blanket around me and ran out of the basement. Somehow I ended up in your backyard. I figured that little building was for storage, but at least it was a place where I could get my head together."

"Instead, you found your mother there," Judith noted.

Terri sighed. "Oh, yes." Her olive skin darkened. "Yes." The last word was barely audible.

"And . . . ?"

Terri put a hand in the pocket of her cutoff jeans. "Is it okay to smoke? I know your mother does."

"Go ahead. I'll get an ashtray." Judith stood up and opened a drawer under the counter, taking out a souvenir from Scotland with a logo depicting a hooded monk stirring a vat of beer. "Go on."

"Mom got all nicey-nicey," Terri replied after exhaling a puff of smoke. "She told me to come with her to that little kitchen and get a glass of juice. That seemed odd—there was barely room for both of us in there. Mom had her own flask and refilled her glass of O.J. She told me my clothes were on her front porch and to get out of town fast. The cops had me high on their suspect list for killing the man in the backyard." Terri paused to sip some beer and take another drag on her cigarette.

"Why?" Judith asked, surprised.

"She thought he might be somebody I knew from Vegas," Terri answered. "The cops would connect the dots. I told her I hadn't been to Vegas in years. Anyway, I was stony-broke. She gave me a hundred-dollar bill and told me to take a bus out of town. Just like that." Terri shook her head in disbelief. "A hunsky wasn't going to take me very far. I didn't know what to do, so I . . . left."

Judith realized Terri was about to cry. "But not before . . . ?" She let the question dangle.

Renie apparently had either hung up the phone or taken her battle outside. For what seemed like a long time, the only sound Judith could hear was the ticking of the schoolhouse clock.

Finally, Terri briefly looked Judith in the eye. "My mother had gone back into the sitting room. I went into the bathroom to sort out my thoughts. I was still . . . fuzzy. When I came out, I looked into the bedroom. Everything is so small in that little place. Anyway . . ." She sighed heavily and wiped a tear from each eye. "I took that ring. I opened the bureau to see if there was any other jewelry. There wasn't, not that I could see. But there was a box of candy and I hadn't eaten since—oh, I'm not sure, I never got any dinner that night, let alone breakfast in the morning. I grabbed the candy, said good-bye, and left."

Judith refrained from rebuking Terri. "But you didn't leave town."

Avoiding Judith's gaze, Terri shook her head. "I took the ring to a couple of pawnshops. The most I could get was eighty dollars. That wasn't going to take me very far, either." She delved into her pocket again. "Here's the ring. I'm so very sorry."

Judith picked up her mother's ring. "Thank you," she said quietly. "Mother will be glad to get it back."

At last, Terri looked at Judith. "Are you going to turn me in?"

"Hardly." She put the ring into the pocket of her cotton slacks. "This is between us. Did you eat any candy?" she asked casually.

Terri's gaze again roamed around the kitchen before she uttered a peculiar little laugh. "No. I put it with my other stuff on the porch, grabbed some of my clothes, and went inside to change. When I came back to leave the house, the candy was gone. Who'd steal a box of chocolates? Besides me, I mean."

"This would've been when on Tuesday?"

Terri frowned. "I'm not sure. Sometime after noon, I guess. I took a bus to the bottom of the hill and stopped at a café to eat. Then I went back to the motel. At least that was paid for with my mother's credit card. I fell asleep and woke up when the kids in the unit next door pounded on my door to show me a picture they'd drawn of the mountains here. They'd never seen mountains. Nice family, nicer than my own. Two teen-age girls, two younger boys, and a mother and a father who love each other. I wonder what that's like?" Terri seemed to drift into reverie. Sensing her visitor's thoughts, Judith waited in silence.

"When I finally got my brain unfogged," Terri went on after at least a full minute, "I began to wonder why Mom thought I was a suspect. It didn't make sense. Yes, I'd worked in Vegas several years ago. No, there wasn't any guy I'd want to kill. Then I was watching TV and learned that the dead man had been misidentified." She stopped to puff and sip. "Finally I decided to confront my mother and ask what the hell she meant. That's when she pitched a fit in your mom's place."

"Did she say anything before she flew off the handle?" Judith asked. "I mean, anything that might enlighten you?"

"Enlighten?" Terri laughed hoarsely. "No. She got mad right from the start, and——"

A knock at the back door interrupted her. Judith excused herself and went down the hall. Doug Campbell stood on the porch. "Is Terri here?" he asked.

"Yes," Judith replied curtly. "Why?"

"Mom's looking for her," Doug said, starting to push past Judith.

"Hold it!" Judith leaned against the door frame, barring Doug's way. "Let me talk to Terri first. She's very upset."

Doug forced a hearty chuckle. "Upset! Man, Terri's always upset. Just tell her to get her butt out here pronto, okay?"

From the kitchen, Judith could hear sounds indicating that Terri was on the move. But she wasn't coming down the hall.

"I'll let her know," Judith said calmly. "Please wait on the porch."

Doug shook his head. "I don't think so. I'll go get her."

"No, you won't," Judith declared loudly. Despite Doug's stocky build and her own always tenuous balance, she realized that help was on the way. "You are not coming into the house!" she said in a loud voice.

Doug's chuckle became sinister. "Who's going to stop me?"

Judith didn't answer. Renie, who apparently had been talking on the phone outside and then gone into the garage to check on her bunny, moved silently down the walk, receiver in one hand, shovel in the other. She moved to the second step and slammed the shovel into Doug's broad back. He let out a horrific yelp and reeled in pain.

"Beat it, buster!" Renie shouted, holding the shovel like a baseball bat. "After dealing with my insurance company, I'm in a mood to kill somebody. It might as well be you. Excuse me," she added, stepping around his writhing form and whacking him with the screen door as she went inside. "Lock it up," she said to Judith. "I'll get the French doors and the front door." She put the phone at the bottom of the back stairs, but kept the shovel as she hurried off down the hall.

Just as Doug was cussing his head off as he tried to straighten up, Judith slammed the back door and locked it. She met Renie in the living room, where she'd finished latching the French doors.

"Where's Terri?" Judith asked.

"Don't know, don't care," Renie shot back, racing to the entry hall. Judith stood by the window seat, trying to calm down. "We're secure," her cousin declared, propping the shovel against the wall just inside the living room. "What was *that* all about?"

"I'll tell you later," Judith said. "I've got to find Terri."

The parlor door that led into the living room opened slowly. Terri peered out and saw Judith. "Is Doug gone?" she whispered.

Movement in the driveway caught Judith's eye. Looking through the bay window, she saw Doug limping away, a hand to his back. "Yes. Come sit down." Judith indicated the sofa.

Terri entered the living room, but gave a start when she saw Renie standing by the shovel. "You! I'm not doing anything, honest!"

"I know." Renie shrugged and went over to one of the side chairs. She rubbed at her bad shoulder and winced. "Damn! I've got to stop attacking people. I keep forgetting I'm semi-crippled."

"I'd hate to see you in full form," Terri murmured, sitting down across from Judith on one of the matching sofas.

"Yeah," Renie agreed. "It's not a pretty sight. You caught me on a bad day."

Judith had mixed feelings concerning Renie's latest outburst. "It might be wise if you kept your rage under control," she said.

"Hunh." Renie looked puzzled. "I thought I was saving your life."

"Well—maybe." Judith's expression was wry. "Between you and Mother, the carnage around this place is mounting. I'm glad that none of the guests are here this time of day." She turned to Terri. "What's your plan? I wouldn't think you'd want to go back to your mother's house."

Terri ran a hand through her dark hair. "I'm not sure. Maybe I should talk to Caitlin. We've never been very sisterly, but she seems like a nice girl. Has she gotten back from carting our mother home?"

"I haven't heard her," Judith replied. "But that's not a bad idea. Caitlin is very responsible. By the way," she went on, "I wanted to ask you a couple of questions. Is it true that your dad married a movie actress after he and your mom split up?"

Terri grimaced. "She *wanted* to be a movie actress. But she never got more than bit parts, hardly any with lines. I guess she gave it up after she and my dad separated. Her real name was Ellen Marx, but she changed it to Ella Di Marco for the movies. The last I heard, she married some rich guy. I think his name was Rosenthal or Rosenberg."

Judith stared at Terri. "Di Marco? Are you sure?"

"Yes," Terri insisted. "I lived with her and Dad in L.A. until I turned eighteen. Why do you ask?"

"Because," Judith said softly, "that's the real last name of the dead man in your mother's backyard."

"I don't get it," Terri said, eyes fixed on the coffee table between the sofas.

"It hasn't been mentioned publicly," Judith explained. "I learned about it from a . . . an old friend in the media. His full name was Carlo Giovanni Di Marco. Does that ring any bells?"

"No." Terri shook her head several times. "But it might explain why my mother thought I was a murder suspect. That is, she knew Ellen's movie name."

Judith started to say that it was unlikely that Vivian would know the man's real name because Mavis hadn't gone public yet. But, Judith thought suddenly, maybe Vivian *had* known all along. "So you've never heard of this man?"

Terri made a helpless gesture with her hands. "Never. I suppose there are other Di Marcos in this world, but I don't know any."

"Was Di Marco one of Ellen's family names?" Judith inquired. "Her mother's maiden name, maybe?"

"I don't know," Terri said. "She'd been married at least once before she met my dad. Marx may have been from a previous marriage." She paused, plucking a loose thread from her cutoffs. "Do you think I should try to contact my dad and ask him?"

Judith shrugged. "It might be a good——" Her jaw dropped. "Your *dad*? What do you mean, *your dad*?"

Terri looked even more befuddled. "My father, Johnny."

Renie let out a little yip. Judith was on the edge of the sofa. "Johnny Agra is alive?"

"Of course," Terri said. "He's alive and well and giving scuba-diving lessons in the Bahamas."

20

Judith's obvious astonishment evoked a curious expression from Terri. "What's wrong?" the younger woman asked. "You look . . . odd."

"I'm sorry," Judith apologized, "but your mother told me your father died some time ago."

Terri uttered a short laugh. "I suppose he might as well have, as far as she's concerned. Seriously, should I try to get hold of him? He's hard to reach, because he also handles boat charters."

"Yes," Judith said. "Maybe he can shed some light on the victim's identity. I assume you're out of touch with your stepmother, Ellen."

"Oh, yes," Terri said, grimacing. "I haven't heard from her in ten, fifteen years."

The doorbell rang. Renie offered to answer it, grabbing the shovel on the way to the front door. "It's Caitlin," she called from the entry hall.

"Oh!" Judith exclaimed in relief, and realized that she'd been worrying about her stepdaughter, though she wasn't exactly sure why.

Renie locked the door behind her and propped the shovel against the wall. "We're secure. I think."

Caitlin had tensed. "What's going on?" she asked.

Judith gestured for her to sit. "Your half-brother, Doug, made a nuisance of himself."

With a wary look at Terri, Caitlin joined Judith on the sofa. "I thought," she said, her gaze returning to her half-sister, "you left town."

"Is that what our mother told you?" Terri replied angrily. "She wants me to go. Are you taking her side?"

Caitlin sighed. "No. This is between you and Mom. Why do you think I live in Switzerland? I'd move to the North Pole if I thought it'd save me from getting embroiled in her antics."

Terri lowered her gaze. "You're smart. I never should have come. I . . . I just didn't have any other place to go."

Caitlin's face softened. "You're *that* desperate?"

Terri wouldn't look at her half-sister. "I guess so."

Judith started to speak, but stopped. Maybe, she thought, it'd be better if she and Renie left the younger women alone to sort things out.

It was Caitlin, however, who broke the brief silence. "Surely Mom will give you some money until you find a job. Doug and Barry have been putting the squeeze on her. Mom can afford to be generous, especially if she sells the ranch in Oklahoma."

"She hasn't been generous with me," Terri said bitterly.

Caitlin's short laugh was harsh. "I wouldn't take it if she offered."

"You don't have to," Terri retorted. "You have a job and a husband. He's a lawyer, isn't he?"

"We all have choices in life. Look," Caitlin went on, leaning closer, "your dustup with Mom hasn't helped your chances of getting any money out of her. Let me help you put together a résumé. I often have to read them when we're hiring somebody at the chemical company. You've done other things besides . . . being a stripper, haven't you?"

"Mostly retail," Terri said glumly. "My last job was in a bookstore. They went broke."

Caitlin nodded. "Are you sure you want to live around here? So close to our mother, I mean."

Terri shrugged. "I've got to start somewhere and get a nest egg."

"Okay." Caitlin paused. "I've seen Help Wanted signs at several places around Heraldsgate Hill. Come upstairs. We'll use my laptop."

Terri looked dubious. "Are you sure?"

"Of course." Caitlin was on her feet. Terri slowly got off the other sofa. "Excuse us," Caitlin said to Judith and Renie. Suddenly she snapped her fingers. "Terri, why did Doug want you to come with him?"

"I've no idea," Terri said.

"Doug didn't say why," Judith put in. "He was very abrupt."

"I wonder," Caitlin mused.

"What?" Terri asked.

"Doug's dad, Ray Campbell, came by the house while I was trying to calm down Mom after your fight," Caitlin explained. "Just before I left, I overheard him say something about talking to Mandrake Stokes."

Terri looked puzzled. "Who's that?"

"Someone who's involved in the ranch sale," Caitlin replied. "Mom asked me to meet with Mr. Stokes because she insists she can't handle it, and Billy . . . well, he's not very smart. Not knowing anything about the ranch, I flunked the meeting. Maybe Ray's leaped into the breach."

"I saw Ray a few times after Mom and my dad broke up," Terri said. "He's no businessman."

"Probably not," Caitlin agreed as the women left the living room. "But I only knew him from when he'd collect Doug for a weekend or . . ." They headed upstairs, their voices fading out of Judith's hearing range.

"My God," Renie exclaimed, "I'm so glad I'm an only child."

"Me, too." Judith smiled at her cousin. "But we had each other."

"That's why we usually get along," Renie pointed out. "When we fought, one of us could always leave and go home."

"A much better arrangement," Judith conceded. She fingered her chin. "So Johnny Agra is still alive. I hope Terri can get hold of him and find out about this Di Marco connection, if there is one, with his ex."

"You look disappointed," Renie remarked. "You wanted him dead?"

Judith shook her head. "Of course not, but it blows my theory about the murder. I had this wild idea that——"

A loud thud and a piercing scream made both cousins jump.

"What was that?" Renie asked, getting out of the chair and hurrying into the entry hall.

Groans and moans could be heard from somewhere in the house. "The kitchen?" Renie said, grabbing the shovel on the run. Judith followed as fast as she could. Before reaching the half-doors, she heard her cousin's voice raised in alarm. "Phyliss! What happened?"

Lying in a heap at the bottom of the back stairs, the cleaning woman let out several more painful yelps, followed by shielding her face with her forearm. "Begone, Satan's handmaid! Help!"

Renie froze, shovel in hand. "I don't think Phyliss likes me."

Judith nudged her cousin aside. "Let me see. Phyliss, what hurts?" she asked calmly.

"Save me!" Phyliss said in an agonized voice. "Your heathen cousin has a pitchfork! She's doing the devil's work before I'm dead!"

"It's a shovel," Judith said, trying to be patient.

Phyliss moaned and groaned. "My ankle!" she wailed. "It's broke!"

Judith tried to bend down, but Renie held her back. "Skip the satanic crap, Phyliss. You drove by 'dumb' a long time ago, and you're coming up on 'stupid' really fast. Let me check. I don't want to call an ambulance for two."

Phyliss's eyes had narrowed. "The Bible has a name for your ilk."

"I know," Renie said. "It's 'woman.'" On her knees, she examined Phyliss's right ankle. "It's a bit swollen," she said. "Come on, let me get you into a more comfortable position."

"Go away!" the cleaning woman shouted. "You, quoting Holy Scripture! It's blasphemy! You're Beelzebub's henchwoman! You've cast your evil spell on me!"

"Oh, for——" Renie took a deep breath. "*Please.* I want to help."

By sheer force, Renie managed to get Phyliss into a half-sitting position against the bottom stairs.

"Maybe," Judith said reluctantly, getting a look at the injured ankle, "we should call nine-one-one. It might only be a bad sprain, but you can't walk on it until you know, Phyliss."

"I need a healer," Phyliss asserted. "A good Christian with godly powers. Oh, how I suffer for the Lord!"

"You need a medic," Renie snapped. She looked up at Judith. "Call nine-one-one."

"You do it," Judith said. "I'm tired of talking to them."

Renie pondered for a moment. "I don't suppose I could take Phyliss to the ER in my car. Unless Carl could help me carry her."

"Carl," Judith reminded her cousin, "broke his leg."

"Damn! I forgot. What's going on around here?" Renie turned to Phyliss, who'd started moaning again. "Can you hop?"

"I'm not a rabbit!" Phyliss cried. "I know you worship them! I saw that furry creature in the garage! He's your familiar!"

"Oh, crap," Renie muttered. "Where's my cell phone? *I'll* call nine-one-one."

Judith gazed around the hallway and into the kitchen. "You had it in your hand when you came in the house after——" She suddenly looked stricken. "Phyliss, are you sitting on my cousin's phone?"

Phyliss's eyes widened. "So that's what I slipped on! I knew it!" She pointed a finger at Renie. "You tried to kill me! You're going to hell!"

"I'm beginning to think I'm already there," Renie retorted. "Move your butt, Phyliss, and let me get my phone."

The cleaning woman recoiled. "Don't touch me!" Struggling to sit straight up, Phyliss pressed both hands on the bottom step and lurched to her feet. "There! Take your infernal contraption! Demon's tools, that's what those walkie-talkies are!"

Renie snatched up her cell phone and stomped off down the hall. "She's all yours, Coz."

As Phyliss tested her ankle, Judith apologized. "Serena was upset when she dropped her phone. A very rude man was trying to barge into the house. That's why we locked the doors."

Phyliss leaned against the wall by the pantry door. "A thief? A sex fiend? A magazine subscription salesman? A rabbit?"

"It was one of Mrs. Buss's connections," Judith explained. "By the way, my stepdaughter and her half-sister are in Room One. They may both stay here tonight."

"Hold on," Phyliss said, with a sharp glance at Judith. "The redhead's Mrs. Buss's daughter, right? Is the other one related to that trollop?"

"Yes," Judith admitted. "But you can't blame either of them for their mother's folly."

"Sins of the fathers and the mothers, too." On that dark note, Phyliss hobbled down the hall.

"Miracle cure?" Renie asked as Judith returned to the living room.

"Phyliss will probably forget about it by the time she leaves for the day," Judith said. "Maybe I should offer her a ride home. Otherwise, she has to walk to the bus."

Renie, who'd been perusing the built-in bookshelves, pulled out a current copy of the *World Almanac*. "Are you going to call Johnny Agra, or will Terri do it? I can check the time change between here and the Bahamas with this. I think it's three hours, but I'm not sure."

Judith fanned herself with her hand. "That sounds right. It's getting stuffy in here. I'm going to unlock the doors and open them before the guests start coming back from their adventures."

"Go ahead." Renie flipped through the almanac. "If Doug hasn't come back by now, I don't think he will."

Judith opened the front door and stepped onto the porch. The sky had grown overcast in the past hour, though the air was very warm and heavy. She saw a sleek red sports car in front of Vivian's house. Billy Buss, Doug Campbell, and Barry Henckel were inspecting what Judith guessed was the Aston Martin DB9 that Herself had said was being shipped from Florida along with her Bentley. Stepping back inside to avoid drawing the men's attention, Judith remarked that it might rain.

"Good," Renie said. "We could use it. I'm sick of this sun."

"If you peek out through the front door," Judith said, "you'll see Billy's expensive toy car."

"I can't tell one car from another," Renie said. "Unless it runs on Pepsi, I don't give a damn."

Judith leaned against the buffet. "I should plan tomorrow's breakfast. If it rains, I might do something heartier than the

usual summer menus. I ought to go to Falstaff's and restock."
She looked at the grandfather clock as it chimed four times.
"Phyliss should be done by four-thirty. I'll offer her a lift and
stop at the store on the way back."

"How can I help?" Renie inquired. "My home repair is on
hold."

"Dream up a dinner for us and make a list in case I don't have
everything you need, okay?"

Renie agreed. Half an hour later, Phyliss had been coaxed
into accepting a ride home. As Judith pulled out of the driveway in her Nissan, she noticed that the Aston Martin was gone,
no doubt for a trial spin around Heraldsgate Hill.

Phyliss lived on the other side of the nearest bridge that
went over the ship canal. Traffic was building up with the late-
afternoon commute. After dropping the cleaning woman off at
her apartment near the zoo, Judith went to Falstaff's. It was just
past five-thirty when she got back to Hillside Manor.

"Are Caitlin and Terri eating with us?" Judith asked, setting
the grocery bags down on the kitchen counter.

"I don't know," Renie replied, picking a couple of green
grapes off of the bunch Judith had bought at Falstaff's. "They
left about ten minutes ago. Caitlin told me they were collecting
the rest of Terri's belongings from the motel and checking her
out. I think they're going to see if there's a vacancy at one of the
hotels at the bottom of the hill."

Judith put a bag of baby spinach into the refrigerator's crisper
drawer. "They're going to bunk together?"

"It makes sense," Renie said. "You need Caitlin's room
tomorrow, right? Terri doesn't want to spend any more time at
that motel with Herself footing the bill. She's fed up with living
off of her mother's table scraps and wants to find a job and an
apartment in the next week or so."

"Good luck with that," Judith murmured. "Of course, it's

August, and all the student summer jobs will end around Labor Day. I wonder how long Caitlin will stay in town?"

"I assume she wants to see Joe," Renie said, opening the package of chicken breasts that she'd requested for dinner. "It's been a while since they've had a visit."

"He'd better get home soon," Judith declared with fervor. "His timing for this trip stinks."

"He's getting paid," Renie pointed out. "When you freelance the way Joe and I do, you take what comes along, or else clients stop asking."

"Oh, I know," Judith allowed, "but if Joe were here, he'd have a lot more insight into the cast of characters than I do."

"If Bill were here," Renie noted, "he'd be able to psychoanalyze them and announce that they're all nuts."

"He'd be right," Judith said, glancing up at the schoolhouse clock. "It's almost six. Nine o'clock in the Bahamas, right?"

"Yes," Renie replied, slicing mushrooms. "You're calling Johnny?"

"I don't know when Terri and Caitlin will get back," Judith said, opening the phone book to the international section. "If they decide to eat out, it could be too late for Terri to call." She dialed international directory information and asked for John Agra's number in the Bahamas.

"There is no such listing," the soft and faintly English-accented operator's voice replied after a long pause.

Judith frowned. "How about a scuba-diving school?"

There were at least two dozen. None of them suggested any connection to Johnny Agra. "Charter boats?" she asked.

The operator recited several names and types. Judith still drew a blank. Frustrated, she thanked the operator and rang off. "I don't know much about the Bahamas," she admitted. "Are they off of Florida?"

Renie put the mushroom slices into a bowl. "Yes. They're

close to Cuba, too." She sat down at the computer. "Let's take a look." A few seconds later, she'd found one of the main sites. "Check it out."

Judith leaned over her cousin's shoulder. "There are several islands. I wouldn't know where to begin to find where Johnny lives."

"You figure he's shacked up with some woman?"

"It'd explain why he doesn't have his own listing," Judith said. She sighed. "Another dead end. Let's put the appetizers out for the guests."

The Californians were already coming downstairs. As usual, they were in a good mood, happily chatting about their day's adventures.

Bob, the former army medic, stood on the bottom step and clapped his hands. "Kudos to you, Mrs. Flynn, for suggesting that Duck tour. It was terrific! That was really fun going out on the lake inside the city."

"Perfect timing," his wife chimed in, "since it clouded up this afternoon. We spent the afternoon shopping downtown. My, but you have a lot of new buildings and construction going on around here."

"Too much," Judith said, smiling ruefully. "It makes for difficult driving. Our transportation system is pathetic compared to other cities."

"But such a lovely downtown!" the other California wife declared. "Very clean, very nice. Oh!" Glancing at her husband, she laughed. "You'll never guess who we saw there."

"Who?" Judith asked, balancing a platter of hors d'oeuvres.

"Those people who stayed here," wife number two replied. "Farmers, I think, from Iowa."

Judith stared at the couple. "The Griggses?"

All four Californians nodded. "They must've bought new clothes," Bob said. "At first we didn't recognize them until we all stopped at a crosswalk. Funny folks, though. They acted as if they didn't know us."

His wife snickered. "She did more than change her wardrobe. Edith and I figure she had a makeover while they were here."

Edith nodded. "A nice one, too, especially her hair."

Renie, who had taken the rest of the appetizers into the living room, joined the little group in the entry hall. "Who got redone?"

"The Iowa farmers," Judith said. "The ones who left suddenly." She turned back to the California quartet. "Did you talk to them?"

"We tried," the other man replied, "but they ignored us, and then the light changed, so they hurried across the street." He shrugged. "Midwesterners are usually friendly. I ought to know. I was born and raised in Minnesota."

"If you ask me," Edith said, "they never were very sociable, not even when we'd try to visit with them here."

"Takes all kinds," her husband murmured, and shrugged.

The Virginia twins and the honeymooners came downstairs in quick succession. Judith finished setting out the food before returning to the kitchen, where Renie was pouring a mixture of mushroom soup, sour cream, and sherry over the chicken breasts.

"Very odd," Judith remarked.

"The farmers?" Renie said, sprinkling paprika on the concoction.

"Yes. I told you I didn't think the Griggses were what they claimed to be." Judith took a big handful of fresh green beans out of the fridge. "But I can't figure it out. They were here the night of the murder. Could they be involved? If so, why stay in the city?"

Sliding the casserole dish into the oven, Renie grinned at her cousin. "You already know the answer. Why ask me?"

"Okay," Judith conceded. "They aren't who they pretended to be. But I ran them through the computer and everything checked out. Wilbur and Patrice Griggs live in Iowa corn farming country. They're using stolen ID, or . . . ?" She waited for Renie to fill in the gaps.

Renie looked blank. "I give up."

Judith was distracted by a flash of lightning, followed almost immediately by the roll of thunder. "Never mind. It's probably one of my loonier ideas. Here comes the rain."

As gray clouds hung over Heraldsgate Hill, big drops poured down, pelting the windows and bouncing off the pavement. The bursts of lightning and thunder grew almost simultaneous. As the cousins made their cocktails, they smiled and mouthed the words of typical natives.

"We need this rain," Judith said.

Renie nodded agreement. "It'll clear the air."

Forty-five minutes later, Judith delivered dinner to her mother. Gertrude griped that "supper" was too darned late, rain or no rain, guests or no guests, dead bodies or no dead bodies.

Judith tried to shut out the litany of complaints. "I've got something for you," she said, reaching into her pocket and placing Gertrude's engagement ring on the card table.

The old lady gaped at the ring and then at her daughter. "Where'd you find it?"

"The laundry basket," Judith lied. "It got tangled with your wash."

"Phyliss shouldn't be so slapdash when she changes my bed." With some difficulty, Gertrude put the ring on her finger. "So where's that candy you were going to buy me?"

"That's another story." Judith frowned. "I'm still sorting out that one. I'll buy another box tomorrow."

"You darned well better," Gertrude muttered.

Making her exit, Judith, however, noticed that her mother's face softened as she gazed at the cherished ring. Memories, no doubt, that could evoke smiles—and tears.

When Judith went back into the kitchen, Caitlin was talking to Renie. "If there isn't enough casserole," Caitlin was saying, "I can have soup."

"There's plenty," Renie replied. "I always make too much Chicken Parisienne. Force of habit, I guess, from when my kids lived at home. What about Terri?"

Caitlin shrugged. "I don't know. When we came back from checking her out at the motel and making reservations for tomorrow night at the Heraldsgate Hotel, our half-brothers were getting out of Billy's sports car and insisted that she go for a ride with them. I suppose they won't be gone long."

For a reason she couldn't quite fathom, an uneasy feeling enveloped Judith. "Did they ask you, too?"

"No," Caitlin replied. "I cut my ties with those two years ago. They teased and bullied me constantly when Dad wasn't around. He tried to straighten them out, but by the time he married Mom, I guess it was too late. After I moved out, I avoided them like the plague."

Judith nodded. "Your father hasn't really kept in touch with them much over the years. He hadn't seen Barry or Doug for a long time until the party Monday night."

"That sounds right," Caitlin said vaguely, staring out through the kitchen window over the sink. "It's still coming down pretty hard. I hope whichever of those morons is driving that hot car remembers how slippery the streets can be around here after we haven't had any rain for a while."

"Was Billy with them?" Judith asked while Renie got out a third place setting and began dishing up the food.

"I didn't see him," Caitlin said, sitting down at the table. "I didn't see my mother, either. That's just as well."

As the last of the B&B guests left for the evening, the three women began eating. The topic switched from family relationships to how much the city—and the hill in particular—had changed over the years. It was inevitable that the conversation went full circle, with Caitlin marveling at her mother's temerity in building a condo in the cul-de-sac.

"Is it legal?" she asked the cousins.

"I don't know," Judith replied, "but if she's applied for permits, we'll find out soon enough."

"It wouldn't surprise me," Renie put in, "if she got a green light. I can't believe how many multifamily residences have been put up in the past few years. Many of them cut off other homeowners' views. But despite all the protests filed and the city holding public hearings, it doesn't seem like there's anything that can be done to stop construction. It's so crowded around here now that the only way builders can go is up."

Judith noted that it was almost seven-thirty. The thunder and lightning had passed over, but it was still raining, though the downpour had dwindled to a drizzle. "Shouldn't Terri be back by now? She did plan to spend the night here with you, right?"

Caitlin glanced at her watch. "Yes. I brought the things she needed with me. The hotel let us put the rest in their baggage room."

The phone rang. Judith got up to grab the receiver.

"Hi," Terri said, her voice sounding a bit odd. "I've decided to go back to L.A. Would you mind shipping my things after I find a place to live down there?"

Judith mouthed Terri's name for the benefit of Renie and Caitlin. "Are you sure about moving back to Los Angeles?" The question evoked a surprised look from Caitlin and a frown from Renie. "Caitlin would be a wonderful person to help you get reestablished."

"Yes, but . . ." Terri paused. "I've lived in L.A. a long time. It's home now." She paused again. Judith thought she heard another voice in the background. "I have friends there, really nice people."

Caitlin had stood up, motioning that she wanted to talk to her half-sister. "Where are you?" Judith asked with a nod at Caitlin. "If you're close, we could bring the items that are here at the B&B."

"I don't need them," Terri replied hurriedly. "I'm right by a drugstore for any necessities. I have to go."

"Wait!" Judith's tone was sharp. "Here's Caitlin." She thrust the phone at her stepdaughter.

"Terri?" Caitlin said—and waited. "Terri? Are you there? *Terri?*"

The tone of Caitlin's voice sent a shiver down Judith's spine. Even Renie, who had actually stopped stuffing her face, looked anxious.

"I think," Caitlin said bleakly, holding the receiver in front of her, "Terri hung up."

"Hit the caller ID button," Judith urged. "The screen will show the number she called from."

Caitlin pressed the CID button. "No," she said helplessly. "It says 'Security Screen' with just a bunch of zeroes."

Judith grimaced. "Try star-sixty-nine for last number dialed."

Caitlin nodded once and hit more buttons. "Unavailable," she said. "Why would Terri hang up on me?"

Judith took the receiver from Caitlin. "I don't think she did. I suspect someone else hung up for her."

21

Caitlin's expression was grim. "What should we do?"

Judith's brain was already grappling with the situation. "I think that car's a two-seater. If Terri went for a ride with one of her brothers or Billy, that Aston Martin should be easy to spot." She started to dial 911 but stopped before she got beyond the first number. Judith simply couldn't deal with so much as a single dollop of sarcasm from the emergency operators. "Coz," she said, speaking rapidly, "get Woody's card from the bulletin board. It's between AAA and Athens Pizza."

Renie removed the pushpin and handed the card to Judith.

"Thanks," Judith said. "Use your cell to phone Holliday's Pharmacy to see if they've seen Terri or the car. Then call Bartleby's Drugs at the bottom of the hill."

"I can do that," Caitlin volunteered, opening the yellow pages.

"Good." Judith, who'd penciled in Woody's private number, waited for him to answer. He picked up on the third ring. "I know you're probably off-duty," she said without preamble, "but I've got a serious problem. I barely know the homicide detectives working this case, and I'm afraid we have a missing person, one of Vivian's daughters."

"Not Caitlin?" Woody said, sounding concerned.

"No, her half-sister, Terri," Judith replied, noting that Caitlin had gone down the hall to use her phone, and Renie had taken her cell into the dining room. "Let me explain what I think may have happened." As concisely as possible, Judith not only related the sequence of events, but gave Woody a detailed description of Terri and her half-brothers. "I hate to ask you to get involved," she went on, "but——"

"Judith," Woody broke in, "don't. I won't step on any toes, but I'll see what I can do. I think the patrol officers on this shift are your old pals, Mercedes Berger and Darnell Hicks. They asked to be switched to the night shift because Darnell's wife had a baby a couple of days ago, and he wanted to be home during the day. I'll contact them ASAP and touch base with the tecs. If I hear anything, I'll let you know."

"Thanks, Woody. Call me at the B&B or on my cell. You have the numbers, right? I know I'm asking a lot, but——" She stopped, aware that she was wasting time, thanked him again, and rang off.

Renie reentered the kitchen. "No sighting of Terri at Holliday's. Everybody who works there knows all the regulars. I had to listen to the pharmacist, Lenny Tripp, describe Olga Broadbutt wearing a halter and short shorts when she picked up her fiber pills."

"Her name's Broadbent," Judith pointed out.

"That may be her name, but have you seen Olga in short shorts?"

"No, thank goodness." Judith frowned. "Of course, we don't know that Terri actually went inside the drugstore." She paused as Caitlin also came back into the kitchen. "Any luck?"

Caitlin grimaced. "The most I could find out was that one of the checkers heard a customer say something about a really hot sports car in the parking lot. Do you think that would be the Aston Martin?"

"I wouldn't be surprised," Judith said, "although there are quite a few expensive cars on Heraldsgate Hill these days."

Caitlin nodded once. "The car was gone when I called."

Judith sighed. "I was afraid of that. Unfortunately, Bartleby's is by the street that leads to both the freeway and the north-south main route through town."

Caitlin leaned against the refrigerator. "What do we do now?"

"We wait," Judith said, and explained about her call to Woody Price. "He'll do what he can," she concluded, "though it's not his case. I can't figure out anything we should be doing at this end. Unless . . ."

Renie held her head. "Oh, God—what? Put targets on our backs?"

"Not quite," Judith replied with a guarded glance at her cousin. "But I think I'll go over to Vivian's and see who's there and who isn't."

"Not alone," Renie declared. "I'll go with you."

"What about me?" Caitlin asked plaintively.

"You stay here," Judith said, "in case Terri calls or comes back."

Caitlin sank into a kitchen chair, her head down and her shoulders slumped. "I wish I were back in Switzerland. It's so . . . calm there. Why did I ever come here?"

Judith put a hand on Caitlin's shoulder. "You meant well. After all, your mother seemed to need you."

"No." She vigorously shook her head. "My mother doesn't *need* people, she *uses* them. Why did I think she might've changed?"

"We often hope for the best," Judith said.

"But we always expect the worst," Renie put in. "I do, anyway."

Judith shot her cousin a reproving glance. "Let's go, Angel of Gloom."

"I think I'll take the shovel," Renie said as they headed for the front door. "Weaponry seems like a good idea."

"Forget it," Judith retorted. "I'm not afraid of Herself."

"It's not her I'm worried about," Renie said, hesitating on the edge of the porch and gazing into the cul-de-sac. "No Aston Martin, just a pickup and the Ericsons' SUV."

"I think the pickup belongs to either Doug or Barry," Judith said, watching her step as she reached the sidewalk. The drizzle continued, leaving a few puddles in the concrete. The cousins barely noticed the rain. Only a downpour forced natives to cover their heads. It wasn't quite eight-thirty, but for the first time since summer began a few lights shone in windows around the cul-de-sac in the early evening.

"Do we have a plan?" Renie inquired as they cut across the open area to Vivian's house.

"Well . . . not exactly," Judith admitted, noting that there was a single light on inside the bungalow. "We're playing it by ear."

Just as they started up the porch steps, a yellow cab pulled into the cul-de-sac. Judith and Renie stopped, waiting to see who got out.

"Mandrake Stokes?" Judith whispered as the dapper gentleman emerged from the taxi.

"So it is," Renie murmured.

As Stokes approached the cousins, he tipped his hat. "Good evening, ladies. A bit dampish, eh?"

"A bit," Judith replied. "Are you here to see Mrs. Buss?"

The man's usually pleasant face hardened slightly. "If you wish to call her that." He tipped his hat a second time and walked past the cousins up to Vivian's front door.

"Now what?" Renie said under her breath.

Judith made a face. "Bad timing on our part." She backstepped a couple of paces so as not to be seen by whoever answered the door. The welcoming voice belonged to Adelita. A moment later, Judith heard the door close. "Damn," she cursed. "I don't have a contingency plan."

"That doesn't bother me, since you didn't know what—" Renie stopped as Judith's cell rang.

Removing the slim phone from her slacks pocket, she saw Woody's private line on the screen. "Yes?" she said eagerly.

"Mercedes and Darnell just checked in," Woody said. "They stopped the driver of an Aston Martin about ten minutes ago after he ran an arterial at the four-way stop just east of the civic center. No valid license plates, just the Florida dealer's temporary sticker, which expired August first. The driver, William Andrew Buss, was alone."

Judith willed herself not to sound too disappointed. "Where was he going?"

"I don't know," Woody replied.

"I do," Judith said, seeing the Aston Martin pull into view. "Billy just arrived. Did Mercedes and Darnell ask him about Terri?"

"Yes. He said he hadn't seen her in the last hour or so. They didn't feel they could press the matter," Woody explained, "but Billy insisted they check the trunk. It was empty except for an unopened half-rack of Corona beer. He seemed to think it was all a big joke. He told them he'd been buying beer at the grocery store at the bottom of the hill."

"Okay," Judith said, standing with Renie by the Ericsons' house and watching Billy open the trunk to remove the half-rack. "I'm going to play neighbor now. Keep in touch?"

Woody promised he would, though Judith didn't hold out much hope that he could discover Terri's whereabouts.

She turned her attention to Herself's current husband. "Billy!" she called. "That's some hot car you've got!"

He looked over his shoulder. "Yeah, custom-built. It's loaded."

Judith moved a few steps closer. "Have you taken it out on the highway?"

"Not here," Billy replied, hoisting the half-rack onto his shoulder. "I took it for a spin on I-10 to I-95 in Florida. Sweet ride all the way."

Judith reached the Busses' garden gate. "How did Terri like it?"

"I dunno." Billy ascended the porch steps two at a time. "Ask her." He went inside and closed the door.

Renie joined Judith. "Is he as dumb as he seems?"

"I think so," Judith said, "but you can be dumb *and* dangerous."

"Oh, yes." Renie glanced up at the low-lying gray clouds. "If we stand here long enough, I won't have to take a bath tonight."

Judith sighed. "We might as well go back to the house."

"Good," Renie said, glancing at her watch. "I'm late for Clarence's tucking in."

"Okay." Judith's response was vague. She strolled aimlessly along the sidewalk toward the through street after Renie had headed for the garage. Daylight was fading fast. The streetlights were on, turning the pavement in the cul-de-sac to glossy black. Judith gazed from house to house, trying to find comfort in the familiar nook that was her home. But there was blight in her surroundings. Mrs. Swanson's house already looked abandoned, an empty shell that would soon be gone, along with Vivian's bungalow. In their place a hulking concrete edifice would rise, not like a phoenix, but an eyesore.

"It's wrong," Judith said to herself. "All wrong." This part of Heraldsgate Hill was a family neighborhood in the truest sense. The Catholics, the Jews, the Protestants, the African-Americans, the Japanese-born widow, had all lived in harmony for many years. They were friends as well as neighbors. There was nothing inherently wrong with people who lived in condominiums. But that wasn't what Judith's small, usually comfortable world was all about. Four generations of Grovers had lived in what had become Hillside Manor. Judith couldn't imagine being squeezed out by the grandiose plans of a misfit such as Vivian Flynn. It simply wasn't right.

Vivian Flynn, she thought, and felt a sudden jolt of realization. It wasn't just Herself's plans that didn't fit, it was the murder case itself. *I'm the one who's been wrong*, she thought. *My usual logic has been there all along, but I haven't accepted my conclusions. I have to start at the beginning.*

But how, she wondered as she walked briskly back to Hillside Manor. And how could she help Terri? Assuming, she thought dismally, that Terri wasn't already beyond help. She entered the front door at about the same time Renie came in through the back entrance. Caitlin was still sitting at the kitchen table, looking morose.

"Is everything okay?" she asked.

"Not exactly," Judith replied. "Have you tried to call your father?"

Caitlin shook her head. "It's kind of late there, isn't it?"

"Yes, midnight." Judith wandered from the kitchen table to the cupboards on the opposite side of the kitchen and back again. "Caitlin," she said, leaning on the table, "did Terri give you any indication she wanted to move back to L.A.?"

"No." Caitlin crumpled a paper napkin and tossed it from hand to hand in a nervous manner. "I did wonder why she'd want to stay around here and be driven crazy by our mother, but she never mentioned pulling up stakes and going to California."

"That's what I figured," Judith said, and suddenly turned pale. "Good God, I can't believe how stupid I've been!"

Renie looked startled. "Huh? You mean by not helping me put Clarence to bed?"

Judith dismissed Renie's latest idiotic suggestion with a wave of her hand. "Aileen Rosenthal. I've got to call Woody and have him put me in touch with those neophyte detectives."

But when Judith phoned Woody, he wasn't keen on the idea. "I've already overstepped the invisible line, Judith. The problem is that they're young and inexperienced. They should never have been put on this case. They're going by the book, trying to make sure they don't jeopardize the investigation."

Judith hesitated, trying to help Woody help her. "Can you tell them I have fresh information?"

"You do?"

The hint of skepticism made Judith wince. She understood that he admired her detecting skills, but she also knew he was aware of her propensity to tell the occasional fib.

"It's something they know, too, but it doesn't mean anything to them," she explained. "It's about the daughter who claimed the vic's body. It's very important that I find out how she surfaced and what she planned to do."

"You mean with the corpse?" Woody still sounded skeptical. "If this daughter got a release from the medical examiner, she probably shipped it to a funeral home wherever the dead guy came from or where she lives."

"That's my point," Judith asserted. "But what worries me most is that Terri's still missing."

Woody expelled a heavy sigh. "Okay, I'll try to reach Almquist and Griffin. They're done for the day, but maybe I can use the gray hairs I've acquired to coax them with my aging wisdom and paternalistic approach. Mentoring, the higher-ups call it. Meddling is how the younger set describes it."

Judith thanked Woody again and hung up. Putting the phone on the counter, she sat down across from Caitlin. "I don't like the waiting game," Judith declared, fighting the old urge to bite her nails. "Not with Terri somewhere out there in the wind."

Caitlin had shredded the paper napkin and was picking up the pieces. "I feel useless. I had no idea how involved you got with these murder cases. I always thought Dad was just teasing you."

"Unfortunately," Judith said, "he's not."

Renie had left the kitchen while Judith was talking to Woody. She returned through the swinging half-doors, her expression ominous. "I thought I heard something outside," she said, standing by the sink. "There's another car over at Herself's. I went out on the porch and heard raised voices, but I couldn't see who was talking."

Judith started to get up from the chair, but the phone rang. She leaned sideways to grab the receiver, hoping it was Woody with encouraging news.

"Hey, it's your Georgia peach," Joe said cheerfully. "How's it going?"

"Ah . . . great. Fine," Judith lied, mouthing Joe's name for the benefit of Renie and Caitlin. "How are you?"

"Just about ready to wind things up here tomorrow," Joe replied, "but don't wait dinner. I probably won't get in until fairly late." His voice took on a more sober note. "I take it you're keeping out of trouble?"

"Absolutely." Judith bolted out of the chair. "Renie and Caitlin and I are just chatting. Would you like to talk to your daughter?"

"Sure, put her on," Joe said. "Say, anything you'd like me to bring back from Atlanta?"

"Ah . . ." Judith was leaning so far across the table that she almost lost her balance. "No, not at the moment. Here's Caitlin." She shoved the phone at her stepdaughter, regained her balance, and followed Renie out to the front porch.

All seemed quiet in the cul-de-sac.

"Are you sure you heard something?" Judith asked.

"Yes." Renie pointed toward Vivian's house. "The voices definitely came from over there. Mrs. Swanson's house is vacant, and the Ericsons never make noise. In fact, I wasn't sure they knew how to talk until about five years ago when I accidentally ran over their recycling bin."

"They are quiet," Judith allowed. "They don't have children. That can make for a more peaceful life."

"Yes." Renie sighed. "Then, if they're like my three, they get married and move far, far away, and you wish they were still under your roof, making noises like the mosh pit at a rock concert."

"I keep worrying that Mike will get transferred to some distant forest service job," Judith said. "Look at Caitlin—she gets back here only once or——hey, is someone there on the sidewalk by Mrs. Swanson's?"

Renie peered toward the corner where the cul-de-sac joined the through street. "Yes. It's a man. He's pacing around. It looks like Mandrake Stokes."

"Let's see what's up with him," Judith said, going down the steps. "Maybe he's waiting for a cab." Halfway across the cul-de-sac, she called his name. "Mr. Stokes! Do you need a ride?"

Standing under the shelter of the maple tree in the parking strip, Mandrake Stokes looked startled. "A car is coming for me," he replied stiffly. "I'm going to the airport."

The cousins reached the corner. "You must've finished your business here," Judith remarked. "I hope it went well."

"It went nowhere," Stokes replied through taut lips. "That's why I'm going elsewhere. This was a wild goose chase." He shook his head. "People are very odd."

"You're referring to the Double UB ranch?" Judith inquired.

"Of course." Stokes peered at a pair of headlights coming

along the street off Heraldsgate Avenue. "I'm a businessman, not an attorney," he said hastily. "I am unable to sort through this ownership problem." The car slowed down. "I believe this must be my ride." He tipped his hat and walked swiftly to the rear passenger door. "Farewell, ladies," he called as he got inside the car.

Judith watched the vehicle make a wide turn to head down the southbound street. For a fleeting moment, she got a look at the car under the streetlight.

"Oh, no!" she cried, digging the cell phone out of her pocket. "That's not a hired car! It's Herself's lavender Bentley!"

"So?" Renie said as Judith dialed the number she'd memorized for Mercedes and Darnell.

"Give me a minute," Judith shot back. "Darnell? It's Judith Flynn. Where are you?"

"By the firehouse on top of the hill," he replied. "What's up?"

Judith quickly gave a description of the car, adding that it might not have a valid state license plate. "It's the other car Mrs. Buss had shipped from Florida. I've no idea who's driving, but they're headed south from the B&B, and I think Mandrake Stokes may be in danger."

"Who?" Darnell sounded puzzled.

"I'll explain later. Just find that car and stop them, okay?"

"If you say so," Darnell responded.

Grateful that Darnell and Mercedes took her seriously, Judith disconnected. "The patrol cops are by the fire station," she said to Renie. "That's only about six or seven blocks from here."

"Now we've got *two* kidnappings?" Renie said in disbelief.

"Maybe." Judith's expression was grim. "Let's hope that's all we have. Why on earth didn't I figure this out——" Her cell phone rang just as she was putting it back in her pocket.

"Mrs. Flynn?" K. C. Griffin's voice was brusque. "Detective

Price asked me to call you. What kind of information do you have?"

"More than I did when Woody talked to you," Judith replied. "Could you stop by the B&B?"

·"Oh . . ." The policewoman sounded pained. "Can't it wait?"

"No. Is Almquist with you?"

"Hardly. I'm home. I don't let him near me after-hours. I mean——" Griffin made a vexed sound. "I separate my work from my private life."

"Then go back to work and get yourselves to Hillside Manor," Judith retorted. *"Please."*

"This better be good," Griffin said sourly, and hung up.

"Mismatched partners," Judith muttered. "Come on, let's do our own surveillance of Vivian's house."

"Good grief!" Renie looked mulish. "It's after nine o'clock, it's dark, it's raining, and I want to watch the Upper Midwest Tractor Pull Competition on TV."

"No, you don't," Judith declared, cautiously opening the gate to Mrs. Swanson's backyard. "We'll get by the fence between the houses and stand under the plum tree. That way, we not only can see Vivian's house, but anybody coming into the cul-de-sac."

"Like the guy from the booby hatch who's going to put a net over your head?"

"Keep your voice down," Judith urged in a whisper. "The Busses may have some windows open."

"Okay, okay." Renie sounded annoyed. "I don't know what you're going to see or hear, but—ow!" Grabbing her foot, she let loose with a string of obscenities.

Judith turned around. "What is it?" she hissed.

"I stepped on a rock," Renie said, hopping up and down while rubbing her injured sole.

"You're barefoot!" Judith exclaimed, trying to keep her voice low.

"It's summer. Since when did I wear shoes in the summer except to drive?"

"You are an idiot," Judith murmured. "I hear music."

"Good for you," Renie said, walking gingerly on the sore foot. "Are they playing our swan song?"

"No, it's big-band stuff," Judith said, crouching down as far as she could against the plum tree's trunk.

Renie knelt beside Judith. "I hear it now. It's pretty loud."

"A good thing, since you won't lower your——" She stopped speaking as the music ended abruptly.

Herself's raised voice could be heard, railing at someone. "It makes not a damned bit of difference, you feebleminded moron! We're still rich! Just keep your mouth shut!"

A man spoke, but not loud enough for the cousins to hear what he said. "Billy?" Judith whispered.

"Maybe." Renie had finally softened her tone.

"Just do as I say," Vivian yelled. "Get your suitcase. You won't need that much because we won't . . ." The words faded away as she, too, spoke more quietly.

Another woman's voice interrupted. Again, the cousins couldn't make out what she was saying. Judith hazarded a guess as to the speaker. "Adelita?"

Before Renie could respond, a car pulled into the cul-de-sac. "The cops, I hope," Judith murmured, standing up to see where the vehicle was stopping. "It's another taxi," she said, "pulling up in front of Herself's. I wonder if Vivian and Billy are doing a bunk."

"I'm not going to guess why, since you won't tell me," Renie snapped, but crept closer to the sidewalk. Judith, who could only see the lighted sign on top of the cab, also moved away from the tree. Renie gestured at her. "Somebody's getting out—a man and a woman."

Keeping a low profile, Judith reached the fence where Renie lurked by a jasmine shrub that grew on a wooden trellis. "Frankie and Marva Lou," Judith whispered.

"Obviously recovered from being poisoned," Renie noted as the couple headed for Vivian's porch, and the taxi drove away.

"It all fits," Judith said, more to herself than to Renie.

"I heard that," her cousin snapped. "If you'd tell me——" She shut up as Judith waved her into silence before scurrying back to the fence between the two houses. Very faintly, the cousins heard the chimes play "How Dry I Am." Twice. And a third time. Then there was pounding on the door, followed by Frankie bellowing to let them in.

Judith and Renie could see Frankie and Marva Lou, but not who finally opened the door.

"Stop playing games," Marva Lou snarled.

"No, no!" The voice belonged to Adelita. "It is wrong for you to——"

The Busses entered, slamming the door behind them.

"Where are those tecs?" Judith asked impatiently. It was starting to rain harder, and a breeze was blowing up from the bay. "Why haven't I heard from Darnell and Mercedes? And where is Terri?"

"Stop fussing," Renie told her cousin, even as the din from inside the house grew more raucous. "Wow! They're really going at it in there!"

Judith cringed as she heard mostly unintelligible sounds from people hurling insults and threats. "Who's on whose side?" she wondered out loud. "Frankie and Marva Lou are the visitors, so Vivian and Billy are the home team. Where does Adelita fit in all this?"

"I thought you knew all the answers," Renie retorted sarcastically.

"Not *all*," Judith said candidly. "In fact, I just thought of something that may or may not fit. The four-way stop east of the center where Billy got cited for running the arterial is by those motels, right?

"Yes. Some kind of residence hotel on one corner, a gas station and a convenience store on another, and two motels on the south side of the east-west street. A Slumber Coach and the Travel Inn." Renie winced at the sound of glass breaking inside the Busses' house. "Hey, hasn't Terri been staying at the Travel Inn?"

"Exactly," Judith said. "I wonder why Billy was in the vicinity. It seems strange that——" She gave a start as the garden gate creaked. Turning slightly, she saw a hooded figure moving stealthily toward their stakeout. "Don't look, don't move, don't breathe," Judith whispered. "I think we have a problem."

22

Frozen in place under the plum tree, Judith sensed rather than saw the hooded outline emerging through the gloom. Renie, however, had ignored her cousin's advice. "Yikes!" she cried, swiveling around to peer at the ominous figure. "It's the Grim Reaper!"

An exasperated sigh emerged from the dark hood. "What's going on in there?" Arlene Rankers demanded, gesturing at Vivian's house. "It sounds like a free-for-all. Is crockery being broken? Or furniture?" She crouched by the cousins. "Should we call the police?"

Brushing moisture from her face, Judith sank back against the plum tree. "You scared us," she said, catching her breath and seeing that Arlene was wearing a rain poncho. "I already called. The detectives investigating the case should be arriving any moment."

"Those two!" Arlene's voice dripped with disdain. "They were so rude to me, especially the young woman. I was sure they were going to haul me off to jail before I could finish folding the laundry."

Judith winced at the sound of shattering glass. "That bunch

is going to be hauled off in ambulances if they don't stop fighting."

She'd barely finished speaking when Billy and Adelita raced out of the house, down the steps, and jumped into the Aston Martin. With a squeal of tires on wet pavement, the sports car headed out of the cul-de-sac and toward Heraldsgate Avenue. Billy had been carrying what looked like a half rack of beer.

"That figures," Judith murmured.

"What?" Arlene's tone was sharp. "You mean . . . those two are . . . what?"

"Having an affair," Judith said.

"Really," Arlene said disapprovingly, "the way younger people carry on!" She shook her head and sighed. "It's s-o-o-o romantic." Briefly, her face looked wistful, but turned serious as she pointed to the street. "Where's that purple car? It was here a few minutes ago."

"Purple?" Judith echoed. "Or lavender?"

"Lavender, yes." Arlene nodded several times. "Very pretty."

"Vivian's Bentley arrived from Florida." Judith slowly straightened up. The departure of Billy and Adelita seemed to have created a lull in the conflict. Voices had been lowered, and household goods were no longer being destroyed. Judith glimpsed someone in her driveway. "It's Caitlin," she said, and moved away from the plum tree. "I'd better stop her. She must have heard the commotion, too."

"Judith?" Caitlin stopped by the Ericson property. "Is that you?"

"Yes," Judith said softly. "Billy and Adelita just took off in his car. Your mother's inside with the other Busses."

Caitlin reached Vivian's walkway. "Is Mom okay? I heard an awful row when I started outside to see your mother. Then a car roared off."

"You heard enough," Judith said, meeting Caitlin in front of Vivian's house. "It's calmed down in the last few minutes."

"I'd better go in," Caitlin said, her green eyes straying anxiously to Herself's front door.

"It might be better if you waited until——" Judith swerved around as she heard the sound of yet another car's arrival. "Finally," she said with a sigh of relief. "The tecs."

Caitlin looked puzzled. "The . . . ? Oh, you mean the detectives." She smiled slightly. "I've been away from Dad for so long that I've forgotten cop lingo."

The white sedan was headed for Hillside Manor, but apparently the detectives spotted Judith and Caitlin. They stopped halfway through the cul-de-sac. Griffin, who was driving, rolled down the window.

"Mrs. Flynn? What's going on?"

"For openers, somebody's getting away with murder," Judith responded. "Meanwhile, there's been an awful row at Mrs. Buss's house. Can we talk somewhere besides on the sidewalk?"

Griffin maneuvered the car to the curb in front of the Ericsons' SUV. She got out first, her no-nonsense manner apparent as she strode briskly toward Vivian's house. Almquist took his time, long legs appearing before the rest of him emerged. Renie and Arlene had come from Mrs. Swanson's garden, joining Judith and Caitlin on the sidewalk.

Griffin stood rigidly by Vivian's walkway. "I don't hear anything."

Judith nodded. "The ruckus stopped when Billy Buss and Adelita Vasquez took off. Mrs. Buss—Vivian—is inside with Frankie and Marva Lou Buss. Obviously, they've been released from the hospital."

Griffin beckoned to Almquist. "Move it. We're going in."

"You first," Almquist said, rubbing his left calf. "I got a leg cramp."

"Oh, for——!" Griffin swallowed the rest of her invective. "Fine. Why don't you go back to the car and order a pizza?"

"Good idea," Almquist said cheerfully.

"I'm not serious," Griffin retorted. "Get over here. Follow procedure. Why did I ever——" Again, she clamped her mouth shut.

Caitlin stepped up to the female detective. "Let me go in first. I'm Mrs. Buss's daughter."

Griffin expelled an exasperated sigh. "I don't care if your mother's the Queen of Sheba. We follow procedure. Move back, please."

Reluctantly, Caitlin obeyed. Almquist ambled to the walkway. "Should we draw our weapons?" he asked in a doubtful voice.

"Yes," his partner snapped. "This may be a hostile situation. Don't you know the rules?"

"Oh, sure," he replied, "but I don't know what's happening."

Griffin uttered a snarl-like sound. Taking out her service automatic, she went up the porch stairs to the front door. "Police!" she shouted. "Open up!"

Watching with obvious anxiety, Caitlin grabbed Judith's arm. "Please—isn't there some way I could go in? I . . . feel so guilty!"

"Of what?" Judith asked in alarm.

The younger woman let go of Judith and hung her head. "Of betrayal. Of being disloyal to my mother. You can't understand."

Before Judith could respond, the front door opened. "Put that gun down," Marva Lou Buss commanded. "We have a truce."

Holding weapons aloft, the detectives went inside. The door closed, but Caitlin rushed up to the porch, opened the door, and disappeared inside.

"That's it," Judith muttered. "I'm going in, too."

"Oh, crap!" Renie exclaimed. "I'll have to go with you."

"Not without me," Arlene declared, following Renie, who was already behind Judith as she went up to the door.

The scene in the living room was deceptively calm. Vivian lay limply on the sofa, gold sandals peeking from under a scarlet, green, and black caftan. Frankie Buss sat in an armchair, looking rumpled and weary. Marva Lou stood in front of the TV, her pallor contrasting with red blotches on each cheek. Evidence of a battle was obvious. The television screen had been shattered, a chair was upended, and a small statue of the Venus de Milo had more than her arms missing. Two lamps had been toppled, a broken beer bottle's contents stained the carpet, and all three of the alleged participants looked spent.

"Now what?" Vivian muttered, narrowing her eyes at the newcomers. "Where's the icebag?" She squinted at the gaudy Murano chandelier, the room's only illumination still in working condition. "Where are my sunglasses? I can't stand that glare!"

Griffin returned her handgun to its holster. "Mrs. Buss," she said to Vivian, "we understand a domestic disturbance has occurred here."

Marva Lou stepped forward, rubbing her upper arm. "A family fracas, that's all. We're fine now."

Vivian darted a malicious glance at her sister-in-law. "Speak for yourself, you viper."

"Now, now," Frankie began, but was interrupted by Caitlin.

"I'll get you an icebag," she said to her mother, whose right eye was red and swollen. "Maybe I can find your sunglasses."

"Don't bother," Vivian snapped, groping under her backside. "I'm sitting on them. They're broken." She glared at Marva Lou. "You owe me four hundred dollars. They're top of the line."

"*I* owe *you*?" Marva Lou sneered as Caitlin went to the kitchen. "Ha!"

Griffin appeared impatient. "Are you people going to act like civilized human beings? If you can't, we're done here."

"They're fine," Almquist said. "Let's go."

"Wait." Judith stood by the front door, willing to bar it if the detectives tried to leave. "You're not done. You've only started."

Griffin swerved to stare at Judith. "What are you talking about?"

"I haven't told you what may be a key to solving this case," Judith said. "I'm sure the rest of these folks would also like to hear it."

"Oh, for——!" Fiercely, Griffin shook her head. "This isn't amateur night. You're wasting our time."

"No, I'm not," Judith insisted. "For starters, tell me about Aileen Rosenthal, the woman who claimed the dead body."

"I talked to her on the phone," Griffin replied, looking defensive. "His daughter knew about his visit here, but she was upset because he didn't return when he said he would. She insisted that was unlike him, so she contacted the local police. The vic's description fit her father. She came up here, IDed him, and asked to claim the body for burial."

Judith cocked her head to one side. "And?"

"There was some confusion at the morgue after Ms. Rosenthal arrived. Since cause of death had been determined, she was allowed to take the body." Griffin shrugged. "That's it."

"Not quite," Judith countered.

"Oh, shut up!" Vivian cried, taking the icebag from Caitlin, who had returned to the living room. "You're the biggest meddler I've ever met! As for your awful neighbor," she went on, pointing to Arlene, "get her out of here—and take your cousin Weenie with you."

Judith shot Vivian a severe look. "I'm not finished."

Marva Lou's expression was malicious. "I like this. I want to hear it. Go ahead, Mrs. Flynn."

Judith turned back to Griffin. "Did you ask Ms. Rosenthal if she had any idea who might have killed her father, or what he was doing at the Buss's house?"

"Of course," Griffin responded. "She insisted he had no known enemies. As for coming to this house, his daughter figured he'd tagged along with some old buddies he'd known when he lived here several years ago. Ms. Rosenthal added that her father had worked for the city and still kept in touch with some of his former colleagues."

Judith persisted. "Such as who?"

"She didn't know. Once she got back to Culver City, she thought she might find some information about his cronies. An address or phone book, maybe. She promised to let us know."

"How," Judith asked, "did she explain her father having someone else's wallet in his possession?"

Griffin made an impatient gesture. "Why are you asking these questions?"

"Bear with me," Judith urged. "I have valid reasons."

"It's fascinating," Marva Lou put in. "Just like watching TV."

Griffin gave the other woman a withering look. "This is real. We don't promise happy endings."

"Speak for yourself," Frankie murmured.

Judith kept her eyes on Griffin. "Well? What about the wallet?"

The female detective took a deep breath. "Ms. Rosenthal guessed he'd found it somewhere. Her father often gambled in Vegas or Laughlin. The wallet was returned to Mr. Brooks in Henderson. There were thirty or forty dollars in it. Mr. Brooks said that was about what he thought he had left when he couldn't find his wallet at New York, New York."

Judith frowned. "At . . . you mean the casino in Vegas?"

"Of course." Griffin looked peeved.

Vivian, who was holding the icebag to her eye, made a clumsy effort to stand up. "I wish you'd all leave. *Now.* I must rest."

"Good idea," Almquist said. "I could use some shut-eye, too."

Judith ignored him. "So," she said to Griffin, "you got no leads out of this Ms. Rosenthal, nor did you ever sit down and talk to her."

"It hardly seemed necessary," Griffin asserted. "She was grief-stricken, she'd been twelve hundred miles away when her father was murdered, and she couldn't think why he'd been killed. We'll follow up when she's had time to go through her father's personal effects."

Vivian had managed to stagger over to Judith. "Do I have to ask these cops to throw you and those two other bitches out of my house?"

"Yes," Renie said. "I'd kind of like that."

"I wouldn't," Arlene declared. "I've never been thrown out of anybody's house in my life, and I'm not starting now. It's—it's unneighborly, that's what it is."

Judith hadn't budged from her stance by the front door. She turned suddenly as a noise outside caught her attention. The doorknob was moving. With a sense of anticipation, she stepped aside.

Terri walked across the threshold but froze in place as she saw the gathering in the living room and the wreckage that was evidence of a brawl. "Oh! What's all this?"

"They're just leaving," Vivian said, bracing herself on the upended chair. "Fix yourself a drink. Get one for me." Her good eye blinked several times. "Wait—why are you here? I thought you'd gone away."

"Not yet," Terri replied, leaving the door open. "Come on in," she said to someone on the porch. "Mom's having a party."

To Judith's surprise, Mandrake Stokes entered, smiled, and removed his hat. What amazed her even more was the couple that followed him into the living room. An almost unrecognizable

Wilbur and Patrice Griggs arrived, wearing Armani suits and smug expressions.

"Hello, Mrs. Flynn," Mrs. Griggs said to Judith. "Hello, Mrs. Flynn," she said to Vivian. "Two Mrs. Flynns in the same room? Or only one?" Her gaze fastened on Vivian.

"Oh, no! *No!*" Vivian cried, and fell to the floor in a dead faint.

Caitlin was the first to rush to Vivian's assistance. Arlene, ever helpful, was right behind her. "Just let her come round," Arlene advised. "She's obviously had a terrible shock."

"It serves her right," Terri declared, standing over her mother's unconscious form like a victorious boxer. "She's responsible for my father's death."

The detectives stared at Terri. "What are you talking about?" Griffin demanded. "Who are you? Who's your father? Mr. Di Marco?"

"Not exactly," Terri replied. "His real name is Johnny Agra. Given name, Carlo Giovanni Agravecchio. He had it changed to John Charles Agra after he dropped out of high school."

Vivian was starting to stir as Caitlin spoke to her softly and put an arm under her mother's shoulders to prop her up. "Could you get me some water, Mrs. Rankers?" she asked.

"Of course." Arlene started to hustle off to the kitchen, but paused after a couple of steps. "Don't any of you dare say anything until I get back! Or else talk louder!"

Griffin had turned to Almquist. "Get us some backup. This case is a mess. Call in the patrol officers, or whoever can get here ASAP."

Almquist seemed embarrassed. "I left my cell in the car. Can I borrow yours?"

"Oh, for—" Griffin once again stopped short. "Here," she

said, shoving her phone at him. "Do you know how to dial the damned thing?"

"I think so." Looking forlorn, he wandered out to the front porch.

Vivian opened her good eye just as Arlene returned with the water.

"I want to put my mother to bed," Caitlin said, looking up at Griffin. "May I?"

"Go ahead," Griffin replied. "She's not much help to us at the moment, and she's taking up a lot of space in this shambles."

Caitlin and Arlene managed to get Vivian to her feet. Herself didn't complain about her erstwhile enemy coming to her aid. In fact, she said nothing at all, merely moaning softly as she was half dragged, half carried to her bedroom.

Judith had sidled up to the Griggses, who seemed to be on friendly terms with Frankie and Marva Lou. Mandrake Stokes, hat in hand, stood off to one side, looking pleased with himself.

"Excuse me," Judith interrupted. "Mr. and Mrs. Griggs, who are you? Wait," she said, holding up a hand. "I have to make a guess. Mrs. Griggs, your family called you Patsy, and your maiden name is Buss."

Patrice Griggs evinced surprise. "How did you guess?"

"I didn't," Judith said. "Everything about you checked out—corn farmers from Iowa. I recalled Marva Lou talking about siblings, and how they could all turn out to be different from each other. Billy was the restless sort, Frankie liked to stay home. She ticked off those qualities along with a third, whose nature was in-between. Marva Lou said, and I quote, 'my own sister.' It occurred to me that in the context of what she'd been saying, that suggested she was differentiating her sister from someone else's. Her husband's would be the most obvious. What also struck me was a note my cousin found in Frankie and Marva

Lou's room that read, 'Could Potsy help?' That's what she told me, but I realized—"

"Hey," Renie broke in, "I wasn't wearing my glasses."

"Exactly," Judith agreed. "Anyway, it didn't make sense because Potsy—your father—was dead. 'Could' implied that Potsy was still alive. I knew your husband called you Trish and that your first name is Patrice. It occurred to me that you might also be known as Patsy, but abandoned the nickname after you got married. I also remembered something Frankie mentioned about Billy and his sporting goods store going bust. He said that Billy might have done better with the farm, which I thought meant the Double UB. It occurred to me later that no one ever referred to Potsy's spread as a *farm*. It was always a *ranch*. The only farm owners involved were Mr. and Mrs. Griggs. I figured Potsy had bought it for his daughter."

"My, my," Trish Griggs said sardonically, "aren't you clever?"

Her husband tapped his wife's arm. "Hold on, Trish. I think this lady wants to help, not hinder."

Mrs. Griggs looked wary. "I don't trust any of these people except Mr. Stokes. And maybe my brother and his wife, since our interests are the same as theirs." She looked at Frankie and Marva Lou. "I hadn't seen either of my brothers in almost thirty years. I am the eldest, and as kids, our parents spoiled both of those boys. I went to the University of Northern Iowa in Cedar Falls, where I met Wilbur. We visited Pa and Ma a few times, but Billy and Frankie were never around. When Ma died, I couldn't go to the funeral—I'd had gallbladder surgery and was laid up for over two weeks with an infection I'd gotten in the hospital. I used to be chubby, and my hair had gone gray, so when we got here neither of them seemed to recognize me."

"Sure didn't," Frankie said, shaking his head. "Not at first, anyway. At the B&B, you reminded me of somebody, but I couldn't think who until the night of the party, when you came out of the B&B to go someplace. It was your walk. You were always kind of pigeon-toed." He turned to Marva Lou. "Didn't I say as much?"

"I thought you were crazy when you insisted I look them up on Mrs. Flynn's computer," his wife confessed. "But I'd never met Patsy. I mean, Trish." Marva Lou cast a rueful glance at Mrs. Griggs.

As Almquist came back inside, Judith looked at the Busses. "The attempt on your lives was a crude and stupid stunt meant to throw suspicion onto Terri for the murder." She turned to Griffin. "I'll turn over the box and what's left of the chocolates as evidence."

"You've been withholding vital information?" Griffin demanded in an irate tone.

"No," Judith said. "I haven't had a chance to do anything about it until now. There were two boxes, the poisoned ones sent via FedEx to the B&B, and the harmless box that was . . ." Glancing at Terri, who looked anxious, Judith decided a white lie was in order. "It was my mother's, but she gave it to Terri, who left it on the front porch here. The killer didn't know it wasn't the candy delivered to the Busses."

"Very confusing," Griffin murmured. "Are you done?"

"No," Judith replied and kept her eyes on Terri. "How did you know your father was the victim, and why did you pretend otherwise?"

Griffin had gotten out a notebook. "That's enough. I need names. All of you are going down to headquarters. We have to follow procedure. You'll be interviewed one-on-one." She turned to Judith. "Your neighbor and that other person," she went on, glancing at Renie, "can stay here with Mrs. Buss until she's able to be questioned."

"I don't babysit lushes," Renie snapped.

"Keep it simple," Judith said to Griffin. "You've got to nail a killer."

"Oh, of course!" the female detective said mockingly. "Why don't you tell us who it is?"

"Let me finish," Judith retorted. "Let Terri answer my question."

Terri's belligerence disappeared. "I always knew," she said, wearily collapsing on the sofa, "but I was scared. I told Dad I was moving up here. I hadn't seen him for a long time, so he told me he'd come, too. He found out my mother had remarried, this time for big bucks. He was doing okay in the Bahamas, but he wanted to put the squeeze on her. What he'd never told me until then was that he and my mother were . . ." Terri closed her eyes for a few seconds and took a deep breath. "They were never divorced. Neither of them had signed the final papers. Legally, my parents were still married."

"Blackmail?" Griffin said in a stern voice.

"Does it matter?" Terri snapped. "He's dead."

"Hey!" Griffin took a few steps closer to Terri. "Your voice! I recognize it now! You're Aileen Rosenthal!"

Terri hung her head. "I borrowed the name from my stepmother. I didn't want to use my own. Let's face it—Dad was always just a whisker away from going to jail. He was a dreamer and a schemer. He'd been calling himself Di Marco for years. That's why my stepmother used it for her so-called movie career. I gave you phony information because I was scared. I was pretty sure who'd killed Dad, so I had to pretend I didn't know he was the victim."

Judith nodded. "You went outside that night, didn't you?"

"Yes." Terri covered her face with her hands. "I found my dad's body. It was awful. I didn't know what to do. I'd been drinking, so I went back to the basement and drank some more until I passed out."

"No wonder," Judith said. "Had you sent letters to your dad?"

"You mean to my mother's house?" Terri nodded. "I thought he was already here. He was always unpredictable."

Judith nodded. "Go on. Let's move up to this evening. I take it you asked for help from Caitlin, who put you in touch with Mr. Stokes."

Terri nodded. "Mr. Stokes turned out to be a big help." She managed a faint smile for the dapper man who was still standing in place, hat in hand. "He represents the buyers for the Buss ranch."

Mandrake Stokes bowed. "Indeed. It was vital for me to find the legal owner before the college moves ahead with the purchase. Given that Mrs . . . Agra? . . . was never married to the late Mr. Buss, the offer must be made to his lawful heirs, William Buss, Franklin Buss, and Patrice Buss Griggs." He sketched another bow. "I'm at your service."

"Swell," Frankie Buss said.

"Finally," Patrice Griggs murmured.

"Incredible!" Caitlin exclaimed, standing in the doorway that led to the bungalow's two bedrooms. "It turns out I'm a bastard!"

"Consider this," Judith said, moving to the younger woman's side. "You were never legitimate in the Catholic Church's eyes. The marriage was invalid because your mother was divorced—or so everyone believed. That's why your dad didn't need an annulment to marry me."

Caitlin shook her head in dismay. "What a muddle! Oh, what's the use? I can't change the past." She grimaced. "I hated betraying my mother, but it was unlawful for her to inherit the estate and leave the rightful heirs with nothing. I couldn't look Claude in the eye if I didn't do the right thing."

The sound of "How Dry I Am" caught everyone's attention. Griffin went to the door, asking who was there. Judith heard Darnell Hicks's muffled voice. "Come in," Griffin said, opening the door for the patrol officer and his partner, Mercedes Berger. "We need to bring in several of these people for questioning."

"How many?" Mercedes asked, looking around the crowded living room. "We don't use a bus for patrolling this neighborhood."

"Speaking of 'bus,'" Judith said, "where are Billy and Adelita?"

Darnell grinned. "They're already at headquarters."

Griffin looked startled. "You arrested them?"

Mercedes shook her head. "They're trying to find a judge or somebody who can marry them."

"We had to cite Billy Buss—again," Darnell explained. "We stopped him for speeding by the civic center. Adelita's family is in town from Campeche, Mexico, staying at the Travel Inn. Billy and Adelita were going to be married in Mexico a couple of years ago, but Mr. and Mrs. Vasquez didn't approve of him, so they headed for Florida, and . . ." Darnell looked bemused. "I guess Billy's been trying to butter up Adelita's parents. The Corona beer in the trunk wasn't for Billy. It was a gift for Mr. Vasquez, but he wouldn't accept it until Billy made an honest woman of his daughter."

Judith slapped her hand to her head. "I should have guessed! Billy's strictly a Miller man!"

Griffin glared at Darnell and Mercedes. "You aren't letting them get away, are you? This case isn't solved."

"We know," Mercedes said, darting a glance at Judith. "But we're confident it will be. We have a tail on Billy and Adelita just in case. The latest word is that they're wondering if a ferry captain could perform the ceremony out in the bay."

Griffin seemed flummoxed. Almquist was gobbling up some Fritos that had been spilled on the floor. "Excuse me," Judith said, "but you can forget about Billy and Adelita? Put out an APB for the real killers."

Griffin glared at Judith. "And who might they be?"

"Barry Henckel and Doug Campbell," Judith replied. "Who else?" She turned to Terri. "Do you know where they might be?"

Terri's face flushed. "Yes. They're in the trunk of my mother's Bentley."

The following Monday was clear and warm under the midday sun. The cousins sat on Renie's deck, taking in the view of the mountains to the east and the sprawl of the city's suburbs up into the foothills.

"So Caitlin's on her way to Switzerland," Renie remarked. "I'm glad she and Joe had a chance to get caught up."

"So am I," Judith agreed. "Thanks again for giving us some of that wonderful salmon Bill caught. Caitlin enjoyed it, too."

Renie looked at her watch. "Bill should be back from the cannery with the fish he had smoked. I ought to check on the plumber to see how he's coming along upstairs."

Judith picked up the empty glass that had been full of lemonade. "I should stop at Falstaff's on the way home." She watched a robin fly from branch to branch in the Joneses' huge Blue Atlas Cedar. "I'm still amazed at Terri managing to trick her two rotten half-bothers and turn them over to the cops."

"Every so often people surprise me," Renie admitted. "Terri's got some smarts. If she puts her mind to it, she can find a decent job."

"True," Judith agreed. "I still wonder where *my* smarts went. Terri laid it all out for me, and I missed the boat."

"Don't beat yourself up," Renie urged. "You fingered the

killers eventually. Besides, there were a couple of crucial pieces she left out."

"You mean Doug overhearing Johnny threaten Vi before the party?" Judith nodded. "That only came out when Barry tried to cut a deal and mentioned it to the cops. I missed some little things—like the casinos. Joe told me that Doug and Barry worked in several places. I interrupted him when he mentioned Paris, Rio, New York—and when he said 'new' again, I thought he was going to say New Jersey or some other place that began with 'new.' If I'd let him finish, he'd have said New York New York, and I would've realized he didn't mean cities, but Vegas casinos. The brothers returned from Vegas at the end of July. Doug found Charles Brooks's wallet and kept it. After the murder, Doug made ID difficult by planting Brooks's wallet in his victim's pants. He must've dumped Johnny's own billfold."

"Maybe," Renie suggested, "it ended up in that Dumpster after the party. That must've been a terrible mess to search."

Judith nodded. "It could've been ditched anywhere." She sighed. "Terri never saw her dad at the party. He came early. Until she found his body, she figured he was a no-show. That didn't surprise her— he wasn't reliable. She probably got there after he was already dead."

"Another factor," Renie pointed out, "was time of death. Johnny was killed much earlier than the M.E. figured."

Judith batted at a bumblebee that was circling her glass. "Yes, before Herself's show got under way. Rochelle mentioned that Hamish Stein had seen a sedan parked in front of Vivian's house that looked like the same one he'd spotted the night before the murder. It was gone by the time the party started. The cops checked out the rental agencies, and learned that someone named Di Marco had rented it Saturday. The car was found late last Friday in the parking garage by the civic center at the bottom of the hill."

Renie nodded. "The brothers had to get it out of the way after they killed Johnny. Good God, they have to be two of the dimmest criminals you've come up against."

"Oh, yes," Judith agreed. "They acted on impulse—no plan, no thinking ahead, just suddenly discovering their mama wasn't a rich widow after all and seeing a Do Not Enter sign on Easy Street. It's a wonder they didn't put the body in the rental car and leave poor Johnny in the parking garage. But they couldn't do that in broad daylight. The freezer was their answer. Except for the party ice, there wasn't anything in it. As the waiters, Doug and Barry were the only ones who needed to go down to the basement to fetch the ice. They took all of it, threw a blanket over Johnny, and put him in there. But they didn't want the body to freeze because it'd be harder to move, so they unplugged the unit. Arlene and I noticed that later, but it didn't sink in. It took a while to defrost, so the chill factor altered the M.E.'s calculations. The basement floor got wet, and so did the blanket. Terri mentioned that, but it went by me. Poor girl—sleeping downstairs with her dead father's body!" Judith shuddered. "No wonder she was a wreck when she got to the toolshed."

"Why didn't she go to the cops?"

"I think she believed that Vivian was in on it," Judith replied. "It made sense. She'd want Johnny dead, too, if he threatened to expose the illegal marriage to Potsy. Terri stalled, trying to figure it out on her own."

"Do you think Vivian knew who killed Johnny?"

Judith shrugged. "Who knows? Her brain's addled by so much booze, straight thinking is questionable."

"So Terri turned the tables on the brothers," Renie murmured. "She was in real danger, too. They may've intended to get rid of her."

"Or at least get her out of town," Judith said. "They couldn't be sure how much she knew. When they offered to take her for a spin in the Aston Martin, she realized that all three of them couldn't fit in it. She thought fast, figuring she could be in danger. Herself's Bentley had just been delivered, so she suggested they try it out. She insisted on calling me when they stopped—not at Bartleby's, but at Buster's Café a couple of blocks away. Then she phoned Billy and told him to come down—fast. That's when Caitlin got into the act. Billy told her Terri sounded scared. Caitlin suspected the worst of the brothers, and with her knowledge of chemicals she whipped up a version of a Mickey Finn so Billy could slip it into the brothers' drinks."

"Caitlin was lucky that Billy was willing to cooperate," Renie said. "Of course, he had nothing to lose and everything to gain by nailing Doug and Barry."

"Right," Judith concurred. "The Bentley was parked behind the café. It didn't take long for Doug and Barry to get groggy. Buster's clientele of hard drinkers are often unable to walk on their own. Billy and Terri hauled the brothers out the back way and into the trunk."

"I'd like to have seen that," Renie mused.

"Me, too," Judith said. "Of course, Terri had no proof, but when she discovered her dad's body, she realized that the only person who'd insisted she stay in the basement was Doug. Somehow he had to be connected to the crime. He had a motive, of course. I'd figured Johnny was there after Ray Campbell mentioned the cop who said, 'Here's Johnny!' adding, 'Where's Johnny?' It indicated he'd been there, but was gone. What threw me off was the stated time of death."

"Wow," Renie said softly. "You're one of the two people in two million who actually listens to what others say." She smiled at her cousin. "Of course, that's why even strangers bend your ear."

"I guess," Judith said modestly. "Hey," she said, glancing at her watch, "I'd better scoot."

Both cousins got out of their deck chairs. "How's Vivian taking it?" Renie asked as they entered the kitchen.

"Not as badly as I hoped," Judith replied ruefully. "She's going ahead with the condo project. Billy is willing to back her, maybe as a thank-you for her generosity to him. Besides, he doesn't want her raising hell, because he and Adelita got married over the weekend. Terri told me he and his bride are heading for a new life in Hawaii."

"Buying off a wife who was never a wife," Renie murmured. "A novel concept. But I'm sorry about the condo thing."

"So am I," Judith said. "I really don't know how I can keep the B&B going with a huge construction project practically on our doorstep. The noise alone will wake up the guests. I'll have to shut down."

"Coz, you can't!" Renie protested. "It could be for several months, and——"

The phone rang. Renie picked it up from the counter. "Oh, hi. What's new?" She listened for a full minute and began to smile. "Really. Very interesting. Tell Bub thanks. Talk to you later, Bippy."

"What's up?" Judith inquired.

Renie didn't look her cousin in the eye but focused on some bananas in a fruit basket on the counter. "Um . . . family stuff with Bill's brother, Bub, and his wife, Bippy." She suddenly clapped a hand to her head. "I forgot to bring Oscar's picture back! How could I? Can I swing by after Bill comes back with Cammy?"

"Glad to see it go," Judith replied. "I put it in a kitchen drawer."

"You're mean," Renie said.

"And you're lucky," Judith responded. "I almost tossed it."

Renie's expression turned menacing. "You want to be the next corpse in your neighborhood?"

"I've had enough excitement lately. 'Bye."

When Judith arrived home with her groceries an hour later, Joe was on the phone in the kitchen. He didn't look happy. "Thanks for the heads-up," he said, and rang off. "That was Smith. Or was it Wesson? I can't keep those patrol cops straight."

"And?" Judith said, setting three Falstaff bags on the counter.

Joe didn't answer right away. He folded his arms across his chest, gazed through the window over the sink, and uttered a big sigh. "Smith and Wesson thought we'd like to know that a bulldozer is heading our way. They had to direct traffic at the bottom of the hill because the bulldozer was blocking an intersection. They asked the guys who were towing it where it was headed. The address is the Swanson house."

"Oh, damn!" Judith exclaimed. "I've been hoping, *praying*, that would never happen! What'll we do?"

Joe shrugged. "What *can* we do? I noticed earlier that a U-Haul was parked in front of Vi's. I suppose her house is next to go."

Judith went to the computer and reviewed her upcoming reservations. "I'm almost completely booked up through Labor Day. How can the guests cope with the noise and the mess and . . . Oh, it's a disaster! I was hoping Herself wouldn't start construction at least until the end of September."

Joe came over to Judith and put his arm around her shoulders. "I know. It's rotten luck. But our hands are tied." He kissed her forehead. "You got more groceries to unload?"

Judith nodded.

"I'll do it," he said, and went out the back way.

When he returned with four more bags, his expression was grim. "The bulldozer is pulling into the cul-de-sac. Renie was just ahead of it."

"She's here?" Judith said. "Oh, that's right. She's come to get Bill and Oscar's picture." Opening the drawer, she removed the framed photo. "I'm too upset to think about how goofy Renie and Bill are."

"I heard that," Renie said, entering the rear hallway.

"Sorry," Judith said, noticing that her cousin was carrying Oscar, but in no mood to ask why. "You saw the bulldozer?"

Renie nodded. "I had to drive around it to get into the cul-de-sac."

Judith handed over the photo. "I'm trying to figure out how to deal with this. I can't bear to call Ingrid Heffelman and ask her to relocate all the guests."

"Wait until you know the construction schedule," Renie advised.

"Well . . . maybe," Judith said as Joe headed into the dining room. "These projects don't always get under way on time."

"Come on," Renie urged. "Let's see what's happening."

"No." Judith refused to budge.

"Stop doing your usual head-in-the-sand thing. I'll bet Joe's out front, taking it all in."

"Let him. It's his ex-wife. Or not his ex-wife."

"I'm going to have a look," Renie said, heading for the front door.

Judith remained in the kitchen, waiting for the racket that she figured the bulldozer would make. *The sound of doom*, she thought. After a few minutes she could hear nothing except the schoolhouse clock ticking away the time. *Ticking away my income. Ruining my B&B. Destroying our cozy neighborhood.*

At last she decided to join Joe and Renie. They were standing on the porch. The bulldozer had been unhitched and was sitting by the corner. Vivian was talking to a young man wearing work clothes and a hard hat. The truck that had brought the bulldozer drove off.

"I decided I might as well see the mayhem," Judith said, noticing that Arlene was on the sidewalk with Rochelle and Naomi. She waved to the three women, who waved back. Rochelle then made a vigorous thumbs-down gesture and shook her head.

Vivian was acting coy, wagging a finger at the young man, who Judith assumed was the bulldozer operator. "But it's the ride of my life!" she cried and tugged gently at the man's sleeve. "Please, sweetheart. I simply have to christen this project myself."

He hesitated, but finally stepped back. "I'll have to drive." Climbing onto the bulldozer, he extended a hand to Vivian. "Here we go."

Vivian went. She slipped, lost her balance, seemed to fly into the air, and came down hard on the concrete in a flurry of purple, magenta, and gold caftan. Her scream was agonizing.

The workman cursed aloud and jumped off of the bulldozer. Vivian's screams turned to moans and groans. Joe hurried from the porch and across the cul-de-sac. Arlene, Rochelle, and Naomi moved closer for a better look.

"Why," Judith said to Renie, "am I unsympathetic?"

"You know why," Renie said, looking smug. "Shall I call nine-one-one?"

Judith stared at her cousin. "I'm not doing it. Go ahead, use your cell. And what's up with you?"

"Nothing," Renie replied, setting Oscar on the porch swing and digging her phone out of her purse. "Nice work," she murmured.

Joe was kneeling next to Vivian, who was still moaning and groaning. The bulldozer operator was talking on his cell.

"Help's on the way," he shouted to Joe and Vivian.

"Good," Renie said, descending the steps. "I don't have to call."

A white sedan with a city logo pulled into the cul-de-sac and stopped. A middle-aged Hispanic man got out, holding a manila envelope. Curious, Judith followed Renie, who'd stopped on the lawn by the small sign bearing the name of Hillside Manor.

"I'm looking for a woman named Vivian Agra," he said, staring at Herself's writhing body. "I hope this isn't her."

"I'm afraid it is," Joe said. "Can I help you?"

"I'm Horacio Benitez," the man said, handing the envelope to Joe. "You can give this to Ms. Agra when . . . she's feeling better."

"What is it?" Joe asked.

"A cease-and-desist order for a condo project," Benitez explained. "The paperwork was signed by a Vivian Buss, which turns out to be an illegal name, voiding the permit requests. Furthermore, the city has reason to believe that the project should never have been green-lighted. There's been a reinterpretation of the zoning and variance laws in this neighborhood." He moved toward his car. "Have a nice day."

"My God!" Judith gasped. "I can't believe it!"

"I can," Renie said calmly as Arlene, Rochelle, and Naomi cheered.

Judith's eyes narrowed. "Coz, what do you know that I don't?"

Renie feigned innocence. "Bub and Bippy came to dinner Sunday to have some of Bill's salmon. I mentioned the project, and that Vivian wasn't who she claimed to be. Bub's legal expertise is developers and zoning and property rights and all that, so he promised to look into it." She shrugged as the city car pulled out and a medic van pulled in.

"Oh, Coz!" Judith hugged Renie. "Thank you! I'm overwhelmed!"

"Don't thank me, thank Bub."

"I will. Truly." She turned her attention back to Herself, where the medics were already on the job. Joe had stood back, watchful but able to offer his wife a V-for-victory sign. The three neighbors, agog over the condo project's demise, joined Judith and Renie.

"I can't believe it," Naomi said.

"What a relief!" Rochelle exclaimed.

"It might be fun to ride a bulldozer," Arlene remarked. "Or not."

Moments later, Vivian was on a gurney and trundled off to the medic van. Joe picked up something from the spot where she'd fallen.

"Broken hip," he said, coming across the cul-de-sac to join the women. "I suppose she'll have to be on a walker for a while."

"A pity." Judith sounded insincere. "What's in your hand?"

"A banana peel," Joe said as the medic drove off. "Where'd that come from?"

Judith looked at her cousin.

"Got to go," Renie said, hurrying up the porch steps. "Come on, Oscar, our work here is done."

Judith could've sworn that Oscar winked.